BREAKING NEWS

Just another crank caller. That's what fashion reporter Lacey Smithsonian was thinking when the explosion rattled the front windows, flashing white light through *The Eye Street Observer*'s newsroom.

Lacey had been trying to finish a column, trying to make it funny, when the phone rang.

"I'm warning you, bitch. Stop writing these stupid stories."

"Who is this and which stupid stories are you referring to?" *I'm on deadline here on a stupid story, you stupid—*

"Look outside and kiss your precious wheels good-bye."

She was puzzled. Her ungrateful Nissan 280ZX was at the shop again, rusting complacently in the humid smog of Washington, D.C. At least she thought it was. She hurried past four rows of reporters' desks to peer out onto the street below. *My Z isn't out there.* Her copy editor Felicity's dismal gray minivan squatted illegally in the fire lane in front of *The Eye*. Lacey was looking straight at it when it blew up.

Lacey streaked back to her desk, grabbed the receiver, and heard expectant breathing. All she could say was:

"YOU THOUGHT I DROVE A *MINIVAN?!*"

Praise for *Killer Hair*,
the first Crime of Fashion mystery

"Cut-wrong hair mingles with cutthroat Washington, D.C., in Ellen Byerrum's rippling debut. Peppered with girlfriends you'd love to have, smoldering romance you can't resist, and Beltway insider insights you've got to read, *Killer Hair* adds a crazy twist to the concept of 'capital murder.' Bubbles may have to visit."—Sarah Strohmeyer, Agatha Award–winning author of *Bubbles Ablaze*

"Ellen Byerrum tailors her debut mystery with a sharp murder plot, entertaining fashion commentary, and gutsy characters. I'll look forward to the next installment."—Nancy J. Cohen, author of the Bad Hair Day Mysteries

"Chock-full of colorful, often hilarious characters. . . . Lacey herself has a delightfully catty wit. The book is interspersed with gems from her 'Crimes of Fashion' column. . . . A load of stylish fun even if you don't know anything or care to know anything about fashion."—Scripps Howard News Service

"Lacey Smithsonian is no fashionista—she's a '40s starlet trapped in style-free D.C., with a feminist agenda, a cadre of delightfully insane friends, and a knack for stumbling on corpses. . . . Lacey slays and sashays through Washington politics, scandal, and Fourth Estate slime, while uncovering whodunit, and dunit and dunit again."—Chloe Green, author of the Dallas O'Connor Fashion Mysteries

"Lacey Smithsonian skewers Washington with style in this new mystery series. *Killer Hair* is a shear delight."—Elaine Viets, national best-selling author of *Shop till You Drop*

Designer Knockoff

A CRIME OF FASHION MYSTERY

Ellen Byerrum

A SIGNET BOOK

SIGNET
Published by New American Library, a division of
Penguin Group (USA) Inc., 375 Hudson Street,
New York, New York 10014, U.S.A.
Penguin Books Ltd, 80 Strand,
London WC2R 0RL, England
Penguin Books Australia Ltd, 250 Camberwell Road,
Camberwell, Victoria 3124, Australia
Penguin Books Canada Ltd, 10 Alcorn Avenue,
Toronto, Ontario, Canada M4V 3B2
Penguin Books (NZ), cnr Airborne and Rosedale Roads,
Albany, Auckland 1310, New Zealand

Penguin Books Ltd, Registered Offices:
80 Strand, London WC2R 0RL, England

First published by Signet, an imprint of New American Library,
a division of Penguin Group (USA) Inc.

First Printing, August 2004
10 9 8 7 6 5 4 3 2 1

This book is dedicated to the late Professor Art Kistner, whose words of encouragement kept me going for years—long after logic dictated otherwise. He suggested that I write novels because I had too much plot for short stories.

ACKNOWLEDGMENTS

It is a long, arduous journey to publishing a book, and I want to recognize the people who helped me with anecdotes, information, and photographs, all of which sparked my imagination in the pursuit of the story. My thanks go to Nancy Adams (no relation to the fictional Gloria Adams), Luis Martinez, Howard Miller, Dotty Sohl, and an unnamed source.

Those who listened to me, encouraged me, and cajoled me include Guy Burdick, Jay Farrell, Barbara McConagha, and Bob Swierczek. I also would like to thank my new editor, Martha Bushko, and my agent, Don Maass.

This list would not be complete without expressing my utter gratitude to my husband, Bob Williams. Without his support, I would never have reached this point. He is, quite simply, the best and smartest man I know.

Chapter 1

If you can't dress up for the United States Senate, what can you dress up for? Lacey Smithsonian wondered. *Apparently, not much,* she surmised, judging from the crowd outside the hearing room at the Dirksen Senate Office Building on a steamy Tuesday morning in September, the ninth to be exact.

A microcosm of the Capital City, they wore their politics on their sleeves, as well as in their position statements. *Dressed for the picket line:* A group of men and women wore blue jeans and identical blue-logoed T-shirts, marking their solidarity—the union workers. A few men in small wire-framed glasses, clad in wrinkled khaki pants, tan jackets, plaid shirts, and earth-toned ties, clasped tattered manila folders—the Democrats: *Dressed for a Save the Endangered Eastern Nuthatch rally at the Unitarian church.* And then there were the trim navy-suited crew carrying sleek leather briefcases and wearing crisp white shirts and red silk ties—the Republicans. *Of course,* Lacey reflected, *they'd be dressed the same way at the beach. Only with Top-Siders.*

And then there were the others.

Poorly dressed, badly coiffed, regrettably groomed? Ah, yes: journalists. Lacey smiled at them. She was a reporter too, albeit on the bottom rung of the news ladder of the Nation's Capital at *The Eye Street Observer.* They didn't smile back.

There is nothing quite like being snubbed by your so-called peers in the halls of Congress, Lacey thought. The high-and-mighty attitude and the preference for flammable fabrics derived from fossil fuels came with the territory of the Fourth Estate. *But why the animosity?* she wondered. *Does polyester cause haughty indifference? Do they hate me because I work for* The Eye, *because I'm a lowly fashion reporter and not a Hill reporter, because I'm not dressed the way they are—or all of the above?*

Lacey had first been cut dead in the hall by a frizzy-haired brunette working for the wire services who wore a rumpled pavement-gray suit and square-cut glasses with heavy black frames. Then she'd been glared at in the ladies' room by a helmet-headed blonde, who wore a lumpy suit that might once have been maroon, paired with a pilled brown sweater. And finally she was nearly tripped at the door of the hearing room by *The Eye*'s own Peter Johnson, clad in his trademark grime-stained tan suit and an equally dingy shirt of an indefinable color. His tie was a misdemeanor of mud and mustard colors. *Dressed in Capital Camo.*

"What are you doing here?" Johnson hissed.

"Still holding a grudge, Peter?" Johnson was a prima donna Hill reporter who had become her sworn enemy after she stumbled onto his territory during that little scandal in the spring. Lacey freely admitted that the whole Marcia Robinson mess technically should have been Johnson's story, because he covered congressional happenings for *The Eye*. But Marcia, the notorious Small Business Committee staffer who pioneered her own political porn site, would speak only to Lacey. It still fried Johnson.

"Stay away from my beat, Smithsonian. I mean it."

"Unless you plan to cover the new American fashion museum, I don't think I'll be trampling on your beat, oh king of the hill."

"Fashion museum? What fashion museum?"

"You hadn't heard? Chairman Dashwood is threatening to withdraw government grant money for it. Museum sponsors are defending their right to wallow in the public trough."

"There's an approps bill for a fashion thing? Good God. The trivial things you cover."

"It's considered a big thing on my beat. Somehow millions sneaked into the approps bill to support the fashion museum and no one is taking credit for it. That's a big oops."

Peter glared down his nose at her as he pushed his oversized aviator glasses back up.

What's the fashion statement there, giant ant in a sci-fi movie?

He puffed up his concave chest, sucked in his rounded belly, and smoothed back his thinning brown hair. He spun on his heel and stalked away to cover a hearing on Homeland Security, the importance of it all weighing heavy on him.

For Lacey Smithsonian, the Senate Appropriations Subcommittee oversight hearing on a new museum dedicated to American fashion was more than just a story—it also provided the perfect occasion to wear a vintage designer suit with jeweled button covers, filigreed gold set with tiny pearls and rubies. Lacey stood out like a swan among the ducks in her tailored black summer-weight wool, a rare vintage 1940s suit styled by the renowned House of Bentley and bequeathed to her by her great-aunt. The suit caressed her hourglass curves, and it fit her better than any modern ready-to-wear or designer knockoff, which was all she could afford on a reporter's salary. The jacket buttoned to just below her collarbone. The skirt, with just enough swing for easy walking, hit right below the knee. The only thing that compromised the outfit was her press identification card with the requisite funhouse headshot, photographed by a vengeful government employee.

Nevertheless, Lacey felt good. Her light brown hair had grown out nicely from a disastrous spring fling with bangs—after receiving an unplanned trim from a psychopath with a razor. Now she had new highlights with a hint of early Lauren Bacall and a devastating vintage suit, and she was here to witness a killer in action.

A lady-killer, to be exact.

According to her late great-aunt Mimi Smith, Hugh "That Bastard" Bentley, the legendary American designer, slated to testify before the committee, was a notorious playboy, a heel, a cad, a louse. A heartbreaking fiend. Lacey had heard tantalizing tidbits over the years about Hugh "That Bastard" Bentley, who wined and dined Mimi during World War II—the same Bentley who designed the suit she was wearing. The subject of the exclusive Bentley's Boutique on Wisconsin Avenue, just outside the District, would occasionally rise like a bubble to be popped. Mimi refused to shop there and only released tiny tempting hints. Mimi never even wore the suit, but she hadn't had the heart to throw it out—she called it a "true Bentley's original." *Did they have a torrid affair, I wonder?*

It was a pathetic comment on Lacey's own lack of romance that she wondered about Great-aunt Mimi's love life. Her most recent heartthrob, ex–Steamboat Springs police chief Vic Donovan, had returned to Colorado in July to deal with "personal family business." He told her he'd be coming back soon, but men said a lot of things. Now it was September and Congress was back in business, but Vic was still missing in action.

But Lacey didn't have time to dwell on Vic. She reviewed her notes. Hugh Bentley was the primary inspiration, constant mover, and major backer (along with the taxpayers) of the Bentley Museum of American Fashion. Besides her Bentley suit and Mimi's tenuous Bentley connection, Lacey figured the hearings and "Hugh the B," as she liked to think of him, were worth a column or two. She was right; the hearing room was nearly packed with media when Lacey arrived. A line of would-be spectators snaked down the halls, held back by security, and they protested every time a reporter or staffer was allowed inside before the doors officially opened.

Wires ran everywhere, festooned with lighting technicians and cameramen. The bright hot lights were already raising the room's temperature to an uncomfortable level. The networks were there, as well as CNN and the other usual suspects from the wonderful world of broadcast. Even *Entertainment Tonight*, that braintrust of political savvy, was on hand.

Luckily the press table had a sliver of available seating. But a female reporter from *The Washington Post* took one look at Lacey and bristled in defense of her territory. "There's room at the other table. It's really crowded here," she said. With a chilly look, the woman indicated another table, stacked tall with press releases, where the overflow trade press were huddled like a boatload of orphans.

"No, thanks, I'll sit with the grown-ups." Lacey smiled at the woman, who scooted over half a millimeter, sniffed, and proceeded to ignore her. The *Post* reporter was outfitted in a stretched-out black-and-white houndstooth jacket and black skirt. Her mouse-brown hair was worn in a short puffy suburban-mom hairdo, although she wore no wedding ring. She raised one eyebrow at Lacey's outfit, then returned to studying her notebook.

David Kenyon, a bearded reporter from *The Washington Times*, made room for Lacey. "So they still let you out of the office."

"Occasionally."

"Isn't that kind of dangerous? The last time they let you out, didn't you stab someone?"

"I haven't stabbed anyone in months, David. Not with scissors anyway."

"Just your barbed wit."

"It's a weapon of class destruction."

Kenyon laughed. The *Post* reporter raised her eyebrows again.

"Well, with all the security here, I guess I'm safe," Kenyon said. "Besides, I don't see where you could possibly hide a pair of scissors in that suit."

"Thanks. I hope I don't need them." *Score one for Mimi's suit.* Lacey surveyed the crowd, trolling for tidbits for "Crimes of Fashion," her weekly column. She spotted most of the usual faces, but something—or, rather, someone—was missing. "David, have you seen Esme?" A well-connected intern who had kept Lacey in the loop when the committee press secretary ignored her calls, Esme Fairchild had been working specifically as a liaison between the museum advocates and the appropriations subcommittee.

Kenyon grimaced. "Unfortunately, no. But the little grumpy

one is here." He pointed to an obviously irritated young staffer who was loaded down with press releases and copies of senators' statements. She was fighting a battle with people who weren't reporters trying to grab the papers out of her hands. She was short. She was outnumbered. It was a losing battle.

"I'm sorry, these are only for the press!" She glared at the press table before turning to her harasser. "Yes, sir, I understand; I will give them to you when I can. After the press gets them. They're for the media!" She sighed in exasperation as she set the releases on the table. True to form, the reporters jumped on them like a pack of dogs.

"Excuse me, is Esme Fairchild here?" Lacey asked, riffling through her copies of testimony and statements and guarding them from attack.

The grumpy baby-faced brunette was dressed in a stodgy style that Lacey called "prematurely serious," which proliferates in Washington like Pentagon budget overruns. Her staff badge identified her as Nancy Mifflin. She peered at Lacey through her trendy little lenses.

"Esme? I wish. She'll probably show up when all the heavy lifting is done. By me."

"I left a message for her yesterday," Lacey said.

"I haven't seen her since then. Esme said she simply had to get a manicure and pedicure before the hearing." Nancy glanced at her own nervously chewed nails. "Heaven knows how important that is when the press is nipping at your heels."

"Listen, Nancy, I really appreciate what you're doing. It can't be easy; we're a pretty rabid bunch sometimes," Lacey said. "Thanks."

Nancy looked a bit surprised. She smiled, then turned her back to stand guard over her precious papers. She was immediately engulfed by a pack of reporters and disappeared from view.

Esme, on the other hand, would have been impossible to miss. She was tall, slender as a postage stamp, with long honey-colored hair and golden eyes, and she always made a point of being seen. She made no secret of the fact that she had done some modeling in college and had her heart set on a fashion career in New York, which was why, Lacey supposed, she had latched onto the Bentley fashion museum project with such fervor. She was all of twenty-one and already worried that time was running out.

The young woman had proven to be a decent news source, if fashion was considered news. Esme Fairchild wore her ambition as boldly as she did her short-skirted suits, which barely met the Senate dress code. Washingtonians like ambition, but the consensus was that Esme's was a little too raw, naked, and desperate. She had even courted coverage by Lacey Smithsonian and that scrappy little newspaper of hers, *The Eye*. Not that Lacey minded; that was part of the game.

"It must have been something big," Kenyon said. "Wild boars wouldn't keep her away from this hearing."

"How well do you know Esme?"

"How much do you want to know?"

"The big-print *USA Today* edition. Not the *National Enquirer* version."

"We've hoisted a few beverages. *The Enquirer* would have been bored. But she's a friendly girl, a very friendly girl. She makes quite an impression. I know that she invested everything in making a good impression on the Bentleys for a job."

"But as what, specifically?" Esme had merely hinted at her game plan with Lacey.

"Company spokesmodel."

"But they have Cordelia Westgate, the party girl with a pedigree."

"Yes, but Cordelia's pushing thirty and Esme thinks she ought to be put out to pasture before old age gets her."

"If Esme thinks she can push Cordelia out of the saddle, she's got a steep learning curve ahead of her. Especially if she made it known. And to a reporter."

The meeting came to order. It looked like the full Senate panel would be in attendance with all senators on deck, not, of course, to listen to the designers, but to rage and rumble about the funding irregularities—and to gawk at Cordelia Westgate, who was more famous for posing nude in *Playboy* than for her role as celebrity spokesmodel for the Bentleys.

They were dressed for the occasion in the full senatorial palette: gray, black, gray, gray, charcoal gray, navy, and one Democrat in olive green, the rebel. The lone female senator on the panel wore a red power suit. She was a Republican. Lacey turned her gaze to the witness table.

Hugh "That Bastard" Bentley in the flesh turned out to be a slightly shrunken octogenarian. However, the old roué had aged well, with his steely blue eyes and his thick mane of silver hair parted on the side, worn long and combed back. His dapper mustache was expertly trimmed in a style from another era, the era of Ronald Coleman and Errol Flynn. He was dressed in one of his own designs, a navy suit that he wore with a silver vest and a blue-and-silver-striped ascot. The silver cuff links on his shirt peeked out beneath the cashmere jacket. Hugh carried a silver-handled walking stick, not a cane, which Lacey had heard was an old affectation. In his prime Hugh had resembled a movie star, with his black hair, strong jaw, and dazzling smile. In his old age he still did. He could pass for sixty-something, and he made the senators look like accountants.

Lacey was itching for details. She scolded herself. The scolding didn't work. *They must have had a fling. If I'd been Aunt Mimi sixty years ago—my God, sixty years ago!—I might have.*

Although Hugh the B came from a hardscrabble early background, no one would know it. He carried himself like royalty. His immigrant grandfather, Hugo Bentbridge, had been a tailor; his father, Harry Bentbridge, had owned a small garment factory; and Hugh had broken into designing women's wear midway through World War II. It was Hugh who had classed up Bentbridge into Bentley, much to Aunt Mimi's amusement. Mimi was a Smithsonian who had "declassed" her name to Smith. "Blame Jimmy Stewart and *Mr. Smith Goes to Washington*," Mimi often said. "That was the kind of Smith I wanted to be. Besides, I was tired of being a phony Smithsonian, like those phony Bentleys."

Despite wartime clothing regulations, Hugh the B made a name for himself and established an American fashion dynasty. *LIFE* magazine once profiled him in the late Forties with a cover story entitled, "A Star Is Worn."

Lacey studied the lineup. The Bentleys and the comely Cordelia were seated front and center at the witness table. Belinda Bentley Holmes, Hugh's younger sister, was seated on his right. Belinda was everything semi-old money and clever cosmetic surgery could achieve on a seventyish canvas. She looked expensive and wore her still golden-blond hair in a sophisticated French twist. Her new Bentley suit was peacock blue. On his left, Marilyn, Hugh's queenly wife and famed muse, was resplendent, if slightly plump, in mauve. She wore her snowy hair in a regal coronet. On her left Aaron Bentley, Hugh's forty-something son, was, if anything, handsomer than his famous father had been. The divorced playboy was a familiar face in the pages of *Vogue* and *W.* Aaron, the reigning king of the fashion house, was expected to plead the family's case for the worthiness of the Bentley Museum of American Fashion, citing fashion's importance to the American economy. *Quite a family photo,* Lacey thought. *Tomorrow's headline? "Senate Dazzled by Royal Family of American Fashion."*

Clinging to Aaron's side was the pseudosociety spokesmodel Cordelia Westgate, who provided the youthful glamour that the Bentleys might lack. It was for a glimpse of Cordelia that the entertainment media were on hand. Cordelia was all legs, collagen-enhanced lips, and fluffy blond hair. She wore a jet-black Bentley trench coat, which Lacey found a puzzling choice, especially in the stifling hearing room.

In his opening salvo, Senator John Dashwood snarled over the forty-million-dollar funding snafu. Seated beneath a huge bronze eagle, he held the appropriations bill in his hand and shook it, looking dignified and rather like an eagle himself. "It was understood that this project was to receive no more grants, and yet millions more for this flimsy excuse for cultural edification were somehow surreptitiously stuffed into the budget like a Thanksgiving turkey, and no one is fessing up." He paused to cast his beady eye over the room. "Well, ladies and gentlemen, I will get to the bottom of this mess. I want our witnesses to tell me how we can justify asking the American people at a time like this to support a fashion museum, at a time when we face terrorist threats from far-flung corners of the earth, at a time when our very souls shake from the responsibilities before us."

The tone of the chairman made it clear he expected to be quoted and he wasn't about to waste the photo opportunity that a little glamour had brought to his hearing room. "Now we can strike this money from the budget or we can approve it. Frankly my vote is no."

The ranking minority member, Senator Demetrius Van Drizzen, offered measured support for the museum, but pledged that continuing oversight of funding would be strict. His statement was brief, just long enough to get camera time. Finally, Hugh the B had his chance to speak. His remarks were unexpectedly concise.

"Mr. Chairman, these are dark days indeed, but we have seen darker and we have triumphed. But we cannot succeed by denying everything that edifies our culture, and fashion has a unique and esteemed place in American life. And to speak to that issue, Mr. Chairman, with your permission, I will yield my time to Miss Cordelia Westgate, who has a message for us—from the First Lady of the United States."

There was a low buzz among the press and the spectators—this development hadn't been revealed in the preprinted statements. All eyes—and cameras—focused on Cordelia, who slipped off the black trench coat and stood up. She wore a uniform of olive drab, a four-button wool jacket and skirt, a tan cotton shirt with a matching mohair tie. On her feet were brown low-heeled service shoes. There was a muted murmur of interest from the crowd. She looked every inch the part of a Women's Army Corps officer from World War II. The cameras closed in on her.

"What the heck is she wearing?" Kenyon asked Lacey. The whole tableful of reporters looked to her expectantly for an answer. "And why?"

"I believe it's a WAC uniform, circa 1943," Lacey whispered back. "However, it's been tailored within an inch of its life. As to why . . ." She shrugged.

Cordelia, with her beautiful, seen-it-all face, was putting her all into her role as a world-weary soldier. She saluted the chairman, pulled a letter from a leather case as if she were a courier from the front, and read.

"From the White House.
"Dear Chairman Dashwood and Respected Members of the Committee:
    "Today, you must determine whether to continue funding for the Bentley Museum of American Fashion. I ask you to consider this question with the gravity it deserves and to vote in the affirmative.
    "There are those who say that fashion is meaningless and that we should not honor it with continuing grants for the future of our new national museum, particularly now. They say it is not the right time or the right place. They say that there are other groups more deserving, and their arguments may have some merit. Yet the American clothing industry brings billions of dollars into our economy each year and at the same time expresses our spirit, our mood, our freedom.
    "The American fashion industry came of age during World War II, another time of great peril for our nation. In addition to doing its part to boost morale at home, the American garment industry clothed our men and women in the armed forces and sent a firm message that the Yanks were coming—and they were coming in style! American industry tooled up to supply uniforms, just as it had to supply our forces with food and ammunition. On the home front—cut off from the traditional fashion leaders in France, Italy, and even in Britain— our designers came up with a new, completely American sensibility in clothes, a sensibility that was flattering, functional, and reflected American freedom,

*from high fashion to sportswear. Images of American
life, the way we dressed and lived our lives, became
ambassadors to the world, spread in movies and magazines.*

*"Consider, please, that one of our most basic needs
after food and shelter is for clothing that expresses who
we are. Fashion can reflect oppression. But in America
it reflects freedom. Please continue to support the Bentley Museum of American Fashion so that it can express
the best that America has to offer.*

*"I look forward to seeing you all at the opening of
the museum in two weeks' time. Thank you."*

Cordelia ended with another salute to the senators and the
famous beguiling smile that moved Bentley merchandise by the
millions. Appreciative chatter rolled through the crowd.

"I wonder if Dashwood's vote is still no," Lacey whispered
to Kenyon. "He doesn't look too happy."

"Wearing the uniform must have been Esme's idea,"
Kenyon told her. "Something patriotic for the cameras. She said
she proposed something dramatic."

"So if it bombs," Lacey said, "Cordelia looks foolish, and if
it goes well, Esme's a genius. Either way, I bet that wool suit
itches."

Their conversation was cut short. Chairman Dashwood
squirmed in his seat and cleared his throat. "Excuse me, Miss,
um, Miss Westgate, would you care to explain what you are
wearing?"

"With pleasure, Senator Dashwood." Cordelia smiled dis-
armingly. "This uniform belonged to my grandmother, who was
a second lieutenant in the Women's Army Corps during World
War Two. She has donated it to the Bentley Museum for a special exhibit on American military uniforms. I'm sure I don't
need to tell you that it was made in America by women who
were members of the International Ladies Garment Workers
Union." At the mention of the ILGWU, there was a cheer from
the union members in the audience, their modern-day counter-

parts who belonged to UNITE, the Union of Needletrades, Industrial, and Textile Employees.

"What do you think of that stunt?" Kenyon asked Lacey. The *Post* reporter looked her way and jotted notes.

"It's great. I only wish her grandmother had been in the Navy. The WAVES uniforms were designed by Mainbocher. Pure class."

"Who designed the Army's uniforms?"

"I heard it was a committee. How democratic."

At the sound of the gavel, Aaron Bentley took his turn as a witness, smoothly clicking off figures that made the fashion industry sound like the engine of the American economy, calculated to warm the hearts of Republicans on the Senate panel. But handsome and glib though he was, he didn't add any sizzle to the proceedings. *Not like a pretty spokesmodel wearing something unexpected*, Lacey thought.

Following his remarks, the Bentleys were on their feet and moving out of the hearing room, and so were half the reporters. They didn't wait for the union witnesses to begin their statements. The glamour was wherever the Bentleys were.

Aaron slid past Lacey's table with Cordelia on his arm and Lacey heard her complain *sotto voce,* "I've got to get out of this thing, darling. You have no idea how hot it is."

"Just be glad we didn't make you wear the khaki rayon panties, the girdle, the rayon stockings, and the jersey slip," Aaron whispered as he squeezed her elbow. "Now smile pretty, Cordy; this is your big moment. Maybe you could salute." Cordelia jabbed him quickly in the ribs before returning to her role and smiling for the cameras.

Khaki panties. It was a lovely tidbit; Lacey wrote it down. The media swarm closed around Aaron Bentley and Cordelia Westgate, and Lacey tried to figure out how best to approach Hugh the B, who was also being swallowed up by a smaller circle of reporters. She was trying to elbow her way in as unobtrusively as possible when she suddenly caught his eye.

For a moment Hugh stared at Lacey; then he drew up his silver-handled walking stick and waved it around like a rapier to carve out some room. He motioned for Lacey to come closer. The crowd grudgingly parted for her.

"Young woman, young woman, is that an original Bentley suit you're wearing, or just a copy? Let me take a look at you— my God, it is my suit! And it's in beautiful shape. I'd know that suit anywhere." He lifted his eyes from her to the crowd and addressed them like a circus barker. "That suit, ladies and gentlemen, was from my very first collection, the one that made my reputation, at least in a small way. Fall of 1944," Hugh said. "And this lovely young lady has brought it back to life. My dear, my dear, come tell me your name. You and I must talk."

Lacey Smithsonian's

Fashion Bites

How to Tell If You're Prematurely Serious

Experienced Washington observers will have taken note of the predominant Washington look. You see it every-where—in the halls of Congress, walking down K Street, or just squeezing the oranges at Safeway. The look that says, "We are serious."

Washington style is serious with a capital S, serious as in we-are-messing-with-your-lives serious, we are writing your laws, we are collecting your taxes, and we are spending your money. (It's for your own good.) And when we say serious, we mean *Serious!*

While this is the accepted look for the gray and gray-ing federal workforce, it seems unnaturally somber in the young. Unfortunately, Washington is positively drenched in the look of the tragically drab Young Fogey. Test your-self to see if you are among the Prematurely Serious:

- You put on your photo ID tag before you leave your home. You wear it everywhere, even to go to the video store. Or perhaps you never take it off. You feel naked without it. You have a serious identity— you need serious identification.
- Casual Fridays make you tense. Casual is not Seri-ous. If you wanted to be casual, you'd live in Cali-fornia, for pity's sake. So you wear a tie anyway, or heels and hose, and a smart navy blazer. "Oh, is it Friday already?" you say. "I've been so busy, I lost track of time. The weekend? Oh, I'll be working all weekend."

- Your wardrobe consists entirely of black, navy, taupe, gray, and white. You think of the taupe outfit as your reckless, devil-may-care look.
- Color makes you nervous, and bright shades of pink, yellow, and purple cause you to break out in a sweat. In fact, those are colors you'd only wear in a sweatshirt, and only at the gym, where exercise is Serious Business.
- Makeup? Contacts? A makeover, a great new haircut, a dress you couldn't possibly wear to the office? Fine for other people, people who don't have Serious Jobs. But when *you* need a new look, there's always your impressive collection of Serious Spectacles, including horn-rims, wire frames, aviators, frameless frames, and those little tiny frames that make you look like Ben Franklin's bookkeeper.
- Hair can be sporty, seductive, creative, carefree, or Serious. Like yours. "Hair? What's wrong with my hair? I don't have time to fuss with my hair. I'm late, I have a meeting, I have Serious Work to do!"

Think about it, Oh ye who are Prematurely Serious. There must be some way to fit into Washington, D.C., without blending into its bland wallpaper. When a thousand identical khaki trench coats march down K Street, it looks like some kind of conspiracy, a convention of federal agents, a conference of the Brotherhood (or Sisterhood) of the Serious. But, hear me, Oh Serious ones, you don't have to be part of the conspiracy of the dull and drab. There is help for the Prematurely Serious, even here in our Nation's Capital. Stick with me, and help is on the way.

chapter 2

Lacey was surprised to find herself seated at Hugh Bentley's side at lunch at SeaWorthy, the exclusive new seafood restaurant on K Street, but she didn't question her good fortune. Hugh had insisted on sweeping her up in the Bentley entourage, ostensibly to discuss her vintage Bentley suit, and Lacey was perfectly willing to let herself be flattered by the old rake.

The Bentley clan was indulging in early cocktails, martinis all around, while Lacey, with her iced tea, enjoyed the gleaming hardwood floors, the polished paneling, and the red leather booths of the elegant restaurant. Background music played swing. The place was packed with lobbyists and lawyers and the occasional deep-pocketed tourist. The Bentleys occupied a secluded corner beneath a stuffed swordfish, and Belinda and Marilyn were discussing the shopping expedition they planned for that afternoon as eagerly as if they were seventeen, not seventyish.

Aaron and Cordelia arrived late from their hotel. She had insisted on changing into a sleek, bare, sleeveless black dress and sky-high heels. She made it clear she had given her all by wearing that itchy WAC uniform. *Apparently posing stark naked is all in a day's work for Cordelia,* Lacey thought, *but wearing wool is above and beyond the call of duty.*

"But you were so fetching, Cordelia. It was a perfect performance," Hugh said. "And it impressed the committee. Far more than I ever could have."

"Not to mention the cameras. Remind me to thank your parents for those perfect cheekbones," Aaron added, stroking her face before introducing Cordelia to Lacey. "She's a reporter with *The Eye Street Observer.* Isn't that a smashing suit? Dad says it's an original Bentley from the first collection."

"You're not from *The Washington Post*?" Cordelia asked Lacey, obviously disappointed.

"I'm sure she's from a much more fair and balanced newspaper," Aaron said. "Isn't that right, Ms. Smithsonian?"

Another member of the clan joined the table. Jeffrey Bentley Holmes, Belinda's son, who designed the stores for the family firm, was another late arrival. He hadn't attended the hearing, being occupied with the museum opening. "Sorry, politics doesn't interest me," he said by way of excuse. "I'd rather hit myself in the head with a hammer."

He smiled winningly at Lacey. "Is this seat taken?" Jeffrey had golden-blond hair and was decidedly not Lacey's type. He was too perfect, he was too wealthy, he was too smooth, and positively too attractive. He could have been a Bentley model himself, with his even features and strong square jaw. He had an easy elegance, even though he was the most casual of the Bentleys, wearing a linen shirt and slacks and sports jacket. Lacey immediately marked him as the type who would pay no attention to her, preferring the allure of a Cordelia or an Esme. In her early thirties, Lacey figured a guy like Jeffrey would be looking for a woman with lower numbers in both age and IQ. He sat down next to her.

"Uncle Hugh loves it when people do their homework," he murmured in her ear.

"Homework?"

"You're wearing an extremely rare vintage Bentley, I gather from Aaron's hyperventilating, and you wear it extremely well. You made a big impression on Uncle Hugh, and you don't even look remotely like a reporter. Unless it's Brenda Starr."

"I'll take that as a compliment." *I love Brenda Starr.*

The last arrival was Aaron Bentley's special assistant, a tall, thin, black man they called Chevalier. He was almost too pretty with his cocoa skin and thick black eyelashes. He seemed ageless, and he could have been twenty-five or forty-five.

"Chevalier, do you know the whereabouts of Miss Esme Fairchild?" Hugh asked. "There was some confusion at the hearing. I expected to see her helping to manage this affair."

"I'm afraid no one has seen her today, Hugh." He busied himself with his napkin.

Cordelia narrowed her eyes at the mention of Esme. "How very odd. I thought she would have Velcroed herself to Aaron today." She lightly touched Aaron's arm with her perfectly manicured nails.

"Surely you didn't mind her absence?" Belinda teased her.

"Of course not, Belinda. I just want to see her wear something as comfy as I had to wear today," Cordelia said. "Something like a straitjacket, in itchy olive-drab wool."

"I'm sure we could design something appropriate, Cordelia, dear," Hugh said.

"Wearing that uniform wasn't that bad, Cordy, and it was a good idea, even if it was Esme's," Aaron said.

"All I said was that I'd like her to wear that damn uniform herself," Cordelia protested, wide-eyed. "Wool! I'll have a rash for a week." Cordelia lifted up her arms to expose an imaginary rash—and much more—to the slightly disconcerted waiter. Then she ordered the lobster. "At least she's not here with us making big cow eyes at Aaron."

"Pay no attention to them, Lacey; Bentleys are all wicked to the core," Jeffrey informed her.

"And you are not a Bentley?" his mother asked in high dudgeon.

"I'm only half a Bentley."

"That's not funny, Jeffrey."

Hugh broke in. "Did you get all of the press statements, Miss Smithsonian? The important ones. Ours." Chevalier assured the patriarch that he had handed out all the statements without Esme Fairchild's help.

"But if you need anything else, please call me." Chevalier produced his personal business card for Lacey. She glanced at it, expecting to read his full name, but it said only *Chevalier.* And a cell phone number. *Even their flunkies are pretentious,* she thought.

Hugh ordered the salmon and turned to Lacey. "Did we put on a good show today?"

"Do you mean Cordelia and the WAC uniform? It was a crowd pleaser." She wasn't sure how the Senate panel would react to "the Bentley show."

"It was all very much spur of the moment. We got that request to appear before the Senate committee just last week," Hugh confided. "All of our communications people are in Paris and Milan preparing for the fashion weeks in October. So we're working with Chevalier here to see if he has what it takes to be our entire PR department for a week or two."

Lacey turned to Chevalier. "What do you normally do?"

"Jack-of-all-trades." He smiled at her.

And master of none? she thought. "How's it going?"

"I'm taking lessons from Hugh in the schmooze department. Generally I work on a variety of jobs for Aaron, sort of his right-hand man."

"Enough chat!" Hugh suddenly declared, and turned to Lacey. "I've been dying to ask you, Miss Smithsonian: Where *did* you get that suit?"

"It's Lacey, please. And the suit was a gift from my aunt. Great-aunt. Her name was Mimi Smith. Mary Margaret Smith, actually, but everyone always called her Mimi." She paused for effect. "I understand that she knew you, once upon a time. During World War Two."

Hugh was silent for a moment. "Mary Margaret Smith." He shook his head. "No, I can't say I remember a lady by that name. Of course, the war—that war—was a long time ago." Lacey thought Mimi was pretty unforgettable. She was a little disappointed—and a little unsure whether she should believe him. "But do you happen to know how she came by the suit?"

"I imagine she bought it. She loved beautiful clothes. She left it to me."

"She's no longer with us?"

Lacey shook her head. *And took your secret, whatever it was, to her grave.*

"I'm sorry. She must have looked lovely in that suit, if her beautiful niece is any indication."

Marilyn addressed Lacey for the first time. "Don't pay any attention to him, Lacey; he's an incorrigible old flirt."

"But a charming one, I hope, Mrs. Bentley," Hugh said.

"So that's where Aaron gets it," Cordelia cut in.

Hugh paused a moment to evaluate his salmon plate. He took a bite, deemed it acceptable. "I should point out that I have been married to this charming lady for almost sixty years," he said, and smiled at his wife.

"And everyone knows that Marilyn has been his biggest inspiration," Belinda said. "It must be true; it's been in all the news stories."

"That's enough, Belinda," Marilyn said. "She's incorrigible as well."

"Incorrigibility runs in the family," Jeffrey cut in.

"I understand there will be a fund-raising gala the night before the museum opens," Lacey said, changing the subject.

"The theme is 'Sixty Years of American Fashion,' starting from the war years," Marilyn said. "Because you have an interest in vintage clothing, perhaps you should come and cover it for your newspaper, Lacey. It's black-tie, but many people will be wearing vintage evening wear, vintage couture, as sort of a style retrospective. I understand there will be some very special Bentley originals." She lifted her glass to her husband and winked.

The thought of seeing all that vintage clothing in action was intoxicating for Lacey. It was true she would have wrestled alligators to get off the fashion beat, but she did love good clothing, especially from the Forties. "I'll have to check with my editor, but thanks. I'd love to."

Belinda cleared her throat. "Of course, you don't have to wear old clothes. I'll be wearing something very sleek and modern from our latest collection."

"Will the First Lady be at the gala?" Lacey hoped that

sounded casual, not like a reporter fishing for a story. There was a moment's silence as the Bentleys exchanged glances.

"We haven't had confirmation from the White House yet," Marilyn said carefully.

"Aren't you going to spill your big news, Hugh?" Belinda teased. She turned to Lacey. "The First Lady will cut the ribbon and open the doors to the museum two weeks from today."

"I'd heard a rumor to that effect," Lacey said.

"These things always get out, especially with a little help from Belinda." Hugh sighed. "But you might as well be the first to know that Aaron is designing a special outfit for her, which is very exclusive. It will become the basis for a new 'First Lady' line of designer wear."

Lacey's fashion reporter senses were quivering. *It's the suit,* she thought. *Wear a great suit, get a great story.* "A special outfit? What does it look like? What color? A dress, a suit?"

"That's enough of a scoop for now," Aaron said testily. "Who knows, maybe someone will leak you a sketch of the design before the opening." He glowered at the others.

"You have to be patient, Lacey. Aaron jealously guards his secrets," Hugh said, rapping the floor with his walking stick for emphasis. "But I can tell you this. We'll be using vintage silk that has been in the vaults for decades. It was too special to use—until now."

By two-thirty, the Bentleys were shopping and Lacey was back at her desk. The office seemed calm, and even Felicity Pickles, the food writer and sometime copy editor at the next desk, was gone. Lacey was making some headway on the First Lady ribbon-cutting story. But too soon, Felicity's new perfume entered the airspace. It cost a hundred and twenty-five dollars an ounce, smelled like a cross between gardenias and metal-working fluids, and spread like a cloud of mustard gas. Felicity lumbered into view behind it.

Dabbing a drop of WD-40 behind each ear would cost a lot less, smell better—and prevent rust! Not to mention attract a certain class of men. Lacey decided not to tell Felicity this. It wouldn't help, and Felicity was a heavyweight contender who could beat her in any fight.

"More old clothes, Lacey?" Felicity clucked sympathetically, as if Lacey had dressed out of a Goodwill grab bag.

"It's an original vintage Bentley suit. You've heard of them. As in 'the Three Bs of American Fashion: Beene, Blass, and Bentley'?"

"If you say so." Felicity chuckled. Lacey knew she was thinking that the fashion beat really should have been hers. *Felicity would be writing about how to accessorize your muumuu with an attractive canvas car cover.*

"You have some crumbs on your chin," Lacey said.

Felicity wiped her face and glared back. To be fair it was very difficult, if not impossible, for someone who wrote about food all day (when she wasn't copyediting Lacey's prose into oblivion) to keep the pounds at bay. And people wouldn't think about it, except that Felicity herself always brought up how much weight she was gaining.

Tony Trujillo's approach saved her from more pointless banter with Felicity. Tony was *The Eye*'s cop reporter and hailed from New Mexico, while Lacey was originally from Colorado. He considered them old neighbors, the Westerners among the Eastern flatlanders.

"Hey, Smithsonian, what's been keeping you?"

"Lunch with the Bentleys at SeaWorthy, that new seafood restaurant on K Street." She said it for Felicity's benefit. Lacey didn't really care for seafood or lobster. *We don't eat bugs that big in the West.* But she knew Felicity would be jealous. "And I'm working on an exclusive about the Bentleys and the First Lady."

"Yeah? Well, I got a real crime of fashion for you."

"What, your new boots? Which endangered species are these made from? Komodo dragon?"

Tony leaned against her desk to show them off. "Ostrich. And they're not endangered. They're— Never mind, we've got an armed robbery. Right up your alley."

"Since when is armed robbery up my alley?"

"Since it happened at Bentley's Boutique yesterday morning. Sort of a coincidence, your being on the Bentley story."

"I hate coincidences, Trujillo."

"It already made the police column. Maybe you could use it in a 'Crimes of Fashion' column." He produced a copy of that day's *Eye Street Observer*, open to a two-paragraph brief, "Bandit Trio Robs Boutique."

"Do you ever notice how you're always trying to give me more work?"

He shrugged and favored her with a brilliant white smile in his smooth tan face. Although Tony was the police reporter, the robbery at Bentley's wasn't the kind of story he would usually cover. Not gory or gaudy enough. No death. And a lot of murders in the District never even hit the newspapers; there were just too many. But he knew that Lacey had ambitions beyond reporting the fickle frippery of fashion, and he was determined to prod that ambition, no matter how much extra work it created for her.

"There's this Bentley's employee, Miguel Flores. Took a beating. He might be willing to tell his story. Says he's a fan of yours. Besides, these are well-dressed crooks hitting a big-money boutique, not the normal scum-on-scum crime that I cover."

"Maybe a sidebar. Your Miguel have a phone number?"

"I knew something was wrong," Miguel said. "Nobody wears Chanel at ten o'clock on a Monday morning."

Miguel Flores was more than happy to tell Lacey about the three overdressed bandits who pulled an armed robbery at Bentley's Chevy Chase boutique, where Miguel was the assistant manager. The robbery went off track, thanks in part to Miguel, and ended with the arrival of not one but two SWAT teams and the capture of two men, one white and one Hispanic. The third suspect, an attractive Chanel-wearing black woman, escaped with the booty. Her trail ended with a discarded wig and one high heel in a nearby parking garage.

Miguel was tall and thin and effortlessly stylish. He sported a flower in his lapel, a yellow rose. His glossy dark hair was worn in a slicked-back ponytail, and he was meticulously dressed, despite his rough handling the day before. Large purple bruises had already formed on his smooth face and neck where one or more of the assailants had kicked him repeatedly. Lacey could see he would be very nice looking when the swelling went down. He met her and Tony, who had come along for the ride, at a small café near the boutique. Miguel was sipping wine. Lacey couldn't write a word if she drank anything, so she was doomed to a decaf coffee, black. Tony slurped some kind of latte. Miguel claimed to be a huge fan of Lacey's column, and he positively purred at seeing Tony again, who was oblivious. "And do you know what else, Lacey? We have the same hairstylist! Stella!"

"Stella Lake? You're kidding!"

"Is there any other? I'm at Stylettos all the time; I can't believe we never run into each other."

"Oh, dear. Then you already know too much." Lacey could just imagine what Stella might have said about her. Stella knew—and told—far too much about her. *About everything.*

Miguel caught her look. "Don't worry; she only told me all the good parts of your innermost secrets, like your big adventure this spring."

"That's what I was afraid of."

"I feel like we're old friends. And Stylettos is so much cooler now that Ratboy isn't her boss anymore. So, like, what about the guy you were seeing? The ex-cop? I hear he was totally hot. I love men from the West." Lacey felt her face color and she glanced at Tony.

"Pay no attention to me," Tony said. "I'll just think about baseball."

"We'll talk about men later, Miguel. Let's get back to the robbery."

Miguel took a sip of wine and his hands trembled. Adrenaline obviously still pumped through his veins at the mention of the robbery. "I had a bad feeling the moment I saw the three of them enter the store," he said. "This overdressed woman and two big fat queens. But what are you going to do? Call the cops on every inappropriate customer? 'Officer, these people are simply not our kind here at Bentley's. Kindly remove them.' Of course, later I wished I had, when I was tied up on the floor next to Kika." He paused for effect.

"They started wandering around with that phony I'm-just-browsing kind of air. I went in the back room for a second, and when I came back out the fat white guy immediately stuck a gun in my face, took my cell phone, and forced me upstairs to the office. Kika was on the floor. Oh, my God! At first I thought she was already dead, but then I saw her breathing. I was tied up too, with duct tape, 'execution style.' That's what the cops said. Then the bitch slaps me for no reason, just no reason at all, and it just made me so mad I said to myself, 'Over my dead body is this bunch of faggots going to rob my store.'"

He smiled and acknowledged what Lacey and Tony were thinking. "Yes, of course, I too am gay. As if that were a big secret. Just ask Stella. But they were, like, *extra* gay. And, like, extra vicious. And I couldn't let them get away with robbing my store, or killing Kika. Or killing me. I object to people killing me, gay or not."

Lacey wrote it down, knowing that all the good quotes would be excised from her copy if Felicity got her hands on it. "So how much do you think they—or rather she—got away with?"

"Furs, leather jackets, and jewelry. Over a million."

"No way!"

"Way! The jewelry accounts for most of it." Designer stores got robbed all the time, Miguel told Lacey. Both Versace and Gucci, located nearby, had recently suffered heavy losses.

Lacey wanted to avoid the typical intrusive journalist questions like, 'How did it feel?' The questions that really mean: 'Would you please cry for the cameras?' Instead she said, "What else can you tell me?"

"After they tied us up, they left the office and went back downstairs for more pillaging and looting. I was so totally pissed. I kept working my hands up and down till they were loose. Maybe it helped that my hands were sweating. But I was still all covered with tape. I crawled to the desk and managed to pull the phone off the desk and dial nine-one-one, and I was great; it was just like a movie. I said, 'Robbery in progress at Bentley's Boutique on Wisconsin!' I gave them my name, so I wouldn't be, like, a nameless victim in an unmarked grave if I was killed. I heard footsteps coming back upstairs, and the cops kept saying, 'Stay on the line, sir, stay on the line.' I dragged the phone under the desk and the door opened. Then it shut. I thought I was in the clear, but then it opened again, like they noticed something was wrong."

"That would be you, under the desk with a phone?" Lacey asked.

"Right. I hung up the phone and she screamed at me, 'The cops, you bastard, did you call the cops?' I said, no, no, it was a wrong number. The woman looked at me. That's when the kicking started."

"You said they were well dressed. What did they look like?"

"The men were big and flash. Lots of leather, jewelry, and bling-bling. Wearing your basic black, but expensive basic black, not your Gap starving artiste collection. Armani suits."

"Not Bentley?" Lacey asked.

Miguel shook his head. "Go figure." The woman was simply overdone, he said, from her nails to her black patent stilettos, the baby blue Chanel suit trimmed in black, and the blue-and-lime-green Hermes scarf she wore around her neck. But what he remembered more was her beautiful, vicious face as she repeatedly kicked him in the head. Then her scarf slipped down, revealing a flaw in her perfection, an unsightly scar on her neck. That Miguel saw this enraged her all the more.

"She screamed at the two guys, 'Shoot him, shoot him.' And she just kept kicking me in the head. The sirens started. The three of them pounded down the stairs. The Montgomery County SWAT team arrived, then another one, and they were all over the place in no time. And they got the two fat boys, but the bitch was long gone." Miguel stopped for breath and another sip of wine. "Thank God we're just over the Maryland line out of the District, or I'd be this year's D.C. homicide number three hundred something."

Lacey didn't know what to make of Miguel's story. *Perhaps simply that stolen clothes make the man—or the woman?* According to Tony, the two captured accomplices lawyered up and were emphatically not talking. They wouldn't discuss the woman. They wouldn't say a word. They knew the drill. Tony said the two flunkies were pros, but the woman in charge sounded like an out-of-control amateur. *Maybe the crime of fashion makes the criminal.*

chapter 3

There was a postcard from Vic when she got home. It was brief and unsatisfying: *Hey, Lacey, the aspen are changing here and turning the mountains to gold. It would be even prettier if you were here. Vic.*

No word as to when he might be coming back. If ever. *How very male.* No "Dear Lacey." No "Love, Vic." She turned the card over. It featured the mythical jackalope, the half jackrabbit, half antelope critter that was the semiofficial symbol of the Western Slope. Was it supposed to be funny? Was it just the first postcard he came across? Or did it carry a hidden meaning, that their relationship was as nonexistent as the elusive jackalope?

After a rocky start, they had decided to take their relationship slowly. Or as Vic put it, "I don't want to spook you. We both know how skittish you are."

She didn't agree, exactly. But with her past history of bolting from boyfriends who wanted to get serious, she wasn't really in a position to argue. Then in July, Vic had to return to Steamboat Springs, Colorado. Partly to take care of business, but mostly it was about Montana—not the state; Montana, his ex-wife. Montana McCandless Donovan, now Montana McCandless Donovan Schmidt.

"She wants to buy my house," Vic said. "She always loved that house."

"I thought she married someone else and they're living somewhere in Wyoming."

"Idaho. And they're getting a divorce."

"So that would make her an ex-ex-wife. An available ex-ex-wife."

"Calm down, Lacey; it's just an easy way to unload the house. I thought you'd be happy." *For a smart man, he can be such an idiot,* Lacey thought. She had seen Montana a couple of times back in Sagebrush when Lacey worked on the local daily newspaper. Vic's soon-to-be ex would occasionally blow into town to whine and complain about something. Montana was aggressively blond and blue-eyed, the girl-next-door-on-skis type. She was all about sheepskin jackets and tight blue jeans and tighter little tops. From what Vic told her, his marriage to Montana broke up partly because he was a cop, and not just a cop but chief of police, first in godforsaken Sagebrush, Colorado, then in the booming metropolis of Steamboat Springs. She couldn't take Vic's hours, his dedication to his job, or the way women throw themselves at cops. But Vic was no longer a cop; now he was a private investigator with his father's security business. He said his future was in Virginia; Colorado (and Montana) were in the past.

"How long will you be gone?" Lacey had asked.

"The house needs some work. Roofing, plumbing, shoring up the foundation."

"What kind of ramshackle shed were you living in?"

"The kind with a view of Rabbit Ears Peak and pronghorns grazing out back. It's a little rustic," he said, "but it's huge and it's got a great fireplace and a deck and a big wood-burning stove. Heats up the whole place on cold winter nights."

"With snow up to your ass." She shivered. She remembered it all too well.

"You never cared for the winters, did you? Are you sure you're really from Colorado, or an alien from some hot planet in a galaxy far away?"

"I was totally broke, my car died, my toilet froze, it was forty below, and in that moment I realized I could be that poor anywhere, but I sure as hell didn't have to freeze to death."

"Alien, then. Yeah, Sagebrush was a hard town, Lacey. Steamboat's a lot more civilized."

"How long will you be gone?"

"I don't know. A month."

"A month!"

"Who knows, maybe less." He kissed her good-bye and said he would call, he would write. It had been two months and a couple of postcards.

Lacey's intuition was on Code Red. She was sure Montana wanted Vic back. The house was just a pretext, and he was too big a dope to see it. A dope with dark curly hair, grass-colored eyes crinkled from the Western sun, and a smile that could wreak havoc on a weak-willed woman like Lacey. He was swimming in an alligator swamp and Lacey was afraid she would lose him. All the better not to have taken the relationship further, to intimacy. This, of course, was the dumbest thing she could do, according to Stella, friend, hairstylist, amateur guidance counselor, and world-class purveyor of gossip.

"You blew it, Lacey," Stella had said. "You should have slept with him right off the bat. Like I do. Guys dig that. You ever hear about catching more flies with honey as opposed to, like, you know, vinegar? And at least you would have had some beautiful memories." Stella had lots of beautiful memories. She was that kind of gal. Lacey put the postcard aside and forced Vic, Montana, and Stella from her thoughts.

Overall it had been an exhausting yet exhilarating day. Lacey had lucked into lunch and a personal interview with the legendary Hugh Bentley and a scoop on the First Lady's opening the fashion museum. *Not just luck*, she reminded herself. *It's the suit. Aunt Mimi's Bentley suit*. The inside story on the Bentley's robbery would also lead to a column, and Miguel was a delight. And there would be another Bentley story from the museum opening. Suddenly there seemed to be Bentleys everywhere she turned.

So what was the Bentley link to her aunt Mimi? Lacey headed for the trunk that Mimi had left her, which doubled as her coffee table and served as her personal security blanket. She

loved to wander through it when she was tired and low on inspiration. Mimi's trunk of patterns and photos was a kind of
combination time capsule and diary of Lacey's favorite aunt. It
was her secret pleasure to roam through the belted wooden
trunk, as full of riches as any pirate's treasure chest. Uncounted
vintage dress patterns filled the chest, and Lacey had barely
begun to explore them. The patterns had been collected and
abandoned in various stages of completion, some still pinned to
fabric, some nearly finished, a fashion archaeologist's dream,
left in stratigraphic context. Mimi had great plans, but limited
time and, apparently, a limited attention span. Lacey delighted
in choosing clothes from the trunk and completing them for her
own wardrobe. Mimi had also tossed mementos, letters, and
photos in the trunk, and sometimes she included a note about a
dress or a picture of a movie star wearing a similar outfit.

Lacey changed into comfort clothes, poured herself a cold
Dos Equis, and slid to the floor in bare feet to undo the brass
buckles. If there were clues to That Bastard Hugh, they would
be in the trunk. After removing about six layers of old patterns
she found a large fat manila envelope marked *Bentley.* She
glanced at it, set it down, and looked for anything else that
might be related. An opening in the lining under the hinges of
the trunk bulged out. Lacey had noticed the slit before, always
telling herself she should fix it, but this time she looked closer,
and she saw that another envelope was tucked inside. On the
outside was a pencil sketch of the Bentley suit Lacey had worn
that very day. It was signed, *Gloria Adams.*

Who is Gloria Adams? She was about to open it when the
phone rang. It was Stella.

"Hey, Lacey, you're on TV. Channel Five. Quick, you're
gonna miss yourself!"

Lacey grabbed the remote. She missed the lead-in to the
story and caught the commercial, and then she had to wait for
the twenty-second news story on Hugh Bentley, with a clip of
the old patriarch parting the crowd with his walking stick and
imperiously demanding their attention. Lacey was featured

prominently in the shot, allowing her to bask in the moment all over again.

"Aren't you the Queen of the May?" Stella said, still on the phone. Lacey was more interested in Bentley's reaction to her in the news footage. In the close-up he had a look of recognition that she hadn't noticed before; she'd been too surprised and flattered by his attention. *He remembers Mimi, not just that suit. I'm sure of it.*

"Wow, Lacey, what a crowd," Stella gushed. "So, is Cordelia Westgate totally supermodel skinny? And can you tell if she's had a little work done, like they say?"

"Yes, she's skinny. Except for her plumped-up lips. Possibly Botoxed. And she's not exactly Miss Congeniality. But I'm totally fried and I still have some work to do, Stella. Can we talk tomorrow?"

"Absolutely. You can tell me what you think of Miguel. He thinks you're a doll, by the way."

Of course she had already conferenced with Miguel. "You're amazing, Stella. Did you ever think of a career in journalism?"

"Nope, I'm doing what I love. Improving people, people like you."

"You're not going to suggest something new with my hair, are you?"

"We'll talk." She hung up and Lacey returned to the trunk. She shook out the envelope that held the sketch of the Bentley suit. Instead of finding answers, another mystery fell in her lap, consisting of a packet of letters, sketches, photos, and a few yellowed news clippings from *The Alexandria Gazette* in May and June of 1944. "Local Woman Disappears in New York," "Friends Fearful After Disappearance of Local Factory Girl," and "Gloria Adams Still Missing."

Lacey read the short news stories, dated from May 24 and June 5, 1944. Twenty-three-year-old Gloria Adams was from Falls Church, Virginia, a little town out in the country at the time, now a booming suburb well inside the Washington Beltway. She was working at the Bentley's dress factory in Manhattan, which also had a contract for sewing shirts for the military, at the time she disappeared. Miss Adams was last seen on Thursday, May 11, at her place of employment, according to other factory workers, and police were following up on leads. She was described as five feet, six inches tall, weighing one hundred fifteen pounds. She had dark curly hair and she wore a light blue Bentley's smock over a navy skirt, white anklets, and navy-and-white saddle shoes. One of the clippings quoted a Miss Mary Margaret Smith, a friend of the missing girl, who said Gloria Adams would not just leave without telling her friends and family.

Mimi in the midst of a mystery? How exciting, Lacey thought. Miss Smith had been in contact with Miss Adams recently and feared foul play. She urged anyone with information to contact the police or the Office of Price Administration, where she worked as an assistant to the director. The factory manager (and the owner's son), Hugh Bentley, expressed his shock and sorrow, and offered a reward of $1,000 for information leading to her return.

So, Hugh, you don't remember Aunt Mimi? I wonder if you remember Gloria Adams. Lacey told herself to be fair; old people had memory lapses. It might also be true that he had so many women in his life, he had forgotten some of them. *The bastard.*

Who was Gloria Adams, and how did her letters and dreams wind up in Aunt Mimi's trunk? Lacey wondered. And how did the long-defunct Office of Price Administration fit in? The only thing Lacey knew about it was that Mimi had worked there during the war. Perhaps Lacey's finding this cache of documents was another gift from Mimi, a glimpse into the nearly forgotten life of the only family member with whom Lacey had had a real bond.

She looked at one old photograph of three young women, including Mimi. On the back Mimi had written, *The Three Musketeers, Spring 1942,* and three names and places: Mimi Smith of Alexandria, "Morning Glory" Adams of New York City, and Mrs. Phillip "Honey" Martin of Georgetown. The black-and-white photo, hand-tinted with a soft wash of pastels, showed a picnic, an ideal day at Great Falls, Virginia. Mimi, so young, so pretty and full of life, wearing blue jeans and bare feet, was balanced on a log overhanging the Potomac. Lacey had never seen this photo, but she would know Mimi anywhere, at any age. Seeing her aunt so young gave her a pang of loss. She wished she could have known her then. Lacey guessed that Honey must be the pretty blond girl-next-door type with the big smile. That left frizzy-haired Morning Glory; she was no beauty, but she had a compelling intensity and a knockout figure. *Obviously Morning Glory must be the missing Gloria Adams*, she thought. *Obvious to me, anyway.*

One mailing envelope with a canceled three-cent stamp contained old letters on blue stationery and written in blue ink. Lacey carefully unfolded the letters one by one.

Dear Mims,   *February 13, 1942*
I still don't understand what your job is at the high-and-mighty Office of Price Administration, but I owe you for putting in a word with Hugh Bentley. I won't have to start on the factory floor but will work as a cutter and draping fabrics for new designs. He's impressed with my skills. By the way, I thought you two were an item. What happened? What's wrong with you? He looks like Tyrone Power!

I'm a little afraid about moving to New York and leaving my friends, but I'm going to be a career girl in fashion design and that's the place to be. Imagine trying to do that in our sleepy southern backwater of Washington, D.C.! I know it's the seat of government, but those trousers are baggy, Mims. That's a joke. Besides, I know you love clothes as much as I do. There's a rooming house for a lot of the factory girls where I can live. I'll write when I can.

Love, Gloria

Dear Mims,   *May 6, 1942*

I may have broken my first rule! Except it isn't written down, so I'm not sure. I've been here two months and I haven't said as much as "Boo!" Really. I have been a model of propriety. And Mims, I know you would be on my side if you could just see this silly smock we have to wear, a puffy powder-blue smock with patch pockets. It pouches in all the wrong places. I simply had to take it all apart and reshape the yoke, and take out some of the excess material. Now I look more like a designer and less like a clown. It fits so much better and looks quite smart when I fold the sleeves back into deep cuffs, even though deep cuffs are outlawed by the new clothing regulations. Can you believe it?

Part of my job as a studio apprentice is to measure cuffs and the like to make sure we're following the accursed L-85. I call it the collar-and-cuffs law, and I always wear my measuring tape around my neck or have it close by in my pocket.

I'm just grateful that I don't have to work on the factory floor. Those poor girls have to wear drab green aprons and green makes me look so sallow! Anyway, my little blue smock looks so much better, and no one has said anything to me yet. Wish me luck.

Love, Glory

Dear Mims,   *July 10, 1942*

I know we have to do our part for the war, but day-to-day factory life is not my idea of the best way to do it. Please don't ever think I'm not grateful for your help in getting this job. Because I am, and I know that it's a stepping-stone. But how on earth do those girls in the airplane factories do it? It's so hot that the sweat trickles all the way down my spine. My shoulders ache and my back hurts and I get so thirsty.

Of course I want to do my part for the war effort. But I've got dreams, Mims. Someday the war will end.

At night when I work on my sketches, somehow I forget about the day. I have to go. Five A.M. comes too soon; guess I'll never be a "Morning Glory."

Love, Glory

Dear Mims,   *August 13, 1942*

    I know I'm a dreadful correspondent. But truly, I'm so tired at the end of the day I can hardly keep my eyes open. Do you remember how I used to think about clothes all the time? Now all I think about is food! I'm so hungry and there's never enough to eat. I dream of fried chicken and mashed potatoes the way my mother fixes it. I know I said I'd never miss anything about home, but now I do: home cooking!

Love, Glory

Dear Mims,   *September 6, 1942*

    This boardinghouse is worse than a convent! We are not allowed to have visitors to our rooms except parents on Sunday afternoon. And men, if there happen to be any, must meet us in the lobby. We might as well meet in Grand Central Station for all the privacy there! My landlady, who thinks she is the queen of Rumania, warns us not to mix with the soldiers or sailors. Curfew is ten o'clock on weeknights and midnight on weekends. Boy, do I feel like Cinderella.

    In spite of the hard work, I love to go to the factory because sometimes Hugh Bentley comes by to see how we're doing. He works down the hall in a glassed-in of-fice, which is nice so that we can see a real live man in the henhouse. He said someday I can show him my de-signs! Of course, "someday" hasn't come yet.

Glory

Honestly, dear Mims,   *January 12, 1943*

    If I have to hear "Use it up, wear it out, make it do, or do without" one more time I am going to scream.

*Marie of Rumania—remember my landlady?—has
posted that sign everywhere. And just try asking for seconds. We have to turn over our ration tickets to her; it
doesn't seem fair. After working all day, a girl gets hungry!*

Your Starving Glory

Lacey wanted to read more, but she couldn't keep her eyes
open. She tucked the remaining letters into her purse to read at
work the next day. When she fell asleep a little later, the
wartime slogan *Use it up, wear it out, make it do, or do without*
was ringing over and over in her head like a nursery rhyme.

chapter 4

Lacey's story on the hearing, "Bentleys Present Uniform Testimony in Olive Drab," complete with photos and the exclusive interview with Hugh the B, "First Lady to Open Museum in Bentley Design of Vintage Silk," were splashed across the front page of the Wednesday LifeStyle section of *The Eye*. The sidebar on the Bentley's robbery was tucked in nicely. Lacey checked *The Post*: a perfunctory couple of paragraphs on the museum and the First Lady's surprise letter. *The Washington Times* had even less; their angle was Senator Dashwood's sudden reverence for the taxpayer's dollars. She had scooped them both with her Bentley interview—not that it mattered to anyone but her. She folded the paper and yawned.

"We keeping you up, Smithsonian?"

Lacey opened her eyes, stifled another yawn, and looked into the smooth, caramel-hued face of her boss, Mac, his bushy black eyebrows drawn together like caterpillars huddling. Her foe, her friend, and sometimes her nemesis. In other words, her editor. She was on the verge of nodding off when he interrupted her reverie. "I hope your column won't put us all to sleep." This was Mac's stab at humor.

"It's riveting, Mac." She squinted at the screen. Her "Crimes of Fashion" column on the boutique bandits filled one line so far. "Armed in Armani? Or, is it chic to rob Versace wearing Gucci?" It was a start. She hit Save.

"Good. Johnson called in. He's afraid you're wreaking havoc on his beat up on the Hill. You seem to frighten him."

"Freak. I merely wrote this little story about the rag trade. And Hansen did a nice job with the photos on Cordelia West-gate testifying before the Senate committee."

Mac picked up the paper and grunted. "She's got a lot of hair," he said before he departed.

Lacey didn't choose fashion. It chose her. Or rather, Mac, with inscrutable editorial wisdom, had thrown her into the beat a couple of years earlier, because it was expedient at the time. He had one dropped-dead-of-a-heart-attack fashion editor on his hands and a looming deadline. Lacey, then bylined as L. B. Smithsonian, Mac's newest city reporter, strolled innocently into his field of vision and voilà! Instant fashion reporter. They had fought about it ever since. She yearned for a real beat. He was happy having her fill the fashion slot. Readers loved her and hated her, but they read her, which was all Mac cared about.

"Crimes of Fashion," by Lacey Smithsonian, and her dos-and-don'ts pieces, "Fashion Bites," sold more than a few papers. So she was stuck. And Lacey wasn't even privy to the usual perks of a fashion reporter's job. *The Eye Street Observer* was too poor—or too cheap—to send her off to cover the real fashion world in New York, Paris, or Milan.

She had to make up her own beat out of whole cloth—so to speak—in Washington, D.C., The City That Fashion Forgot. Lacey believed that the clothing people chose always told a story. Unfortunately, in Washington, a peculiar little world of its own with its own baffling rules of dress and culture, the story was usually a dull one. Lacey often found herself working harder than she would have with a normal beat.

The phone rang. "*Eye Street Observer*, Smithsonian."

"So, what are you going to wear to that fancy-schmancy fund-raiser?"

"Nice of you to call, Stella."

"So, like, I just read your story on that museum ball and it's right up your vintage alley."

"I know, it sounds great, but I haven't checked with Mac yet. And I'm not sure they would let an *Eye Street* reporter in with the hoity-toity press like *The New York Times* and *Entertainment Tonight*."

"Is it really five thousand bucks a plate?"

"More like a grand—for the civilians, that is. It's major-league fancy-schmancy. And you know Mac; he wouldn't pop for a grande latte at Starbucks."

"You're going, you know you're going. Forget the money; you'll find a way. But what to wear?"

"I don't know yet, Stel. It's not about me."

"You are so wrong! It is totally all about you, if you look good enough. And it's totally about me, because I'm doing your hair! So of course you will look fabulous. We just need to find you the right look." Lacey heard a bell tinkling in Stella's background. "Damn, my eleven-thirty is here. I'll call you later. So the look. What do you think: Hedy Lamarr? She was the total package. Or maybe Barbara Stanwyck, femme fatale? Think about it." Stella hung up.

"Hey, Smithsonian," Tony was hollering from across the room. His boots du jour traveled swiftly to her desk.

"Hey, yourself. What's up?"

"You were up on the Hill yesterday morning in the appropriations hearing on that museum thing, right?" She nodded. "I saw you on TV last night; nice work snagging that interview."

"Hold the flattery. You're only interested in criminals."

"And criminal activity. We've got a missing woman." Irrationally, Lacey's first thoughts were of Mimi's friend Gloria Adams, who'd apparently been missing for sixty years. *But how did Trujillo know about Gloria?* "You know an intern named Esme Fairchild?" Tony said.

"Oh, right. Esme." *Not Gloria, you dope, Lacey.* "I've talked with her, but she wasn't there yesterday."

"Aha!" Trujillo was bursting to let go of his information. "And she's not there again today."

"You've got my attention. Tell me."

"She hasn't been seen since Monday. Her parents filed a missing-persons report."

"But aren't they in Tennessee or someplace like that?"

"They're flying in. Apparently they're overprotective. When she didn't call them as scheduled, they started calling her office, her friends, her housemates. No one's seen her. I'm working on the story, but I thought you might—"

"More work for me?"

"—help out. I'm sure there's a fashion angle. Mac thinks so too," Tony said, indicating the burly editor who was steaming back down the aisle toward them. Lacey was often struck by Mac's appearance—something like a black G. Gordon Liddy, with all of the intensity and the eyebrows, and none of the politics. "She knows her, Mac," Trujillo said. "Told you she would."

"Smithsonian. You know this Fairchild woman?"

"A little. You want me to work on a fashion angle?"

"There's a fashion angle?" The eyebrows danced.

"Do you read my stories, Mac, or just doodle in the margins?"

"Just help Tony with some background. You know the woman, and we need a more personal view to beef up our coverage. Everyone's going to be all over this story. Another missing intern. You know what that means."

It means that Kenyon over at the Times *might have some inside info. I wonder if he'll share?* "Media circus day?" Lacey asked.

"She's an intern! Missing interns never turn up alive here. Be a miracle if they actually find her. Now get on it." Mac stomped off to put out other journalistic fires.

Lacey first called Kenyon, who swore he didn't know any more than he'd told her at the hearing. Esme was friendly; he assumed she had many boyfriends. He knew what Lacey knew; she was ambitious. In other words, he wasn't sharing.

Lacey hit a little pay dirt with Nancy Mifflin, the subcommittee's guardian of the press releases. Less grumpy today, Nancy didn't have any insight into Esme's possible whereabouts, but she told Lacey that Esme had left some modeling shots in a folder at her desk—would that help? Lacey immediately dispatched a bike messenger to pick up the photos. Nancy also gave her the names of a few other people who might have information, including a housemate where Esme lived. Lacey left a lot of messages and started to wonder about lunch.

The phone rang, but it wasn't a return call from any of the people she was hunting. It was Brooke, her conspiracy-crazed friend, a top-drawer Washington attorney who wasn't above the occasional down-and-dirty surveillance. Brooke Barton, Esquire, managed to pump out billable hours with CNN blaring in the background all day long. She never suffered from network news burnout, unlike mere mortals like Lacey. Brooke's favorite tongue-in-cheek theory of the moment, which Lacey almost believed, was that Washington had top-secret "pheromone jammers." Sinister microwaves transmitted from the basement of the Pentagon were jamming all natural pheromones within the Beltway, derailing all hopes for male-female romance in the Nation's Capital. Why? To ensure that thousands of government wonks mindlessly toiled away at their desks, building empires of red tape, using building blocks made of lawyer's briefs. They knew something was missing in their lives, but they weren't quite sure what. (Brooke and Lacey were pretty sure what was missing from their lives: men.) Brooke's latest twist was that the jamming rays were now color-coded to match the Homeland Security alert level, pumping up the power whenever the country lurched from Yellow to Orange. *Attention, Washingtonians: No fooling around, or the terrorists will win!*

"Lacey, it's me. Listen, I read your appropriations story, I heard about the missing intern, and I put two and two together—"

"And no doubt got sixty-four."

"Why quibble over the math? Are you working on this? What do you know? Did you know this Esme Fairchild? What can you tell me? By the way, I saw you on TV last night—wow, great suit. So what's the story?"

"Take a breath, Brooke."

"No time for that. Are you free? Let's go to lunch, across from the square. I can be there in ten minutes."

"What, no briefs to file? No testimony to prepare? No witnesses to intimidate?"

"Everything is under control. Well, you know what I mean, under control for D.C."

"I'd love to meet you for lunch, but I don't know anything yet. Do you read me?"

"I read you every day, Lacey. See you soon."

Lacey grabbed her purse before anyone else could give her more work. She cut through Farragut Square to reach the restaurant. The day was glorious and warmer than the day before. There was no hint of the crushing Code Red humidity that had dogged the summer. Lacey even detected a slight crispness in the air, announcing a hint of the fall to come. She breathed deeply.

Following her success with the vintage Bentley, it was the perfect day for another Forties suit. This one had a long fitted jacket in a golden tan, with square-cut lapels and a skirt in a warm brown. She wore it with a matching brown shell. Unfortunately there was no label to tell her where it came from; Lacey had picked it up at a vintage store in Vermont. A pair of brown-and-tan spectator pumps with a Cuban heel, not too tall to walk in, were perfect with it.

"Lacey Smithsonian?" She glanced up to see an intense-looking man about thirty staring at her. He was stationed just under the statue of Adm. David Farragut. "Damon Newhouse, Conspiracy Clearinghouse. You know, 'DeadFed dot com'?" He offered his hand.

She stopped and stared at him; then she remembered the Web site that had prominently featured her stories that spring about dead hairstylists, too many suspicious suicides, and a missing seamy videotape. She took his hand.

"I see you're speechless at the sight of me in the flesh. I bet you thought I only existed in the blue glow of a computer screen," he said.

"Right, we've only spoken on the phone. And e-mail."

"When I've been able to get ahold of you. And you don't much like e-mail, do you?"

"You're not going to make me feel guilty, Damon. Not on such a beautiful day."

"Oh, right. Beautiful day. I don't get outside much." He was compact, thin, and dark; boyish, with a delicate face that he tried to toughen up with black wire-framed glasses and a neatly trimmed mustache and goatee. He was dressed all in black, and he looked like he should be carrying bongos and a copy of Allen Ginsberg's *Howl*. It didn't work—he was too cute to look convincingly tough. *Are there lots of these little-boy beatniks lost in cyberspace?* Lacey wondered.

"I've e-mailed you about fifty times," he broke into her thoughts.

"I'm not very good about managing my mailbox," she said.

"I've called a dozen times, too," he said. "You have a sexy voice-mail message."

"I thought you'd be . . ." She groped for something to say.

"Taller?"

Nerdier, creepier, and crazier-looking. "Right. Taller."

"That's what everybody says." He sighed. "I'm taller and handsomer on the Web." He had a nice smile.

"Look, I'd love to talk, but I'm on my way to lunch." She began to walk away.

"That's cool. I'll walk with you. I thought it was time we met in person. Then maybe you'll take my calls. Now that you know I'm real, not computer generated." He matched her step for step. *All too real.* His enthusiasm amused her. She had been enthusiastic once.

The Conspiracy Clearinghouse Web site, better known as DeadFed dot com, was Newhouse's baby, a compendium of all the known, alleged, suspected, or hoped-for conspiracies afoot in Washington since the 1950s. Damon worked by day as a mild-mannered news editor for a trade association for Web-based technologies. By night he was an avenging loose cannon of a journalist whose ambition was to break big news stories on the Web, like *The Drudge Report* and *The Smoking Gun*. He strove to be a force for truth, a concept that in Washington was both malleable and elusive.

"And you would be calling me about what, exactly?" Lacey inquired.

"These things go in cycles. Time for something new to break. Something big."

"And that involves me how?"

"Esme Fairchild." Lacey said nothing, so he continued. "You were at that appropriations hearing yesterday. The fair Esme Fairchild, missing Washington intern, worked for the committee. I saw you in the background of a news report. Last time that happened, all hell broke loose. You brought down the Stylettos Slasher."

She stopped and took in a big breath of air. "Just for the record, I did not intend to stab Razor Boy."

He turned toward her and whispered conspiratorially. "But aren't you glad you did?"

"I'm glad I'm alive. Besides, anyone would have done the same in self-defense."

"You think just anybody could hold off a killer with a hair-spray blowtorch, sizzle him with a hot curling iron, and skewer him with styling shears? Ha. You've got an instinct for this stuff. So what does your instinct tell you about Esme?"

"Nothing. You know everything I know, Damon. You probably know more than I do."

"You might have the inside track and not even be aware of it."

"And why, pray tell, would I give you information?"

"Because you want to move into the big time."

"And you can help me do that?" *So I can be considered a complete nutcase too.*

"I can link to your stories. Lots of other sites link to me. Major linkage, premier placement. Maybe feature an interview with you, a live Webcast? Before you know it, you're not just local anymore; you're all over the Web. Lacey Smithsonian dot com."

"Hold on. I hate to break it to you, Damon. Everyone thinks you and your DeadFed are stone crazy."

"Yeah, and they check it every day, more than a million hits a month. How many hits does your column in *The Eye* get a month? I may not even need your stories. Maybe I'll just watch what you do, see what happens, then connect the dots."

"Then you don't actually need me." Lacey studied the pretty little park of Farragut Square. It was early September, the leaves still a rich green, the flowers gold and scarlet. She should be enjoying its lush promise of a lovely autumn. She thought about asking Mac for time off. She deserved it. Maybe a long weekend up in Bucks County, north of Philly . . .

Damon sensed he was losing her. "But Lacey, teamwork is crucial. The longer Esme Fairchild is gone, the less chance there is of finding her alive. The faster we find out why it happened, the sooner we find her and whoever did it. Was it politically motivated? Does she have enemies? Is it part of something bigger? Was she just unlucky?"

"Do you stop for air?" Lacey cut in. He reminded her of someone.

He took a breath. "Never. Esme's a lowly worker in the hometown industry. Young, eager, enticing. One more victim for the Washington vortex."

"She's only missing. You've already concluded she's dead."

"Or kidnapped as a sex slave and shipped to the Middle East."

"You believe everything you see on your own Web site, don't you?"

"I present everything. I suppress nothing. It's a forum for varied opinions."

"Maybe Esme just walked away. People do that." *Do they? Did Gloria Adams just walk away?*

Damon stared at her. She put her sunglasses on. "Even you don't believe that." He kept pace with her in silence all the way to the upscale joint that mostly served salads to young K Street lawyers.

Lacey and her new puppy, Damon, reached the front door, where Brooke was waiting. *That's who he reminds me of,* Lacey thought. Ms. Barton, Esquire, looked pretty, cool, and casual in her khaki slacks and red linen jacket. Her long blond hair was French braided, and she glanced at Damon with interest.

Warning, disaster ahead! But Lacey didn't have a chance to steer him away before Brooke reached out her hand to Damon. "Hi, I'm Brooke Barton, and you are . . . ?"

His hand met hers. "Damon Newhouse. I run a little Web site. I'm a friend of Lacey's." Their eyes locked, and Lacey's jaw dropped. Code Orange–level pheromone-jamming microwaves met fierce resistance and bounced back, retreating in defeat to the depths of the Pentagon subbasement from whence they came. Lacey watched them exchange exotic chemistry, imagining a mushroom cloud of heat and lunatic conspiracies. "I knew I should have ditched this puppy in the park," she muttered to the air, as they were clearly paying no attention to her.

"Damon Newhouse?" Brooke stood rapt. "You're DeadFed!"

"Didn't I see you at Fort Marcy on July twentieth?" Damon finally blurted out.

"At the Vince Foster Assisted Suicide Tenth Anniversary Vigil?" Brooke's voice betrayed an unusual breathiness. "You were in black, wearing shades."

"You were wearing red, writing down license plate numbers," he said. "The truth is out there."

"DeadFed dot com? 'A little Web site'? Good God!" Brooke said. "I check it first thing every morning. And the last thing at night." Her eyes opened wide with delight. "This is destiny. And we're all here to talk about Esme Fairchild's disappearance."

Lacey cut in. "No, we're not."

Brooke ignored her. "Damon, you are joining us for lunch, aren't you?"

"I'd be delighted. Do you think we can rule out alien abduction?"

I'll be jiggered, Lacey thought. *I've just fixed up a blind date for Mulder and Scully. No, wait: Mulder and Mulderer. Against my will!*

Brooke ushered them in and waved to the waiter for a table. She was a regular, so they were seated immediately. Brooke and Damon kept up a lovely game of conversational Ping-

Pong, with a heady mix of pumping pheromones and dark talk of "evildoers." Damon mentioned something about a "vortex of evil," but he could have been talking about anything from the latest terrorist alert to the salad bar. They knew nothing about Esme Fairchild, so it was easy to theorize. *Unconstrained by the straitjacket of facts,* Lacey sighed to herself. They pressed Lacey for her nonexistent inside information.

"All I can tell you is that Anthony Trujillo is the lead on this story. You should call him."

The waiter bearing lunch forced them to take a break. True to form, Brooke slathered her Cobb salad in dressing. Brooke had a mania for salads and a serious addiction to salad dressing. Damon, a skinny carbohydrate loader, dug into a mountain of pasta, and Lacey had a steak, rare. She needed it to keep up her strength among her high-octane companions.

"She was only an intern, and only twenty-one. Unlikely that she had a heavy political background. Or motivation," Damon said.

"Twenty-one is not too young to be in over your head in a real mess, especially here," Lacey observed.

"Who was she sleeping with? That's the real question," Brooke said, attacking an artichoke with relish.

"If she had an affair with a married congressman, she's probably already dead and partially buried in Rock Creek Park," Damon offered. He twirled his linguini with his fork and spoon.

"We could go look. Together," Brooke purred. "How's your afternoon?"

Lacey communed with her filet and remembered the letters from Gloria Adams to Aunt Mimi. What would they tell her? Women went missing every day; they melted into the background or the soil, and they faded from memory. Lacey hated coincidence. She didn't trust the curious juxtaposition of two missing women suddenly pressing in on her. She also thought of her aunt. *What would Mimi think? Or do?* In each case there was a Bentley connection, no matter how tenuous. Lacey didn't know what it meant for her, but she was going to find out, if only for the light it might shed on Mimi. Lacey kept her musings to herself. Instead she said, "Maybe it's not a conspiracy at all, and Esme was just in the wrong place at the wrong time." Brooke and Damon took a break from their tête-à-tête and looked at Lacey.

"Nah," they said in unison, before resuming their conversation.

She decided to leave them in peace. Besides, she had to get back to *The Eye*. She tossed her money on the table. "You two crazy kids have fun. I'm due back on planet Earth."

chapter 5

Like her thoughts, Lacey's desk was a jumbled mess, with notes scattered everywhere and press releases tossed to the side. She stared at the pile of papers. She didn't remember leaving it in such a state, but it was a possibility; she'd been in such a rush to get to lunch with the ever-urgent Brooke. Lacey glanced over at Felicity's empty desk, with a nagging suspicion that the food editor had rummaged through her things. There was no overt reason, just the feeling that Felicity was still after her job. She shrugged it off, then made a note to lock anything important in her desk drawer every time she left it.

Lacey checked her voice mail and e-mail: nothing. She cleared a space and started calling likely sources all over again, finally scoring pay dirt: Tyler Stone was a housemate of Esme's and she was at home, waiting for the missing woman's parents. Tyler worked for Senator John Dashwood's state office, while Esme worked for Dashwood in his capacity as chairman of the Appropriations Subcommittee. Tyler remembered seeing Lacey and told her she thought the vintage Bentley suit was pretty radical.

"And you probably saw me; I was wearing the Ralph Lauren suit."

"Of course, the gray one, black piping." Lacey remembered. In her early twenties, Tyler was tall and thin. She had shoulder-length shiny dark hair and wore the ubiquitous tiny dark-framed glasses. *Another Prematurely Serious Hill staffer.*

However, she had a wardrobe that came with old money. Very old money.

"When did you last see Esme?" Lacey asked.

"Monday morning, day before yesterday. This is definitely too close to home."

Esme lived with three roommates in a townhouse on Capitol Hill. The other two were also there, but they declined to comment, except to say that Esme was a great girl and a great roommate and they were hopeful of her safe return. *Blah, blah, blah. You can tell all these women work for politicians.*

"Could you tell me what she was like?" Lacey asked the more talkative Tyler.

Tyler repeated what Kenyon had told Lacey: Esme was consumed with her career plans. "We were friendly, but we didn't hang out much."

"What was her schedule like?"

"Like mine. Get home late, leave early. I mean, you can go days without seeing all your housemates. I guess that's why no one really thought about it when we didn't see Esme for a while. You just assume she'll show up."

"Do you still think she will?"

"Not now, with the police involved," Tyler said on a dour note. "A D.C. cop talked with us last night, but we couldn't really tell him anything."

"Was she dating anyone?"

"I guess, but it wasn't like I ever met anyone. She'd just say she had a date after work and ask me to lend her something to wear."

"Did she do that a lot? Borrow clothes, I mean."

"At first. But after a while I started to say no. I mean, she wanted to wear things I hadn't even worn yet, which seemed rather presumptuous. Because we weren't really close friends. And, well, it's not like I'm going to wear her clothes."

"Why not? Didn't she have nice clothes?" Lacey remembered that Esme was a little thinner than Tyler, and while she could apparently wear Tyler's clothes, it probably didn't work the other way around. Esme had certainly seemed well dressed when Lacey saw her, and she had a knack for accessories that made her stand out. That and the fact that she had somehow escaped the ubiquitous, ugly little black-framed glasses that so many under-thirty types on Capitol Hill seemed to be wearing these days.

"Sure, but, um, she didn't really have that much," Tyler said. "Off the record, okay?" Tyler seemed to want to talk, and Lacey agreed. "Esme wanted people to think she had more, you know, independent means, like the rest of us. It's not as if you can live in Washington on a lowly staffer's salary, not on Capitol Hill. And she was only an intern. Come on, her salary is like lunch money. Mine is like lunch money plus drinks."

"And a line on the résumé?" Lacey prompted.

"Connections. The name of the game."

"The name of the game for trust-fund babies on the Hill? No offense meant."

"None taken. If the shoe fits, make mine Manolo Blahnik. Or Jimmy Choo." Tyler's family, she revealed, had a substantial mansion overlooking the Hudson River above Manhattan. Sharing a group home on the Hill in D.C. must have been a constant trial for a girl used to serious closet space.

"And Esme's shoes?"

"Nordstrom's Rack. Or some designer-knockoff discount place. I admit she had a good eye, but she had to work for it. That's so boring."

"Did you notice if anything was missing?"

"Nothing of hers. I looked in her room and found a couple of my things she borrowed. Things I'd lost track of. But I'm still missing a new Bentley suit in jade green. It's not carried in the Washington store. The tags were still on it. I won't say she took it, but I don't know where else it could be."

Is that a crime of fashion? "So why did she want everyone to think she was a TFB?"

"You don't know much about working on the Hill, do you?"

"That's why I talk to people like you." *People who know everything.*

"So people would *think* she's connected," Tyler continued.

"So she could get that big job with the Bentleys. Big New York fashion houses don't exactly take people off the streets with a degree from Old Hickory Junior College or whatever it was. Come to think of it, she never even told me where she went to school."

"But she was beautiful, not your average Jill."

"She certainly thought so." Tyler sniffed. "Look, she was working it the right way. I admire that."

"You weren't friends?"

"We weren't. I don't want to sound mean, and please don't quote me, but quite frankly, she couldn't keep up with the rest of us. Even though she wanted to. Okay, we're, like, totally privileged, we know that, but we work hard. So when Congress is out of session, we want to do something cool, like do the Hamptons for the weekend, or Key West, or go skiing in Aspen. But Esme could never go. If she could manage to scrounge up a plane ticket, then she didn't have skis, or an outfit, or the price of the lift ticket. She had this attitude going like she was Little Orphan Esme and we were supposed to be her big sisters or Mommy Warbucks or something. She wasn't our charity project. I mean, you just can't carry someone forever. She was an okay roommate. But we hadn't really talked recently." Lacey could hear someone in the background, and Tyler muffled the receiver for a moment. "Look, I really have to go."

The conversation with Tyler Stone and her sense of entitlement gave Lacey a headache, as well as some more sympathy for Esme. She was rummaging in her bag for some Advil when the courier arrived with the packet from Nancy Mifflin, who turned out to be surprisingly helpful and organized. No doubt Tyler Stone would think Nancy was one of the boring staffers who had to budget. The envelope's three eight-by-ten photos of Esme Fairchild were designed to give the viewer a full-bore blast of budding cover-girl beauty. Looking through them, Lacey could tell that whatever additional cash the missing intern may have been able to put together had gone into her portfolio. They looked expensive. And the photos reminded Lacey of something. They had the same look and flavor as the latest

Bentley advertising campaigns in *Vogue* and *Elle*. Not a coincidence, she assumed.

There was Esme with her honey hair burnished by the sun as she stared intently into the camera. She wore a black wool Bentley jacket, an unbuttoned white tuxedo shirt showing off her almost imaginary cleavage, and a gold-beaded choker. Her lips were slightly parted, not quite a smile. *Is it a look of seduction or arrogance?* Lacey wondered. Another shot had Esme wearing a jean jacket on a windswept beach, no blouse, the jacket, presumably a Bentley, secured tenuously by one button.

The first two felt deliberately staged, but the third managed to look both natural and glamorous. In it, Esme was the golden girl in the sunset, her glorious hair backlit. She was dressed in a buttery suede skirt and jacket, which she teamed with a soft pink-and-gold patchwork satin bustier. Suede boots completed the picture, all Bentley, no doubt. This time a real smile beguiled the viewer. This was a shot that might make a Bentley's executive reach for the phone. Esme glowed, and she made Bentley's suede glow with her. And she was younger and fresher than Bentley's current spokesmodel, Cordelia, who, though only twenty-eight, was living the hard life of a hard-partying celebrity, and it showed in the dark circles under her eyes.

"What you got there, Smithsonian?" It was Mac, the stealth editor.

She held up the photos. "Meet Ms. Esme Fairchild, missing intern du jour. This one is my favorite." She indicated the golden-girl shot.

He snatched them away with interest. "She's awfully young for something like this to happen. What a waste."

"We don't know she's dead yet." Every time Lacey said that it sounded more hollow.

Mac shrugged. "Not yet." He lifted the golden-girl photo up to the light. "This one. Definitely above the fold. How did you get ahold of these?"

"I have my secret methods." *Luck, sheer luck.* "There's not that much personal information that I can cadge, except that she was trying to look like old money on a moderate-money budget. All anyone really knows is that she wants to be a Bentley model. She made like the Sphinx with her housemates."

"Give me what you got. Looks like you got that fashion angle nailed. It's a gift, Smithsonian. Accept it."

"You know we don't cover real fashion here. How come you never send me to New York? Or Paris for Fashion Week? I've never even been to Paris."

He smirked at her as he collected the photos. "Now why would you want to be one of the pack when you can blaze your own trail? Smithsonian, you puzzle me."

"I'm out of the fashion loop here, Mac. I don't even know all the designers or the newest trends in New York or the buzz in Paris or Milan or—"

"Why should you? You cover Washington. Besides, it might ruin that special gift you got. That special hot, buttered scorn you've perfected. And once in a while, a soft spot for the underdog, which we approve of here at *The Eye*. By the way, when are we finally going to put your photo at the top of your column? This would be a good time. You know, a simple news shot."

Yeah, preferably with my eyes crossed. News shot, yuck. "Never, Mac. Never. That's when." Mac chuckled and lumbered back to his office. *No doubt congratulating himself on choosing me for this thankless job.* Lacey wrote up what she had so far and forwarded it to Trujillo. *Too bad I didn't find out who Esme is dating. Maybe I'll get a call back from someone in her crowd.*

Lacey was about to congratulate herself on finishing up early when Felicity's toxic perfume once again invaded the airspace. This was odd, as Felicity normally preferred to torture Lacey with the aroma of freshly baked goodies packed with fats, sugar, and calories. Lacey sniffed the air. There was no food in the nearby environment. *Did Felicity break both arms?*

"Hi, Felicity, you didn't happen to see anyone messing with my stuff, did you?"

Felicity shook her head and turned away. "I've been busy."

"Cooking something up?"

Felicity looked peevish. "I'm on a diet. I don't want to talk about it. And there will be no more temptation around here. Don't even ask for a brownie; I'm not kidding." She snapped a carrot stick in half and bit into it. She crunched unhappily.

Lacey peeked around Felicity into the ample food editor's cubicle. Instead of the usual platters of artery-choking goodies, Felicity's desk was overrun with rabbit food, chopped vegetable heaven, a blizzard of plastic Baggies full of green and orange.

"You have my sympathy." Lacey looked up: Mac was heading her way again, looking way too pleased with himself. She was about to run for cover and a cup of coffee when her phone rang. It was Miguel Flores.

"Lacey, we have to talk. The Bentleys fired me!"

"Miguel, that's terrible! How did it happen? When?"

"First things first. Want to go shopping?"

Lacey Smithsonian's

FASHION BITES

Shopping Under the Influence

We've all done it. Gone shopping under the influence, that is. Guilty, guilty, guilty, Your Honor. And I don't mean drugs or alcohol, which can lead to risky behaviors other than shopping. You may think you've won your black belt in bargain hunting, but even expert shoppers can be sabotaged by temptation. Do these sound familiar?

- *Chocolate.* Endorphin mood enhancers like chocolate deaden the pain of a long day and make you susceptible to temptations you might ordinarily shrug off. Outlandishly expensive shoes? No sale. Expensive shoes plus chocolate? Charge 'em!
- *Bargains.* Oh yeah, we've all been there. That five-hundred-dollar suit that's been marked down to seventy dollars? A bargain—in an unwearable neon Jello-mold color. It has ruffles—and you're not a ruffles person. It starred in a bad 1980s sitcom. Don't give it a rerun. Repeat: It's not a bargain if I'm never going to wear it. It's not a bargain. . . .
- *Friends.* Can't shop with 'em, can't shop without 'em. But beware of competitive shopping with a friend who has deeper pockets—and double-dares you to go toe to toe with her. And then there is the more insidious temptation, sympathetic shopping. She's blue and you just want to cheer her up. So the two of you buy and buy and buy . . . till your budget's in the red. Uh-oh. Who's blue now?
- *Sexy sizes.* So maybe it runs large, but just because

it says it's a four or a six or an eight, that doesn't mean it fits. You can zip it, but can you breathe? You can squeeze into it, but how soon will you pop out of it? You can walk in those dainty heels in the shoe store, but can you walk outside for even five minutes? Don't shop by the numbers—unless all you want to wear is the size tag.

- *Fantasies.* Perhaps the most dangerous trap of all. You walk past a slinky white dress and it whispers to you, "Barcelona." You turn and look and the little temptress dares you to buy her—and fly off to Spain. The fantasy dress has a tenacious hold all its own, because the dream of Barcelona has lingered in your subconscious for years and somehow has manifested itself in front of you in living, breathing Lycra. You can only hope that the price tag jerks you back to reality. (Unless you're ready to turn fantasy into reality. See you at the bullfights!)

Just remember, stylish reader, you're the one who's going to wear those clothes. Or not. You deserve to be clearheaded about it. Don't shop under the influence. You'll respect yourself in the morning.

chapter 6

With Miguel on one side and Stella on the other, Lacey felt cornered. Ambushed. Shanghaied. Her instinct was to get away by herself to contemplate what to wear to the grand fashion museum gala. Out of the clear blue, Mac had gleefully given her the go-ahead to cover it; in fact it was a mandate. Apparently Claudia Darnell, *The Eye*'s publisher and a legendary fashion plate herself, found the whole idea irresistible. The paper was not only buying Lacey a ticket; they were buying a table for staff so she didn't have to muscle her way into the press table. Claudia promised to be there too, even if it meant flying back from Paris a little early—and Claudia was still mourning the demise of her beloved transatlantic Concorde.

That meant Lacey needed something spectacular to follow up her vintage Bentley suit, but she didn't have a vintage evening dress, much less a spectacular vintage evening dress. She dreaded ending up in something safe, boring, and black, rendering her totally invisible. Every upscale event she attended in D.C. resembled a funeral directors' convention, a sea of black; black tie, black tuxedos, black dresses, black limos. *You're a reporter. No one cares what you wear,* she told herself. But she still didn't want to wear the black-evening-dress uniform. And as Stella said, "Of course, it's all about you—if you *look* like it's all about you."

This was where Miguel and Stella came in. Apparently Miguel's idea of talking out a deeply personal crisis was to go shopping. And Stella found retail therapy a perfectly reasonable solution to any problem. Besides, Stella had a project: Lacey's new look for the gala. Lacey felt she needed time to contemplate, to imagine a look, to wander through some of Mimi's patterns, maybe fondle some material in a quiet fabric store. Instead, she was being marched to the chichi shops on upper Wisconsin Avenue in Chevy Chase with Stella and Miguel on either side to go shopping for—shoes. *Shoes? I don't even have a dress yet. Shoes are the last thing I need!* There was no time for dinner, but she had managed to grab a handful of Hershey's Kisses off Trujillo's desk on her way over from *The Eye.* He had laid in a supply during Felicity's diet.

"Honestly, Lacey, you have the most boring shoes," Stella, her friend, hairstylist, and footwear consultant, announced loudly.

"My shoes are boring because I like to use my feet. I walk on them." They were in the appallingly expensive shoe store known as Scarpabellas, which Lacey had never before even dared to enter.

"You haven't been there yet?" Miguel had said. "Then that's our secret destination. It's so exclusive that people who don't need to know don't even know it exists."

The oh-so-exclusive store was snuggled between two town houses and had the air of a private club. The carved oak door bore a simple brass plaque: *Scarpabellas. Beautiful Shoes.*

The door opened at Miguel's knock. *"Buenos días, amigo,"* he said to the gamine-faced redhaired salesman.

"Hi, doll!" The salesman turned out to be an old friend of Miguel's. His name was Chad. They air-kissed. "Welcome to Scarpabellas." He gave Stella and Lacey a skeptical once-over, but allowed them in on Miguel's say-so. "My poor, poor Miguel, I heard the news. Those Bentley bitches will pay."

"Not now, Chad. We have a mission."

"But you're bruised, you poor thing."

"Dramatically, I hope."

"Absolutely. I couldn't have done it better if I'd designed them."

While they chatted about the merits of Miguel's bruises,

Lacey looked over the store. It was a tasteful mixture of hard-wood floors, soft taupe carpets, and softer chairs. The shoes were arranged carefully on the walls like art. In fact, it looked like an expensive art gallery. She was surprised the displays weren't signed by the artist.

She looked down at her vintage spectator pumps that were actually beginning to hurt. But after a full day on her feet in the salon, chirpy little Stella was still wearing strappy black high heels. She also wore a painful-looking strappy black bustier. *She looks like a cover girl for* Goths Gone Wild.

Stella picked up a pair of impossibly smooth ankle boots with a Wicked Witch of the West toe and a spike heel. "Beauty knows no pain, you know."

"Beauty is in the eye of the beholder. With a sharp stick in it," Lacey said.

"Ladies, ladies, calm down," Miguel cut in. "The festivities have only just begun." He was wearing sunglasses and a black beret that dipped low over the side of his face that showed the most bruises. Although the day was warm, he wore a black turtleneck and a black jacket, accented by a red rose. He called it his French look. "We're here to shop, schmooze, and be merry, for tomorrow we hit the unemployment lines. And I am *so* going to collect. I have to get there before the bruises fade. If they fade too soon, I'll have Stella give me another little beating, just for color. And then I'm going to sue."

Stella nodded. "See, Lacey, it's a celebration, and I will celebrate tonight if we find you a decent pair of shoes for the *gala.*" Stella stretched out the vowels for emphasis. Lacey counted at least seven As in that *gala.* She turned and caught a glimpse of the three of them in one of the full-length mirrors. *Career woman, Goth princess, French philosopher. We look like we're going to a costume party, and it's only September.*

"We're having a good time. I am. You are too, Miss Grumpy Two-Shoes," Miguel said.

"I am, I am," Lacey said, "but I thought you wanted to talk about the Bentleys."

"When I have your undivided attention. Over drinks. First

we have a mission. Phase one: shoes. Fabulous shoes." He turned her toward a shoe display. "We are in Scarpabellas, Washington's best-kept secret, a shrine to fabulous footwear. Well, at least it's a local branch of the shrine. The main shrine is in Milan. Just look, Lacey. They're like little sculptures. Sculptures you can wear."

Lacey looked. There were shiny, sparkling things with impossible heels and impossible prices. There were lots of hand-crafted Italian and Spanish shoes with buttery soft leather and tags that had way too many zeroes. Lacey picked up a nice pair of casual shoes that looked like someone actually could walk in them. They carried a price of nearly nine hundred dollars. She put them back immediately.

"Mission? What mission?"

Stella picked up a very pointed shoe in scarlet patent leather and aimed it at her. "Geez, Lacey, I thought you were clear on the concept here. *You're* the mission. We're going to be your stylists for the big glamorous gala. I'm hair and makeup, and Miguel is costume and accessories. What do you think of these?"

"I'd rather not say, and what are you talking about? Stylists? Costume?" Lacey's head was buzzing from the Hershey's Kisses.

"And the story you wrote about the Bentley's Boutique bandits was totally fab," Miguel cooed, "even though there's no picture of me and my beautiful bruises. So I'm helping you dress for the ball, Cinderelly."

"Look, Miguel, I'm not Cinderella. I'm a reporter. Writing stories is what I do. You don't have to do anything for me. It might actually be a conflict of interest."

"This isn't a payback thing, it's a friend thing. But you could offer to pay us if it would help ease your conscience," he said. "You can pay me a million dollars. It will be psychic revenge on Aaron Bentley."

"Aaron's the bastard who fired Miguel." Stella jumped in with both high heels.

"Not here, Stella, not now," Miguel said. "This is a temple

of fine footwear, and we are here for Lacey on a mission of aesthetic mercy."

"With all due respect, guys," Lacey pleaded, "we may not share the same aesthetic."

"Don't go all hoity-toity on me, Lacey, I got your style down," Stella proclaimed. "And I know this fancy-schmancy party is vintage-optional. For you that means vintage-mandatory. So Miguel and me, we already worked this out. We're going to make you a Forties movie star."

"A Forties goddess," Miguel corrected. "Those cheekbones deserve it. Only first you simply *must, must, must* have some sexy shoes, dear." He scanned the wall of shoes, and after a couple of false starts that drew frowns from Stella, and one that got a head shake from Chad, Miguel picked out a pair for their approval. Stella nodded. They were a luminescent shade of bone, with faux jewels that reflected all the colors around them. They would pick up all the colors of her fabulous dress, whatever that turned out to be. They had thin ankle straps and heels that could give a sensible woman airsickness. "And who do you suppose designed these babies?"

"Torquemada? No? Perhaps the Marquis de Sade," Lacey said, backing away from the heels.

Miguel made a face and waved one little finger. "Alessandro Scarpabella himself, the master shoemaker."

"For that price I should have Geppetto and a puppet boy to go along with them."

"We'd all like a puppet boy to go along with them."

Chad appeared silently out of nowhere with a pair in Lacey's exact size. He complimented her on the delicacy of her small feet, and Miguel on his excellent taste in shoes. "And they're on sale," he murmured.

Lacey blanched. "Six hundred and sixty dollars? On sale?" She tried them on under duress. They were not quite as uncomfortable as they looked, but she was sure that would come. But on her feet they simply dazzled.

The salesman beamed. Miguel said it was a steal. "Reduced from twelve hundred dollars!" Stella rolled her eyes at the price, but she touched Lacey's arm. "Once in a lifetime, you know? And you can wear them if you ever get married. And if I ever get married. And if Miguel ever . . . well, gets another job."

Lacey's head was spinning from the fabulous but horribly expensive shoes, the chocolate, the price, and Stella and Miguel ganging up on her to turn her into Cinderella for the Bentleys' gala. She protested; then suddenly she thought of humble congressional staffer Tyler Stone, almost ten years younger, ten million dollars richer, with her jets to Aspen and her limos to the Hamptons. *If the shoe fits* . . . Tyler had said.

"What do you think, Lacey?" Stella asked.

Lacey snapped her credit card down and gripped the counter to steady herself.

"I think I'm having an out-of-body experience." *I can always bring them back tomorrow. Alone.*

After the emotionally draining—at least for Lacey—experience of shoe shopping, the trio sought refuge in Richwood's, a faux-Tudor restaurant just off Wisconsin tucked into a side street. It was cozy and quiet and had the atmosphere of backroom political dealmaking. A television picture flickered soundlessly above the bar. After the sleek, shiny "New D.C." experience of Scarpabellas, this place was comforting Old Washington. Lacey expected any minute to see a fat congressman go by chasing a not-so-sweet young thing. Over a glass of sparkling red wine that went with the chocolate mousse, Lacey listened to Miguel's story. She had no idea why she ordered the mousse. *Am I drunk on chocolate—or drunk on shoe shopping?* Stella and Miguel were downing Brie and white wine.

"The bastards," Miguel was saying. "They say I violated Bentley company policy by resisting the robbery."

"Like there was a book with this rule in it." Stella supplied the punctuation. "The Bentley company policy is whatever the boss makes up at any given minute." She had plenty of experience with crazy bosses; Lacey gave her that.

"As if anyone in the history of the world has read the Bentley company policy book!" Miguel lamented. "I thought I was going to die! I was thoroughly beaten and kicked in the head with higher heels than you just bought, Lacey, and in a larger size, and believe me, pain is not my thing, no matter what that cute little shoe salesman back there might tell you."

"So what happened?"

"No one showed up for work today. Except me, and I was late. Everyone else was too freaked out about the robbery. Aaron Bentley, the big man himself, shows up and the store's locked. When I get there twenty minutes later to open up, he fires me."

"Is there really such a policy?"

"Who knows? But when your life is on the line, that 'no resistance' crap goes right out the window. If that bitch in the Chanel suit had just said, 'This is a robbery, honey, just be calm and no one is going to get hurt,' like they do in the movies and on TV, I'd have said, 'Darling! Welcome to Bentley's! So lovely to see you, what a fabulous suit! Right this way, boys and girl! Here, take my keys, here's the combo to the safe, let me show you the really good stuff, oh, let me help you with those bags, big fella. Are you parked in front? Let me get the door for you, bye-bye, don't be strangers!' But it wasn't like that. The Rainbow Coalition had the duct tape and the guns, and when they do that, it's serious business. Like the detective said, 'execution style.' I wouldn't have resisted if I didn't think it was curtains, the end, *fini, adios,* Miguel. So I get fired for not getting killed. If I'd gotten killed, maybe they'd have given me a bonus."

"I'm so sorry, Miguel. I don't know what to say," Lacey said. "The whole thing doesn't make sense. With the Senate hearing and the screwy museum funding and the Bentleys in town courting the press, why would they want to look like jerks by firing their heroic assistant manager?"

"They're divas. Divas don't make sense," Stella cut in.

"The stupid thing is I always wanted to meet Aaron Bentley, 'cause he's a babe. He's just as gorgeous in person as he is in the photos, but he's totally ice inside. He has ice-blue eyes,"

Miguel said. "Sexy, though. Wouldn't we like to see him tied up at someone's mercy?"

Not wanting to further explore that image, Lacey changed the subject. "Did you think Aaron himself would come to the store today?"

"I don't know. God. I guess I thought the Bentleys would have enough class to tell me they were sorry for putting our lives at risk." Miguel ordered another pinot grigio.

"Oh, Lacey, did he tell you that Aaron's little trophy model, Cordelia, was there too?" Stella asked, always ready for good gossip.

"I guessed they were a couple," Lacey said, recalling her luncheon with the Bentley clan.

"They were together, totally cozy," Miguel said. "All the ugly rumors are true—Aaron Bentley is a flaming heterosexual. He's also a flaming bastard. So I guess that rumor is true too. Oh, I almost forgot, while he's sacking me, a very famous actress who is currently at the Kennedy Center in some forgettable Broadway-bound extravaganza waltzes into the store and in her plummiest English accent says, 'Darlings, I simply had no idea there was a Bentley's Boutique in Washington!' Then she looks at me and says, 'I saw you on the news. Aren't you one of the Bentley Bandits?'"

"Oh, my God! What actress?" Stella was dying to know.

"I can't say, but a *very* famous actress. And maybe she was on television? On a famous soap opera? And I can't reveal the name of the show, but its initials are, like, maybe *Dallas*?"

"No!" Stella screamed.

"Yes!" Miguel shouted.

"Which bitch?"

"Queen bitch!"

"Oh, my God! The queen bitch herself!" Stella would be entertaining all her clients for days with this little tidbit.

"But then she ruined it by informing us that she always gets a thirty-percent discount at the Bentley's in Manhattan."

"She's already rich. Let her pay," said Stella the egalitarian.

"What happened next?" Lacey asked.

"Cordelia personally escorted the famous actress with the English accent through the store and I was personally shown the door by Aaron, that big bully. And now I alone am left to tell the tale."

Lacey realized that between Miguel's story and her aunt Mimi's legendary loathing for Hugh "That Bastard," not to mention the wine and the chocolate, she was perfectly prepared to believe the worst about the Bentleys. She thought it must be time for a little journalistic balance. *Just a little*, she thought. *It's an experiment.*

"Miguel, just to play devil's advocate for a second, could Bentley's have been looking for a reason to get rid of you and this was an easy out?"

Miguel was nonchalantly unoffended. "No way, my sales were sky-high, and I just got an outstanding review from the regional manager. Whom I have never ever even slept with."

Because she seemed to be on good terms with Hugh Bentley, Lacey resolved to ask the old devil about Miguel's firing. *He probably never even heard about it. Aaron must handle all the dirty work now.*

The flickering of the television behind the bar caught her attention. A picture of Esme Fairchild stared back. It was a plain head shot, released by her parents; probably a yearbook photo, better than a driver's license, but not nearly the equal of the photos that would be featured in the morning in *The Eye Street Observer*. Her companions followed Lacey's gaze.

"Hey, I know that chick!" Miguel said.

"You do? How?" Lacey once would have been dumbfounded, but she was beginning to get used to the weird way that in Washington everyone in a certain class seemed to know everyone else in the same class—and no one in any other class. *It's like a layer cake of small towns.*

"She shops at Bentley's. Well, let's say she browses at Bentley's. She never buys anything."

"She's the intern who's missing," Stella announced. Miguel hadn't seen the news, being wrapped up in his own troubles as the dishonored hero of the Battle of Bentley's.

"Get out!"

"Yeah, and I bet Lacey knows something about her. I got a feeling." They both stared intently at Lacey.

"I only know she wanted a job with the Bentleys."

"Wow, they got rid of her even before she started working for them. Now that's efficient," Miguel quipped. Lacey and Stella just stared at him. "So sue me; it just popped out. Do you have any more gossip, Lacey?"

She begged off from more drinks and begged to go home. "You'll just have to buy the morning paper if you want to know what I know." She hoped she'd given Esme a fair shake.

Lacey stayed up late that night, alternately looking at her new shoes, trying them on in utter amazement, and reading more letters to Aunt Mimi from Gloria Adams.

Dear Mims,   *September 8, 1943*

We traveled upstate for a company picnic on Saturday afternoon. Schoolchildren are collecting milkweed pods—you wouldn't believe it, Mims—big onion sacks full of them, for the boys in the service. Imagine! They say the fibers inside are used to fill life jackets. I even heard a rumor they're going to use them to produce nylon. I wish I knew how to do that. I haven't had stockings in ever so long. There are rumors they can be had for $5 or $10 a pair. Good golly Moses! Who has that kind of money to spend on hosiery?

Don't be mad, but I wouldn't turn in some poor woman who spends her life savings on a pair of stockings. The fact is, stockings are out there. Yes, I know all about your big important job and the war effort and I know that everybody hates the OPA! You should have been at the picnic. We even had chicken and tubs of potato salad.

Your stuffed Glory

Darling Mims,   *January 8, 1944*
   *You would hardly know me, I'm so sophisticated
these days. I'm wearing my hair differently. You know
what a cross it is to bear, but now I wear it in a twist at
the nape of my neck caught up a hairnet. On top, I wear
finger curls that dip over my forehead. I saw something
like it at the pictures last week. Maybe it was Ann
Sheridan.*
   *At any rate, it looks quite nice and is finally under
control! When I go out with Hugh, I wear a bit of mascara, brow pencil, and ruby-red lipstick. What a vamp!
Ha! I know what you're going to say, but believe me,
he's never going to marry her.*
                                   Your Glamorous Glory

Lacey read the letter several times. *When I go out with
Hugh.* Gloria had changed, even by her own admission. She
had to know he was engaged to Marilyn. But was she in fact
going out with the handsome Hugh Bentley? Or was that just a
fantasy?

Lacey didn't know what to think, and she wondered what
her great-aunt really did during the war. All she knew was that
Mimi had had a government job. She had never really bothered
to find out more, and Mimi had already been an old woman, if
a sassy old woman, when Lacey was a young girl.

There are so many questions you never bother to ask, Lacey
thought. *You think there will plenty of time to ask them later. But
there's never enough time.*

chapter 7

Thursday was September 11. *The Eye Street Observer* featured
news of the remembrance ceremony for the victims of the Pentagon and World Trade Center attacks, which had transformed
life in the country forever. Mac's editorial reflected briefly on
how life had changed since that September day in 2001 and
how life in the Capital City continued on with some sense of
normalcy despite increased security and the Department of
Homeland Security's ever-present color-coded security alert
system. Mac closed with a question: *Will there ever be another
Code Green day?*

Lacey reflected that she had pretty much assumed there
would never again be a Code Green day. She was just grateful
that people refrained from color-coordinating their clothes to
the security alerts. It would be a nightmare painted in yellow
and orange. But maybe, once in a while, that would be better
than the constant gray palette the city wore. Ah, for a day of
Code Green—Code Innocence.

The Thursday morning papers also featured front page stories about missing Senate intern Esme Fairchild. *The Post*
began its story below the fold and tucked her yearbook photo
inside the A section. *The Times* gave it two columns and the
same photo below the fold. But *The Eye* led with a dazzling
two-column glamour shot of Esme the Golden Girl, above the
fold, placed top left. The day's lead story was bylined by Trujillo
and Smithsonian. Mac had all three papers on his desk. He

exuded satisfaction, which, of course, was a temporary mirage. He complimented Lacey as she passed by his office.

"Nice work on those photos, Smithsonian."

She silently thanked Nancy Mifflin again. Lacey was glad that her contribution to that story was out of the way. Because Trujillo was the lead, she'd copied him with all her notes and phone numbers relating to Esme, and she didn't anticipate any more work on it from her end. At the moment she hoped her own beat might open a small window into a side of her aunt she hadn't known. *What exactly was Mimi's job at the Office of Price Administration? Did it have something to do with Hugh the B? Is that how they met? And then what? A steamy, doomed love affair?*

The first order of the day was to check out DeadFed on the Web. After yesterday's lunch with Brooke and Damon, anything could happen. Damon had linked her story to his site with his own introduction, which mentioned that *Eye Street* fashion reporter Lacey Smithsonian, who had covered the Marcia Robinson scandal and wound up stabbing a serial killer, was now on the Fairchild story. *Stay tuned for further developments from this veteran Washington investigative reporter,* he promised, implying that Lacey would uncover something any second. *"Veteran" makes me sound so old!* Lacey thought.

She had brief e-mails from both Brooke and Damon. His said, *More to come?* Hers said, *Sorry you had to run off; we were all having such a great time,* and implied she would forever be grateful for introducing her to Damon. Lacey sighed.

Her number one desire was to get hold of Hugh Bentley and grill him about those pesky company policies that required firing heroic employees who fought for their lives—and for Bentley's precious overpriced inventory. Perhaps it would lead to other threads of information. She had chosen to wear another suit of Aunt Mimi's, a Black Watch plaid that made her feel like a femme fatale in a pulp fiction novel: strong, attractive, capable of facing the bad guys. It had a green velvet Chesterfield collar and cuffs. She wore a pair of green leather pumps, though not the kind that Stella might approve. She hoped the suit would help inspire her to ask the right questions. Too often the right questions came at deadline—or right after the story went to press.

A call to the cell phone of the Bentleys' jack-of-all-trades, Chevalier, went to voice mail. Hugh had told her at lunch on Tuesday that the Bentleys were overseeing the placement of the exhibits. *The museum.*

Lacey grabbed her purse and made a quick exit from the office. She grabbed a cab and headed to the handsome edifice of the yet-unopened Bentley Museum of American Fashion, near Judiciary Square and the National Building Museum, where the fund-raising "Sixty Years of American Fashion" gala would be held.

The new museum was housed in a corner building that presented a facade of three connected redbrick and white-trimmed Victorian row houses, from behind which rose an impressive modern steel-and-glass block. The doors designated the office entrance, the museum shop, and the public entrance, which was open for workmen coming and going.

Lacey entered through the unlocked front door and saw the metal detectors already in place. A security guard at the front desk put his newspaper down and glanced at her with a sour expression. "We're not open yet, ma'am." She explained what she wanted. Looking at a clipboard, he said, "You're not on the list."

"You're not even open and there's already a list?" Lacey inquired sweetly. She flashed her press badge. Reluctantly he picked up his two-way radio.

"We got a woman here, says she's a reporter." He paused. "Who you with?"

"Lacey Smithsonian. *The Eye Street Observer*," she said. "I'm here to see Hugh Bentley or Aaron Bentley. Or Jeffrey Bentley Holmes. Or Marilyn Bentley, or Belinda Holmes, or Cordelia—"

"You hear all that?" The guard shouted into the speaker. He indicated Lacey should stay put. "Someone will be up soon."

It was Jeffrey Bentley Holmes who greeted her with a welcoming smile. He looked darn good for a man wearing a tool belt full of hammers and nails slung from his hips. The sleeves of his blue work shirt were rolled up, his jeans fit well, and his scuffed steel-toed boots indicated he meant business. This was not the Bentley fashion statement she had expected.

"Lacey, so nice to see you. But I'm confused. Why are you here? Is anyone expecting you?"

"I'm completely unexpected. I hope you don't mind."

"Not at all." He wiped his hands on his jeans and offered her his hand. "It's great to see you again."

"You're dressed like one of the guys on *This Old House*. Or is it *This Old Museum*?"

"Our new collection, the Bent-nail Look, by Bentley. We're a hands-on family, as you can see. Anyway, I'm not a fashion guy; I'm the build-the-stores guy. Would you like an advance tour of the museum?"

"I'd love it, but I also have some questions about the robbery at the boutique," she said. She briefly explained the purpose of her visit.

"Well, that's a CEO type of problem, not a square-footage-of-display-area type of problem," Jeffrey said. "You do need Hugh or Aaron. They're around somewhere. Follow me." Jeffrey signed her in on the guard's clipboard. The guard looked sulky and resumed reading the sports pages.

"Only workmen are coming in right now," Jeffrey said. "Last-minute things, a million of 'em, and I suspect the curator is going mad." His sense of composure and good humor was comforting. She hoped the other Bentleys would be as welcoming, but she doubted it. "Everyone with a stake in an exhibit wants to oversee their own little piece of genius."

"Is that what the Bentley clan is doing?"

He laughed. "Absolutely. We are the worst by far. Trust me. Are you sure you care to step into the lion's den?" They turned a corner into the Bentley wing. Squadrons of display designers, drapers, technicians, and workmen were scurrying everywhere, surrounded by sixty years of the work of a fashion dynasty. But it was full of eye candy for someone like Lacey. Several originals from the fledgling first collection adorned the mannequins just inside the doorway. The exhibit was chronological, from 1944 to the present. Huge photos of Bentley's humble beginnings contrasted with the sleek imperial castle of gleaming chrome and glass it now occupied in Manhattan. There were even pictures from the first factory floor and the various workrooms. One featured a dressmaker's dummy draped in fabric with a woman pinning a pattern together. *Is that the studio where Gloria Adams worked?*

"But the museum features other American designers? Other work?"

"Oh, yes, they're all here, but I imagine Uncle Hugh and Aaron have supplied the most headaches, as well as the most money. Ah, here's Ms. Mandrake, the curator of the museum. Penelope, I'd like you to meet Lacey Smithsonian. With the—"

"Eye Street Observer," Lacey filled in. She put out her hand and wore a determined smile.

A bony woman with a perpetually worried look turned at his voice. She was perhaps forty, perhaps a little younger, but she underwent a transformation in his presence. It was subtle, but Penelope Mandrake glowed in the presence of the handsome Jeffrey, who, Lacey assumed, probably had that effect on any woman between seventeen and death. Penelope then peered suspiciously at Lacey through her decorative lenses. She was dressed in black slacks and top, which were smeared with dust; she looked as if she'd already been moving exhibits and crawling under displays. Her dingy brown hair was pulled back into a no-nonsense ponytail, and makeup obviously had no place in her life. She shook Lacey's hand firmly. "We aren't really ready for the media. In fact, I didn't know any media were scheduled." She checked her notebook. "Of course, we have *The New York Times* slated for a special tour on Monday. Then Tuesday is *The Post*, and I believe there are some other special arrangements. And the networks are coming in next Thursday. Oh, and the *Discovery Channel,* the *Learning Channel,* people like that."

Special arrangements? Why am I not surprised that The Eye *isn't on that list?*

"It's all right, Penelope. I'll vouch for her." Jeffrey stepped in and protectively placed his hand on Lacey's shoulder.

"Very well. Nice meeting you. Call if you need me, Jeffrey." The woman looked at her watch, then at Jeffrey; then she clutched her large notebook full of tasks and scurried off, adjusting her glasses as she went. She passed Hugh Bentley coming in. He wore casual attire today, as if he were sailing a yacht: navy blazer with the Bentley insignia, light slacks, a light blue ascot at the neck, and an immaculate white linen shirt. His stick today was an impressive hand-carved oak with a plain but graceful silver handle.

"Why, Lacey Smithsonian. You're the last person I expected to see here, though you are certainly dressed for the early exhibit period. You could step right into a display case."

"It's not a Bentley."

"No, but it's a good example of its kind. It's not mass market, but perhaps the work of a clever seamstress copying an original of the time. Probably something similar in our archive."

"I like it," she said lightly. "And that's really all that matters."

"Don't let him intimidate you, Lacey," Jeffrey cut in. "He's really just an old softie at heart."

Hugh tapped his cane on the floor. "Don't you have something to do, Jeffrey? I will be happy to entertain Miss Smithsonian for a moment or two."

"Sure thing, Uncle Hugh." Jeffrey winked at Lacey, and he and his well-hung tool belt sauntered gracefully over to adjust the navy velvet drapes adorned with silver stars that fell gracefully behind a pale blue Bentley evening gown with a full net skirt, circa 1956.

Hugh offered Lacey his arm for a leisurely stroll. "Now you must tell me. What is it about these old clothes that you like so well?"

"First of all, they have more detail, they're better constructed, they're built to last, and they fit me better because they're tailored for someone with a shape like mine. And they have a certain something, an elegance, a glamour, that doesn't exist anymore," Lacey said. "At least not on a reporter's salary."

"Do I take it that you don't shop at Bentley's?" He played mock affronted.

She thought of Mimi. *If you only knew.* "Let's just say it's way above my pay scale." She smiled at him.

"You're right about one thing. Those clothes suit you." He studied her for a moment. "Women were more petite, more curvy in those days. Even our models were only five-foot-six or -seven. More real." He indicated the mannequins from the Forties, stylized papier-mâché, with molded curls and waves. Recently refreshed with glamorous Old Hollywood makeup and red lips and fingertips, they looked startlingly innocent and knowing at the same time, like any Forties starlet in any Forties B movie. A look that said, "I know exactly what you're after, Joe, and you're not getting any—not unless those are real nylons in your pocket." They were far more interesting to Lacey than the later dummies, which were taller and thinner and blanker, and constructed from glass fibers and polyester resins. There was even a tableau from the latest collection, with a mannequin based on Cordelia Westgate. *The haughty gaze appears anatomically correct. Right down to the collagen in her lips?* Lacey wondered. Hugh hit a button on a display, and "Long Ago and Far Away," a love song that was a hit for Jo Stafford in 1944, played softly in the background. Lacey realized that she and the legendary Hugh the B were alone. Jeffrey must have slipped away, leaving his Uncle Hugh at her mercy. *Or is it the other way around?*

Lacey hated to break the moment, but she had to do it before she found herself liking old Hugh the Bastard. "I called your press guy. Did he let you know?"

"Oh, no, Chevalier believes it is his duty to protect us from inquisitive reporters." Hugh sounded amused. "His idea of press relations is no relations at all. But what does it matter? We are teaching him how to accommodate the important media. And you took the initiative to show up unannounced."

"We all have jobs to do, Hugh."

"I would have thought you were too busy with the hearing and the interview to fit in a story about our unfortunate little robbery."

So he had read T*he Eye* that morning. "It's the robbery I want to discuss. Actually its aftermath."

"Are you not sick of us by now?" He tapped his stick impatiently.

"I'll let you know. In the meantime, though, I'd like some answers."

"Then you'll have to tag along with me as I inspect these mannequins. I don't know if I have the answers you want."

"My pleasure. I understand that Miguel Flores, the assistant manager of Bentley's Boutique in Chevy Chase, was fired yesterday because of some company policy."

"I'm really not involved in the day-to-day business anymore. You'd have to ask Aaron." Hugh readjusted a suit on one of the papier-mâché dolls. He retucked a pocket hankie with infinite care, then patted it like a proud parent.

"This is your baby now?" Lacey indicated the exhibit.

He stood gazing at the best examples of his empire. "An old man's dream, I suppose. Knowing that something of mine will outlast me. Fashion is ephemeral. Museums last a little longer."

"About Miguel Flores—"

"I was sorry it came to that, but it was Aaron's decision, and he is a fiend about safety. As proud as we are of our merchandise, we simply can't have employees risking their lives for a few trinkets."

Aaron chose that moment to stroll in with his favorite accessory of the moment, Cordelia, who looked slightly hungover. "Someone mention my name? Ah, Ms. Smithsonian, you are ubiquitous. And to think I had never even met you before yesterday."

"I hope you don't mind if I ask a question," Lacey said.

Aaron smiled. "Not at all, for a guest of Dad's."

"Does Bentley's really have a company policy of not resisting a robbery? Was it necessary to fire Miguel Flores?"

"Absolutely. We have the policy, and my decision to let an employee go is just that. I have no other comment on internal company matters." His eyes traveled up her body. "However, I will applaud your suit today. It suits your coloring." He favored her with a dazzling smile. Cordelia bristled slightly, then smiled with just a hint of sneer. "Isn't it charming, Cordy?"

"It's charming," she said, towering unsteadily over Lacey.

"May I see a copy of the policy?"

"You're doing a follow-up then? I trust you will print our side of the story?"

"If you have a written policy, it will help your side."

"Chevalier can help you with that. He'll give you our associates' handbook of company policies. Everyone we hire is given one, and they are expected to follow the rules. Is that all?"

"Actually, no."

Aaron laughed. "Are you sure you're not a New York reporter?"

"I'm sure you heard that Esme Fairchild seems to be missing."

"Yes. She worked with us on our presentation to the senators," he said smoothly. "A terrible thing. We were saddened to hear about it. I believe Chevalier will have an official statement later."

"What can you tell me about her?"

"Only that she seemed quite competent. Chevalier found her invaluable as our liaison for our impromptu senatorial appearance. She had a brilliant future in front of her."

"In PR? Or as a model?" Lacey kept her eyes on Cordelia. The woman took Aaron's arm protectively but said nothing and closed her eyes as if the dim light bothered them.

"Very possibly as a model," Aaron said. "She was going to show me her portfolio." Cordelia's color seemed to fade through her makeup.

"And do you have any comment, Ms. Westgate?"

Cordelia scratched the inside of her left arm where the woolen WAC uniform had irritated it two days before. "I really didn't know her, but she seemed very clever. Too clever by half."

Aaron cut in. "Of course, we all hope for a happy conclusion."

"Of course, a happy conclusion," Cordelia echoed.

"Do you have any idea what could have happened? Did she tell you her plans?"

"We have no idea what could have happened to her, Ms. Smithsonian. But then, the Nation's Capital is a dangerous place, isn't it?" Aaron made excuses for the two of them, leaving Lacey alone again with Hugh, who was leaning against a wall, balancing the oak cane in front of him.

"May I ask you something else, Hugh?"

"Could I stop you?"

"Probably not."

He indicated a plum-colored sofa, positioned to view part of a display. "Fire away."

Lacey sat down on the other end of the sofa. The clean scent of new-sawn lumber was in the air, and the dust tickled her nose. Workmen toiled in other rooms, leaving a distant scrim of noise surrounding the Bentley exhibit. "Do you remember a Gloria Adams?"

He closed his eyes. "I haven't heard that name in almost sixty years."

"What can you tell me about her?"

"She was a factory girl at Bentley's who disappeared one day and no one ever heard from her again. It was always troubling." He sounded a little sad about it. He opened his eyes and looked directly at her. "Where did you hear about Gloria Adams?"

"She was a friend of my aunt's. I saw an old newspaper clipping."

"Well, who knows, perhaps I did meet your aunt once or twice. I'm sorry I don't remember her. What do you know about Gloria?"

"Only that she disappeared."

"And now another young woman has disappeared." An edge hardened his voice. "That always makes for good reading in the newspapers, doesn't it?"

"I'm not planning a story about it yet." *Could there be a link?* "Women disappear every day, don't they? Do you remember anything about her?"

Hugh recalled Gloria as a competent, even talented worker. Gloria Adams came to Bentley's sometime during 1942. The factory was beefing up production for both military and domestic needs. The company had always sewn shirts and dresses, but Hugh had bigger dreams. He wanted to make a name for Bentley's, and he would start with a full line of women's clothing, not drab housedresses but something with a snap to it, something more professional for the women who had been moving into new jobs even before the war, something more sophisticated. Women were clamoring to wear the clothes they saw in the movies, clothes that were designed by Adrian, Edith Head, and Dolly Tree. Of course, those designs were too extreme for real life, but Hugh saw that a smart designer could take glamorous elements and make them more moderate, more wearable, but still alluring and exciting.

The market was ready to explode; then the war happened. Hugh didn't enlist, he told her, because his father was ill and someone who knew the business had to run the factory. The industry was hamstrung by government regulations and he had to deal with endless bureaucrats.

"Imagine, having the government outlaw French cuffs! That was the order of L-85." Hugh chuckled at the memory. "Shirts could have only one pocket, skirts could be only so wide, hems only so deep. It was like learning how to juggle wearing a straitjacket." But he worked with and around the regulations and the bureaucracies, never giving up on his goal. "We all knew the war couldn't last forever." His first—and some said his most brilliant—collection debuted in the fall of 1944. It was a memorable year. Gloria disappeared in May and Hugh married Marilyn Hutton in late June of the same year. Then in September, despite the war, his collection came out.

Gloria had a future at Bentley's, according to Hugh. But her disappearance also took a toll on everyone. She might not have been that memorable before, but afterward no one would ever forget her, certainly no one at Bentley's.

"There was a war going on in the rest of the world, and we tended to think that all the evil things were happening over there. Something like Gloria disappearing . . . you don't think it can happen so close to home," Hugh said. "But it wasn't an immediate thing we were aware of. Gloria didn't show up to work for a few days. No one was very worried at first. Then people started asking questions. I wasn't so sure she didn't just run off with a GI and get married."

The disappearance had a devastating effect on his sister, Belinda, and his fiancée, Marilyn, who refused to go anywhere alone after that. According to Hugh, the two women became the best of friends, and they were still more like sisters than sisters-in-law.

"Were you ever romantically involved with Gloria?" *Or my aunt?*

"Oh, heavens, no. I was engaged, and things were different in those days."

Bet me, Lacey thought. "You've always had a reputation as a ladies' man, you know."

"A reputation, yes. Many of the girls flirted with me. But their own boys were off to war and they were lonely. It was only flirting, and it is only a reputation. I'll tell you a little secret, my dear: A little 'reputation' is good for a man, if you know what I mean. And I've been married to Marilyn for nigh onto sixty years."

"But I had the impression that Gloria—"

"I don't want to say anything negative about her." He shifted around in his chair, tapping his stick on the floor and stroking the smooth wood handle. "But she had fantasies, fantasies about me that were unrealistic, to say the least. Today they would probably call her a stalker."

Gloria? A stalker? But then, Hugh had been incredibly handsome in his youth, still dashing at eighty-something. And Gloria? She had the bloom of youth, the freshness that was always alluring. But she was no beauty. Certainly not in comparison with Marilyn Hutton, who had been graced with classic good looks, and a healthy income to make the most of those looks. Yet Gloria had written, *When Hugh and I go out.* Lacey thought it was ironic that today someone like frizzy-haired Gloria could come pretty close to being a knockout, with her figure and all the cosmetic and hairstyling options available. That and a good eyebrow waxing. She could imagine Stella saying, "Let me at her, I'll turn her into a silk purse, no prob." Lacey was about to stand up to go when Hugh took her hand.

"I have a question for you now, Lacey Smithsonian. Would you consider donating your Bentley suit to this collection? The one you wore to the Senate. It's quite smashing. Particularly with the button covers. I was always very fond of those button covers."

"*My suit?*" *Give away Mimi's suit? That bastard!* It was as if Lacey could hear Aunt Mimi shouting clear through her thoughts. She didn't know whether the thought of Mimi's indignation or Hugh's question startled her more.

"It would be your legacy, or your aunt's, if you wish. It would be one of our premier ensembles from the Forties. I could even commission a special mannequin to wear it, one that would look just like you." He took her stunned silence for a serious consideration of his question. "Just think about it."

That suit was one of Lacey's treasures. Even though Mimi had refused to wear it, the old woman had kept it forever. It must have had some strong sentimental pull. The last thing she would want was for "That Bastard" to get his hands on it. *Mimi would return from the grave just to haunt me.*

"I'm sorry, Mr. Bentley. A plaque with my name on it is no equal for the suit. For you the suit is just a great example of its kind. For me it's truly one of a kind. And I plan to wear it, not visit it." She stood up to leave.

"Don't be so hasty." He leaned on the cane to stand up and

moved close to her. "You say you don't shop at Bentley's, but what would you say to a trade?" Her head was spinning. He was crafty; she gave him that. "Any Bentley couture gown that you desire, for the suit," Hugh went on. "No, no, make it any *two* gowns. That suit of yours really is more than just a great example of its kind to me. It brings back an entire era for me. A lifetime."

She smiled broadly, hoping to outcharm him. "That's very kind of you, Hugh. But really, I'm keeping the suit."

He patted her hand. "Think about it, Lacey Smithsonian. The offer remains open. Call me anytime, or leave word with Chevalier. I trust I'll see you at the gala?"

"You can count on it."

chapter 8

"What I'm saying is that Esme was seeing Aaron Bentley, as in *seeing him*, not just, you know, seeing him around."

Miss Marcia Robinson herself, a glossier version of the famous former frump who had been Washington's favorite scandal pinup girl in the spring, was sitting across from Lacey at Starbucks, slumped down in a plush olive-green velvet armchair. Between bursts of conversation, she was ogling all the male latte sippers, and Lacey was taking notes.

Lacey had barely gotten back to the office when she received a frantic call from Marcia, who claimed to have hot information on Esme that just might help Lacey—and might even, quote, "get me killed!" With the promise of a near-tabloid-sized news story, Lacey was off like a shot to have coffee with a very self-possessed Ms. Robinson, who hardly seemed in fear for her life. Marcia claimed she had just learned to look calmer than she felt after being in the media spotlight so long.

"Wait a minute, Marcia; you're saying that Esme Fairchild was seeing Aaron?" Lacey asked. "Exactly up until when?"

"Exactly up until she disappeared." Marcia swirled a straw around and around her latte.

"Well, he seemed pretty cozy with Cordelia Westgate when I saw him last. About half an hour ago."

"Oh, yeah, they're having a thing, too. Common knowledge. Esme was just, you know."

"No, I don't just 'you know.' What? She was sleeping with him?"

"Duh! Yes, she was sleeping with him."

No wonder Cordelia flinches every time her name is mentioned. "Why? Other than animal attraction."

"It just happened, I guess. He's gorgeous, he's rich and powerful, and she's a lowly intern on the Hill. It's a Hill thing. I've been there." Marcia sipped her coffee with a straw to avoid mussing her lipstick. "And she wanted a job." Lacey reflected that Marcia had embraced her glamorous new look with a vengeance. She wasn't about to go back to being the chubby congressional staffer whose dumpy driver's-license photo had been splattered across the covers of a dozen tabloids. "But I really am scared, Lacey. I could be next!"

Why Marcia would be eager to talk to her after all the stories that she'd written on the notorious former Small Business Committee staffer was a mystery in itself. Lacey suspected Marcia was now addicted to that spotlight.

"Here's the inside scoop, Lacey: Esme was kind of a silent partner in my Web site."

"You're kidding. Your pornography empire?"

"As if. It was *so* not porno. It was never that bad. You ever heard of *Girls Gone Wild*? Well, this was sort of *Wonks Gone Mild*. Only with, like, naked wonks."

"What did Esme do? Was she one of your, um, naked wonks?"

"No way. She did the marketing plan. And she helped set up the whole tape and DVD ordering, billing, and shipping deal. Fulfillment, she called it. I love that word. But when the scandal broke, she stopped talking to me for a while. Of course, she started calling me again to dish on Aaron Bentley. She went to New York on the weekends a couple of times to see him, and do you know what else?" Marcia leaned in close to Lacey and lowered her voice. "She said that Cordelia Westgate would soon be history." Sighing, she leaned back. "Anyway, when I saw that you wrote the story on her, I had to call. If Esme's dead . . . I mean, who knows who's next? I thought this whole scandal thing of mine was pretty much over, but it's never really over, is it?"

Lacey put her coffee down. "Marcia, if Esme was killed, it was probably because she was in her own kind of trouble, or she was in the wrong place at the wrong time. Or maybe she had a secret. You, on the other hand, exposed everything. I think."

"The Web site wasn't that bad," Marcia protested.

"I mean you spilled your guts to the special prosecutor and to me. You're safe because you don't have any more secrets. Now, do you know anything else about Esme that might be a secret?"

"Well, she was screwing this senator."

Lacey narrowly avoided wearing her double latte decaf on her Black Watch plaid vintage suit. Apparently there were no pheromone jammers strong enough to stop Esme Fairchild. "Oh, no! You don't really mean at the same time?" Lacey wasn't sure she wanted to hear this. *Of course you do.*

"And that was a real affair, not just a fling. He was going to buy her something very nice—expensive—for their six-month anniversary, I heard. Her choice."

"You said Aaron Bentley was a real affair. So who is this senator, anyone I should know?"

"I don't know. Ever hear of Demetrius Van Drizzen?"

"Van Drizzen? He's a member of the Appropriations Subcommittee." Oh, yes, Lacey had heard of him. "Wow, she liked them old. I mean, old for her."

"Yeah, but he's cute too, in kind of a distinguished senatorial kind of way. He's not exactly awesome like Aaron Bentley."

"She was a busy girl."

"You're only young once. You can sleep when you're dead, you know? Oops—wrong thing to say. Sorry."

"Wait a minute, Marcia. You don't have proof, do you? Like a videotape or something?"

"No, no, no, I swore off videotaping forever, Lacey. Swear

to God. But she told me because we were friends, and she wouldn't have just made this stuff up, would she?"

"So it's hearsay. You don't have proof."

"Isn't that your job, Ms. *Eye Street* reporter? Besides, I feel better just telling somebody. I don't know if those guys have anything to do with Esme disappearing, but you'll look into it?"

One more question, Senator. Were you having an affair with a missing intern half your age? "I'll look into it."

After she left Marcia, Lacey realized she was starving, and, decaffeinated or not, she was on a high buzz. She picked up a quick sandwich to bring back to the office. *No going home early for this girl,* she thought. *But where to start? It's not often that I'm handed the ammunition to torment so many people in one day.*

She strolled past Mac's office. Through the glass she could see Esme's parents being interviewed on CNN. Mac waved her in. Trujillo was leaning against the wall, watching the show.

"Please, whoever you are, bring Esme back home," her mother pleaded, looking haggard and desperate.

"We just want to know she's safe," her father urged, trying to maintain his composure, but his eyes were red and watering. The head shot of Esme filled the screen with the words, *Missing from her D.C. home.*

Mac clicked the mute button on his remote control. "This story is hotter than D.C. in August, and just as humid."

"It's a weeper," Tony agreed. He arched an eyebrow at Lacey. "Who is it today, Lois Lane?" He was the only man at *The Eye* who ever noticed her clothes.

"Smile when you say that, Clark Kent. And I see you're taking the armadillos out for a stroll." He clicked his boots together and smiled. "So what's the latest?"

"Group of senators on the committee made a press statement, expressed their sympathy for the family, and announced a reward of thirty thousand smackers for information leading to her return. The Bentley family just pledged another twenty grand; makes it an even fifty."

"Van Drizzen wouldn't be one of those senators, would he?"

When Tony nodded in the affirmative, Lacey grimaced. *How nice; both her lovers contributed. Gives a girl a warm glow.*

"What's that look supposed to mean?" Mac demanded. "Spill it, Smithsonian."

"It's just hearsay from a slightly unreliable source. No confirmation, no witness, no second source. I really shouldn't even repeat it. . . ."

Mac's eyebrows rose. Tony's arched. She wished she could capture them on film.

"Why don't you let your editor be the judge of that?" Mac growled.

"Esme was supposedly having an affair with Senator Van Drizzen."

Tony whistled. "How come I haven't been hearing that?"

"Girl talk." Lacey shrugged. "And here's more hearsay: At the same time she's been having a fling with Aaron Bentley."

"Interesting. Does she have a twin sister?" Trujillo again. She ignored him.

"Does anyone else have this?" Mac wanted to know.

"I don't think so, and my unreliable source can be overly dramatic."

"In that case, be delicate, Lacey, when you get statements from both those guys." It was an order. "Work with Tony—he's the lead—but stay on this thing."

"I plan to." Nevertheless, she cringed inside at the icky tabloid feel of the whole thing. Mac's phone rang, busting up their little tea party. Mac knit his brows and rumbled into the phone while Lacey and Tony exited quietly. "What do you suppose he means by 'delicate'?" she asked.

"He means don't get us involved with any special meetings with our publisher and her lawyers and the FBI, but get the story anyway." Tony socked her in the arm. "Go make those calls. Don't stab anybody unless I get to watch."

"That is so not fair. It was only one time." She jabbed him in the ribs, then eyed him meaningfully. "But you never know when I could snap."

Tony had walked to her desk instead of back to his own, so

he could sniff around Felicity's desk. Oddly, the food maven was not around. He picked up some of the chopped veggies left there. "Oh, man, what is this? Sliced green peppers! No cinnamon rolls? What's happened to the Felicity we know and love?" He looked so bereft it made Lacey laugh.

"She's on a diet."

"Man, I hate it when women diet. They get so mean and skinny. It's not natural."

"Why worry? She's already mean and she'll never be skinny."

"Felicity's a doll. She's always bringing little treats in for everybody. I don't know why you don't like her." Tony picked up some papers, hoping to find a more delectable snack.

That was just like a man, she thought. Trujillo had the metabolism of a wolverine; he could eat anything, and it never showed up on his thirty-two-inch waist. He munched on a green pepper, still poking around Felicity's desk. Finding nothing, he gave up and grabbed a couple of cherry tomatoes for the long stroll back down the hall to his police beat fiefdom.

Waiting on Lacey's desk was a messengered package from Chevalier, with Bentley's company handbook. It did, in fact, back up Aaron's position about no resistance in a robbery, but still, Lacey thought, it was cold. As if they counted on robberies as a cost of doing business. She didn't especially want to talk with Aaron Bentley again that day, but she dutifully called Chevalier and gave him a message for Aaron. No doubt she was getting on the Bentleys' collective nerves, with the possible exception of Jeffrey, the handsome nephew who seemed to be unfailingly polite and good-humored. She was astonished when Aaron called her right back, and even more so when he readily admitted his fling with Esme.

"Of course, I was hoping you, of all people, would not find out, but it would be foolish to deny it," Aaron said. "Look at what happens to all those politicians when they lie. I may not be perfect, but I don't lie about things like that." He told her it was just a casual relationship, and besides, he was divorced, she was single, neither of them were breaking any laws or marital vows. "I enjoy women," he said, with a hint of a come-on.

"Do you have any idea what happened to her?"

"No. I have no idea. She is a clever girl and I'm very fond of her. I would love it if she could turn up safe. Now is that all for today, Ms. Smithsonian?"

"When did you last see her?"

"Last Thursday, I think; then I returned to New York until just before the hearing. And my secretary can confirm that."

Predictably, Lacey had less success with Senator Van Drizzen's office. She knew his press secretary, Doug Cable, slightly, but he wouldn't let her speak with him, even when Lacey said it was a personal matter. Finally, after too much time spent wrangling pointlessly with the press flack, Lacey decided to just drop the bomb and see what happened: She said she'd heard that the senator was having an affair with the missing intern, and would he care to comment?

Outraged, Cable simply hung up on her. It made her laugh. *Don't they train press flacks not to do that? Would he have hung up if I were with* The Post? She made a few other fruitless calls on her Esme list. It seemed that Esme's crowd, what there was of it, either didn't know enough or care enough to return Lacey's calls.

She also made another call to Tyler Stone, who denied knowing whom Esme was seeing. Lacey confronted her with her new information about Esme's two lovers; Tyler was unfazed.

"If that's true, it's no wonder we never saw her around the house," Tyler said. "I don't know where she slept."

"Did you know she was seeing Van Drizzen?" There was silence. "You did."

"You can't use my name in connection with this."

"I'm just trying to confirm what another source told me."

"In that case, let's say there were rumors to that effect." Tyler hung up.

Forty-five minutes later the phone rang. It was Senator Demetrius Van Drizzen himself, taking a most imperious tone.

He flatly denied the rumor and apologized for his press secretary's rudeness. Mr. Cable had been too shocked by the idea to think clearly, he said. Mr. Cable would be taking the rest of the day off.

"Elected officials are too often the victims of these baseless allegations. I am a happily married man, Ms. Smithsonian."

Aren't you all, Lacey thought, but did not say. "And where is your wife, Senator?"

"She's visiting our son, who is a freshman at Princeton. She is unavailable for comment."

Until the wagons are circled; then she'll be out front catching arrows. "When did you last see Miss Fairchild?"

"I don't recall. Certainly she worked for the committee, but I'm not aware of her comings and goings." He continued with his lecture. "From now on I suggest you cover the facts, not these scurrilous rumors that are clearly politically motivated."

"I'd be happy to. And the facts are . . . ?"

"That a young woman is missing and we are all hoping that she is returned safely to her family. Good day to you." He hung up.

"Thank you, Senator," she said to dead air, and put down her receiver.

Lacey put together a few paragraphs with the statements of Esme's paramours, both admitted and alleged, and sent them to Trujillo to work into his update. Then she wrote a preview of the museum collection she had seen that day, for which she had taken extensive mental notes while talking with Hugh Bentley. Even though other media had been promised exclusives, no one had embargoed Lacey from writing about it. The Bentleys would just have to get used to her being the barnacle on their boat.

An hour later, Lacey finished up her story, shut down her computer, and began packing up her stuff. She headlined it, "Master Designer Spins Yarns—and History," knowing Mac would probably change it.

"Leaving, Lacey?" Felicity was back at her desk. She ostentatiously looked at the wall clock. Like the martyr she was, Felicity took pride in often staying later than anyone else.

"Don't be silly. I've offended my quota of sources for the day. I'd like to quit while I'm ahead."

chapter 9

When Lacey got home, the expensive shoes from Scarpabellas were still perched on the trunk, where she had left them last night, beckoning to her. *I'm sorry, beautiful shoes, but you have to go back.* She tried them on anyway and admired their sleek sauciness. She pranced in front of the hall mirror and admitted they weren't quite as high and uncomfortable as they could be. She wondered what on earth had possessed her to buy them and promised herself they would go back. *Soon.*

A call flashing on her machine diverted her attention. She pressed the button. "Lacey, it's Marie Largesse. I just had the strongest urge to ask if y'all're planting morning glories? It's fine weather to dig in the dirt, but I don't know why morning glories. I'm just the messenger, *cher.* You'll understand. Just make sure they're morning-glory blue." Marie's smoky Cajun accent flavored the message.

Another cryptic bulletin from the friendly neighborhood psychic. Marie was a psychic, all right, but she seemed to be forever getting her astral wires crossed. The one time Lacey had relied on Marie to pull something spectacular from the ether of the psychic network, she'd fainted dead away.

"Maybe blue is my color today," Lacey said aloud.

"Y'all come on down to the Little Shop of Horus. It's been ever so long," Marie signed off.

Lacey removed the glittering fantasy heels and returned to the bedroom to change into her comfort clothes, black shorts and a light knit top. She put Esme Fairchild out of her mind.

She would either turn up or not. Tony would get the story or not. Mac would be happy or not. *Gee, it's nice not being the lead reporter on this story.*

But one thing nagged at her: Why on earth did Hugh want Mimi's suit so badly? He had offered Lacey a very expensive trade, and no doubt many women would be tempted. She pulled the black Bentley suit from her closet and took it from its special cloth garment bag. Hugh had even remembered the jeweled button covers fondly. They could be removed to reveal plain black buttons for a more subdued look. She peered at the suit closely.

So what are you woven out of, kryptonite? Could it be carrying contraband microfilm from the Forties, or was there a treasure map drawn on silk and cleverly sewn into the lining? Silk maps had been sewn into the linings of jackets during the war for bomber pilots—and spies. *No, Aunt Mimi wasn't a master spy and I am way too fond of melodrama.* She laid the suit gently on the bed, turned it inside out, and felt for anything suspicious or lumpy in the lining. There didn't seem to be anything. She took the jeweled covers off and rolled them around in her hands, admiring the gold filigree that cradled the pearls and rubies. *Priceless gems? Don't be silly.* Mimi spent a lot of money on clothing, but she could never afford real jewels for the button covers. *And if she had, I'd have heard about it.* Though they were lovely, they were just costume jewels.

She thoroughly examined the suit, the perfectly spaced stitches, the cleverness of the set-in shoulders and sleeves. The only oddity was the lack of the distinctive Bentley label inside the jacket, the label that would have said, *Premiere Collection.* It would have been black, embroidered with gold silk thread. That the label was missing made a certain kind of sense to Lacey. Mimi had such a distaste for Hugh, she could easily have snipped it out in a fit of pique. In fact, the label could be in the "Bentley" envelope that Lacey had set aside the other night when she became so distracted by the Gloria Adams letters. She went and retrieved the fat packet from the trunk now, sat down on the floor, and spilled the contents out onto her blue-and-rose Chinese carpet.

In front of her lay several articles snipped from glossy magazines about Bentley's premiere collection in 1944 and a couple of patterns in smaller envelopes, with sketches and notes attached. In a full-color spread, Lacey saw her own suit, although shown in a blue-gray wool rather than black. Even with plain dark blue buttons the suit still carried lots of sass. The model wore it with an enormous matching hat with a navy ribbon, navy gloves, and navy pumps. *Too bad I couldn't get away with that hat.* The Bentley story continued on a page that shared advertising space for Woodbury Facial Soap, their slogan: "It Keeps the Debs A-Glow with Glamour," and a testimonial to the power of Camel cigarettes to relieve "nervous tension."

Handsome Hugh Bentley modestly said he was doing his patriotic job to keep America's women beautiful during the war and was also keeping them employed in his factory. Some worked on the domestic side, while others stitched shirts for the military. Just an all-around peach of a guy, according to *LIFE* magazine.

The other article, also on the dashing young Bentley, was clipped from *Woman's Home Companion* and featured evening attire for the "modern career woman" who needed to entertain at home, and for the "darling debutante" making her first appearance in society. It was a collection that borrowed heavily from movie glamour and featured dewy-eyed young starlets, a dream collection designed to help the female consumer forget about the war that intruded into so many other parts of their lives.

Lacey set the clippings aside and looked through the smaller envelopes. To her surprise, the first envelope contained another note from Gloria Adams, along with several sketches of details of the suit in question, and a cartoon featuring Mimi in the suit, popping a bottle of champagne. Gloria proved to be a talented cartoonist. Lacey immediately picked out Mimi's distinctive pert chin, high cheekbones, and luxurious hair.

Dear Mims,   *July 7, 1943*
   As you can see by this package, I finished the suit that I promised to make you so long ago when I first came to New York. There are all kinds of excuses I can

offer—too busy at work, too tired when I get home. You know me. But when I heard that your Eddie died, I felt so bad and I didn't know what to do. Saying I'm sorry just doesn't make a dent in it. But maybe the suit will tell you how much I care, so here it is. It took me a while, but I wanted every stitch to be perfect. Thinking about you and Eddie and how I was going to be your maid of honor makes me cry. Is it really true his parachute didn't open?

There are a few spilled tears on the wool, but because it's black I don't think they hurt anything. The beautiful wool you bought was a dream to sew, and I don't want you to feel bad about wearing it. Remember, you bought it before we got into the war, so it isn't like you didn't come by it honorably.

I have to tell you a secret, Mims, and you cannot tell anyone, not yet. I couldn't work on your suit at the studio, so I had to use the sewing machine in the living room of the boardinghouse while the other girls played Scrabble and listened to the radio. I'd try it on in my room and step on a chair and try to see what it looked like in the bureau mirror, but I couldn't see the whole suit and how it would hang in the back. So I took it to the workroom at Bentley's and stayed after I clocked out. I adjusted it on the dressmaker's dummy so I could really take a good look. Then Hugh Bentley walked in behind me. When he spoke I swear I nearly died. I explained real fast that I hadn't done it on company time and I had this material and it was for you and it would never happen again. He didn't say a word and he walked around looking at the suit, feeling the material, testing the seams. I waited to be fired. He asked me where I got it. I said I designed it. I didn't tell him I had a drawerful of designs and patterns.

He didn't fire me, Mims! He looked at me, I mean really looked at me for the first time, and he wanted to know if I had any more! Then he took me out to dinner—

*spaghetti at a fancy Italian restaurant—and we talked
all night. He wants to do his own line of clothes. He's
not bad, but he's more of a tailor than a designer, technically very good, but his sketching . . . well, he's not so
much of an artist, you know? We talked about that,
mostly. Now I have so many ideas running through my
head. I sketch new designs whenever I have free time.*

*Mr. Bentley had to explain personally to the land-
lady why I was out working so late. He took full respon-
sibility. Only you and my roommate know. Wasn't she
the suspicious one when I came home after one in the
morning! I stayed up till three telling her all about it,
but she's sworn to secrecy.*

*It all sounds so crazy, but there you have it, Mims;
I'm in New York to stay. And I have you to thank.*

Love to you, Gloria

Lacey read the letter twice. It was written in July of 1943,
almost a year before Gloria vanished. And if what Gloria wrote
was true, then it was she, not Hugh Bentley, who designed
Mimi's gorgeous black suit. And yet Hugh recognized it immediately. *What's going on here?*

She put the note aside and drew a deep breath. Mimi had a
fiancé who died in the war and Lacey never knew it. *Maybe
that's why she never got married.* If Lacey had a fifth of
whiskey, she'd have poured herself a double. She went to the
fridge. All she found was an open bottle of champagne leftover
from an afternoon with Brooke on the balcony last weekend. Its
bubbles were long gone, but it would do.

Her glass of flat champagne in hand, she lifted a second
puffy envelope. A brief note, also from Gloria, was attached.

Mims,   *April 20, 1944*

*Don't show it to anyone. It's my newest design, all
the pattern pieces. I won't let Hugh have it and I know
he can't copy the details. He wants to ruin it in rayon
crepe in a grayish lilac because he says it looks good*

on Marilyn. It doesn't! I can't believe that's what he wants to do to it. This dress is too important to me. I don't care if I have to wait till the war is over to see it made. And I want my name on this dress, not Hugh Bentley's! I will not let him make it for her!

It simply must be made in silk, morning-glory blue, to be exact. My color, as you know. Besides, Hugh could have it made right. He knows how to get silk even now. He has his ways. And his customers are buying silk dresses on the QT. It didn't all go for the war effort. If anyone asks, he says it's prewar stock and when it runs out, there will be no more, so he can charge an arm and a leg for it, but Hugh's private stocks never seem to run out. I've learned a lot, Mims, and I've learned there are some people who get everything they want, even in a war, and I'm going to get my hands on some of it. I'll write when I have more time. Hide this envelope! Oh, and don't turn me in!

Love, Gloria

Morning-glory blue sent chills down Lacey's spine. She wished that Marie's wayward psychic messages would come with a little bit more detail. Turning the envelope over, Lacey noted that Mimi had scrawled a few words—*Last letter from Gloria.*

Lacey opened the envelope. Several sketches of Gloria's dream dress tumbled out, again including drawings of details, the bodice, the midriff, and patterns of beadwork. There was a somewhat idealized drawing of Gloria herself in the dress as well, making her far more glamorous. In it her hair was more controlled, the nose a touch smaller, the eyes the exact color of the dress. *Morning-glory blue,* it said in Gloria's hand. The pictures were colored in pencil, and just to be sure Mimi would know what it should look like, Gloria included a small piece of the blue silk and a sample of embroidering with crystal beads and faux pearls. The rest of the contents appeared to be all the pattern pieces, each hand-initialed and numbered with the notation, *Blue evening gown—G.A.*

But Gloria disappeared—and she never wore her fantasy dress.

The dress featured an intricate beaded midriff and a long skirt that flirted with the limits of L-85, the notorious clothing regulation. The bodice was low, but not scandalous. Lacey examined the sketches and the pattern pieces. The dress was beautifully designed and the pattern was expertly cut. It bore the telltale lines of the early Bentley designs, but Lacey had never seen this one. Whether Hugh had ever designed a similar one, Lacey had no clue. Maybe for one of those clients who could buy whatever they wanted during the war, whether it was red meat, gasoline—or silk.

Lacey arranged the stiff pattern pieces on Aunt Mimi's cherry dining room table to make sure they were all there. They would have to be pressed flat. She knew that the fabric and the color, stipulated by Gloria Adams and reinforced by Marie the psychic, would enhance her eyes. The dress was an impossible fantasy, like the Scarpabella heels that mocked her, but she fell in love with the dress, just as Gloria had. In fact, the shoes were just right for the dress; they would pick up the color of the silk. They would be amazing together. She gazed at the dress, lying in pattern pieces on the table, and then at the shoes. And then at the sketch. Lacey poured herself more flat champagne. Champagne was always dangerous for her. Flat or not, she could have sworn she felt the tickle of the bubbles. She told herself it was an utterly mad idea even to contemplate finishing the dress—it couldn't possibly really work—it wasn't tailored for her— where would she find the silk?—and the pattern was sixty years old! It would be like rebuilding a vintage Rolls-Royce from a paint chip and a box of plans found in a barn. *No way,* Lacey thought. *But . . . what if there* were *a way?*

The phone rang. Stella and Miguel were in the lobby of her building, waiting for her to buzz them up. Lacey had completely forgotten they were supposed to come over and discuss their big plan to remake her for the gala. *Forgotten on purpose.*

It rubbed her the wrong way, as if she had some giant flaw they wanted to take care of. She also worried that whatever they decided would be weird and extreme—an avenging Goth warrior via Versace. *Never!*

Lacey opened the door to a heavenly aroma spiced with oregano, and her defenses melted temporarily. Miguel carried a pizza and Stella carried beer and a bundle of magazines, including a vintage 1941 *Vogue* for inspiration. Miguel glided past Lacey, deftly handing her the pizza and heading unerringly for the pattern and fabric spread out on the table. She quickly set the tantalizing box down on a trivet in the kitchen, then rushed over as he picked up Gloria's sketches with Stella crowding his elbow.

"Careful, Miguel. Those are old—and priceless."

"You started without us?" Stella demanded. "And you're already into the champagne? Before the pizza?"

"Trust me, Lacey," Miguel said. "I have the hands of an artist." He handled the sketches. "And this has possibilities. Definite possibilities. I presume you have all the pieces? And how old is this?"

"Who's Mims?" Stella wanted to know. "The chick in the dress?"

"Yes, I think all the pieces are here, but the dress was never made, and Mims was my great-aunt Mimi, and no, it's not my aunt; it's a woman named Gloria Adams in the dress, and it's from nineteen-forty—"

"Well, then!" Miguel gazed at Lacey, then the sketches, several times, until he was satisfied. He picked up the sample of blue silk and held it against her skin, nodding. He also spied Lacey's new shoes and tested them against the silk. "Yes, see how they pick up the blue? This is the dress. This is the fabric. This is amazing. Lacey, the dress gods—or goddesses—have smiled on you. Stella, can you work with this?"

Stella was nodding in sync with her new Svengali. "I'm thinking a French twist, doing something high with her hair. It'll make that bodice look even lower."

"But it's impossible," Lacey protested. They merely stared

at her. "I mean, it's only a pattern, and the tailoring, the silk, the beading, the details—"

"Nothing is impossible," Miguel declared. "How much time do we have?"

"A week and a half."

"You must work on your abs every day. This dress is all about the midriff."

"Hey! My abs are just . . . But how on earth . . ." *Maybe I should skip the pizza.* It was crazy, it was impossible, but she wanted the dress.

"He's a genius, Lacey." Stella was merely nodding at Miguel's every suggestion. Lacey was no match for this dynamic duo.

"And the cost," Lacey said. She glared at the shoes.

"Don't be ridiculous; you have to have something fabulous to go with those shoes."

"And Stella, about the shoes—"

"This is so much better than going *prêt-à-porter*, which I was simply dreading," Miguel said. "You're so goosey about money. I'm the one who's unemployed here, remember?"

"It's only because I don't have any money."

"Nonsense. Stella tells me you have a little credit-union account that you raid all the time to treat yourself. What better treat than the fabulous Dress That Never Was?"

"Stella!"

The stylist shrugged and her dangling earrings brushed a bare shoulder. Stella was wearing some sort of jungle-princess one-strap leather dress in gold with a stripe of leopard down the sides. "It musta come up in conversation or something."

Miguel flipped open his cell phone. "I have some calls to make if we're going to beat your deadline. Can you slice me some pizza, darling? And bring a fork if you have one."

"I have a phone too, you know," Lacey said. "A real one."

He smiled and winked. "It has my speed dial." He stalked around her apartment while he punched buttons and stepped out on her balcony to admire the view of the Potomac as the sun descended. By the time Lacey and Stella had heated up the pizza, set the plates on the table, and opened the beer, Miguel had made a half dozen calls, some in English, some in Spanish, some in a little of both. He knew someone who could bead anything, someone who was a wizard with pearls, and a tailor who could put it all together and make it snuggle her curves. "My little dream team. They're trying to get green cards, so they really need the work, and overtime is no *problemo*."

"I will not be responsible for running a private little sweatshop."

"Then feel free to right the wrongs of mankind, darling, and even better, you can pay the going wage." Miguel also had a friend in New York's Garment District who dealt in silks. "I'll need this sample to match the dye lot." He snatched up Lacey's solitary scrap of morning-glory blue silk, folded it carefully, and slipped it into his wallet before Lacey could protest. In a daze she removed the patterns and made everyone sit to eat their pizza.

"So who is Gloria Adams?" Stella was gazing at the sketch: Gloria triumphant, wearing the blue dress.

Lacey retrieved the photo of Mimi and her friends, including the woman she assumed was Gloria Adams, "Morning Glory." She dished out the short version, that Gloria was a friend of her aunt's who wanted to be a designer and walked off the face of the earth one day in 1944. *Like Esme Fairchild did the other day.* Lacey left out Gloria's connection to Hugh Bentley, basically because she didn't know exactly what the connection was. Hugh claimed Gloria was a mentally unbalanced stalker and he knew nothing about her ambition, but he could be lying. No doubt there were little lies on both sides.

"This looks like an early Bentley to me," Miguel said. Lacey felt a little dizzy. *So Miguel sees it too.*

"You've been holding out on me." Stella pouted and grabbed another slice of pepperoni-laden pizza. "Is all this stuff out of that magic trunk of yours?"

"Why, Stella, you mean there might be a few tiny pockets of my life you don't know about? I'm shocked."

"So, if this dress was Gloria Adams's design, what happened?"

"She never got to wear it. She vanished a month after she sent this letter to my aunt."

"Someone has to bring her dream to life then," Miguel ordained. "It might as well be us."

"But would she want me to wear it instead of her?" *Pay no attention to things that don't matter, Lacey. Follow your instincts. That's what Mimi would say.* "Maybe she would. She'd want the world to see it."

Or at least, Hugh Bentley. Wait till he sees me wearing Gloria's gown!

chapter 10

"In the Mood" had been playing in Lacey's head. It was one of her favorite Glenn Miller tunes, and she had been in a Forties frame of mind all week. She was wearing a navy crepe dress with three-quarter-length sleeves and a pocket and collar embroidered with gold thread and beads. The slim silhouette suited her, but as usual she felt more dressed up than necessary. Most of the crew at *The Eye Street Observer* demonstrated their fervent belief that casual Friday was in effect every day of the week. *And casual Friday here means Freaky Friday.*

Lacey was grateful that summer was over and hairy-legged men had stopped wearing shorts to the office with tank tops and open-toed sandals. With September she was also spared the tattoo parade on display during the humidity-whipped months, the flaming hearts not quite tucked into revealing décolletage, the sunbursts framing pierced navels, the surprise of an Art Deco flourish in a saucy "butt banner" on the lower back, kissing the thong as the waistband dipped low. *Would it be such an affront to civil rights to institute a dress code?* she often wondered, but wouldn't dare suggest it. She was content to see the cover-up of sloppy khakis and T-shirts. She was also grateful for handsome Tony Trujillo, who always dressed well and enjoyed strutting around in his collection of cowboy boots and tight jeans.

As if she expected something wonderful to happen to sweep her off into the weekend, Lacey always seemed to dress up on Friday. She thought she looked eminently sweepable in the navy crepe. *Now all I need is a devastatingly handsome guy who's in the mood to sweep with me,* she thought. *Oops, that didn't come out right.*

On Friday morning, the talk radio shows were abuzz with the news that missing intern Esme had been playing two guys at the same time. And they had to credit *The Eye* with breaking Esme's connections to Senator Van Drizzen and Aaron Bentley. Mac had given her a byline along with Trujillo: "Two Powerful Men—One Missing Intern." The same edition also ran her column on the Bentley armed robbery and her preview of the Bentley collection in the museum. It was altogether too much Bentley for Lacey.

When she arrived at the paper, she learned Van Drizzen had scheduled a press conference for eleven A.M. An e-mail from Brooke demanded all the secret details she was sure Lacey had declined to print. A second e-mail from Damon Newhouse echoed Brooke's message. Lacey noted that Brooke's e-mail cc'd Damon, and Damon's e-mail cc'd Brooke. *Oh, no, they're already e-mail buddies.*

At ten-thirty, Tony and Lacey grabbed a cab to Capitol Hill to hear the venerable Senator Van Drizzen once again deny the allegations that he had an affair with Esme Fairchild and condemn *The Eye* for printing scurrilous, unconfirmed allegations from its gossip columnist. "I'm not a gossip columnist," she whispered to Tony.

"He's on the run now, and everyone knows it," he said with a grin.

"How long do you want to bet it takes before Mrs. Van Drizzen is by his side vouching for the sanctity of their marriage?"

"Next week. I'll say Monday morning. Want to start a pool?"

Van Drizzen wasn't taking questions, and he had fallen into the trap of vigorously denying the charges rather than simply letting them die. The farther the story inched ahead, the more true it began to look, regardless of the facts: a time-honored way of judging guilt in D.C.

For Lacey, the biggest surprise of the morning was the sight of Felicity in a suit. Granted, it was just a plain black number with a white blouse worn without accessories, and the effect was rather like a secular nun. But Felicity never wore suits. She was a slave to puffy dresses with large patterns, the louder the better. The occasional jumper was her only attempt at widening her fashion horizons. First a diet. Then the suit. It could mean only one thing: a job interview?

Lacey didn't dare ask, but she could hope. "You look nice, Felicity." And she did look nice, for Felicity. "Special occasion?"

"I'm going out on a story." Felicity fumbled in her drawer looking for a pen, then tried to unearth a notebook among the crumbs of past culinary triumphs.

"A story?" Lacey asked. "A food story?"

Felicity shifted her gaze. *She looks as guilty as Van Drizzen*, Lacey thought. The office busybody seldom left the office, though she was rarely seen at her desk. In fact, now that she was thinking about it, Lacey had no idea how Felicity managed her job; she just tried to steer clear of her. Felicity battered away at Lacey's stories as a part-time copy editor, and she wrote about food and it showed. *A lot.*

Finally, latching on to a dog-eared notebook, Felicity grabbed her purse and left. Lacey briefly entertained the thought of scanning the food editor's desk. The furtive way Felicity was acting tickled Lacey's suspicions. There could be a telltale résumé lying around. However, notwithstanding Felicity's new diet, Lacey feared finding deadly little food bombs: M&M's in the file cabinet, Twinkies tucked behind the dictionary, handfuls of hard candy in the pencil drawer. And recipes, everywhere there were recipes. It was too frightening to consider.

Lacey turned away, picked up her copy of *The Eye,* and read her column.

CRIMES OF FASHION

The Well Dressed Criminal—Armed in Armani?

by Lacey Smithsonian

We knew it all along. Even criminals follow a dress code. Most people are bound in some small way to wear the garb of their chosen profession. So it is with the bad guys too. Our clothing tells stories about us.

Perhaps our lessons are informed by Hollywood. We all know that cat burglars wear black, old-time gangsters wear pinstripes with dark shirts, and jewel thieves are immaculately groomed in evening dress. And, of course, don't white-collar criminals wear white collars? The street pimp wears flash and gold chains, the prostitute hot pants and cruel heels. If it is true that clothes make the man, does the crime of fashion make the criminal?

Bentley's Boutique on Wisconsin Avenue was robbed this week by three overdressed bandits, one of them an attractive woman wearing Chanel. The men were apparently armed in Armani. What the salespeople did not expect was that the chic-looking thieves who robbed the boutique of more than a million bucks in jewelry and other sundries turned out to be low-class vicious thugs. . . .

The fashion beat, Mac once told her, was her oyster. She could do with it what she liked. Lacey retrieved Mimi's picture of the three young women from her purse and placed it in front of her. Next to it she placed the pictures of Esme. At the moment she liked the connection of Esme and Gloria—and the Bentleys. Esme was ambitious, trying to boost herself to another level. As far as Lacey was concerned, the jury was still out on Gloria Adams. *Obsessed lying stalker or wronged woman?* She opened one of the letters from Gloria that she had brought with her.

Dear Mims,   *March 17, 1942*
    Mother is still mad at me for moving here. She says factory girls have bad reputations and there are plenty of office jobs in Washington, although she really thinks the only respectable work for a woman is teaching. When I tell her I'm not really a factory girl and I have bigger plans, she says I'm a fool. She doesn't think

*clothes are important. Well, neither did Adam and Eve,
but they found out!*

*Every time I see someone walking down the street
their clothes tell me stories. I can tell who's a nurse,
who stays at home with her baby, who's a factory girl,
who's up to no good, who's got a dream that's a little
too big for whatever shabby uniform she's got to wear
to the factory.*

*My mother said I was crazy and you don't get ahead
by dreaming. But you know, Mims, I think you have to
dream or you go crazy. You always believed I could design wonderful clothes, and I'll always be grateful for
that.*

See you in the funny papers!

Your Glory

There couldn't be many people left after sixty years who had
known any of the principals in the Gloria Adams story, but she
might know one or two. There was Duffy, Frank Duffy, Mimi's
old boyfriend, or whatever you called someone you lived with
for years without benefit of marriage. Her family pretended not
to know, and Duffy would move out temporarily when Mimi's
relations came to town, to "keep up appearances." Lacey
caught on to the affair early one morning during a summer visit
when she was a teenager. She looked out her window to see
Frank kissing Mimi good-bye and getting in his car. If anyone
would know more about Mimi's past, it would be Frank Duffy.

Although she hadn't kept in close contact after Mimi died,
Lacey was fond of Frank. He'd moved to Frederick, Maryland,
a few years ago, where he hooked up with an amorous and pos-
sessive widow. Lacey exchanged Christmas cards with him, but
now she picked up the phone. Duffy was surprised when she
called, but he said he would be delighted to see her. They made
a lunch date for the next day, Saturday. His lady friend was
making a shopping trip to New York with some gal pals and he
was on his own.

The other possibility was that "Honey" (Mrs. Phillip) Martin, who lived in Georgetown when the "Three Musketeers" photo was taken, was still alive. *By now she might be "Honey" Zimmerman and long since deceased,* Lacey realized, *but you gotta start somewhere.* She ran Web searches on several variations on the names and came up with a couple of thousand leads. But only a handful were local. On her deceptively logical principle of "look in the easy places first," she ruled out any lead that was too far out of the Beltway. *Plenty of time to comb the earth later.* After a couple of false starts, she got lucky and found that a Mrs. Phillip (Honey) Martin had moved to Cleveland Park, only a mile or two from Georgetown.

Lacey sat before the screen, a little dumbfounded at finding her presumed quarry alive and living not five miles away after sixty years. *It's that weird small-town Washington effect,* she thought. *It's a sprawling metropolis and a bunch of little villages, and it's the most transient place on earth—except for all the people who never leave.* Lacey called Mrs. Martin, introduced herself, mentioned that her great-aunt was Mimi Smith, and was promptly invited to tea that afternoon. Mrs. Phillip Martin was indeed "Honey," the third Musketeer.

Lacey waved to Mac, caught a taxi to the very verdant and upscale neighborhood, and was charmed by Honey Martin's pale yellow-and-white three-story house. A round turret overlooked the front walk, which was flanked by two handsome magnolias and a hedge of holly.

Honey opened the door herself, even though a housekeeper was bustling about. Following brief introductions, she ushered Lacey into her lush garden, where they enjoyed a view of a host of climbing roses, pots of mums in a riot of colors, and beds of autumn flowers. Honey was happy for the company, she said. She had lost her husband the previous year and missed him terribly. Her children were trying to persuade her to move into a senior residence, but she would have none of it.

"Can you imagine? They want to lock me up in the suburbs. They'll have to wait until after I lose my mind completely. Not before." Honey had lively brown eyes and short curly white hair. Her skin was thoroughly lined and parchment white. Full of energy, she seemed younger than her eighty-one years, except for the telltale osteoporosis. Wearing purple slacks, a lilac sweater, and a colorful silk scarf wrapped around her neck, she looked like a slightly withered flower in her own garden, perhaps an old-fashioned tea rose. Silver drop earrings and a large emerald-cut diamond set in platinum were her only jewelry. She mentioned that she had lost touch with Mimi over the years. Their lives had grown in different directions and she was sorry for it.

"I can see the resemblance. Yes, about the mouth and the chin. And your carriage too," Honey said. A look of puzzlement crossed her face; then her eyes lit with enjoyment. "Weren't you involved in some shocking events at one of those fashion shows sometime back? You didn't kill someone, did you? No, no, I remember, it was the young man who was the killer; you just stuck a fork in him."

Lacey nodded, not knowing quite what to say. "Scissors, actually."

"Now I remember." Honey's laugh crackled. "Mimi would have loved that. I do believe she would like that dress you're wearing too. She was quite the clotheshorse."

"Thank you. It's vintage."

"All the rage, I've heard. And perfect for tea. Now, where is my Ruby?" As she spoke, a woman in her sixties came bustling out the door into the garden, a very handsome light-skinned black woman with a bouffant hairdo.

"I'm coming. Don't wrinkle your underpants." The woman wore a yellow sweatshirt and blue jeans. Lacey introduced herself to the woman. "How do. It's nice to know that someone has some manners around here."

"There's nothing I can do about her, Lacey; she's been with me for the last thirty years."

"Thirty-*five* years and no dental plan." Ruby showed her perfect teeth.

"She thinks she runs my life," Honey lamented.

Ruby set down a tray with two tall iced teas and slices of nut bread. "I do run her life. Now you just holler if you need any-

thing. She doesn't know where anything goes in this house."
The woman gave Honey an indulgent look. "Don't forget to
take your pill, Honey."

"Cholesterol or some damn thing." She swallowed it with a
gulp of tea. "What can I say? She cooks like an angel. Now,
why do you want to talk to an old woman like me?"

"There's so much about Mimi that I don't know—I thought
perhaps you might have some answers." Lacey produced the
"Three Musketeers" photograph and handed it over. "Do you
recognize this photograph?"

Honey's hands trembled slightly and her face softened as
she took it. "Oh, yes, I do. We were so young. So alive," she
whispered. "So full of promise. So long ago."

"What can you tell me about that day?"

"There were several days like that." She turned the photo
over, then turned it back. "Would you look at that hairdo? I suppose I thought that looked clever." In the picture Honey's hair
was braided and crossed over her head, rather like a milkmaid's,
with a flower tucked into it. Mimi's was pulled back and tied
with a scarf, and Gloria's was wild, perhaps from the humidity.
"We called ourselves the Three Musketeers, not terribly original."

"Was it a special occasion?"

"Well, let me think." Honey closed her eyes for a moment.
"Phillip was in the Navy then, and I missed him so. Mimi used
to keep my spirits up with impromptu picnics. We would wrap
up some sandwiches and pack a thermos of coffee and off we'd
go. We'd catch a ride to the park. Gloria came down once or
twice to visit her family. This must have been around Easter.
Yes, you see, the dogwoods are in bloom."

"Who took the picture?"

Honey looked up and blinked. "I have no idea. You don't expect me to remember, after sixty years?"

"Of course, how silly of me," Lacey said. "It's funny I never
heard about you."

Honey continued to gaze at the photo. "Why should you, my
dear? It was so long ago. I was very caught up with my new

role as a Navy wife. All my time was spent trying to learn how to cook. I was going to be the perfect housewife when he got home from the war."

"Do you remember when Gloria disappeared?"

Honey focused on Lacey. "It wasn't like she disappeared suddenly. No one heard from her for a while. She was in New York and we didn't hear from her every week. But time went by and then Mimi started asking questions. She was at loose ends, you see. She needed to forget about Eddie. A year had gone by, but she was still devastated."

"Tell me about Eddie." Burning with curiosity, she wished she could remember everything without the tricks of memory coloring part of the tale and fading others.

"Eddie Franconi. It was terrible; they had just decided to marry. I was going to be a bridesmaid."

"What was he like? Was he handsome?"

"Oh, yes," Honey said, smiling. "He was dark and handsome and charming, long lashes and the most unexpected blue eyes. They were all so handsome in their uniforms." Honey took a moment and sipped her tea before continuing. "He was a paratrooper, and his parachute failed to open. A streamer. That's what they called them as they streamed down. Eddie was a streamer. And then, one day we realized that Gloria had vanished."

"Did Mimi try to find out what happened?"

Honey shrugged. "That job of hers at OPA gave her ideas. Everyone hated OPA. It was a terrible agency, fining little old ladies for abuse of ration tickets. And sending men to prison for buying their girls a few nylons in the black market. But Mimi got caught up in it. She was idealistic."

"Where does Hugh Bentley fit in?"

Honey looked around her garden. She rose from her chair. "Would you like some flowers to take home? I bet you would."

"They are gorgeous." Lacey let Honey tell it her own way. The old woman slipped on her gardening gloves and retrieved a pair of garden shears from a side table. Carefully she selected a pale yellow rose and snipped it. Then another and another.

"I heard a lot about Hugh Bentley," Honey finally said. Mimi had met him in the course of government business. Hugh had to deal regularly with the War Production Board and the Office of Price Administration in producing military clothing for the war effort. He wanted to raise prices, but he was denied. Mimi had gone out with him a few times before she was engaged to Eddie Franconi—and before she heard that the dashing Mr. Bentley had a fiancée in Connecticut.

"Was it a torrid affair?" Lacey blurted out. "And why did Mimi end up hating Hugh? I know she recommended Gloria for a job with him."

"If they had an affair, she didn't tell me. I think she was certainly attracted to him, until she found out about the fiancée, and then she felt downright foolish. There were lots of reasons to hate Hugh Bentley. He was something of a rogue, I heard."

Honey set the flowers down and picked up the photo again. "You might think by looking at this picture that Gloria— 'Morning Glory,' we called her—wasn't terribly attractive, but she was. She was so full of spirit that she drew people to her. Maybe the wrong sort. She probably threw herself at him," Honey surmised.

"What about Hugh's fiancée? Didn't that bother Gloria?"

Honey turned again toward a bed of brilliant dahlias in autumn colors. "In a way it's hard to blame Gloria; there were so few men around. All our strong young boys were shipped off to foreign places with names we couldn't pronounce. And here comes a handsome rascal like Hugh Bentley with money to buy nice dinners and a tankful of gas. That alone might tempt you to let him buy you dinner and take you for a drive in the country."

"If he had so many women on the string, what did his fiancée, Marilyn, see in him? Why did she put up with that?" Lacey asked. "She must have known."

"Some women are very good at turning a blind eye when they put their minds to it. You must remember that everywhere you turned there were women. Women taxi drivers. Women running service stations. That's not a bad thing, of course, but sometimes you have a hankering to see a good-looking man, a young man with all his limbs." Honey snipped a pair of dahlias, bright orange with yellow tips.

"But there must have been lots of men in Washington during the war," Lacey protested.

"Washington was stuffed to the gills. Mimi shared a room with three other girls on bunk beds. But it seemed to me that the men were all so old. There was a song at the time, 'They're Either Too Young or Too Old!' Or else they were taken or married or unfit for active duty or just plain dull. Bureaucrats, you know. I suppose it was natural for Gloria to throw herself at Hugh. I simply never believed she had a chance."

"Why didn't she have a chance?"

Honey raised her face and gave Lacey a look. "Hugh Bentley was just her fantasy. He had his pick of women. And I was afraid that Gloria fell in with a fast crowd in New York, you know."

Lacey followed Honey to another batch of bright blossoms. "What made you think that?"

"Gloria had acquired some expensive things at a time when they were especially hard to come by. Now, Gloria's people in Falls Church didn't come from money, but she showed up with a new camera. One of those German Leicas. And I noticed one time that she was wearing diamond earrings. Gloria told me they were rhinestones. Rhinestones indeed. They were small, but they were diamonds." Honey set the shears down, shook her head, and took a sip of her iced tea. "My father was a jeweler and I worked in his shop. As if I would be fooled by rhinestones."

"So there was a man? Was it Hugh Bentley?"

"That's what we thought, because factory girls didn't make enough to be buying a camera and diamond earrings. But Gloria said she worked so hard there was no time for a man."

"Did Gloria Adams want to design clothes?"

"Oh, my, yes. It was all she talked about. That's why she went to New York."

"Did she make anything for you?"

"Well, no, she didn't."

"Do you think she had the talent for it?"

"She was clever with a needle. She always made her own clothes. And she was quite a fashion plate, even with the cheaper materials. I remember, it must have been that Easter, she made clever pinafores for her little sisters out of tablecloths, the kind with printed borders, clusters of red cherries. They looked as charming as if they had come from Garfinkel's department store. But as for the rest, I'm no judge. Mimi was her special confidante." Honey seemed to run out of steam and concentrated on some memory outside her garden. "And then one day she went missing."

"And the Three Musketeers fell apart?" Lacey prodded. Honey moved to a patch of chrysanthemums that ranged from pale to deep reds and added them to the pile of flowers. Lacey found herself agog at the sight of the bouquet Honey was making for her.

The shears paused in the air. "With all our boys overseas who were dying and maimed . . . quite frankly I didn't think Gloria deserved the attention."

Maybe Honey was the odd man out in their little trio. "You didn't like Gloria, did you?"

"I thought she was a tramp. Maybe I wouldn't think that today." A cool breeze ruffled Lacey's hair. "Things happen, my dear. Life goes on. It was years and years ago."

"What if we could find out what happened to her?"

"If Mimi couldn't find out what happened, I don't think you can." Honey said it a little sharply; nevertheless, she smiled warmly and placed the bouquet of flowers in Lacey's arms, grabbing a piece of newspaper from a side table to wrap the ends in. "I'm feeling a chill. Now you place those in water as soon as you get home, dear. So nice of you to visit me. I'll have Ruby call a taxi for you." Then Honey disappeared into the house, saying she had dinner plans and she simply had to get ready.

The flowers fragrant in her arms, Lacey was dismissed.

chapter 11

Bouquets weren't part of the office's usual decor. Lacey scrounged through *The Eye Street Observer*'s kitchen cabinets for a vase, finally settling on a chipped red ceramic pitcher stashed under the sink behind some cleaning supplies. She heard the distinctive beat of cowboy boots. She glanced behind her. Today they had lizard toes and calfskin uppers. "Nice boots."

"Nice buds," Tony said. "So who's the guy, Lacey?"

"Bored, Tony?" She tried to arrange Honey's flowers artfully.

"Just nosy, as you know." Tony was content to watch and hand her the occasional flower to insert. "Very pretty. So who is this guy who gives you flowers?"

"No guy. A little old lady with a ferocious green thumb."

"Aha. So I guess the famous Vic Donovan is still missing in action?"

"That's what I like about reporters: We're so subtle and diplomatic."

"Have you heard from him?"

"He doesn't call, he doesn't write."

"Maybe he can't spell."

"He can spell. And he's spelling it out quite clearly."

"Doesn't mean he doesn't care. You know guys. A guy figures that *not* saying he *doesn't* love you is the same thing as saying he loves you. Some guys, anyway."

"Thanks for that puzzling insight into interspecies commu-

nication, Tony." She had to move the conversation away from
Vic. "So. Any more news on Esme?"

"Nothing much. The reward's gone up another ten grand.
Van Drizzen's been on CNN all day. And his wife is returning
to Washington."

"The old stand-by-her-man ploy."

"Until she finds the smoking garter. Or the little blue Gap
dress."

"Political wives: They're a breed apart."

Lacey picked up the vase and headed back to her desk. She
had to admit that the bouquet, with its white and yellow snap-
dragons peeking through peach and blush-colored roses, regal
dahlias, sturdy chrysanthemums, and sprays of bittersweet, in a
full spectrum of autumn hues, classed up her shabby environment at *The Eye*. It was a very impressive show. But now that
Tony had mentioned Vic, they only reminded her of him. Vic
had never given her flowers. Maybe he had changed his mind
about coming back to Virginia. She imagined him sucked into
a giant Montana fly trap.

Nearby, Felicity watched with interest as Lacey cleared off
her desk and set the vase of flowers down. Felicity made herself look busy.

"How did your story go, Felicity?"

The food editor shrugged. "It didn't pan out. No big deal."

*Darn, looks like her job interview fell through. Maybe I
should offer to punch up her résumé for her.* As Lacey moved
the flowers to block her view of Felicity, she noticed her phone
message light blinking and was surprised to discover that Jeffrey Bentley Holmes had left her a voice mail. *Now what have
I done?* To her surprise, when she returned the call, he asked
her out to dinner. She was immediately on guard.

"I don't know, Jeffrey. I can't be too popular among the
Bentleys." *What's your angle?*

"Nonsense. With you around, Uncle Hugh won't need a
pacemaker. And Aaron will."

"You've read my stories, then?"

"Every word. Darn those rascally Bentleys: designing visionaries, philandering womanizers questionably involved with a missing intern, grossly insensitive employers. What can I look forward to tomorrow?"

She groaned, and she heard him laugh. "I think dinner would be a bad idea, Jeffrey."

"Don't be ridiculous; I'm not upset. After all, you didn't mention me. And really, Lacey, I'd love to take you to dinner."

"Why, may I ask?"

"Why not? You might be one of the few honest people in Washington."

"You're not spying for your family? To ferret out what I might write next?"

"Maybe I'm a counterspy or a double spy. Would that help you make up your mind?"

A vision of Vic whooping it up with his ex-ex-wife crossed her mind along with a chill of loneliness. The thought of having dinner with a terribly attractive man would be pure balm to her ego. It was against her better judgment. *But what has better judgment ever gotten me?*

"Just dinner, Jeffrey. No stone throwing allowed."

The salmon was fresh and the view of the Washington Monument fabulous at the Hotel Columbia's Pinnacle Room, close to the Willard, where Jeffrey was staying. It was disconcerting that he looked so perfect. But she wore self-assurance as well as her elegant navy dress. Heads turned as they walked into the dining room. He was wearing gray flannel slacks, a navy blazer, an impeccable white shirt, and a blue-and-green-striped tie. He exuded utter confidence. This was a way for her to see how the other half lived, she rationalized, and not think about how much the entrée cost. It wasn't exactly like snagging a bowl of chili and a beer at Hard Times Café in Old Town and listening to Marty Robbins on the jukebox, as she often had with Vic.

Lacey tried to blot Vic Donovan from her mind for most of the evening, but she couldn't help making comparisons. Jeffrey was handsome, but in an Ivy League, pretty-boy way, with blue eyes, blond hair, tan skin, and perfect teeth. *He could grow on you.* Vic, on the other hand, was a more muscular physical presence, ruggedly good-looking with his dark, wavy hair and unreadable green eyes. He always looked like he had just climbed out of a Jeep, while Jeffrey looked as if he had just climbed out of, well, a Bentley.

Jeffrey smiled. "That's a wonderful dress. You look beautiful."

"Reporters hear a lot of things, but that's not usually part of the dialogue."

"I can't imagine why not." He waited for her to be seated.

"You're flirting with me." She briefly wondered if her alert level had been downgraded to Green, pheromone jammers put on hold—although the jammers never had an effect on how Donovan tripped her wires. "Jeffrey, I'm not denigrating my appeal as a sparkling dinner partner, but I really have to ask—why?"

"Why am I flirting or why did I ask you out? Well, I knew you'd make a sparkling dinner partner, and I felt safe asking you out because you've already met the family. You have no illusions about them," Jeffrey said. "You already know that Uncle Hugh is positively dying to get his hands on that original Bentley suit."

"But how far would he go to get it?"

"What do you mean? Did he offer you something?" Jeffrey's complete command wavered briefly.

"Did he ever. Not one but two Bentley's couture gowns, anything I wanted." She flipped open the menu and glanced at the choices. "He reminds me of a little boy who wants all the toys."

"That's Hugh, all right. And Aaron too. Runs in the family. But don't let him intimidate you." Lacey thought it was a good sign that Jeffrey hadn't asked for anything or complained about her writing. *Not yet.*

"He's probably just trying to get you on his side. He can't be happy with the publicity. He doesn't want anything to mar the opening of the museum. He's an old man. It's the most important thing in his life right now."

A man alone at a nearby table rattled his newspaper, turning his page to a picture of Esme Fairchild. It threw an immediate pall over Lacey and Jeffrey. "The Bentleys seem to be at the center of several big stories," she said.

"Yes, of course, the robbery and the missing intern." Jeffrey's face lost some of its good humor. "Is there any news on her?"

"No news. What happens to all the young women who disappear? A few of them run away. Many of them turn up dead." *What happened to Gloria Adams?*

"Horrible." Jeffrey picked up his glass and played with it. "Do you think Aaron is involved somehow? It's not a trick question. I'd like your opinion."

"This is D.C.; anything could happen," Lacey said carefully. "It's a toss-up between the men she knew and the random stranger in the street."

"The men she knew—meaning Aaron."

"Don't forget the senator." She also thought of Kenyon, the reporter Esme had been drinking with. "There may be others."

"Yes, but Aaron is my cousin, though he's considerably older."

"Do you think he's involved?"

"Honestly, I'd have to say that paying people off is more his style."

"He doesn't like to get his hands dirty?" There was no response. "Did you know Esme?"

"I didn't have an opportunity to meet her," he said. "From what I hear she's not my type."

Lacey wondered. Esme and Jeffrey would make an even handsomer couple than Esme and Aaron, and certainly one that was more age-appropriate. They would shimmer with a warm golden glow made for the media. A waiter quietly left a fresh basket of bread in front of them.

"Fashion is a cutthroat business, but I'd like to think we're not that bad. I'm just not always convinced of it."

"But you're not in the fashion end of it." Jeffrey did get his hands dirty with his carpentry. She reflected on how attractively his tool belt had hung when she interrupted him at the museum.

"Thank God. Lord knows I'm much better with a hammer and drywall than with all the rag trade's infighting and back-biting. I was pretty happy running my own little residential design-and-build construction company up in Westchester, but Uncle Hugh said he needed someone he could trust to build the stores, and Aaron made me one of those offers you can't refuse."

"It must be nice to have a family business to join. No résumé problems."

Jeffrey sighed. "Only if you want to work in the dark heart of the Bentley empire, and I'm not sure you would."

"Dark heart?" Her ears were practically quivering. "You mean something more than just money, and the family business, and the glamour of the fashion scene? Something mysterious?" *Like a sixty-year-old murder? And maybe a recent one?*

"Something that holds us all together." He picked up a slice of aromatic rosemary bread. "If my family has anything to do with it, this Fairchild mess, I have to know."

"Why do you have to know?"

"Because there are no consequences in my family," he said quietly. She wondered briefly whether he was still talking to her, or to himself. " 'No consequences' was the first lesson I learned. If you're a Bentley, things get cleaned up. They never happened."

"But you're a Bentley."

"Only half."

"You said that the other day. And aren't you all only half? Technically speaking."

"Sorry, it's automatic."

"What's the worst thing you ever did, Jeffrey?"

"You really want to know?"

Of course not. I want to know the soup of the day. One of Lacey's strongest traits as a reporter, she thought, or perhaps it was a flaw, was that she always wanted to know the ending.

And perhaps people sensed she couldn't resist a good story. Or perhaps they had simply worn out everyone else they knew with endless repetitions. He grimaced at her and waved for the waiter. "Okay, but this is off the record." She raised her eyebrows at that. "Because I don't want to read something like, 'Another Bad Bentley. Juvenile Delinquent Shames Fashion Family.'"

"You, a delinquent? But you said there were no consequences."

"I did, didn't I? Well, in my case, there were consequences," Jeffrey admitted. "I crashed my mother's brand-new sports car when I was fifteen."

"And she threw you in jail?" Lacey asked. Jeffrey nearly choked on his drink.

"Not exactly. Besides, she never exactly told me not to drive it."

"What about your dad?"

"He died when I was ten. My mother was not terribly interested in me. She was busy with boyfriends, trips, the whole Bentley haute couture scene. I wasn't terribly interested in her either, but I did like her brand-new sports car, a little red Mercedes-Benz. With my brand-new learner's permit I was determined to take the Benz out for a joyride while she was gone on some trip. So I spun out into a bridge abutment way out in the countryside late one Saturday night and totaled the car. I didn't have a scratch on me—the little Benz gave its all for me—but I didn't know what to do. I had only the vaguest idea of where I was, so I just sat in the car."

Lacey refolded her napkin to keep herself from grabbing her pen and notebook. She visualized the poor smashed Mercedes. She hated movies that ended in the carnage of beautiful automobiles. "And then the cops came. Did they nail you?"

Jeffrey approved the bottle of merlot and poured for her. "Officer Michael O'Leary and Officer Rocco Rappoli were about to arrest me for reckless driving, speeding, driving without a license, hell, probably even grand theft auto, when I announced, in my snottiest teenage lord-of-the-manor tone, that I

was Jeffrey Bentley Holmes. That backed them up a bit. Then
Rappoli said, 'Well, he didn't get himself killed, so let's just
beat the crap out of him.' I felt the blood run out of my face. No
one had ever so much as raised their hand to me. O'Leary
stopped him. 'He's part of that Bentley clan, you know those
filthy-rich bastards. Think, Rocco, what good would it do you?
You got four kids and one in college next year.' Rappoli said
something like, 'A guy can dream, can't he?' Rappoli stomped
off to the cruiser, no doubt to call a tow truck. Big beefy-faced
O'Leary turned to me and said, 'You don't know how lucky
you are, kid. Rocco Rappoli here was one of the finest welter-
weight boxing champions in New York. His hands are lethal
weapons.' O'Leary told me to get in the backseat of the cruiser.
'Take some advice from me, kid. You keep your mouth shut and
don't say a word. It's going to be a long drive back to your
mother's house. I ain't gonna touch you, but I'm not taking any
lip from some bratty rich kid. Do you understand? And I won't
be held responsible for Rappoli if you open your trap.' By this
time I was so scared I couldn't have said a word, even if I
wanted to. Rappoli looked like he could have been a mob en-
forcer in another life." Jeffrey laughed at the memory.

"Oh, my God. I was such a wimpy goody-goody as a
teenager. If I'd been picked up by the cops I would have died
on the spot," Lacey said.

"I doubt that very much."

Lacey picked up her glass of merlot and toyed with it. "And
did you mouth off on the long way home? And how long was
it?"

"It was much longer than it needed to be. I think we took
several laps of Westchester County before they dropped me off.
And boy, did I get an earful. 'Those Bentleys,' O'Leary said,
'they may be rich as royalty, but they are the scum of the earth.'
I was vaguely embarrassed by my family, as most kids that age
are, but I had no idea how deep the resentment ran against my
family. We Bentleys and Bentley Holmeses were so smugly superior. These two working-class cops lashed me with their
scorn. I began to think getting the crap beat out of me would be

easier than listening to it. O'Leary, who could never afford a Mercedes like the one I had just casually totaled, had been a cop for twenty years. He unleashed a litany of the offenses of the Bentleys that started with me and had no end."

"Did that include your mother?" She wondered about the cool Belinda who had not one hair out of place.

"Oh, yeah. He spared no one. 'With a mother like that, what can you expect? She's a Bentley too.'"

"Everything is off the record for now, Jeffrey. But what exactly is included in that litany of offenses?" Their entrées arrived, seafood for Jeffrey, filet for Lacey, artfully arranged platters with artistic mounds of mashed potatoes and curled vegetables.

"The usual, I suppose. Uncle Hugh treated the factory girls as his own private harem. Women who said no were given the worst work, the worst hours, or they were simply fired. The cops had names and case histories, but no one dared defy him because he could ruin them. And Hugh was a smuggler, a black marketeer, a war profiteer who bought off politicians."

This story is tilting again in Gloria's favor, Lacey thought as Jeffrey continued.

"Cousin Aaron had a little drug business in his high school, where he got A's in chemistry. And there was a girl that he got pregnant. Rappoli knew her family. The girl was fifteen. Hugh arranged and paid for an abortion. She killed herself when Aaron refused to see her again." Lacey noticed Jeffrey hadn't touched his swordfish. "Rappoli would turn around and glare at me and say things like, 'I still think we should knock some sense into the kid.'"

"It sounds pretty punishing, even without the corporal punishment."

"I had no idea what people thought of us. After all, it wasn't exactly dinner conversation, not at our dinner table, even if we provided entertainment far and wide. We thought we were getting away with it all, and we were, but it was no secret. Bentley dirty laundry was hung out all over town. I had to wipe my eyes on my sleeve so they wouldn't see I was crying. As I said, it was a long drive home."

Lacey realized she had hung out a bit more of that Bentley dirty laundry on a line called *The Eye Street Observer. What does he really think of me?* she wondered.

"Eventually they got tired of the Bentleys and started talking about other things." Jeffrey stopped and took another bite.

"That must have been a relief," Lacey said.

"O'Leary said he was going to the eight-o'clock Mass at St. Timothy's on Sunday morning. Rappoli wondered where my family might be going to church. O'Leary just laughed and said Bentleys worshiped money, not God. But I thanked God myself when we finally drove up to my house. No punishment my mother could think of could compare with that trip home with O'Leary and Rappoli."

Lacey could imagine the glamorous and beautiful Belinda, haughty and superior, meeting the police officers at the front door like the lady of the manor in some Bentley dressing gown.

"My mother thanked them graciously. After they left she just looked at me and said, 'Well, Jeffrey, perhaps you are a Bentley after all.' " He took a long swallow of wine. "A Bentley was the last thing on earth I wanted to be at that moment."

A few sleepless hours later, Jeffrey had found himself in front of the arched oak doors at the stone church of St. Timothy's. He eased open the heavy door and stepped inside.

He paused in his narrative. Lacey took another bite and swallowed. "Okay, go on. I'm listening. You're at the church. You're inside the door. Then what?"

"That's all for now." Jeffrey leaned back and sighed.

"No, wait a minute. I'm a Catholic. I can take it. I really want to know what happened."

"Really?"

"Yes."

"Good, then I have something to tell you next time."

"Next time? No fair!"

He laughed out loud. "You should see your face."

She grabbed her napkin, making a show of wiping her mouth, hoping to hide her expression.

"Next time, Lacey. Have some patience. I know, I know, you're a reporter. But you have to wait. Besides, I can't stand talking ancient Bentley history all night. I want to know about you."

No matter how she tried he wouldn't budge. He was good at it, very good. The evening wound down and Jeffrey proved to be the perfect gentleman. He escorted her to the parking lot where she'd left her Z, and he left her with a dazzling smile.

There were too many contradictory thoughts scrambling around in her head as she navigated the Fourteenth Street Bridge back to the George Washington Parkway. *Could there really be one white sheep in the Bentley wolf pack? And when the wolves find out, will they fire him—or eat him?*

chapter 12

Saturday's weather was jewel-like in its perfection, the azure horizon punctuated with cotton clouds as Lacey drove up to meet Frank Duffy. It was warm, with the slightest hint of coolness in the breeze. The trees still wore their deepest summer green, though a red leaf or two peeked out now in anticipation of fall. The Z was in prime shape, and the sixty or so miles between Old Town Alexandria and Frederick, Maryland, slipped away pleasantly, without much traffic. Everyone in Washington was searching for Esme Fairchild, and Tony Trujillo knew everything about Esme that Lacey knew. She felt free to pursue her own story: the common thread between Esme and Gloria—the Bentleys.

She was early to meet Duffy. Lacey parked the Z on North Market and ducked into Venus on the Half Shell, one of her favorite vintage clothing stores. A pair of platform pumps in alligator, enclosed in a glass case, called to her, but the very thought of buying more shoes made her shudder. Peering between two mannequins dressed in Twenties flapper garb in the front window, Lacey suddenly caught a glimpse of Duffy passing by on the sidewalk, smiling, as usual.

Younger than Mimi by ten years, Frank Duffy was now a spry seventy-something with soulful blue eyes. He was still fit and trim. He and Lacey had planned to meet at a little café on Market Street, just down the block from the vintage store. Lacey had dressed casually and comfortably in black jeans and a violet V-necked sweater to prepare for the sinful dessert that

Duffy would no doubt talk her into. When she darted out of the shop to meet him, he greeted her with a big grin and a question.

"Lacey, my pet, it's wonderful to see you, but what's up? You drove all the way up here for lunch with an old rogue like me?"

"You're not that old, but you are a rogue. And yes, I would like a little information. I want to pick your brains."

"Good for you. Still a reporter, aren't you? I've been following your latest exploits up on Capitol Hill. And if you keep stabbing those bastards, they'll give you a real beat yet." He took her arm and patted her hand gently. Duffy had been a reporter himself for a few years before law school and a long career as a trial attorney. It seemed to Lacey that nearly everyone she met had put in time on a newspaper somewhere in America; Duffy had been a city beat reporter at *The Minneapolis Star-Tribune*. They decided to stroll down the street window-shopping and select a restaurant on whim.

"So you met That Bastard Bentley in the flesh," Duffy said. "And you've come to ask me what I know."

"Am I that transparent?"

"I'd be disappointed if you didn't want to interrogate every possible witness. And you'd better hurry; your witnesses are getting a little long in the tooth, like me."

"So what can you tell me, Methuselah?"

"Not much, I'm afraid. Mimi held her cards very close to the vest. When it came to That Bastard Bentley, she didn't dwell in the past. It was one of her charms. Did they have an affair? Maybe, but she never told me." Duffy paused and shot Lacey a knowing look. "You were going to ask me, weren't you?"

"I was going to be subtle."

"A reporter, subtle? Never."

They selected an inviting restaurant decorated with dark wood and shades of green. The sandwich board on the sidewalk trumpeted fresh fish and chips and Killian's Irish Red on tap, and those were the exact words Duffy said to the waitress after they were seated in their booth near the window. Lacey ordered the soup-and-sandwich special, and if she ordered a Killian's, she told Duffy, she would have to sleep it off before heading home.

"Did she ever explain why Hugh was officially Hugh 'That Bastard'?"

He shook his head. "Mimi only said Bentley took what didn't belong to him."

"Like someone else's designs?"

"She never did say, just changed the subject." Duffy had heard a little about Gloria, and he thought he remembered seeing the Three Musketeers photo, or one like it, but not many details. "She called it all ancient history. Our own history started when we met."

Lacey asked if he ever heard about Gloria Adams's disappearance.

"Yes, but I wouldn't have known about her at all, except that one day about ten years ago Mimi announced that we were going to a funeral in Falls Church. It turned out to be Gloria Adams's sister. Mimi saw the obituary in the paper and we went. It had been years, but the family welcomed Mimi like some long-lost relative. We met the woman's daughter—that would be Gloria's niece. The niece told us her mother never got over losing Gloria, and Mimi said neither had she. I was a little surprised because before that day I had never heard of Gloria Adams."

"What were they like, Duffy? Her relatives."

"I have only the vaguest memory of the woman and her daughter, who was a teenager at the time. They were timid, colorless women. I wouldn't recognize them if I passed them on the street." The waitress delivered their drinks, iced tea for Lacey and the Killian's Irish Red for Duffy. "After the funeral, Mimi and I went to lunch and hoisted a few stiff ones. Mimi was of the mind that Bentley had used Miss Adams quite shabbily. Mimi had barely escaped his amorous advances herself, and she stopped just short of accusing him of having something to do with the girl's disappearance. Mimi tried to find out what happened, and I gathered she nearly lost her job with the Feds over it."

"Really? What exactly was her job?"

"Until the war ended she worked for the Office of Price Administration, which investigated, among other things, black marketeering. She had their investigators crawling all over Bentley's factory." Duffy chuckled. "Mimi could get people moving." He reached for his plate as the waitress reappeared.

"Don't leave me in suspense, Duffy. What did they find?"

"Not Gloria. But they did find a truckload of contraband nylon stockings and silk and other fabrics."

"That doesn't sound like much."

"It was another age." He winked at Lacey. "Those things were worth their weight in gold. All production of nylons had supposedly ceased. No one knew it at the time, but the U.S. government secretly reopened a factory and was making nylons exclusively for espionage purposes."

She looked up at Duffy, puzzled. "Girl spies just gotta have their nylons?"

Duffy laughed. "And male spies too. For use as currency. Better than cash. Nylons would buy you a lot during the war."

"Did Bentley manufacture them?"

"No, but he must have known about them. Shipments occasionally were hijacked. OPA managed to nail only a couple of Bentley's drivers, but they never nailed the big fish. And Hugh Bentley finally filed a formal complaint against Mimi for harrassment. She managed to keep her job, but his complaint just convinced her even more strongly that he had something to hide."

"Hugh Bentley looked me in the face and told me he didn't remember Mimi Smith."

Duffy laughed again. "Oh, I doubt that very sincerely. There was a lot of bad blood between them."

"But she really managed to shut down some of his profiteering?"

"She made it a lot harder for him, anyway."

"Good for her!" Lacey took a moment to digest the information and play with her food. Hugh hadn't forgotten Mimi. He wanted her suit back. It was personal for him. Lacey realized she shouldn't underestimate any of the Bentleys, including the charming Jeffrey.

"Now, Lacey, darlin', I have to say this because I'm an old man and it's the kind of thing an old man says, and because I care about you. Don't be playing games with Hugh Bentley. If he's the snake that Mimi thought him to be, he's only more poisonous now. He may be old, but he has his own little empire, and no doubt he has others to do his dirty business for him."

Lacey stood up and kissed him on the forehead. "You're a sweetheart and I will be careful."

"Sit down and order dessert."

He ordered the cheesecake and she restrained herself to the sorbet. "And Gloria's family, where are they?" Lacey asked. "Maybe they would have some more information."

"I believe they were still in Falls Church, where Gloria was from," he said. "Perhaps they're still around."

"Wait a minute, what was their name?"

"I can't remember, Lacey."

"What about the sister who died?"

"Mosby, like the highway."

Over dessert Lacey tried to extract a little information about their romantic life and why they never married. Duffy found this amusing. "I adored her. I asked her many times to marry me. She loved me, but she was almost fifty when we met and she said it wasn't important, that there wouldn't be any children. She said I'd get tired of her." His eyes misted over. "Silly, that was. I was afraid she'd get tired of me."

"Oh, Duffy, how could you think that?"

After Lacey got home, she powered up her new-slash-old computer, Trujillo's old laptop, her reluctant concession to the information age and getting e-mails from people who refused to write letters or pick up their phones or cell phones. It was parked in the small second bedroom that she planned to someday turn into a guest room. She didn't like Googling at home or tying up her phone line, but it beat going into the office, and the Alexandria library closed at five on Saturday.

She found some information about black-market silk and nylons, but nothing useful about Bentley Industries, as it was called during World War II. The Internet eventually, after much searching, offered up a *Washington Post* obituary of one Gladys Mosby. She was survived by her daughter, a Mrs. Wilhelmina Tremain, and a granddaughter, Annette Tremain, both of Falls Church, Virginia. She found the phone number on the Web. *So much for privacy.* Her first call was a success, and Mrs. Tremain agreed to talk on Sunday after church. She was a Presbyterian. Her daughter, Annette, preferred to stay home. Lacey made plans to visit about two o'clock.

Before she went to bed, the new Scarpabella shoes caught her eye. "Okay! Monday! You go back on Monday!" she said out loud. She wished she had tried on the vintage alligator pumps in Frederick: sixty years old, like new, and only a hundred bucks. *Beat that, Scarpabella.*

chapter 13

Damn. It's too early for telemarketers. Lacey picked up the receiver of her faux vintage phone on the nightstand. The glow of her digital clock informed her that it was six A.M. *It's too early for emergencies, too.*

"Hello?" She was too groggy to say anything clever.

"Hey, Lacey, do you know where Huntley Meadows is?"

"What? Trujillo, is that you?"

"Yeah, so, Huntley Meadows? Supposed to be a nature preserve? Near Route One?"

"Sort of. But do you know what time it is?" She lifted her foot out of bed to move the drapes. It was still dark.

"News time, Smithsonian. Focus. Huntley Meadows?"

"Okay, yes, I've been there. It's not far from here, and what the hell—"

"Cool. I'll be there in twenty minutes. Get dressed."

"What!" She sat bolt upright in her bed. "Why?"

"You are alone, right? I mean, it's cool if you're not, but—"

"Tony, what is going on?"

"They found Esme there."

"Esme! Esme Fairchild?"

"So you're up now? At least they think it's Esme; you know they're not saying. We've got to get there before the scene is disturbed, and while the local cops still might talk. I never heard of a nature preserve off Route One. Is it in a strip mall or what? I need a guide. You're it. Meet me out front." He hung up without waiting for a response.

"Good-bye to you too," she said to the dial tone.

There was no time to bathe, and that was just too bad. Lacey did not like early-morning expeditions, but if it was true, this was a scoop. She threw on a pair of jeans, a blue work shirt, and a pair of sneakers. She also grabbed a black hooded sweatshirt and knotted it around her shoulders. Makeup, although minimal, was necessary. If the building were on fire, Lacey would grab mascara and lipstick on her way out, which was how she dashed it on that morning, along with some brown pencil for her eyes and a spot of blush. On the way out the door she grabbed her purse and tape recorder and a small pair of binoculars from the Spy Store in the District. On the elevator down to the lobby, she calmed her hair in a securely tied band. It would simply have to do.

Trujillo's black Mustang pulled into her circle driveway as she exited the front door of her building. He leaned over and opened the passenger door for her. "Nice timing." Lacey guided him down the George Washington Parkway, then to a squealing right on Belle View up to Route One, and then a left and over the hill down to Lockheed. The Huntley Meadows wetlands preserve was just a few blocks west of the busy Route One corridor, lurking incongruously behind the endless strip malls. Tony pulled into the parking lot at the north entrance. It all seemed so smooth, but as they jogged down the path past the nature center they were stopped by a Fairfax County police officer.

Lacey flashed a smile at the cop. "We're just looking for some early-morning cardinals."

The cop shrugged. "You can't go this way, ma'am."

"Really? Well, we'll just go the other way." She tossed him another flirtatious smile. "Thanks, Officer." She grabbed Tony's arm and led him away.

The policeman tipped his cap, and Tony said nothing until they were out of earshot. "So, birdwatcher, what's this about an early-morning cardinal?"

"I have no idea. Cardinals should be in bed now. Like me."

Huntley Meadows early in the morning is full of sounds—

chirping birds, the honking of Canada geese, small creatures slithering over dried leaves, and the splash of water as the geese land in the marshy pond. The strong scent of marsh grass and mud permeates the atmosphere. Nevertheless, there is the feeling of stillness that could, on any other morning, impart a contented peacefulness. Today it felt hostile, under the eye of unseen predators.

Lacey and Tony picked their way through the trees behind the nature center to a small observation tower, which was outside the yellow crime-scene tape but still allowed them good visibility of the small knot of police at the curve of the boardwalk. They climbed to the upper platform, where cheerful placards explained the ecosystem and wildlife of the protected wetlands, including the great blue heron, egrets, ducks, beavers, deer, and geese. Lacey could see part of the boardwalk that led from the nature center into the northern end of the marsh. It circled part of the pond and then trailed off into the woods leading to the observation tower where she and Tony were now standing.

"You see anything?" Tony asked. Lacey lifted her small ten-power binoculars to her eyes. "Binoculars, Smithsonian? I had no idea you were such a child of nature. Let me see." He reached out for them, but she pulled away.

"Hold your horses." She kept her eyes on the slow-moving crime-scene investigators. Some were standing on the boardwalk taking photos. Two in rubber hip boots were in the swamp up to their knees. They seemed to be extracting a large mud-caked object from underneath the boardwalk.

"What do you see?" Tony demanded.

"Tell me what you know."

"I heard she was stashed underneath the wooden walkway, but this morning a couple of birdwatchers saw what they thought was a foot peeking out. What's going on down there?" Trujillo was reaching for the binoculars, but Lacey jerked away again.

"Grabby. There's more than just a foot." The binoculars helped, but she was wishing they were closer. But then as two policemen moved aside she saw a nightmare in the morning light, one that twisted her stomach into a knot. She stifled a gag, thankful now for the distance.

The bloated body bore little resemblance to a living thing. Muddy hanks of hair were wrapped around the head, but a gaping hole with bone protruding was all that was left of Esme's lovely face, savaged by decomposition and creatures in the muck. *If it is Esme.* It would be impossible to identify her without forensics. Although filthy, the clothing on the corpse could be a jade-green jacket and a short skirt. It could be Tyler Stone's missing unworn Bentley suit. Tyler would never wear it now.

Lacey choked and coughed and handed the binoculars to Trujillo, who uttered a "Madre de Dios" after focusing the lens.

She sat down on a nearby bench and propped her face in her shaking hands. Unexpected tears spilled down her cheeks. She had stared into the face of a murdered woman before. But this felt worse somehow. Esme clearly did not belong out here in the wild marsh among the muskrats and the herons and Canada geese. Someone had taken her suddenly from life to death. And there was no face to stare into.

Lacey glanced across the pond and saw a small group of people on the opposite shore standing on another observation platform. "Tony, look over there." He turned the binoculars in that direction. News crews were setting up cameras.

"Hey, I think that's one of our guys taking photos. I think it's Hansen. We're covered. He's great with a long lens. Let's go see if we can get any comments."

The Fairfax County police at the tape line weren't saying much, but someone let it slip that something was tied around her throat. They seemed to be waiting for someone. "FBI," Tony murmured in her ear. Tony said he knew someone there he could call. They made their way back through the woods to Tony's Mustang. He offered to take her to breakfast, but she declined. There were other things on her schedule and she needed to take a shower, a long hot shower, even though she knew it wouldn't help wash away the memory of the end of Esme Fairchild.

A half hour later Lacey stepped out of the shower to answer the ringing phone. *That will be Brooke.* She had an understanding with her friends not to call before ten. She glanced at the clock. Ten sharp. She picked up the receiver.

"You know I sleep in on Sunday mornings."

"They found Esme. Dead, of course."

"I was there. It's not confirmed." The faceless body clung to her memory.

"No, but we know it's her," Brooke said with complete assurance. "Wait, you were there? What were you doing up before the crack of ten?"

"Hang on; let me turn on the television." The phone had a long cord and she carried it with her into the small den where she kept the TV. She clicked the remote. Esme's formerly lovely face filled the screen.

"Well?" Brooke was on the other end. "And who tipped you?"

"Trujillo. And yes, it's probably her."

"Okay, who are your main suspects?"

"The world at large." Lacey had to change the subject. "By the way, where were you last night?" *No doubt out with Damon.*

"Tell you later. Van Drizzen's a tempting suspect, but naturally a senator wouldn't get his hands dirty personally; he'd let someone else do it. Of course, the police aren't releasing any information on the cause of death, but the guy who found her, an early-morning wildlife enthusiast, according to the news, said there was something wrapped around her neck. So my guess is strangulation. Did you see anything on her neck?"

"Let's talk later, okay?"

"Sure thing, Lacey. But I, uh, have a date this afternoon."

"Oh, yeah? Afternoon delight? Who's the lucky guy?"

"Damon and I are going to the Spy Museum. There's a new exhibit on high-tech surveillance."

"Happy spooking." Lacey figured that would keep them out of trouble and out of her hair, but of course their theories, fanciful and otherwise, about the intern's death would already be flying off into deep cyberspace. She hung up and watched the news. They ran video clips from the night before: Esme's mother on the eleven-o'clock news. Police search teams combing the wooded parks in and around the District. A broadcast reporter caught her mother, Frances Fairchild, bursting into tears. In her frustration she cried out, "They're not looking for a girl anymore; they're looking for a body!"

There was small comfort for the Fairchild family in that even though their daughter was dead, they had finality. Unlike Gloria Adams's family, they had a body to bury, a body to mourn. What little there was of it. Even if someone eventually discovered what happened to Gloria Adams, what comfort could that be at this late date?

The phone rang again. It was only ten-thirty. Maybe she should let the machine answer it. Or maybe she should unplug the phone, she thought. She answered it.

"Oh, my God, Lacey, I could be next!" The hysterical voice was unmistakable.

"Good morning, Marcia. I gather you've seen the news."

"What am I going to do? It could be me in that swamp." Marcia's voice caught on unshed tears. "They'll be finding me dead in a swamp next!"

"Try calming down. Now, why would they want her dead? Or you?"

"All I can think of is that it's because she knew me. This is all because of me!"

On Planet Marcia, Lacey thought, *everything is about Marcia. Terrorists are attacking America to get to Marcia! The alert level has been raised to Code Marcia!* "Get a grip, Marcia. You've told all your secrets to the special prosecutor, right?"

"Well, yeah, I guess so." She didn't sound that sure.

"Then no one has a reason to get rid of you. People get killed in this town to keep them from talking, not to punish them after the fact for talking and talking and talking, like you did. That would be considered backward. Believe it or not, Marcia, you actually were protected by the press. Your notoriety is your best life insurance!" *It's a theory, anyway.*

"Are you sure?" Lacey eventually managed to calm Marcia down and get off the phone. She could only imagine who would call next. Stella? Marie? Mac? The FBI? *My mother?* She pulled the plug.

She put on clean black slacks, a red-and-white sweater, and a black wool blazer with gold buttons. It was suitable for church—and for calling on the last family link to Gloria Adams.

chapter 14

The Tremains, mother and daughter, lived in a small two-story redbrick colonial with a neatly trimmed lawn and matching maple and dogwood trees on either side of the walkway. A few bright orange leaves poked out of the bottom branches of the maples.

The white front door opened and a small round woman stepped out to greet her. She wore a flower-print shirtwaist dress with a blue sweater, plain sensible navy pumps, and a strand of pearls around her neck, which must have been her church outfit. She wasn't much on makeup, and her hair was worn in a serviceable puffy bob; streaks of gray shot through the pale brown. Lacey estimated her age at around fifty-five, though there could have been a five-year difference on either side.

"You must be Lacey Smithsonian. I'm Wilhelmina Mosby Tremain. Gloria Adams was my aunt. Call me Willie. Annette is inside." Even though Northern Virginia has become pretty Yankeefied, Willie struck Lacey as quiet and dignified in an Old Dominion way, with a soft Southern affect. "Do come on in. Please excuse the house. We don't get visitors that often."

"Thank you so much for seeing me on such short notice." Lacey followed Willie into the small hallway and set her purse down on a side table. "Something smells good," she said.

"Annette just made some banana bread, and she'll have tea out shortly." Lacey realized she was hungry and thanked heaven the Tremains embraced old-fashioned Virginia hospitality.

The house was comfortable and clean, though its furnishings had seen better days. It had an overstuffed feeling and just missed being "shabby chic." Magazines and paperbacks were piled everywhere. A worn burgundy Oriental carpet lay in front of the fireplace, where two ancient wing chairs were placed. The sofa, likewise, had seen a lot of use. Annette entered quietly from the kitchen carrying a tray set with treats and, obviously, the good china. "This is my daughter, Annette." She was probably in her late twenties, but she looked younger. She also seemed terribly soft, as if exercise were a sinister concept to her. Perfectly plain mousy brown hair, parted down the middle, hung lankly to her shoulders. She had pale green eyes and pale lashes. She might have been pretty, Lacey thought, with some color in her face. Annette wore a wispy light blue blouse and jeans and sandals on her feet.

Willie indicated that Lacey should take a seat. "I didn't mean to put you to so much trouble," Lacey said, suddenly feeling guilty for their effort.

"No, no, no trouble at all."

"It's our pleasure," Annette said, looking very interested.

Lacey's immediate impression was that Annette was standing at the front door of life, waiting for someone to open it up for her and escort her in. *Too shy to ring the bell?* Lacey remembered that Duffy said they seemed to be timid women.

They settled down around the coffee table. Lacey handled the china carefully, afraid to break it. Willie had thoughtfully gathered pictures of Gloria for Lacey, including a studio shot of a serious-looking young woman wearing wire-framed glasses: Gloria at twenty-one, a year or so before she went missing. Her unruly hair was subdued into a large poof on top, revealing her ears, and brushed down in the back. *Her thick eyebrows could use a trim,* Lacey thought. But her gaze was direct, hungry for something. A later photograph, taken when she was living in New York, showed she had abandoned the glasses and developed a bit more polish. And she wore lipstick. *You'll hardly rec-*

ognize me, Mims, one of her letters had said. It was just a snapshot, but it had a lot more life than the professional shot. She looked happier, freer, with finger curls spilling over her forehead. There was also a picture of Gloria and her sister, Gladys, Willie's mother. They strongly resembled each other.

"That one was taken in the spring of 1944, right before she disappeared," Willie said. "Of course, I wasn't even born then, but I grew up knowing about her. Here's another one."

She handed Lacey a picture that must have been taken the same day as Mimi's photo of the Three Musketeers: Mimi, Gloria, and Honey. Lacey had brought it with her, slipped carefully into a stiff envelope, and she pulled it out to compare them. Annette leaned in intently. Both photos had the same Great Falls background. But Honey was missing in this shot; instead the photo showed Mimi, Gloria, and another young woman, linked arm in arm.

"That's Gloria and my aunt Mimi," Lacey pointed out, "but who is the other woman?"

Willie just shrugged and Lacey turned over the photo. There was nothing written on the back of this one. The same dogwoods were in bloom, the light was the same, and Mimi and Gloria were wearing the same outfits as in Lacey's photo. It had to have been taken at the same time. Lacey looked closely at the new woman. The third woman was small and she wore a faint smile between the grinning Mimi and the fierce Gloria, who may have been scowling at the sun in her eyes. She couldn't have been more than five feet tall, and was built like a squat fireplug, wearing a plain white blouse and blue jeans. There was something very pragmatic about her squared-off Dutchboy haircut. So there was a fourth at that picnic, taking pictures in turn. Not just a passing stranger. *Did Honey really forget? And will she remember when I call her back?*

"Have you seen these?" Annette asked. She had a handful of news clippings on Gloria, including a few that Lacey hadn't seen. But they all told the same story, and none had a satisfying conclusion. Willie also produced a small packet of letters from Gloria to her sister, Gladys. Willie said she might have read them once when her mother died. They meant nothing to her; she had read a few and then put the rest away. "Gloria wrote a lot about clothes and sewing, and I hated to sew. So if all the letters were about that, I just didn't find them that interesting," Willie said with apologies.

"May I copy them? I'll bring the originals right back."

"Well, I suppose it would be all right." Willie sounded doubtful. She placed her china cup and saucer down. "Somehow I feel it's rude to rummage through dead people's things."

"Dead?"

"Oh, surely by now. Don't you think? Even if she just ran away and abandoned all of us. After all, Mother died ten years ago." Willie wavered. "Maybe I should just burn them."

"Wait a minute, Willie." Lacey's pulse raced. "Maybe there's something important in the letters. What if there was some way to find out what happened to her?"

"Why do you care about Gloria?" Annette broke in.

"I'm not quite sure, except that my aunt cared about her and wanted to find out. And maybe I can find out more about Mimi and her life." Lacey hesitated. *Be honest.* "And I'm a reporter. Curiosity is a real bad habit of reporters."

Willie looked at Lacey. "Do you really think it's possible to find something in the letters?"

"I don't know, but I'd hate to see you torch them without knowing for sure."

"At least you're honest." She hesitated; then she handed over the photos and the letters.

Lacey felt terrible. Some days she wasn't sure what honesty was. She was only sure that she wanted to know more. "And I'd like to write about Gloria and compare her story with Esme Fairchild's."

"Who on earth is . . . ?" Willie was stumped, but Annette was showing definite signs of animation. In fact, she looked like she was about to jump out of her skin.

"Mother, that intern whose body was found this morning! In some park down on Route One. It was on the radio; I told you I heard about it. Lacey, were you there, did you see it?"

"Yes, I was. And Esme Fairchild was involved with Aaron Bentley, Hugh's son."

"Oh, wow," Annette said, "the fatal-romance-with-a-Bentley angle, right?"

"Now, don't get carried away, Annette," Willie cautioned her daughter. "More tea, Lacey?"

Lacey suspected that Annette might be too shy to have much firsthand experience with romance, but her secondhand experience filled the room. Bodice rippers and romances of every stripe crowded the bookshelves by the fireplace, supported one end of the dilapidated sofa, and formed a pyramid of purple-tinged literature on a scarred mahogany end table. Annette came alive with the possibility of seeing her missing great-aunt Gloria as a tragic romantic figure in the same vein as a murdered Washington intern. *And if Annette can't have fifteen minutes of fame for herself, perhaps a minute or two of reflected glory—or Gloria—would be enough.*

"I suppose if it keeps some other young woman from disappearing or getting killed it's all right with me if you look at the letters—that is, if it's all right with Annette," Willie said. "There's no one else left to shame in this family." She sighed deeply. "Annette and I know the whole sad story about the scandalous affair with Hugh Bentley." Willie stirred herself. "Oh, dear, look at the time!" She stood up and grabbed her purse. "I have to leave for choir practice."

"I'm sorry," Lacey said, and started to rise from her seat.

"You don't have to leave," Annette said. "Really."

Willie made her apologies and left. Annette picked up the tea tray, and Lacey followed her through an arched door into a small kitchen. It was painted bright yellow in an attempt at cheerfulness, but had accumulated years of grime that scrubbing couldn't obliterate. The kitchen was woefully behind the times, although a microwave oven took up most of the space on one countertop and appeared to be well used. The small refrigerator must have been fifty years old. As if reading Lacey's thoughts, Annette said, "It's the original GE."

"They made them to last," Lacey said.

"Good thing. It's not like we could afford a new one." Annette moved a few things aside to set the tray down on a yellow-and-chrome Formica-topped table for two. "I can take care of these things later."

"What do you do, Annette? For work, I mean."

"I work for the phone company in the District. It's boring, but they have a pension plan. I don't pay much attention to those things, but Mother does." She rinsed her hands in the sink and dried them with a faded towel. "I just started there one summer and it turned into a full-time job after I finished my associate degree at NOVA. You know, the community college."

"What's your degree in?"

She shrugged. "I just took a lot of courses where I could read a ton. That's my passion." She pointed to another stack of books wobbling on top of the old GE.

The Tremains' house felt small and stuffy, and Lacey had a sudden urge to get a breath of fresh air. Real air. "Hey, why don't we run over to Kinko's? I can make some copies of the letters and the clippings; then we can grab coffee somewhere. My treat."

Annette looked surprised. "Sure." Lacey wondered if she got out much with people her age. Annette didn't talk like women her own age; she didn't use current jargon or popular phrases. And she was dressed for a quiet afternoon at home with Ozzie and Harriet Nelson. *I'm in a house where time moves very s-l-o-w-l-y. In fact, I think I heard it just screech to a halt. Get me out of here!*

Over coffee and a caramel brownie, Annette revealed that Gloria's disappearance had affected the family in many ways that her mother would never admit. It had taken away their interest in adventure, in expanded horizons, and replaced it with fear.

"I grew up listening to the tale of Auntie Gloria, who had great ambitions, and look what happened to her. She went to New York with dreams of glory and then disappeared one day. It was used to keep my mother in line ever since she was a teenager. And then it was used on me. I'm sorry to say it worked. My mother and grandmother could tell the story in their sleep."

"Sounds like a real drag." Lacey savored the aroma of the coffee and the air of the wider world beyond the Tremains' constricted horizon. Their tea had been decidedly weak.

"I halfway hated Gloria Adams all my life. It's not her fault, but she wrecked everything for the rest of us." Annette picked up the brownie and threw Lacey a guilty look. "I wish I had the courage to run away to New York and do something exciting."

"Did you read the letters?"

She nodded with obvious pleasure. "Sure I did. Gloria was having a big romance with Hugh Bentley, which I found fascinating. I skipped the boring parts about sleeves and hems and some damned clothing regulations. But Mother said Gloria was a liar and made it all up. So I don't really know what was true. And Mother could be right. I mean, have you seen the pictures of Hugh Bentley? He looked like George Clooney."

Gloria said he looked like Tyrone Power. "He was very handsome."

"And Gloria . . . well, you've seen the pictures. Even though she looked better after she left here, she just wasn't in his class."

No wonder Gloria left home. "Your family is really big on building self-esteem."

Annette ducked her head, embarrassed. "I know. I know. You're right. Who knows, maybe he saw through her looks, you know? Maybe she really had something after all."

Lacey thought about all the romances that Annette must have read. "Like Mr. Rochester and Jane Eyre?"

"That would be too much to hope for. But I like to think it was possible. She said they were going to get married, but it was a big secret because of Marilyn somebody."

"Married? Sounds like you know the letters pretty well."

"I found them when I was about sixteen. I was in my grandma Gladys's house, looking through the linen closet for a fresh tablecloth or something. They were tucked in an old shoe box with the pictures and the news clippings." Annette leaned toward Lacey in a conspiratorial manner. "I am so boring. I never did anything bad in my life. But when I saw those letters, I had to read them. I didn't dare ask. I just jammed them into my pocket and took them home with me. There really aren't that many, only five. But I felt so guilty and so excited 'cause I'd finally put one over on Granny and my mother."

"Does Willie know you took them?"

"Of course not. It's my one guilty secret and I cherish it. You can't tell; promise me you won't."

"I promise. Did you put them back?"

"Yeah, a couple weeks later. After I'd memorized all the good parts, like 'Hugh kissed me in the closet.' Or, 'We can't tell anyone yet, because Marilyn is temperamental and he's waiting for the right moment.' After Granny Gladys died a couple years later, we got the box and Mother said I could read the letters if I wanted. I acted very blasé. 'Oh, *those* old letters.'"

"What do you think happened to Gloria?"

"I used to tell myself stories about her." Annette explained that she used to imagine that Gloria Adams one day simply decided to change her name and sail away to a new life in Paris or London or Madrid, where she was a spy during the war. "I always hoped she'd come back someday and take me with her. I knew she was nothing like my grandmother, Granny Gladys. Auntie Gloria would be one of those wild aunts who did crazy things, like in *Travels with My Aunt* or *Auntie Mame*."

Or Aunt Mimi, Lacey thought. "Hugh Bentley also took my aunt out a few times."

"Get out of here!"

"Yeah. But after she found out he was engaged she stopped seeing him. And she blamed him for Gloria's disappearance."

"Really?" Annette leaned in close on her elbows. "I mean, my grandma and my mother always said it was probably some 'rough trade' who worked in the factory. Not even a man, just 'rough trade.' Scared me to death when I was little. I thought it was his name. Mr. Rough Trade, or maybe Ralph, Ralph Trade." They shared a laugh. "My family blamed Gloria's fate on her decision to work in a factory, even though it was a garment factory. It wasn't like it was bombs or torpedoes or airplane parts."Annette wiped the crumbs from her hands, then opened the envelope and looked at the photos again. "Your aunt was really pretty."

"She was a lot more than that," Lacey said, fondly looking at the young, indomitable Mimi. "I'll return the photos as soon as I can. I'll get professional copies made at the paper." She sorted out the copies of the letters, giving Annette the originals. She dropped Annette off at the Tremains' home, where time was still stuck in molasses, and decided to swing back into the District. Parking in front of Honey Martin's perfect yellow-and-white house, she climbed the twenty steps to the front door. Ruby opened it.

"I'm not sure I should let you in, Ms. Smithsonian. She's been one cranky old white woman since you visited."

"I'm so sorry about that. Do you think she'll see me?"

"Sure, she will. Follow me. Her bark's worse than her bite. She wears dentures these days."

Ruby led the way into the front sitting room, tastefully appointed in dark wainscoting and a cream-colored sofa and wing chairs. Sitting by the bay window was Honey Martin, today dressed in lemon yellow and working on a needlepoint. She turned to Lacey in surprise. "I don't recall that we had an appointment. Ruby?"

"You tell her yourself if you don't want her here. I'll be in the kitchen." With that, Ruby left the room.

"I do apologize for disturbing you, Mrs. Martin," Lacey said. "But I have another photograph and I wonder if you could identify a woman in it. It seems to be from the same day as the picnic."

With a deep sigh, Honey held out her hand and received the photograph. "Your visit brought back a lot of memories. Memories I'm not so proud of. I suppose I judged Gloria too harshly. And I lost a dear friendship over it. Things have changed so much. Now, let me look at this." Honey peered at the photo through her glasses, then turned it over. "Dotty? No, Dorrie, I think. Dorrie Rogers, I believe it was. I didn't remember that she was there. She was such a quiet little thing."

"Who was she?"

"Someone Gloria knew in New York. Yes, she was her roommate."

"Do you remember anything about her?"

"Not really, I never got the impression they were friends. Mimi felt sorry for Dorrie, and that must be why she invited her along on a picnic over Easter. Mimi was always doing things like that. Things that made you feel that you weren't quite as good or as charitable as she was. It could be a little irritating, I'll tell you. But we all went along with her so she wouldn't think we were as mean or petty as we really were." Honey set the photo down on a round cherry tilt-top table with scalloped edges.

"Do you know what happened to Dorrie Rogers? And her full name? What was Dorrie short for?"

"Child, I don't know what happened to Gloria, or what happened with my friendship with Mimi. How on earth can you suppose I know what happened to that little woman? I have no earthly idea." Honey gestured, then let her hands fall in her lap.

Lacey supposed she had just made the top of Honey Martin's list of exasperating people. However, she couldn't resist one more question. "But she was a factory girl?"

"Oh, yes, they both worked at Bentley's. Beyond that, I don't know. I'm sorry; I really don't know." Honey picked up her needlework and focused her attention.

"I'll just show myself out," Lacey said. She retrieved the picture from the table and exited quietly, waving to Ruby in the kitchen door.

That evening she settled down on her sofa. She hadn't exactly run a marathon, but she felt like it. She opened her new folder of the Tremain letters, which also had Gloria's telltale sketches.

Dear Glad—   *March 10, 1943*
    Everything I've ever wanted is about to come true.
I'm going to marry the man I love and we're going to
be a design team. Of course, there is one big complica-
tion. Her name is Marilyn. But things will work out.
You'll see. . . .

Chapter 15

At six o'clock Monday morning, Lacey had cause to regret her decision the night before to plug the phone back in and return it to the bedroom. It started ringing, crashing insistently into her dreams no matter how hard she tried to ignore it. She reached for the receiver. She didn't even get a word out.

"Lacey, you've got to come down to Stylettos right away. I've got a brilliant idea."

"Stella, it's too early for brilliant ideas."

"Trust me."

Lacey snuggled down in her comforter. She had no desire to get up. She yawned. "I'm listening. Dazzle me."

"We have to create your look for the fashion gala. And not just one look, but, like, a whole gallery of looks, you know? Different Forties styles and makeup, to see what goes with the dress. Miguel and I tried calling you all day yesterday, but your machine didn't pick up."

"I gave it the day off. And it's too early."

"Wake up! If we don't do it this morning, we'll be a whole day behind on the game plan. Meet me at eight o'clock. Come with clean, dry hair, but don't style it. And dress the part so we can see if it goes." Lacey groaned. There was always an implied threat that when she didn't please Stella, retribution would rain down on her hair. Besides, it now seemed that she wasn't going to the gala for herself, but as the point woman for a whole team. *I wouldn't want to let the team down.*

At eight o'clock, fortified with a large Starbucks latte, Lacy arrived at Stylettos. Stella unlocked the door. The salon didn't officially open until ten. "What? You didn't get me a coffee?"

Lacey glared at her. "I don't remember that order, milady."

"Never mind, I have a Coke." Stella handed Lacey the early edition of *The Eye*. "Body Found in Swamp May Be Missing Intern." The stylist's dragon-lady nail pointed to the double by-line. "I knew it; you were there. She was wearing a jade-green suit. 'Body showed signs of violence.' What was it like? I want all the details."

"It was heartbreaking."

"You poor thing. Don't worry about a thing; I'll take care of you," Stella said. Lacey wore a vintage navy wool crepe suit with pearl buttons. The sleeves ended in buttoned cuffs. She also wore Mimi's three-strand pearl necklace. She sat in the chair and Stella went to work. "Nothing too extreme," Lacey warned her. "And if I fall asleep, I'd better recognize myself when I wake up."

"But the blue mohawk will match your suit." Armed with a comb, hairpins, and a curling iron, Stella proceeded to transform Lacey. By nine o'clock she stared back at herself in a time warp from 1943, wearing an upswept twist spilling over with saucy pin curls on top, rather like Gloria's finger curls. *I'm so sophisticated you won't know me.* Gloria's words echoed again in her head. Lacey marveled at her heavily mascaraed eyes, seductively arched brows, and bright red lips. Stella brushed a little more blush on Lacy's cheeks. "Voilà! What did I tell you? Forties, right? Fabulous, right?" Stella whipped out a Polaroid camera and took a picture.

"Whoa! What's that for?"

"For the judges, of course. Me and Miguel. This is Look Number One. We're going to vote. So I want you back here tomorrow. Same time, same place, same station."

Lacey groaned.

When she got to the office, people noticed. Trujillo was, of course, the first to comment. "Hey, it's *His Girl Friday.*"

"And it's only Monday, you lucky fella."

Trujillo just grinned. "Did you see the story? We nailed it, Lacey! You can be my nature guide anytime."

Mac wandered over to her desk, looking at her quizzically. "Good job on that Fairchild story. Tragic as hell, but a nice job. What the hell are you all dressed up for? The Pulitzer Prize?"

She ignored this question. "They haven't officially verified it's her yet, have they?"

"No, but they will. She was wearing a suit she borrowed from one of her roommates; they ID'd it. But you're late, Smithsonian. Explanation?"

Explanation? Yes, I have one of those. "I was researching some styles for the Bentley Museum gala, Mac. 'Sixty Years of American Fashion.' You remember."

"Impress me." He looked like he might believe her.

"Well, the gala will feature a lot of women in vintage looks. Like this. So I'm going to try one out every day to, um"—*Think fast, Lacey*—"to see what it takes to get the right look, what kind of preparation women went through. It's just an idea for a column."

Mac's eyebrows were dubious. One went up; one went down. "What do you think, Trujillo?"

"I think she looks hot." He winked at Lacey. "In an old-movie kind of way. I can't wait to see who she is tomorrow."

"Different every day, huh?" Mac was thinking. His eyebrows were doing the rhumba across his forehead. Lacey didn't know what it was he was thinking, but she had a pretty good idea she wouldn't like it. "I have an idea, Smithsonian. A fashion idea."

Mac with a fashion idea? She and Tony were both struck dumb at the thought. Mac picked up the phone. "Hansen? Mac Jones here. Come on up to the newsroom and bring some cameras. I'm gonna need—"

Disaster loomed. "Hold on, Mac," Lacey said. *Am I so photogenic all of a sudden? First Stella, now Mac.* She had a sinking feeling.

"—a photo spread. A fashion thing. Yeah, of course it's for Smithsonian. She's gonna model five different hairdos for the fashion gala thing. We'll run it on Sunday as a prelude to that museum thing. How big a spread? Oh, big, really big."

"Oh, no, not me, Mac. We should get a professional model; this is just an experiment—"

"It's not like you're hard news, Lacey. You're on the fashion beat. Hell, you *are* the fashion beat. You already got the silly hairdo. What's a few snaps? I gotta go talk to Hansen."

"Wait a minute, buster! It's not silly!" But he was out of earshot. Mac was getting the wrong idea about her. At this rate she'd never get away from the fashion beat.

Her phone rang. Miguel reported from New York that he had found the right fabric and he narrowed it down to two color choices. He had her twist of silk with him, and he would try for an exact match. Did she trust him to select it? She did. Did she want bugle beads, faux pearls, or both? Gloria's design stipulated both. Lacey went out on a limb. Both.

"Good choice, and I take it that cost is no object?" Miguel said cheerily.

"Wait a minute, Miguel—"

"'Bye." He hung up.

She felt like she'd been rolled over by a truck, and the rest of the convoy was due to arrive any minute. She decided to stop trying to solve the mystery of what she'd gotten herself into and concentrate on the mystery at hand. She wanted to find Dorrie Rogers, Gloria's roommate, who worked for Bentley during the war. Bentley had had a union contract—it was part of his deal in supplying military clothing—so Lacey put in a call to UNITE, the garment workers' union. After being transferred to a number of different people she eventually found a courteous woman in the press office who said it would be a long shot.

"The only way we could find her is through a pension, if she got one, if she's still alive," the woman said in distinctive New York tones. "What if she quit, got married, and changed her name?"

After depressing Lacey with the seeming futility of her quest, she said she would put in a call to the pension people. But if they found her, they would have to contact Miss Rogers first to see if she wanted to talk with Lacey. "Who did you say you were?"

"A reporter with a Washington newspaper."

"And this is about?"

"She might have witnessed management abuses that may have taken place in that factory." Lacey thought the union would like the sound of that. It was too early to go hollering *murder.*

"I'll try," the woman promised, but not before pointing out that another problem was that no one knew what name Dorrie was a diminutive for. Dorothy seemed the best bet, but she might have been Doreen or Dora or Eudora or something completely unexpected. Worse, it might be her middle name; the pension rolls might list dozens of Mary D. Rogerses and Martha E. Rogerses—and which one was she? "And in the end she might be already dead." Lacey had a headache, and it wasn't even ten A.M. yet.

Lacey also made another call to Chevalier and gave him a message for Hugh, saying that she planned to write about both Esme and Gloria, two young women who aimed for the stars but fell to earth too soon. History repeating itself, with the House of Bentley playing a key role in both tragedies. His comments would be welcome. *But unlikely,* Lacey added silently.

Chevalier suggested politely that she give it a rest. "It doesn't do anyone any good to keep dragging this up." He would pass her message along, though, and to her surprise, Hugh called back shortly.

"Is this necessary, Lacey? It's old news. I thought you had more class than that."

You hoped I'd roll over. "I'm a reporter. I have a job to do. I'm just letting you know as a courtesy."

"Don't you have something else to write about?"

"I choose my own stories, and this one is running whether you like it or not." Hugh was silent for too long. She wasn't going to speak first, so she said good-bye, hung up, and sighed.

"Another happy customer, Smithsonian?" Mac reappeared, ready for the photo session.

"Hugh Bentley. There's a tiny chance that a story I'm writing is not going to please him."

"And this is different from your other stories how?"

"He might try to bar me from the fashion gala. Even with a ticket." Disappointment washed over her. The dress, the preparations, the cost all seemed overwhelming. And now this special humiliation with the photos. She liked the look, but Mac's photo spread idea was an open invitation to mockery. *I much prefer to be the mocker, not the mockee.*

"Ha. Let him try. And you're not getting out of the photo shoot." He laughed diabolically. " 'Retro Makeover Turns Tables on *Eye Street Observer* Fashion Maven.' Or something like that."

"You'd better not make me look like an idiot. I'm not kidding about this, Mac."

She gazed down the hall. Long, lanky Hansen was striding into view with a couple of Nikons hanging around his neck and a bag of film. His scruffy blond hair was in need of a cut. He was wearing his usual blue jeans and oxford-cloth shirt, and some sort of grubby athletic shoes. Lacey ran to the ladies' room to check her makeup. The red lips startled her, but it went with the hair and the suit. She returned to her desk, where a small crowd had gathered. Trujillo materialized again to watch, and there was Mac, always a fashion heart attack.

Not surprisingly Felicity was also on duty, watching everything. Today Felicity wore some sort of hippie dress that could have been left over from 1967, or brand-new from some catalog. The yards of tie-dyed purple gauze trimmed in purple ribbon had a sort of wistful Ophelia feel to it and would have nicely suited a lovelorn hippie teenager in the Summer of Love. Seeing Felicity wearing a suit and pumps the day before had given Lacey hope that the food editor was climbing the food chain up and out of *The Eye Street Observer*—and out of Lacey's life. This dress said she was going nowhere. It depressed Lacey. *Probably Felicity too.*

"She says she's going to look different every day," Mac told

Hansen, and raised the old bushy mood indicators over his eyes, daring Lacey to defy him. He was way too amused.

"He doesn't believe me, does he?" Lacey asked Trujillo. *I'll really have to do it now.*

"I think he's beginning to see your point."

"Hansen, could you shoot from my left side, please?" Lacey asked.

Todd Hansen was a news photographer. He didn't care about his subjects' good sides and bad sides. He liked to catch people looking silly. He looked through the viewfinder. "Whatever." He switched sides.

"Bounce that flash so there aren't any gross shadows. And get up off your knees, buddy, because if you take one frame of me from that angle I guarantee you will never get up again. And Mac, don't get any ideas; you are not going to put a photo with my column." They had been wrangling over this idea for months. Hansen snapped off a few shots while she was talking. "I mean it, Hansen. If even one picture bears any resemblance to my congressional press pass, you will suffer."

"Relax, Lois Lane; you look very cool. Clark Kent, Jimmy Olsen, and the rest of the gang are all here to support you in your hour of need," Trujillo said. "Superman will be here soon to fly you around the *Daily Planet.*"

"Smart-ass." She relaxed and Hansen got his photos. She wished the photographer good luck and told him that if she didn't get to see the proofs, the whole proofs, and all the proofs, and approve the final choice, she would hunt him down and make him eat his Nikons. Hansen laughed and ambled off to his darkroom.

"Lacey." Mac settled against her desk. "Now tell me about the story that's going to piss off Hugh Bentley."

"Maybe I should just write it first; then you can judge." Sometimes she had to write out a story and let it make its own point, rather than share an idea that he could squash in an instant.

"The judge is waiting."

"Esme Fairchild isn't the first woman involved with the Bentleys who has gone missing."

"What? Damn it all to hell. When did you find this out?" He stood up straight, all of his six-foot, broad-shouldered presence on full editorial alert.

"Don't get too excited. It happened sixty years ago. Hugh was involved with this woman before Aaron was even born. It's just one of those weird-coincidence stories that catch the imagination, with a fashion angle. But her family never got over it. It still haunts them." *Well, one of them.*

"Hmmm." Mac was thinking, but he looked doubtful. His eyebrows were static; they didn't know which way to jump.

"Think about all the women who disappear from Washington, Mac. What happens to them? Lots of high-profile cases that just trail off. The last one was never solved, although there are plenty of theories. And that woman who was found in the Potomac a couple of years ago? Not even a suspect."

"You're thinking we could do something like Washington's top ten unsolved mysteries?"

It was a good idea. "We might even have to go back a month or two to capture that many," she said.

"That sounded suspiciously like sarcasm, Smithsonian. The District is not that bad."

"Right. We almost took back the murder capital title this year, and now the chief of police has declared a state of crime emergency. How is it not that bad? But that would be a big research piece. I'm tapped out, and this Bentley story will take all day."

Mac gazed around the newsroom looking for an easy mark. He settled on Trujillo and quickly moved off toward him. *Ha. Payback time!* she thought. Before she could get started on her story, however, her phone rang.

"You're the one who wrote the Esme Fairchild story?" The male voice sounded vaguely familiar.

"Who is this?"

"An affair with a U.S. senator isn't enough of a motive to kill somebody these days. You'd have to kill half the women on the Hill. And a few of the men."

"I take it you have a better reason? And a name?" Lacey automatically started typing up what he was telling her.

"For motive try forty million dollars that mysteriously landed in that appropriations bill."

"I'm listening."

"It's a madhouse during appropriations. Put that together with any number of people with access to computers where the bills are put together. A clever young intern or staffer could have inserted doctored numbers in the final bill, which was passed without debate, because they'd already talked all the line items to death." Lacey recalled that despite Senator Dashwood's assertions that they would find the person behind the additional funding, no one had turned up.

"So all you're telling me is that pork is everywhere. Pork winds up in just about every appropriation bill. Why is this a motive for murder?"

"Women disappear here. It's almost routine. Everybody blames it on sex—it's a boyfriend, a psycho, a serial killer. What's everybody looking for? A body out in the woods or in the river. What's everybody *not* looking for? Numbers in a column in a computer file. There are people on the Hill who'd much rather have a bunch of dopey homicide cops poking around than a bunch of smart accountants with a special prosecutor, adding up columns of numbers that don't match up."

"And a dead woman is a pretty easy place to lay the blame for some sort of financial trickery," Lacey said. "So the same clever person could easily leave a phony trail leading to Esme."

"Maybe. Sounds like the kind of questions a reporter might ask. If a reporter were asking questions at all."

"Here's a question. Who am I talking to?"

"You don't need to know, and you can't trace this call," he said.

Big deal, she thought. *Like I could trace a call if I wanted to. The Eye* didn't even have caller ID, anyway. The paper was too cheap to give such a luxury to mere reporters.

"So why would Esme Fairchild mess with that?"

"To please the fashion fat cats who could make it all happen for her."

"Like Aaron Bentley? Then if the fat cats are happy, why kill her?"

"Dead interns tattle no tales. Try following a road map, if somebody hands it to you." He was mocking her. *Some days it feels like the national sport.*

"What do you really want?"

"Maybe I'm a troublemaker. I want to see this story break big. On DeadFed."

"Then call them yourselves. Better yet, e-mail. Tell 'em you're Deep Throat. They'll like that."

"Very funny. It's better if it comes from a legitimate paper first."

"Did you call *The Post*?"

"Give me a break."

At least he called us legit. "I think it's pretty easy to blame a dead girl."

"It is, but you'll be hearing rumors to that effect soon, very soon. Want to be first or last?"

"So, the question is, who is going to scapegoat Esme Fairchild?"

"It's a start."

"Why don't you just tell me that?"

"Maybe I don't know. Maybe she did it. I'm just passing on information. *Ciao,* Ms. Smithsonian. Use it in good health."

Her caller hung up. Lacey didn't know what to make of this. It could be partly true and partly the fevered imagination of some paranoid wonk, like many Washington rumors. There are people who love to float rumors in the media, just to see how they play, to see who bites, who sticks her neck out. *Throw us a bone and we all go galumphing after it.* But if this rumor was going to see daylight in the other media, she'd feel like a fool to have missed it. The easiest thing in the world was to blame the victim. Her challenge was how to write it without condemning Esme, who couldn't defend herself.

When she contacted the staff spokesman for the Appropriations Subcommittee to check on the status of the so-far-informal inquiry into the forty-million-dollar mistake, he admitted that Esme Fairchild would have been a target for questioning, but so were two dozen other committee staffers and interns, not to mention the senators and their own staffers and interns. A call to Marcia Robinson revealed nothing new. Or as Marcia said, "Of course Esme could have figured out how to do that. I mean, duh. She crunched all the numbers for my Web site. But I totally don't think she did it. I mean, she told me everything. Or at least she told me a lot. She told me all the really important stuff, like who she was sleeping with."

A call to Tyler Stone told her that no one wanted to comment, but she persisted. "Did Esme have anything to do with inputting those figures into the appropriations bill?"

"It appears she was too busy sleeping around to do that," Tyler responded before hanging up.

By the time she got off the phone, the police had confirmed that the remains found in Huntley Meadows were those of Esme Fairchild. The dental records matched. Lacey finally wrote what she could, noting that rumors were expected to fly about Esme's possible involvement in tampering with figures in an appropriations bill. It was bound to cause trouble.

The vultures are gathering around the bones of a woman who no longer can defend herself . . . she wrote.

Lacey sent what she had along to Trujillo. Thus freed from the burden of the ugly Washington rumor of the day, she felt free to return to her story on Gloria Adams and Esme Fairchild. There were similarities: Both were ambitious, both wanted a career in fashion, both slept with the boss. But Gloria's story was unfinished, and Esme's was finished all too soon. Where did they converge? She was getting nowhere fast when Brooke called.

"Hey, we didn't get a chance to talk. So why don't I pick you up? You didn't drive, did you?"

"No, the Z's in the shop again. Oil change and inspection sticker."

"Great, I'll pick you up. How's sevenish?"

*　　*　　*

The loading zone in front of *The Eye* held Brooke's slate-gray Acura. Lacey opened the door and sank gratefully into the deep leather seat and fastened the seat belt. "Thanks for the lift, Brooke. I'm wasted."

"No prob. Whoa, what happened to you? Hair and lips, I mean. Wait, don't tell me. Stella happened. Now what? Don't tell me." Brooke slipped into Q&A mode as she pulled into late-rush-hour traffic on I Street and headed toward Fourteenth and the bridge to Virginia. "Does it have anything to do with past-life regression? Were you Veronica Lake in a previous life?"

"No, this is not Veronica Lake hair. Watch where you're going."

"Okay, what about that strange gypsy psychic woman? The imposing one who dresses in veils?"

"Marie Largesse? No."

Brooke looked confused. "Are you in a play at a theatre I'm not familiar with?"

Lacey checked her image in the mirror on the visor. "You don't like it?"

"I like it! It's just so, you know, *Out of the Past*. Wait, is it so retro-nouveau that I'm not even up to date yet?" Brooke looked so seriously concerned that Lacey laughed.

"Yeah, that's me, Lacey Smithsonian, trendsetter. You'll find out in Sunday's paper. Wait and see."

"No way." Brooke slammed on the brakes like somebody's mother with an intransigent child. "Do you want to walk home?"

"Okay, okay. Stella's trying out vintage looks for me to match the dress I'm wearing to the fashion gala next week. This is Look Number One. You can probably call in your vote, if you want. Just dial 1-800-MAKE-A-FOOL-OUT-OF-LACEY-SMITHSONIAN."

The Acura sped up again. "Well, that explains everything. Was that so hard? So what's new? Anything I should know about the Fairchild case? I've been in court all day; I feel totally out of contact."

"Read tomorrow's paper. It might even interest your little coconspirator."

Brooke pulled her cell phone from her purse. "I'd better call Damon."

"If you use that thing while you're driving, I'm exiting this car. I'm serious; I will not be a party to a cell-phone-related accident." The cell phone wavered in midair. "I mean it, Brooke. Do you know how many people fall to their deaths off communication towers so that selfish people like you can talk on their cell phones in their cars and kill even more people on the highway?"

"Fanatic." The phone went back in the purse. "But if Damon knows there's something coming, he can pick up the paper's first edition and get the story on his Web site before anyone else. Then he can interpret and context it before the story gets spun out of all recognition. And did you know there's sometimes a huge delay before the information gets posted to the Web?"

"Don't stress about it; my information might not even make it into the paper. I have no control over copy editors. And Mac."

"He wouldn't do that."

"You never know." Lacey enjoyed taunting Brooke. "He thinks he runs *The Eye.* Oh, yeah, he does run *The Eye.*"

Brooke maneuvered the Acura deftly onto the can of worms known as the Fourteenth Street Bridge. "Did I tell you that Barton, Barton and Barton is buying a table at the museum gala? You're going, of course."

"No, you didn't. And yes, I am. I think."

"So you're doing a vintage look? Wait a minute, you don't have any vintage evening wear. That I know of. And I would know."

"I will. Sort of. Maybe. At least there's a plan."

"Aha! A pattern from Aunt Mimi's trunk?" Lacey nodded and Brooke continued. "But I can wear something modern, right?"

"The conceit is that everyone is wearing American black tie. Evening wear by American designers. It can be new, but rumor has it that many women are going to wear vintage, all the rage now. Hadn't you heard? So—are you bringing a date?" For once she hoped Brooke would bring someone dull who couldn't care less about Lacey's job.

Brooke tried not to smile too broadly, but failed. "I thought I would."

"You're not bringing Newhouse?"

"We wouldn't miss it. Who are you bringing?"

"I'm working. So what are you going to wear?"

"I don't know. What do you think?"

"Make me happy. Don't wear black, gray, or taupe, or anything Burberry."

"You know that's all I have!" Brooke pouted. "You're telling me I need something new, aren't you?" Brooke pulled up to a trendy restaurant and martini bar just off the waterfront in Old Town Alexandria and managed with unexpected luck to grab a parking space by the door.

"Drinks? Oh, Brooke, I'm really tired."

"Are you kidding? We're not wasting that new—or old, or new-slash-old—look that crazy Stella gave you. That lipstick's got a lot of voltage. Let's try it out."

Settling into a divan with a tall padded back, they ordered martinis and appetizers. But while a couple of men shot subtle looks their way, Lacey knew they would not approach. It was nearly eight o'clock and the men all still wore their suit jackets, their ties tightly knotted, their photo ID cards on little metal chains, courtesy of their various government bureaus, agencies, and departments. And the ones who weren't Feds were probably Alexandria or Virginia employees—they were only a block or two from the Alexandria Town Hall, the Alexandria courthouse, and the Federal District Court. They all looked vaguely the same: pale skin proudly won through endless overtime under fluorescent lighting and pudgy physiques, because nobody but the President had time or made time to work out, unless they were in the military. And to a man they wore tiny glasses: gold wire frames, silver wire frames, black wire frames, and a few brave iconoclasts who held out for tiny horn-rims.

Lacey strongly suspected they would change directly from those crisp blue suits and knotted red ties into their starched and pressed jammies at bedtime, and the ID tags probably didn't come off at all if they worked for the Department of Homeland Security. As Brooke commented to her over their martinis, they looked as if their pheromones were jammed so hard they squeaked. They wouldn't approach. You might as well ask them to paint themselves blue and run naked into the Potomac—unless it was a Code Blue day.

Lacey closed her eyes and pictured a different sort of man. The first man who popped into her head was Jeffrey Bentley Holmes, so handsome and perfectly groomed. No ID tags for him. Yet he was troubled—but who wouldn't be in "the dark heart of the Bentleys"? Then she was seized with the picture of a hard-bodied man who liked blue jeans and black leather jackets and muddy Jeeps. A man with sea-green eyes who preferred action to bureaucracy. A man who seemed to prefer Colorado—or was it Montana?—to Alexandria, Virginia. And her.

"Lacey, it's Vic. Sorry I missed you." She played the message again to hear his deep, melodious voice. That was all that was waiting for her when she arrived home with her eye makeup smudged and her lipstick faded. There were no clues or cues or nuances for her to seize on. She reflected that Vic must believe wholeheartedly in leaving no incriminating personal information, like where he was or where he'd been or when he was coming home, and certainly no emotional information, like how he felt about her or his ex, or whether he called to say good-bye forever, or to save Saturday night because he'd be coming home with bells on. *Anonymous informants call me and they just can't shut up, but Vic? Seven words.*

"Damn you, Vic Donovan. What's up with you?" She said it aloud in her empty living room. She didn't even have a picture of him, but she remembered every line in his face, his eyes, his buttery low voice. The question of why he called drove her nuts. *As Stella would say, I need a man bad. One in particular.*

She washed away the last of Stella's Look Number One and went straight to bed, knowing that the martini Brooke had insisted on would make six A.M.— and Stella's Look Number Two—arrive far too soon.

FASHION BITES

Thank Heaven It's Not Code Taupe. Or Is It?

What are you going to do when the Homeland Security alert is Code Orange, the air quality is Code Purple, the Beltway has you seeing red, and you're feeling blue?

Whatever you do, for heaven's sake, don't color coordinate. Whacked-out fashionistas will be running around the District looking like deranged crayons. Holy Code Crayola!

Theoretically, the government alert system is simplicity itself, featuring the primary and secondary colors every first-grader learns: red, orange, yellow, blue, green. So simple, so easy to understand. But ask yourself: Is it, perhaps, too simple? Are these the same people who live to tangle you up in red tape, the people who wrote the grim, gray federal regulations, the people who gave us the *tax code*?

Why would Washington bureaucrats pick a system that is so bold, so colorful? To judge by most Feds' clothing, they've never heard of the rainbow. The fact is, color frightens most bureaucrats. Wouldn't they be more likely to create a code that they could understand—a comfortable, neutral color code designed to baffle outsiders? Could it be the publicized code is not the *real* code at all? Yes, the government would have a *secret* color code. A code based on taupes, beiges, and oatmeals; the colors of a bureaucrat's soul.

We might be told the country is on Code Orange, but the top dogs in Homeland Security might actually be working in Code Gray, Code Umber, Code Puce. Or heaven forbid, Code Mushroom (the cloud, not the soup).

No doubt they silently signal each other via their ties and lapel pins, or the background colors of their shabby photo ID cards. Keep your eyes open for the little signature notes. For the Washington man, keep an eye on the tie. As ugly as it may be, this is where the most information resides in their garb. For all we civilians know, the knot could be a subtle signal. Does a Windsor mean we tied the knot with Great Britain? A four-in-hand an impending alliance with the European Union? A bow tie that we're secretly in bed with the French? What about the patterns? Regimental stripes: Code Souza. March in formation until further notice. Tiny geometric foulard patterns: Code Microbe. Anthrax spores! Stop breathing now! Psychedelic paisley: Code Groovy. All civilians are advised to party down and skip naked through the Reflecting Pool.

With the Washington woman, look to the accessories. If she's already on the run with her grubby but functional jogging shoes, it could be Code Dusty Tan. Run away immediately! Sporting a green and brown backpack instead of an attache: Code Camouflage. Evacuate and take shelter in Rock Creek Park. And if you see women streaming out of congressional office buildings wearing "escape hoods" accessorized with their Burberry scarves, you can be sure that the alert status is now Code Mustard (the gas, not the spice).

Haven't heard of escape hoods? Snazzy over-the-head garments featuring a clear window over the face. They're not pretty, but they give the wearer enough air to evacuate the building in the event of a biological incident, and Congress has a boatload of them. Where's yours?

Meanwhile the rest of us are bungling around somewhere in Code Yellow, blissfully ignorant of the threats revealed by the super-secret codes that lurk around us. My advice: Hold on to your optimism, wear what you please in colors you like, whether azure or emerald, and to counter the blues, although I don't recommend it for courtroom attire: Think Pink.

chapter 16

Lacey's little black dress from 1942 seemed demure, but it had a saucy scarlet kick pleat and matching piping and buttons, which of course matched her bright red 1942 lips. She tucked a red hankie in the pocket and secured it with her jeweled cardinal pin, one of her favorites. Tuesday morning's approximation of a Forties style, courtesy of Stella, parted her hair in the middle with the sides rolled up and caught in a clip in the back; the rest of it curled into a pageboy. Lacey successfully fought the planned addition of a bow. "I'm not going anywhere as June Allyson," she told Stella, who was wearing black kohl ringed around her eyes for that dramatic I've-been-up-all-night-doing-God-knows-what look. In Stella's case, it might not be just a look.

"Fine. But it would complete the look and it would be more authentic. And what have you got against June Allyson? I've got a great photo of this look right here, *LIFE* magazine, 1949."

"It's way too *Little Women*. And I am no ingenue. I am a woman, a dangerous woman."

"You need a man, Lacey. You blew off the last one, Mr. Curly Lashes Vic Donovan. And he was so cute. Have I mentioned that before? Have you heard from him?"

Lacey bit her scarlet lips.

Lacey's voice mail was flashing furiously when she finally made it into the newsroom. Hansen was waiting for her, sitting at her desk, sipping a cup of black coffee and perusing the

LifeStyle section of *The Eye Street Observer.* He was on the in-side jump of Lacey's Gloria and Esme story, "Separated by Sixty Years, the Same Old Story: Ambitious, Young, and Gone." The Tremains' photos of Gloria joined with the Esme photos peered out at the reading world. Hansen glanced up at Lacey, taking in her vintage Look Number Two.

"So, are you, like, channeling her? This Gloria Adams of yours?"

"That's a pretty gruesome thought. But I'd like to channel some black coffee."

"You think she bought the farm? I mean the Adams chick; we know about Esme."

"Yeah, I think she did. And she wasn't a farm girl."

Hansen set the paper back down, open to Trujillo's compan-ion piece, "Ten Who Never Came Home." It featured *The Eye*'s list of the top ten unsolved murders of young women who had disappeared in Washington. Their photos showed they were as diverse a lot as Washington was becoming: black, white, Asian, Hispanic. They were last seen at a bar, at a bus stop, going out to jog, picking up the mail, leaving the office, meeting a friend. Some of their bodies had been found—in the Potomac, in Rock Creek Park, in an abandoned building in Southeast D.C.; some had never been found and their murdered status was only pre-sumed. But they had a sad sameness: young, attractive, ambi-tious, female, missing.

"Reading this stuff you'd think the District of Columbia is not a safe place to live," Hansen said.

"No kidding. Remember when Mayor Marion Barry said that 'except for the killings' D.C. had a really low crime rate? And we haven't even mentioned the ones who weren't quite so young or pretty or well-off. I guess the pretty ones make better copy."

"Feeling upbeat this morning?"

"I'm fine." Stella had scolded her for arriving at the salon with puffy eyes and made her sit with wet tea bags on her eye-lids for twenty minutes. Lacey looked refreshed, but she didn't feel it. "I only had one martini."

"Must have been a double. Look alive, Lacey, Mac is interested in this little project for some reason." Hansen readied his Nikons.

"The humiliation aspect, no doubt." She made a face at him.

"You'll have to do better than that."

She tried a sultry look, but she felt her eyes go wide when Felicity walked over to her desk. Felicity's long auburn hair was parted on the side in a wild profusion of pin curls, an exaggerated approximation of a Forties hairstyle. *Is she mocking me? Along with the rest of the world?* But she found no conscious irony in what Felicity wore: another one of her flowered prairie dresses that tied in the back.

"Hey, wide-eyed innocence. I like that," Hansen said. "Give me more angles like that." He took some photos. He even got busy moving Lacey's flowers around the desk for a more interesting background. The second photo session was much less painful, she decided. As soon as he left her in peace for a moment to reload and change lenses, Lacey picked up the phone and punched in the number for her voice mail and listened.

"Lacey, I knew there was some kind of conspiracy with that appropriations bill! You could have told me about this last night." It was Brooke, of course. The call was logged at five twenty-five A.M. "Boy, can you keep a secret! I should have made you drink that second martini. Wait till you see DeadFed. But I don't know what to make of the Bentley connection. Call me."

Lacey logged on to her computer while listening to a call from Damon Newhouse expressing his faith in her and hoping for more developments. DeadFed had picked up the story, "Dead Intern Linked to Approps Bill Scandal."

In the meantime, Peter Johnson cruised past her desk, crumpled the front page, threw it at her, and walked on by without saying a word. She opened it up and was amazed to see she shared a byline with Trujillo and the insufferable Johnson. Mac had decided to mix in the rumors about Esme's possible involvement with the mystery money and Tony's reporting on the discovery of her body and asked Peter to include the Hill angle.

Lacey recrumpled it and threw it at Johnson's head. Peter was steamed. He turned on his heel. "I told you to stay off my beat."

"I'm not on your beat. And I'm not exactly thrilled to have my name associated with you either." Hansen had reloaded his camera and was happily snapping pictures of their angry exchange. At the sound, they turned toward him with their mouths open. He shot another frame.

Mac showed up just in time for the tail end of the photo shoot. "Children, children, we're all supposed to get along. Now play nice." Johnson huffed away. Hansen was still shooting. He was trying to sneak in a forbidden photograph of her right profile.

"Hansen, either shoot me straight on or from the left side or you'll be changing lenses with a broken arm."

"What is your problem, Lacey? You look good from any angle."

"Men!" *The next thing, he'll be crawling on the floor for an up-the-nostrils shot.*

"It's not exactly *Glamour* or *Vogue*, you know."

"Believe me, I know. Sorry. I hope I don't look as grumpy as I feel."

Mac stepped in. "Thanks, Hansen. I think we've got enough. This might be a fun feature, kids, if nobody kills each other before it comes out and we have to use it for an obit." He gave her a meaningful look, a lift of his expressive brows, and moved on to other editorial duties.

The only cure for the aftereffects of Lacey's martini was spicy Mexican food, so she called Miguel, who was back from New York, and proposed an early lunch. The restaurant was Salvadoran-Mexican and one of his favorites, "Though I don't normally eat it for breakfast." He sat across from her. The décor was unprepossessing, but the food was delicious.

"It's lunch. It's eleven-thirty, " she protested, and ordered a platter of cheese enchiladas.

"Like I said, breakfast." He ordered tortillas, butter, and strong coffee. "I'm not usually up before the crack of noon. I love today's look, by the way, you ingenue you. And your look deserves a little peek at something special."

He pulled a wrapped package from a sleek black Bentley's bag and set it down. It was covered in white paper, wrapped in string. Lacey waited expectantly. Miguel untied the string slowly, pulled back the white paper and then several layers of pink tissue paper to reveal his prize—the beaded midriff for the Gloria Adams gown. Lacey was clearly expected to gasp with pleasure, and she did. He held it up for her, the heavenly blue shade of silk embroidered with shooting stars, a pattern that would also be beaded on shoulder inserts.

Gloria Adams had stipulated the beading and had sketched several patterns to pick from. Miguel chose the shooting stars because Gloria, he said, was "a falling star."

"It's perfect." Lacey reached out for it, but Miguel held it away from her.

"Don't touch it; you have greasy fingers."

"You're awfully persnickety."

"I have not yet begun to persnicket. This is a work of art— a tribute to a poor dead woman who was robbed of her life's work."

"Allegedly."

"Allegedly, smegedly. You know it's true."

"But how do we know it's true?"

"I worked for Bentley's for five years. I know Bentley. This dress has all the classic marks of his early lines. And it has something more—genius. That unknowable quality that seemed to disappear from his later work. Now we know why. Gloria Adams was the original. Hugh Bentley was the copy. There, I said it." He also pulled Lacey's story from his coat pocket and he gazed at Gloria's photo and sighed deeply. "Nice work, Lacey. She could have been a star. But instead we'll use you. I'd love to see Hugh Bentley's face when he sees you wearing the Adams dress. That's what you've been thinking all along, isn't it?"

"Maybe that's what he's afraid of—that I'll pull a rabbit out of a hat."

"Or a skeleton from a closet?"

"The Bentleys are very careful with their skeletons, if not their reputations."

"Too bad." Miguel folded the material carefully and sealed it in a plastic bag. "I've been trying to reconstruct it all, the fateful moments that led to my untimely demise as a loyal Bentley's employee. Why Bentley's? Why Monday? The bandits concentrated on old-stock, pricey items that weren't selling, items that were heavily insured. It doesn't make sense."

"You think the robbery was a setup? But why? The Bentleys were in town testifying before Congress. It's a huge embarrassment."

Miguel thought about it. "Miscalculation?"

Lacey tried to concentrate on her enchiladas. There was something about hot, spicy enchiladas covered in melting cheese that was curing her martini-induced headache. "Okay, the Bentleys planned their own robbery? For the insurance?"

He shrugged. "A mere question, but a good one." He savored his coffee and warm tortillas and butter before he suddenly slammed down his mug. "Oh, my God, I just remembered something. We have to get to Bentley's."

"But you've been banned."

"Oh, please. Do you think I'm afraid of big, bad Aaron Bentley? He's not there. Believe me, I am informed of his every move by my former compatriots in the slave shop. Let's go."

"I'm eating."

He paid no attention, instead flagging the cute waiter. "*Hola, hombre*, could you wrap that up for her?" Miguel whipped out his handy cell phone and pressed one button. "Hey, doll, it's Miguel; you haven't messed with the storage drawer, have you?" He seemed satisfied with the answer and nodded to Lacey. "I'm coming right over. Touch nothing."

The efficient waiter grabbed Lacey's platter in mid bite. She had just been beginning to feel better when she saw her plate of enchiladas sail away.

"You can eat it later. Besides, you shouldn't be eating anything before the gala. Not a bite. Have you been doing those ab exercises?"

"I'm starving. What is so important that we have to leave?"

"A scoop. A scoop for my favorite fashion reporter." He refused to tell her what the fuss was about on the way over to Bentley's Boutique in his blue VW Beetle convertible. His D.C. vanity plate read FLORES. He didn't believe in anonymity. Miguel knew so many shortcuts through the city, and he drove so fast that she was queasy by the time they arrived. She was glad her enchiladas were in a Styrofoam box, rather than in her stomach.

At the front door, a woman dressed in a sleek black Bentley's pantsuit threw herself at the handsome Latino. "Miguel, darling, we've missed you. Come in; the coast is clear."

"Hug, hug, kiss kiss. Naomi, where's Kika?"

"Still on leave. I don't know that she'll be back; she was pretty freaked out."

Lacey felt a little odd walking through the door for the first time. She could just imagine what Aunt Mimi would say. *In the lion's den now?* Bentley's Boutique was a bright, open space with sparkling crystal fixtures and mirrors everywhere. This was the temple of couture where Hugh had invited her to select any two gowns in exchange for Aunt Mimi's suit. Her eyes roamed hungrily over the racks of beautiful suits and dresses. The clothes were striking, they were fabulously made, but they were not enough to make her change her mind.

"Naomi, this is the notorious Lacey Smithsonian. 'Crimes of Fashion,' you know."

The woman was dark and exotic-looking, with an extremely short haircut glued down sleekly to her shapely head. "Of course. I loved your story on El Florito here." Naomi smiled warmly, although she had that natural unconscious haughtiness that the Bentley's staff was known for.

"No one's touched the drawer?" Miguel demanded.

"Are you kidding? Inventory is months away."

Lacey was tiring of this little game. "What's with the drawer?"

He put his arm around her shoulder and steered her toward a small storage room in the back of the store. "It's our deep, dark secret compartment, where things get tossed that we have no idea what to do with, including the occasional item that people ask us to hold for longer than the prescribed two days. It's a total mess, but the important part is it generally is cleaned out only before inventory."

"If then," Naomi said. "What are you up to, Miguel?"

Miguel looked over her shoulder. "You have a customer, dear." He turned Naomi around and gave her a gentle shove toward her customer service duties, then turned to Lacey with a smug look on his face. "Follow me."

He led her through an arch. On the right were dressing rooms. On the left was the storage room, which was stocked with shelves and rolling racks of clothing hung in plastic bags. Shoes and accessories occupied another aisle, at the end of which was a huge old dresser from a previous generation of store décor. Now scarred with years of use, it served as a makeshift desk. On the top were stock tickets and hold tags, pencils and pens. Taped to the mirror were various official announcements. ALL SALES ASSOCIATES MUST SIGN OUT FOR LUNCH, THEN SIGN BACK IN. BREAKS ARE TWENTY MINUTES LONG, NOT THIRTY! ACCESSORIZE!

Miguel opened the bottom drawer, moved socks, boxes, and wrapped items, and finally pulled out a long, thin, shiny black box with *Bentley's* written across the top in gold script, with a hold tag taped to it. He stood up and presented it to Lacey.

"Behold Exhibit A: *Hold for Esme Fairchild. Will be in at ten Monday morning, September eighth.* There's a phone number with it."

"The eighth?" Lacey said. That had been the day before the hearing. The day of the robbery, the day Esme disappeared. "She was picking this up on the eighth?"

"She was supposed to be here right when it happened. Voilà! I give you the scoop."

Did Esme somehow get caught up in the robbery? Or did

she never make it here? Either way it was a scoop. "What can I say?"

"Say, 'thank you, Fairy Godmother.'"

"Thank you, Miguel." She hugged him. He lifted the lid to reveal the thinnest silk in a pattern of swirls in blues and greens and black. It came with a price tag of two hundred and fifty dollars. It would be beautiful with a jade-green Bentley suit. He interrupted her thoughts.

"I don't know why I forgot about this, except that I had my own insignificant troubles. Robbed. Beaten. Unemployed. Underappreciated."

"It's okay; your head was being kicked in. I'm not surprised a few little details got kicked out of it." Lacey noticed that most of the bruising had faded; there were just a couple of sickly yellow patches left. Was he wearing cover-up? "But did you see her that morning? Do you remember her coming in?" He shook his head. "I have to call Mac."

He handed her his cell phone. "Here, use mine. Dial. Press this button. Smile. Welcome to the phone of the future."

Naomi popped her head in the back room while Lacey dialed. "What are we up to? May I help?"

Miguel steered her back into the salesroom. "Just clearing out a few personal things. Lacey has to make a call."

"Mac, it's Lacey. I'm at Bentley's Boutique on Wisconsin in Chevy Chase. Can you send Hansen here for a photo?"

"What's up, another funny hairdo?"

"I've got something potentially very big. But it's mine, my story."

"Explain yourself."

"It's something about someone who disappeared and recently resurfaced. Got it? I'm on an unsecured cell phone. Just send Hansen; we need a photo."

"I don't get it. Is this a fashion photo?"

"There is a fashion angle. And this person who resurfaced—get it?—we may have some insight into her last day. I can't take it with me, so I need a photo. Good enough for you?"

"Why are you talking in code? It is code, isn't it? Damn it.

Oh, all right, I'll send Hansen. Keep it nailed down, Lacey, whatever the hell it is. I'll find Hansen. You said the store's on Wisconsin?"

"Right over the D.C. line."

"Hansen or his replacement will be there in half an hour. Depending on traffic."

Lacey handed back the phone and wandered around the store while she waited. Miguel went out for coffee, and Naomi subtly bullied a few people into making purchases they hadn't quite intended. *Accessorize!* Lacey thought about the scarf. The Bentley's exclusive silk scarf collection was displayed in a glass case. She imagined that Esme wanted to wear something to the committee hearing to signal to the Bentleys how much she wanted that job with the fashion empire. With the borrowed Bentley suit it would be perfect. That made sense, but the scarf would have been a large purchase for an intern. But didn't Marcia say Esme was expecting an expensive present from Van Drizzen?

The front door opened to the sound of a tinkling bell. Lacey looked up to see Miguel strolling in with several skim-milk lattes. He was handing them out to Lacey and Naomi when she sighted Hansen walking past the front windows. There were more tinkling bells as the photographer, wearing his trademark dual Nikons and camera bag and blue jeans, strode in, followed by Tony Trujillo. *Trujillo? What's the big idea? This is my story!*

"I asked for Hansen. Are you two a package now?"

"Hey, Smithsonian." He stopped at a display for sunglasses and tried on a pair. They set off his even white teeth as he grinned at her. "Stylin'! What do you think?"

Hansen waited for some instruction while Naomi sidled up to Tony and purred. Tony often had that effect on women. Miguel looked a little put-out.

"They're fabulous," Naomi said, picking up an even more expensive pair. "Try these."

Tony took off the shades and turned his attention to Lacey. "What's up?"

"I told Mac not to tell anyone." He turned his hundred-watt smile on her.

"Look at it this way: He didn't tell Peter Johnson, who is still in a sniffling snit about yesterday's addition to his story. I, on the other hand, take no offense. So what is it?"

Lacey pulled him into the back room, leaving Miguel and Naomi to gossip over lattes.

"I've got a lead on what Esme planned to do her last day," she offered.

"And I got an interview with her folks," he countered.

"Double byline."

"Of course. Explain."

"Esme planned to come here that day to buy the perfect accessory to make an impressive show at the Appropriations Subcommittee hearing the following day. Her housemates had tried to cut off free access to their closets, but she wanted to continue to impress the Bentleys. And she had managed to put her competition, Cordelia, in an itchy World War Two uniform. It was her moment of victory. But no one heard from Esme after that Monday." She showed him the scarf and the hold tag. Tony seemed unimpressed. *Come on, Tony, do I have to do the math for you?*

Lacey directed Hansen to take photos of the box, the scarf, and the tag. He snapped away while Miguel hovered at the door outside camera range. Naomi finally caught on that a photo essay was being shot in her back room and grabbed Miguel. "Oh, my God, you mean this scarf was being held for that woman they found dead?"

"Yeah, the blonde."

"The one who never bought anything?"

"Yeah, she asked me to hold this for her. She said she was going to buy it that Monday. Would have been a first for her."

"I guess she never did buy anything after all. Wow, I wonder how many of these scarves I can sell now?" Naomi clearly worked on commission in addition to her base salary. "I'll call it 'the Esme.'"

Watching Tony's eyes stray toward Naomi, Lacey grabbed

his arm. "Tony, focus. Look at the date and time on the hold tag," she commanded. "Esme was supposed to come here and buy this scarf at the *same time* the armed robbery was in progress. Get it?"

"The same time." His face lit up. He got it. "Aha! You think she got caught up in the robbery?" He turned to Miguel. "Did you see her?"

"You will recall that my coworker Kika and I were sprawled on the floor of the upstairs office wearing gray duct-tape handcuffs, which is not my color. If she came in, I didn't see her."

"Don't forget the female robber got away, and no one knows how," Lacey said. "And I understand Esme's VW Cabriolet still hasn't been found."

"It probably won't. Not in one piece, anyway. No doubt it's made a trip to some chop shop in D.C., Baltimore, or New Jersey." Tony socked her in the arm; it was one of his compliments. "I like it, Lacey. By the way, has anyone called the police with this?" Hearing no affirmative answer, Tony flourished his cell phone. "Allow me. Hansen, you have enough photos? Get the whole store, for context. And more when the cops get on the scene."

Naomi was more than happy to pose anywhere they wanted her. Lacey was sure that if Tony had asked, she would be posing nude, draped in the soon-to-be-famous "Esme" scarf. While Hansen finished up, Tony called a number and asked for the lead FBI investigator on the case, one Gary Braddock. Aside to Lacey he said, "Oh, the Bureau is so going to hate this."

chapter 17

At first Lacey found it hard to believe Gary Braddock was an FBI agent. The others she knew looked like bookkeepers in cheap suits. But Braddock was dressed all in black—jacket, slacks, and sweater, looking like an I'm-so-cool advertisement. According to Trujillo, he was known in some circles as "the Undertaker." Lacey wondered if that referred to his attitude or because he was the agent who had recently put several major bad guys on death row. She estimated his age at about forty, his sandy-blond hair sprinkled with gray. *Nice-looking for a Fed. Even for a non-Fed.*

Tony had briefed her on Braddock while they waited for him. She had met only FBI Headquarters types, he pointed out. "Bureaucrats." He snorted. "This guy is Washington Field Office. It makes all the difference. Plus he's like the Zen master of this stuff." Braddock was described as cool, even by criminals he arrested, interrogated, and sent to prison. Lacey assumed his was a studied and perfected image. And of course, he would naturally assume he was smarter than anyone else, particularly a reporter. *Particularly a fashion reporter.*

Tony told her the Bureau requested that they stay at the store until the police team arrived. Miguel polished his statement about how he just wanted to help the cause of justice. He left out his sheer joy in being able to embarrass the Bentleys once again.

Gary Braddock entered the store followed by a Maryland homicide cop, who wore a rumpled shirt, tie, and tan khaki jacket. He had obviously been briefed on the players. He made straight for Miguel, took his statement, appropriated the scarf for evidence, and issued a receipt to a dazzled Naomi, who even dropped the Bentley's snob act for him. Naomi's statement confirmed Miguel's. The Maryland cop stood by the door and didn't say a word. It was clear who was in charge here. Tony and Braddock shook hands.

"Gary, hey, man, good to see you."

"Trujillo. Nice boots. And thanks for the call. I imagine I can look forward to seeing this on the front page of *The Eye Street Observer* tomorrow."

"Courtesy of Lacey here. What can I say? She's got good sources." He made the introductions. "Agent Braddock, Lacey Smithsonian, she writes 'Crimes of Fashion.' "

She detected the slightest movement in his eyebrows and a subtle upturning of his mouth. *Oh, good,* she thought, *yet another man who finds me amusing.* After Tony's brief tutorial, Lacey had prepared herself for a sparring match with the Undertaker. However, she wasn't prepared for his sense of humor and his empathy. And he didn't show that he believed he was smarter, if he did. He could be very dangerous, she thought.

"So when Miguel Flores remembered the scarf and told you about it—"

"He didn't tell me then; he brought me to Bentley's to make sure it was still here and that he remembered it correctly."

"You didn't think he made it up, set up the scarf and the note to get more publicity?"

"No. Naomi backed him up, didn't she?"

"What do you think of the scarf?"

"I think it's a fashion clue. And maybe more."

"Ah, a fashion clue. Agent Thorn, whom I believe you met last spring, told me that you, quote, 'mock people with your tasteless opinions.' "

"Tasteless or not, I get paid to write them. Who's doing the mocking here?"

"I'm not mocking anybody. What do you think this fashion clue means?"

"I thought putting together scenarios was your job."

He grinned. "So I guess I'm going to read your scenario in the paper tomorrow." He rubbed his hands together and checked one of four cell phones attached to his belt.

Am I the only one in the universe who doesn't have a cell phone? Lacey wondered.

He fiddled with one, then looked back up at her. "I know you're guarding your turf, but I appreciate that you gave us a heads-up about this information. The more pieces, the less puzzle."

She didn't know whether to trust him. "You're not going to leak it to *The Post* just to screw us over, are you?"

"You have my word." He shook her hand and effectively dismissed her. "Nice work, Lacey Smithsonian, 'Crimes of Fashion.' "

Trujillo gave her a ride back to the office in his black Mustang with the white ragtop. "I feel honored, Tony. Getting a ride in the love of your life."

"Speaking of love, or at least attraction, I think Braddock likes you."

"Oh, please. He was playing me. And this Zen master interrogator of yours barely asked me the time of day."

"He got what he wanted. And on top of that he practically winked at you. That's a lot from the Undertaker."

She glared at him and he burst out laughing. "You're a real comedian, Tony."

They returned to the office and went to their respective desks, where they would file their separate stories and let Mac stitch it together. She looked around. "Hey, Mac, where's Ms. Pickles?"

"Out. She had a lead on a story."

"Out? You're kidding. A food story?"

"I dunno. Something to help you out."

"She's helping me? How on earth could she help me out?"

"She said she was picking up a press release or something."

"What was she wearing?"

"How do I know? Clothes." Mac wasn't about clothes.

Something Lacey should remember, but he'd been so interested in the photo shoot and hairstyles that she'd forgotten. *So much for fashion clues.* Even without evidence that Felicity was wearing interview clothes, Lacey held out hope that the job interview hadn't fallen through. She wondered where Felicity would go. *The Post* would scarcely deign to hire anyone from *The Eye,* and she doubted that even *The Washington Times* would hire reporters from the feisty third daily. No, Lacey thought, Felicity was probably going all-out for some high-paying job at a trade association, some in-house publication job with the American Snack Food Association or the National Federation of Baked Goods Wholesalers or some such group. With that happy thought, Lacey buckled down to finish the Esme Fairchild scarf story. She had a sudden picture of Esme with Gloria standing behind her and winking. Lacey began to write.

The merest twist of silk, an expensive Bentley's scarf placed on hold but never purchased, could send investigators down an entirely different path in the mysterious death of Washington intern Esme Fairchild. The multicolored silk scarf was just something to finish her look for the appropriations hearing the next day. She wanted to impress the Bentleys, fashion's royalty. But this decision may have lead to a fatal conclusion. Did the scarf bring her to Bentley's Boutique during an armed robbery last week?

With a nod to FBI Agent Gary Braddock's subtle scoffing at her, she thought she might have something for her Friday column, "No Such Thing as a Fashion Clue," but she was spent. Not so with Tony, who was still energetic. In fact, he was positively high.

"What do you say we go out for a drink and celebrate this story? It's not often that we scoop the world like that." He pinched a wilting blossom from Lacey's bouquet.

"I'll take a rain check, okay? I'm fried."

"I'm buying."

"I'll miss my golden opportunity to see you pick up a check." She didn't tell him she wanted to be at home watching her answering machine, waiting for a call from Vic—a call that would probably never come.

Mac strolled over. "Nice teamwork on that story. Take the afternoon off."

It was way past time to go home. "Very funny, Mac."

When Lacey stepped off the elevator she saw someone dressed in blue work clothes and a blue baseball cap down at the end of her hallway, trying to get into her apartment.

"Hey, what's going on?" she called from the center hall, not wanting to get too close until she knew what he was up to.

He didn't look at her, but simply said, "Maintenance. Must have the wrong key." He turned and walked down the hall toward her, keeping his head down. "No problem, I'll be back."

"Wait a minute," she said as he pushed open the door to the stairs exit that was next to the elevators. "It's after hours. What do you want in my apartment?" She moved after him, and held the exit door open. "Hey—who the hell are you?" She reached out for his arm to stop him, but he jerked away and slammed her into the wall, hitting her shoulder.

His rapid steps downward echoed back. Her heart was beating fast. Everything about this was wrong. She realized his shirt didn't have a name tag like those of the rest of the staff. She looked behind her as she walked back to her apartment to make sure he was gone. Then she noticed the fresh scratches in the paint on her door and the doorjamb. He didn't have a key; he had a screwdriver or a pry bar. *Way to go, slick.* Once inside, she slipped on the chain and called the management office's emergency number just to make sure. The woman said there was no maintenance call logged and suggested that if Lacey was concerned she should call the police. *So much for caring and concerned building management.*

She grabbed an old baseball bat from her closet and propped it by the door, just in case her visitor came back. She made a brief report to the Alexandria police officer who came to check out her call, but she didn't feel any safer. Her description of the guy was inadequate, especially for a reporter. She thought about calling Brooke or Stella to keep her company, but she couldn't face their interrogation, which would be much more intense than the police. She thought about the Smith & Wesson that Vic had insisted she borrow last spring, but she had given it back before he returned to Colorado. She couldn't sleep that night. She had no Vic, no gun, and no idea what was going on. *I have nothing of value—except a trunk full of an old woman's memories.*

chapter 18

"Genius. Am I a genius or what?" Stella paused to let Lacey appreciate her vast intelligence during Wednesday morning's vintage hair experiment. "I put you together with Miguel Flores and voilà! You almost have the whole thing wrapped up. In a Bentley's scarf, no less." She stood behind the salon chair, looking at Lacey in the mirror, contemplating today's hairstyle: Look Number Three. It was the seventeenth of September; the gala was scheduled for the twenty-third. Stella was soon putting hot rollers in, even though Lacey said they weren't period. It was to give her "extra fullness."

"Did you see my story?"

The Eye played up its role in the discovery of the Bentley's scarf the next morning and its possible connection to Esme's possible last moments. The story was also all over the television stations and radio. But the other newspapers didn't have it. They would have to play catch-up the following day and counter with some other aspect of the case. Mac played it above the fold on the front page, double-bylined by Smithsonian and Trujillo.

"Yeah, there's a link on DeadFed dot com."

Damon Newhouse strikes again.

"You could buy a paper, you know. One of the last great bargains in this country."

"Oh, I plan to. For my scrapbook, and I'll buy one for the salon, too."

"That's seventy cents we can count on, and by the way, I don't almost have the whole thing wrapped up."

Stella smacked her on the head with a comb. "Listen to her. You said the same thing the whole time you were looking into Angie's death."

"I was just doing my job. And that hurt." Lacey rubbed the spot.

"I'm just doing my job too." Stella swooped up Lacey's hair, which reached her shoulders, twisting it around for inspiration. "So who killed Esme Fairchild?"

"I don't know." *And who tried to break into my apartment last night?* Lacey felt on edge. She'd even placed a match in her doorjamb so that if it was out of place later, she would know someone had gotten in, but she didn't feel like sharing that with Stella.

"C'mon, Lacey, use your imagination," Stella said. "I think it's the senator guy. That's what most of my clients think. Not that he did it himself, but that he made it happen, you know. His goons. Henchmen, thugs, and goons."

"Or it could have something to do with the robbery at Bentley's."

"True. You know what they say. This is a small town; everything is connected. Like some kind of conspiracy."

"Stella, you have to stop reading that DeadFed Web site."

"Nah, it gives me a knowledge edge." She dropped Lacey's hair. "I'm glad you're wearing that green suit today." It was a very fitted forest-green suit with covered buttons. Lacey wore it with a rose pin at the throat. "I have just the thing," Stella said, whipping out a small piece of mesh material trimmed in green velvet.

"A snood? Where'd you find that?" *Oh, dear, there will be merriment today at* The Eye. Lacey examained it carefully. It looked new.

"I was thinking of Lana Turner in *The Postman Always Rings Twice.*"

"She wore a turban, not a snood. Hedy Lamarr wore a snood in some movie."

"Whatever, but isn't it cute? I kind of made it myself, knowing how you like green. Totally radical, huh? I'd wear one myself if my hair wasn't so short." Stella ran her hand through her short spiky ends and blew a kiss at her reflection in preparation for concentrating on today's masterpiece. She parted Lacey's hair in the middle again, caught the sides up with combs, and fitted the snood over Lacey's lightly highlighted locks. Stella also insisted on putting the finishing touches on Lacey's makeup and surveyed her work in the mirror.

"Damn, I'm good. What do you think?"

Not being a veteran snood wearer, Lacey wasn't quite sure what she thought. It was unusual, efficient, pretty. "I like it, but—"

"But what?"

"What happens when I go outside wearing this?"

"That's your problem, kiddo." Stella reached for her first Coke of the day. "But you shouldn't care; you look dangerous."

"Dangerous, huh? In that case, look out, world; here I come, snood and all. Thanks, Stella. By the way, give me a receipt and I'll have the paper pay for this. Mac's insisting on taking my picture every day. He wants to do a feature on these styles for the gala."

"Oh, my God, and you didn't tell me! Lacey! What's wrong with you?"

"I must have forgotten. Imagine that."

"Imagine—My work in *The Eye*! Do you want my picture too?" She was so excited, Lacey didn't have the heart to say no.

"I'll ask Mac." She squared her shoulders and left the salon, wary of strange looks. But her fears were unfounded. The glorious morning compelled her to walk to the office. She strolled through Dupont Circle, down Connecticut, left on K Street, and through Farragut Square. Lacey's fitted late Forties suit and matching snood didn't log one look. Not one that she noticed, anyway. It was D.C., after all.

However, once she hit the office, the snood was an object of much interest. Hansen was again waiting at her desk, ready to snap away. "I'm getting to dig this high-fashion biz," he said.

"I'm ready for a gig at *Vogue*. But we need a different background for this one."

"Yeah, something very 'girl reporter.'" Tony Trujillo jumped up from Felicity's desk, where he had no doubt been rummaging, in hopes that her diet was over.

"Morning, Tony. Didn't see you there. Pawing through somebody else's desk?"

"Not at all. I'm here to see you. I wouldn't miss the wacky 'do of the day."

"You don't like it?"

Trujillo circled around her. "Yeah, I like it; it's like some old newsreel. 'Girl Reporter Snags Exclusive for *Daily Planet*.' But what I really want to know is, when are you going to come in with the stack of bananas on your head?"

Lacey grabbed a pencil from her desk and launched it at him, only to have it bounce off his chest. "You're wearing out your welcome, Lizard Boots." She didn't wait for a comment. She logged in and checked her voice mail. There were only three: Brooke, of course, was first at six forty-five A.M., congratulating her on yet another Esme story, but complaining that she hadn't been alerted first. The second was from Aaron Bentley.

"I trust you've exhausted all the possibilities for writing unpleasant stories about the Bentley family. Really, this must stop or our attorneys shall lodge a complaint against your newspaper."

One more message was from someone she didn't know, someone with a raspy voice. "Reporters can disappear too, you know. Knock off the Fairchild stories."

Lacey instantly thought about the phony maintenance man and her sore shoulder and held her breath expecting to hear more, but was thankful there wasn't any. She'd had threats before. It was never pleasant, but she sure as hell wasn't going to back off of her story.

The lanky photographer stretched his long legs and grinned. "Let's try it outside, Lacey. The square's got nice scenery." Hansen stood up, grabbed his bag of lenses, and slung it over his shoulder. Lacey checked her makeup in a small mirror. "Bring the mirror; I like it. It's classic," Hansen said.

"Classic," Trujillo echoed as he followed them out. Mac merely pulled his nose out of *The New York Times* and grunted as they trooped past his window.

Lacey endured yet another photo shoot, with Trujillo offering suggestions and several tourists stopping to observe. After it was finished, all she wanted was a quiet day. She was cleaning off her desk when Hugh Bentley called. "You're too late," she said. "Aaron already called to say he hoped I was through writing about the Bentleys."

"Let's not be too hasty. Aaron is always so . . . abrupt. There might be something you could write that we could all agree is a good story." He paused. Lacey waited. "I wanted you to be the first to know: Bentley's will provide complementary tickets to the gala for Wilhelmina Tremain and her daughter, Annette."

"That's very generous, Hugh." *Trying to throw me off a track I haven't found yet?*

"That's not all. Bentley's will also provide them with gowns and a day of beauty before the event."

"That's a story, all right. Sort of a Cinderella story." She could see the possibilities, and she was a total sucker for makeovers and magic moments. No matter what Hugh's motivation was.

"Your story about Gloria Adams brought back some sad memories. And reading about her family made me think about how they might feel, even after all these years." *He's really pouring it on,* Lacey thought. "I thought they might like to have a taste of glamour. The kind that Gloria craved."

"And help turn the negative publicity around."

"Exactly. Bentley's can provide a little sparkle to their lives, at least for one night. You made them seem terribly woebegone."

Oh, good, now it's my fault. She opened the newspaper on her desk. "Sorry, that wasn't my intent."

"Think about what you've written. A woman disappears, things go bump in the night, and evil walks the earth. Her family suffers forever after. It has mythic qualities. Mythmaking is tricky business, Lacey."

You should know, she thought.

"Nevertheless . . ."

She realized she hadn't had enough coffee that morning and started looking for her coffee cup, rummaging through papers, when she saw it sitting on Felicity's desk. She wondered what on earth the woman was up to. "But, Hugh, why call me?"

"Because after implicating Bentleys in that tragic story, you now have the chance to be fair to us. Objectivity and all that, and because you like myths. You've got one tailor-made for you: Cinderella Annette goes to the ball."

"And meets her prince?"

Hugh laughed. "I can only do so much, Lacey."

"Are you giving this to *The Post?*"

"Of course I am, but not until tomorrow. For today the story is all yours."

Then I have to get an exclusive with Annette, before The Post *gets to her.* Hugh's flack, Chevalier, arrived at the paper to deliver the official press release to Lacey before she could even find Annette's phone number. The receptionist was all but drooling when Lacey walked out to the reception area to meet him.

"Hugh Bentley asked me to deliver this personally." He smiled, showing even white teeth.

"That wasn't necessary."

"Of course, it's my pleasure. I wanted to see where your offices were located. And my job is to keep the Bentleys happy. And this is going to be a happy story, right?" He squeezed her elbow. "I certainly hope so. A positive story." He bared his teeth in a smile, then left.

As soon as he was out of sight, Lacey made a beeline for her desk and called Annette's office in the District, only a few blocks away. Annette was in and said she'd take an early lunch so that she could meet Lacey right away. Lacey grabbed her purse and headed for the door. She ran into Mac on her way out.

"Any more surprises today, Smithsonian? I don't think I

could take any more after your snood, or whatever Trujillo
called it."

"Just business as usual." She smiled brightly and Mac
looked doubtful but she ran out before he had a chance to utter
any protests.

Hugh's gesture was a good story. It blatantly pushed all the
sentiment buttons, and Lacey hoped with all her heart that Annette would emerge as a beauty. Yet Lacey couldn't dismiss the
tingle of apprehension running up her spine. The master of the
PR game was playing her, just as surely as she would shape
the story to suit her own sensibilities. *It's still a good story*,
she told herself.

Aside from the possibility of turning the story around, Hugh
sounded genuinely interested in the Tremains. Did he think
other designs by Gloria Adams might be hidden at their house?
Annette and Willie said they didn't have anything, but maybe
there was something stuffed in a box, a drawer, a corner of the
basement that hadn't been explored in years.

How far would Hugh go to find out?

She met Annette in Farragut Square. They bought coffee
from a little stand and strolled around, taking in the statute of
the admiral in the middle of the square before settling on a
bench in the crystal fall air. Lacey pulled an envelope out of her
purse and handed it to Annette. "Thanks for the photos."

"No, thank you! Of course, Mother was mortified when she
opened the paper." Lacey drew in her breath, but Annette reassured her. "Nothing you did; it was just that the story was so
big, what with the photos of Aunt Gloria and Esme Fairchild.
And it is all so tragic. But that's why Mr. Bentley called. And
he came over to our house last night to meet us, he and his
driver."

"To your house?" *He is after Gloria's designs! He could
have even sent someone to break into my apartment for the suit.*
"Did he want anything else?"

"He asked Mother if she had anything that Gloria might
have made. Things like that. But who'd have that kind of thing?
I mean, she vanished sixty years ago."

"You still have the same refrigerator," Lacey pointed out.

"Yeah, but Mother said we didn't have anything except the photos we gave you. She said everything we knew about Gloria was in your article."

"But what about her letters about Hugh? I didn't write about those."

Annette's eyes grew wide. "She'd never tell him about those. They're private, and she thinks they're all lies anyway." But that was all she would say on the topic. It was clear that she didn't want to talk about Gloria; she was too excited about the invitation to the gala.

She had a glow that was missing before. It defied the clothing she wore, a pair of gray slacks missing a belt and a wrinkled white shirt, her hair held back in a ponytail and not a shred of makeup. But there was promise in Annette's face, Lacey was sure of it.

"Can you believe it? It's like a dream come true." Annette was on high bubble. "We're going to Bentley's Boutique on Saturday to select our gowns. Bentley's! It's so hard to imagine."

"What do you have in mind?"

"Mr. Bentley said he would provide a stylist. Someone to help us decide what looks best."

"You don't mind?"

"Really, Lacey, I have no idea about what looks good. Given my druthers, I'd probably go for the full heaving-bodice, romance-novel, cover-girl look." Annette sighed with happy pleasure.

"Annette, *The Eye* would like to follow your makeover and dress selection with a photographer, if you don't mind. And I'd like it to be an exclusive."

"Oh, my God! You're kidding." Annette's squeal probably communicated with dolphins somewhere. Lacey assumed that was a yes. Now all she had to do was tell Mac that she was turning *The Eye* into *Lacey's Daily Makeover Magazine*.

*   *   *

"You have a visitor, Lacey," the guard told her as she passed through the newspaper's reception area after saying good-bye to Annette. He read from a piece of paper: " 'Belinda Bentley Holmes,' " and he indicated the woman sitting on a plum-colored sofa beneath framed front pages of *The Eye.*

Lacey greeted Belinda in a small conference room off the lobby. Clad in tailored navy slacks, a red blazer, and a matching red sweater, Jeffrey's mother looked composed, wrapped serenely in her status as a Bentley. Gold jewelry complemented the buttons of her jacket, and every strand of her platinum page-boy was locked into place. Belinda was too thin, Lacey thought. It looked like she lived on cigarettes and black coffee, even though she turned down the offer of a cup from Lacey.

"I realize, Ms. Smithsonian, you are a busy woman, and no doubt I'm keeping you from dragging up another tawdry little scandal."

"Can I help you with something?"

"I hope so. I am not a busy woman in the same way you are, but I have one overriding interest in life, and that is my son, Jeffrey."

That's not the way I heard it, Lacey thought.

"I was an older mother, you see, and therefore he is every-thing to me. I understand he took you out."

"For dinner. He was a perfect gentleman." She didn't think it was a big deal.

"Of course he was. Let's keep it that way, shall we?"

"Excuse me?"

"I have been waiting for Jeffrey to show some interest in a suitable young woman."

"You're saying I'm not suitable?" Lacey didn't know whether to be offended or amused.

Belinda surveyed Lacey's outfit, complete with snood, and shrugged her shoulders with a dismissive smile. "It would hardly be seemly for him to be associated with a . . . with a reporter who persists in digging up tragic news from the past and dwelling on unfortunate recent events. So distressing for his family."

"I'm surprised you didn't bring me a nice juicy apple,"

Lacey said. *A poison apple.* But Belinda didn't seem to have much in the way of a sense of humor. Lacey was more amused than offended. *Mothers usually like me,* Lacey thought. *I've never been warned off by anyone's mother before.*

"Mrs. Holmes, Jeffrey is an adult. I doubt if he asks his mother for permission to ask someone out. I don't."

"I see. Then let's be businesslike. What would it cost to keep you away from him?"

"You're bribing me?" Lacey couldn't help it; she started laughing. "It was only dinner!" *Poor Jeffrey.*

"You don't understand what being a Bentley means." Belinda picked up her smart little bag and stood up. "When you come to your senses we can do business." She stood up stiffly with perfectly erect posture.

"You are wrong about one thing, Mrs. Holmes. I am completely aware of what being a Bentley means," Lacey said, but Belinda strode out and showed no signs that she'd heard her.

Lacey wondered if this was standard behavior for Belinda Bentley Holmes. She had moved across the country to rid herself of her own family. It had been a long time since her own mother embarrassed her in front of dates, but the memories lingered on. Of course, that was in high school, when a mother is the most embarrassing burden a daughter could possibly carry, although her father and sister ranked right up there as well. Lacey remembered her house as a constant agony of cheap furniture, lurid colors, bizarre food combinations, blaring TV, and tacky behavior. Her mother so often plied Lacey's dates with vile concoctions: Rice Krispies Treats and something indescribable made out of cornflakes and melted chocolate chips. But Rose Smithsonian never warned anyone off, and high school boys loved her wacky cereal-based goodies, from her own recipes. One favorite combined shredded wheat, marshmallows, peanut butter, and caramel sauce. She had, however, given up trying to get Lacey matched with anyone. She sighed a lot and pinned her hopes on Cherise, Lacey's sister.

Lacey hoped Belinda's visit was the last surprise of the day. It was a vain hope.

chapter 19

Just another crank caller. This makes two today. Unless you count Belinda Bentley Holmes.

That's what Lacey thought, until the explosion rattled the front windows, flashing white light through the newsroom. A momentary shock; then reporters flew to the windows, crowding her to the side. She upgraded the crank's status to lunatic.

Lacey had been trying to finish a Fashion Bite, something at last that had nothing to do with the Bentleys, trying to make it funny, when the phone rang.

"I'm warning you, bitch. Stop writing those stupid stories."

"Who is this, and which stupid stories are you referring to?" *I'm on deadline here, gumball.*

"Look outside and say good-bye to your wheels."

She was puzzled. Her ungrateful Nissan 280ZX was still at Paul's shop, rusting complacently in the humid air of Washington, no doubt waiting for someone to swim to Japan for new parts. At least she thought it was. She hurried past four rows of desks to peer out to the street below. *My Z isn't out there.* The only mode of transportation she recognized was Felicity's dismal gray monstrosity of a minivan parked illegally in the fire lane outside *The Eye* offices.

The impact of the explosion took only a moment, but Lacey remembered it in slow motion. Shards of metal flew up from what was left of the hulking frame. It sat on melted wheels, showering twisted metal minivan bits onto the street, along with several open tins of home-baked cookies, now cookie dust. Lacey was horrified. Outraged. She streaked back to her desk, snood flying, hoping the creep was still on the phone. She grabbed the receiver and listened to the sound of expectant breathing.

"YOU THOUGHT I DROVE A MINIVAN?!"

There was silence on the other end. A thoughtful silence. Then, "Uh-oh."

"Listen, you brain-dead piece of protoplasm, if you think I'm going to stop writing stories because you're blowing up other people's minivans, you're out of your freaking skull." The caller hung up, leaving the dial tone buzzing in her ear. "What stupid story?" *Why on earth did this nameless idiot think that Felicity's minivan was mine? Oh, my God—Felicity.*

"Felicity?" Lacey had seen her just a minute ago. She looked around to see if the evil food writer was still in the newsroom. Unfortunately she wound up nose-to-nose with Mac. He was wearing the Unhappy Editor's face.

"You have something to tell me, Smithsonian?"

"Mac, I . . ." There were people standing around the window, people crowding around her desk. A distant wailing of sirens drew closer.

Mac twitched his eyebrows dangerously. "Smithsonian. In my office now." She closed her eyes for a moment, then marched into his lair. Mac slammed the door shut behind her, then pulled the blinds over the glass. He took a breath and glowered before trusting himself to speak.

"I see you pick up the phone, I see you run to the window, I hear the big bang. So who's on the phone, what's the stupid story, and just what in the ever-loving hell is going on?"

Lacey felt sick inside, but struggled for composure. "I don't know; someone blew up Felicity's van."

"Who was it?"

"I don't know. Some idiot with a low voice. I had a similar call this morning on voice mail, but I don't know if it was the same guy. Maybe if I had caller ID we could trace it." Mac grumbled. The policy was that reporters should answer the phone no matter who was on the other end. No screening allowed.

"This is a fine mess. They blow up Felicity's van and they call you? Are they stupid or are you involved in the middle of some mess?"

"Maybe they meant to call Felicity and got me by mistake."

"Or maybe they meant to blow up your car and got hers by mistake. So what did you do?"

Men. They're all alike. Always looking for someone to blame. "My job, Mac! I was just doing my job. Maybe somebody meant to get Felicity."

"Nah, everybody likes Felicity. Must be you; you're always pissing someone off." Lacey was about to spit out a reply when someone knocked at the door.

"Yeah?"

Trujillo stuck his head in. "We have some people here who'd like a word with Lacey. They're trying to talk to Felicity, but she's a little—upset." Tony opened the door wider so Mac and Lacey could take a peek. Felicity appeared to be in shock, frozen at her desk, while a couple of D.C. cops tried to talk with her. "There's a fire truck out front too. I wonder if they'll give her a ticket for parking in the fire lane," Trujillo said.

Lacey walked back to the window. The still smoking van was surrounded by cop cars. Firemen were dousing the smoldering ruin. No doubt there were agents from the Bureau of Alcohol, Tobacco and Firearms out there too. Could Homeland Security and the Federal Bureau of Investigation be far behind? She watched, mesmerized by the scene. She was vaguely aware of Mac shouting orders. "I want an editorial, front page, that's right, front page. We will not be intimidated." He was getting into the swing of it now. It was an impressive display of bravery. But then, she reflected, the smoldering wreckage wasn't Douglas MacArthur Jones's burgundy Lincoln Town Car with the plushy seats. *I regret that I have only one of Felicity's minivans to give for my newspaper,* she imagined him saying.

Aware of a presence near her, Lacey turned to see a man

wearing black. Agent Gary Braddock quietly took in the chaos of the newsroom. "Ms. Smithsonian."

"Always good to see you, Agent Braddock."

"Glad to see you're in one piece. Unlike your car."

"Not mine. I don't drive a minivan." Lacey indicated Felicity, who was now tearfully wiping at her eyes. "Felicity Pickles. Food editor. It's her car."

"But you got a phone call and then ran to the window?"

"I gather there were witnesses."

"Cops told me the car was yours."

"They got it wrong. And the bomber got it wrong. I've got no idea why everyone thinks that minivan was mine. But hey, at least my car got lucky. My lucky day, huh?"

Mac waved them into his office for some semblance of privacy. He issued a general order to the newsroom at large. "Deadline, people. We are still on deadline, you can gawk after you've filed your stories."

Mac left them alone and closed the door. Lacey sat down while Braddock leaned on the windowsill. He pulled out a small notebook. "I don't have a full statement from her yet, but Ms. Pickles says she was helping you with your beat."

"Helping me?!" *I'm sure she was helping me.* In spite of herself, Lacey felt her eyebrows rise and her eyes roll. *She was also rummaging through my desk.* "That would be novel."

"She told me that she answered a call that came for you last week, while you were out. She knew how busy you were, so she picked up a story. She neglected to tell the caller she wasn't you."

"She neglected to tell me."

He didn't appear surprised. "Gave the name of Lawrence Zasker. We're chasing the name. And the phone records. Apparently said he had a scoop about the new museum. That fashion museum. Ring a bell?"

"The museum, yes; Zasker, no. What kind of scoop?" Lacey peeked through the closed blinds into the newsroom. She saw a female police officer escorting a weeping Felicity out.

"According to Ms. Pickles, he didn't say. They set up a couple of meetings, but he didn't show up. He told her to wear a black suit so he would know her."

"Damn, I thought she had a job interview."

"Fashion clue?" Braddock deadpanned.

"Red herring."

"You don't like her."

"I don't think she was helping me. I think she was helping herself to my story."

"This message . . . whoever sent it waited until she was out of the car, no one was around, no one was hurt. No witnesses yet, either, but we're still canvassing."

"Maybe it was the Minivan Liberation Army."

The faintest flicker of amusement showed in Braddock's face. "Maybe the message was for you."

"They never send roses. Of course it was for me. They called me to say, 'Watch us blow up your car'! Only they didn't bother to say who or why or which stories pissed them off."

"This is a pretty emphatic message for insulting someone's tie. You must have hit a nerve."

Lacey picked up a copy of *The Eye* and showed it to him: the pictures of Esme Fairchild and Gloria Adams. "Take your pick—the Bentleys, the senator, the Fairchilds, Esme's killer— who knows? And there's always my column. And my anonymous callers. Hell, someone tried to break into my apartment last night." Braddock opened his mouth to speak. "And no, I didn't recognize him; he was trying to play maintenance man. And yes, I filed a police report in Alexandria."

"Now that we've narrowed the field of suspects to the entire capital region, I'm sure we'll get someplace," Braddock said. "We'll be looking at your phone records too."

"But they didn't get my car. The morons."

"Nobody said these guys are smart, Ms. Smithsonian. After all, they took Ms. Pickles for you, and I have to say the resemblance is minimal. Nice snood, by the way."

"Thanks. Felicity won't be answering my phone anymore."

"Probably not. Now what's your cell phone number?"

"I don't have one. I hate them. Don't believe in them."

Braddock opened the door. "Mr. Jones, would you join us, please?" he called out.

Mac, shirtsleeves rolled up and tie loosened, returned to his office. He handed Lacey a small black object as he walked in. "This is your new cell phone, courtesy of *The Eye.* I want you to keep it with you at all times. Sleep with it under your pillow. Oh, and Lacey, I want you to use it when you get in trouble."

"*When* I get in trouble? Show some faith, Mac."

Agent Braddock held out his hand. "May I?"

She gave it to him and he punched in a direct dial number to one of his phones. "Call me if you get another threat, any kind of threat. We don't want to see any more smoking vehicles. They're an environmental problem." Braddock handed the phone to Mac, who coded in *The Eye*'s phone number. "Any questions?"

"Does this thing come with an instruction book?" Lacey had no idea how it worked, so Braddock gave her a brief tutorial. He gave her a look that Lacey interpreted as his I'd-tell-you-to-stay-out-of-trouble-but-I-know-it-won't-do-any-good look and left. She saw him laughing with Trujillo across the newsroom before Mac shut the door again.

Her boss wiped his face with a handkerchief. "Honest to God, whoever thought the bag-and-shoes beat would be such a problem?" He saw the hopeful look on her face. "And don't entertain any ideas about a new beat. If this kind of thing happens to you on fashion, I don't know what you'd do in the news pen."

"You could try me. I'm fresh out of minivans to blow up."

Mac indicated the cell phone. "You are to carry that with you wherever you go. I have told you *The Eye* does not ask its reporters to put themselves in danger. As you apparently already are, we will try to mitigate those circumstances. First, you can take a leave of absence."

"No way, Mac. You know I can't do that." She said it automatically, but then wondered about the wisdom of that decision.

"Felicity is going to take a few weeks off. Effective immediately. Think about it."

It was way past time to go home. Mac agreed to let her turn in her column the next day. Lacey went back to her desk to collect her things. She found someone replacing her phone. The new one had a little screen with caller identification. She'd learn all about that tomorrow. Her glorious bouquet was drooping and she picked off a few more dead blossoms.

As Lacey headed for the door she was greeted by the unexpected sight of her friend Brooke Barton waiting for her at the reception desk.

"Lacey, I gather you were the intended target?" There was an unhealthy glow of excitement about her.

"News travels fast when you're having fun. How'd you find out so quickly?"

"Guess. Okay, I'm taking you out of here, Ms. Bomb Bait. You are officially under my protection as of this minute, and don't even think about making a break for freedom."

"Thanks for the lift. I'll be fine," Lacey said as they pulled into the parking lot of her building. "I'll get my car back tomorrow. You don't have to come up on my account." Lacey was as exhausted as if she'd built the bomb and blown up the minivan herself. She planned to throw her accursed new cell phone under the sofa and go straight to bed.

"I'm not leaving you in your hour of need. Let's order a pizza." Brooke took her keys from the ignition and locked the Club on the steering wheel.

Lacey thought for a moment. Spending the evening alone suddenly sounded less and less attractive. "Pepperoni?"

"And mushrooms and black olives and onions," Brooke agreed.

Lacey figured she'd regret that. But life was short, and she might as well pile up a few more regrets. On her way in, she noticed the match still in her door. Her apartment had not been tampered with.

Lacey's brush with disaster apparently offered the perfect excuse for an impromptu party at her apartment. Damon Newhouse, with a personal invitation from Brooke, showed up following the pizza boy. He strode triumphantly into the living room with a six-pack of Magic Hat Number Nine. Brooke loosened her top button, kicked off her heels, took the beer, and kissed him as passionately as if someone had tried to blow up her Acura. Damon hugged Lacey like a long-lost sister. Lacey changed out of her green Forties suit and into a lavender knit top and comfortable navy shorts.

Wearing beat-up boots and denim, Trujillo showed up soon after with a bottle of tequila with a worm in the bottom. Lacey urged him to drink up. Mac and his wife, Kim, brought a big bucket of fried chicken. Kim was Japanese-American and turned out to be the total California girl. She actually had a mellowing effect on Mac away from the office. Mac and Damon were soon doing tequila shots together.

Another visitor showed up. "Having a party?" he accused Lacey. "I came here with an update. And a thing of beauty." Miguel produced the completed bodice with embroidered midriff and shoulder insets.

"It's exquisite. And it's not a party, Miguel; it's a pizza that got out of control. After the car exploded."

"A car exploded?"

"Outside the office. Somebody blew up my imaginary minivan. Oh, never mind. Come on in and have a drink."

Trujillo offered him the tequila and a lime. Miguel took one look at the worm. "You've got to be kidding, amigo. Is there any decent wine? Say, a nice pinot grigio, for example?"

"I brought wine and chocolate." The tiny but strong-voiced Stella popped through the open door. "Lacey, I came the minute I heard about the explosion at *The Eye*. I knew you had to be involved somehow. And you need your friends."

"And now you're even psychic."

"Right. I'm not. But Marie is. She'll be over as soon as she locks up the Little Shop of Horus. I called her, but she already knew! Psychic."

"Why not? Barnum and Bailey are dropping by later. You said you brought chocolate?"

"Godiva." She handed the box to Lacey, who opened it, selected one, took a bite, and let the flavor explode in her mouth. The bite of chocolate felt like it saved her life. Saved her from screaming, at least. She directed Miguel to drink Stella's wine and after thoroughly washing her hands, took the bodice into the bedroom to see if it fit. Brooke, Stella, and Kim followed, drawn by the irresistible lure of viewing another woman's closet. Damon, Trujillo, and Mac were out on the balcony drinking their individual poisons and measuring each other's little journalistic empires.

When Lacey reemerged for Miguel to oversee the fit, the ladies followed. Brooke was in a dither. "My God, Lacey, I didn't know it was that fancy! Now I really have to shop."

By this time Marie, the friendly neighborhood psychic, stood majestic in the middle of the room, her black gypsy curls tumbling over a gauzy gown of purples and blues. Bangles decorated her wrists, and a tattooed vine snaked down her right arm. She smiled at Lacey, who was wearing the bodice with her shorts. "Perfect, Lacey. You must protect it with your life," she said. "There are those who would covet it." Her pronouncement amused the crowd.

"Yeah, they'll be pea green with envy," Stella said.

"It'll be a dress to die for," Miguel said, "but if it's me or the dress, I'll choose me every time. Now turn around and let me see." He made a few adjustments in the shoulder line and the back darts. "Be careful; you're full of pins. And stop wiggling or you'll look like a dartboard."

Lacey tried not to let Marie's words disturb her. Her predictions usually made little or no sense, except when they were about clothing or the weather. *So maybe this one should be heeded?*

Lacey changed, returned the bodice to Miguel, and rejoined the party, which could have been thrown by the Three Stooges. Mac announced that "someone named Vic phoned while you were doing your girly thing. I told him you were busy."

"Did he leave a message?"

He shrugged. "He said he might catch up with you later, if you're not too busy." Mac picked up a chicken leg and took a bite. He resumed a conversation with Damon, who seemed to be angling for a job at *The Eye. Or just developing a new source.*

Trujillo dragged her to the tiny kitchen, where he opened the fridge, looking for a beer chaser. "So, who was it, Lacey?"

"Who was what?"

"Don't play coy, Smithsonian." He got in close, conspiratorial. "The van. It was meant for you. Who did it?"

Could it be the Bentleys? Belinda was certainly displeased with her, but Hugh had just teased her with a new story that presumably he *wanted* her to write. Was it her talkative anonymous caller, unhappy that Lacey hadn't done exactly as he wished? How about Van Drizzen or whoever killed Esme?

"I don't know, but my dance card is full. I'm going to need more minivans."

Once everyone was stuffed with pizza and chicken, and the tequila and even the worm were gone, the party wound down. Mac announced he and Kim were taking their leave and everyone else followed. Everyone was out the door by eleven-thirty. But Stella refused to go home.

"No way, Lacey. You need me."

"I'll be fine alone."

"You'll be finer with me here. I'll be here in the morning and we'll do your hair." It was hopeless. Stella took the pillows off the couch, pulled out the sofa bed, and made herself comfortable. "Of course, you could put a real bed in that other room, you know."

"It's on my list of one hundred most important things to do next."

Lacey gave up and went to bed. She tossed and turned all night, her dreams full of exploding minivans.

chapter 20

Lacey finally awoke about eight Thursday morning, stumbled toward the shower, and remembered Stella. The stylist was asleep on Lacey's sofa bed, her red crew cut peeking out from under the baby-blue blanket. Lacey crept past her to start a pot of coffee before she took a shower. At least she didn't need to go into the salon this morning.

"Morning, Stella," she said once the coffee was ready. The blanket emitted a groan. "Want some coffee?" Another groan that could have been yea or nay. Lacey figured Stella could help herself.

Lacey poured herself a cup, then stepped out on the balcony to decide what to wear. The sky was gray and gloomy, threatening to rain, which matched her mood. The only good thing was that Vic was not around for one of his special lectures, accompanied with a trip to the range to practice her shooting skills. And the radio said a hurricane would miss Washington after all.

After the previous day's stress, Lacey decided to be comfortable today. She selected high-waisted black slacks, a light blue sweater, and a short black leather bomber jacket, which Stella had talked her into buying in a weak moment. It wasn't vintage, but it was a classic look. *I'll be the bomber today.*

After dressing she came out of the bedroom to find Stella opening her eyes over a steamy cup of black coffee. She wore the large T-shirt she had borrowed from Lacey to sleep in. She squinted at Lacey. "Okay, I'm thinking of a French twist today.

It's classic; everyone wore one, from Joan Crawford to Audrey Hepburn. And it's easy. Where's my bag?"

Stella's large black leather bag must have weighed thirty pounds. It was a mobile salon, and Stella hunched over it like a surgeon selecting tools.

Lacey didn't even argue this morning. Her hair was swept up into a twist with the bangs dipping low on the side. She glanced in the mirror. It was a good look, very uptown, professional, with just a hint of hard edge thrown in. It would go great with the black jacket. Lacey grabbed for her bag, and the new cell phone rang. It was Mac. "Why are you calling me on this thing?" she demanded.

"To see if it works."

She thanked him and tossed the cell phone back in the bag before saying good-bye to Stella, who was back under the covers, fluffing the pillow.

"Uh, don't you have to go to work, Stel?" Lacey hesitated.

"No. Not until one today. Go on. What, you don't trust me here alone?"

"I trust you with my life, Stella. I'd tell you not to let any strange men in, but I know that's your favorite kind. Just lock up when you leave. And put that match in the door, like I showed you."

"Got it." She was asleep again before her head hit the pillow.

Lacey was aching to drive to work in her own car for a change, but with a bomber on the loose, the Z was safer locked up at Asian Engines, and Lacey thought she would be safer on the Metro. She settled into a window seat and tried to empty her mind in that meditative Metro trance that she sometimes managed to achieve. But at the Pentagon station the doors shut and her eyes opened to meet those of a lean man with short cropped hair and a face as spare as a hawk's. Senator Van Drizzen's press secretary, Doug Cable, was swaying over her, gripping the overhead bar. She had seen him at the Appropriations Subcommittee hearing, and if she were in any doubt, his staff ID badge was dangling in front of her face. He wore a subtle moss-green glen-plaid suit, white shirt, and yellow tie. Cable was chewing gum, which struck Lacey as odd because he looked like a tough guy, not a gum-chewing kid. She could see his muscles working from his jaw to the veins in his temples. He leaned into her face and chomped harder on his gum.

"Hey, you're that reporter, right?" She looked up at him blankly. "Ha! Sure you are. Smithsonian, Lacey Smithsonian." He said it with a sneer. He blew a bubble, then stuffed it back in his mouth. "I'm Cable, Doug Cable. With Senator Van Drizzen." He had ignored her at the hearing, but he was not ignoring her now. "You work for that rag, *The Eye Street Observer*. What is your problem, Smithsonian?" His voice carried throughout the rush-hour crowd on the subway car. People were staring, unusual behavior on the Metro.

"I don't have a problem. Not yet."

"That's good. Because the senator had nothing to do with Fairchild. And you're giving him a problem he doesn't need." Chomp, chomp. His jaw muscles threatened to jump out of his skin. She wondered if he were an ex-smoker. "Do you read me?" He shouted it.

"Loud and clear," she answered.

A woman next to her muttered, "Really loud." Cable popped a bubble at her.

"Just what are you doing messing around in libelous accusations? Don't you cover some girly beat? Don't mess with the big boys."

His words didn't bother her, but his voice did.

"Wait a minute," Lacey said. "You're the one who called me, trying to blame the whole budget mess on Ésme Fairchild. That was you, wasn't it?"

Cable swallowed his gum. His eyes were angry slits and his mouth a tight line. "You're sick, you know that? Stay away from my senator, Smithsonian. I'm warning you. Far away."

A copy of the newspaper was in Lacey's lap, the editorial boxed on the front page with a picture of Felicity's still-smoking van. The headline read, "We Will Not Be Intimidated!" She picked it up and snapped it right in Cable's face. He turned his back on her. He got off at the next stop, Archives, a long walk from the Senate. *What the hell?* Lacey thought, *Did he get on this line just to badger me?*

"Don't worry, honey; you turned the tables on him," the woman next to her said. "He's a real lunatic."

The run-in with Cable had done nothing to improve her already dreadful mood. And on top of that, Hansen greeted her with a quick photo shoot for Look Number Four, which he tried to make too arty. Her photographer was getting bored, she thought. But what seemed to make everything worse was that her outfit had turned on her, and she didn't care if the thought was irrational. When Lacey'd gotten dressed, she'd thought her black-slacks-and-blue-sweater outfit was perfectly good, but as soon as she got to the office bad things began to happen to the sweater. It stretched out and hung unevenly. It made her look really fat, she thought, and every time she caught her reflection in the windows of Mac's office, she seemed to grow to huge proportions. The hem unraveled. It drove her crazy. *My God, did the freshness date expire?* She also managed to spill coffee on the sleeve. She tried to clean the spot off, but merely succeeded in creating a ring around the stain and pilling the fabric. She knew she shouldn't worry about such a small thing, especially at the newsroom, where high style meant wearing socks that matched. But she knew that because of her column people held her to a higher standard. *Drat!*

Lacey would never be a slave to the latest styles. She didn't make that kind of money. Nor did she expect other people to be perfect. But they expected her to be at least presentable, if not downright entertaining. She believed that a woman should be able to put together a decent outfit that would complement her size and shape and offer up clues to her basic personality, or at least as much of it as she took to the office. It wasn't too much to ask, but today she was rapidly becoming her own fashion victim. *I'm turning into a "Crimes of Fashion" column,* she thought. *"When Good Clothes Go Bad?" "When Angora At-*

tacks?" Even if it was a great color, the blue sweater was history. It wasn't even noon, but it was time to go shopping.

"I have to get out of here," Lacey said to no one in particular. She took an early lunch and dashed to Filene's Basement on Connecticut Avenue. She tried on half a dozen sweaters before she was satisfied. She settled on a fitted yellow sweater with black piping around the sleeves and square neck. Satisfied that she finally met the Smithsonian standard, she felt she could go on with her day.

When she returned to the office her brand-new desk phone rang. "You didn't hear it from me, but Senator Van Drizzen's wife is moving back to Arkansas today." It was Tyler Stone, Esme Fairchild's Capitol Hill housemate and a staffer for Senator Dashwood. Lacey looked at her new high-tech caller identification screen. It said CALLER UNKNOWN. *That's a big help.*

"Where are you calling from?"

"A pay phone. I can't make this call from the office."

Or the ubiquitous cell phone. "Why are you calling me?"

"I feel bad. For Esme. I had no idea that she would die. I mean, who did?"

"So Mrs. Van Drizzen is really moving out?"

"The van will be there at three."

"Why now?"

"It's all because of that damn scarf that you wrote about. That Bentley scarf that Esme had her eye on? It was the same as the one the senator bought his wife for her birthday three weeks ago. When his wife saw it in the paper, she figured out that he didn't pick it out it for her all by himself."

"Hang on, Tyler. I'm looking for something." Something tickled Lacey's brain. She grabbed a paper from the Van Drizzen press conference. It was a photo of the loving senator and his wife. She hadn't noticed it before, but sure enough—it was the same Bentley scarf. Mrs. Van Drizzen had secured it on one shoulder with an American-eagle pin. "I found it. You're right; it's right there in black and white. The same scarf."

"Van Drizzen sent Esme to Bentley's for it. I guess Esme decided she just had to have one for herself. It made the perfect accessory for my Bentley's suit that she swiped." Tyler paused. "I didn't mean that how it sounds."

Marcia had told Lacey that Van Drizzen was going to buy Esme something very special. Perhaps that would be a Bentley's scarf and the good senator intended to pick up the bill?

"Do people on the Hill think he's involved with Esme's death?"

"Not really. Esme wasn't Van Drizzen's first forbidden intern, and none of the others are dead, right? Lots of people think it's just the fickle finger of fate shining a light on his sins. His turn, you know?"

"Then Esme wasn't the only one he was sleeping with right now, was she?"

"There are rumors of some others. But I don't know any names."

For interns, Washington was a big game of musical beds, and yet grown-up women couldn't get dates. "I appreciate the information, but why are you so interested in telling me all this?"

"You want to find out the truth about Esme. I'm down with that, and squawking to a fashion reporter is more amusing than tipping off the political reporters."

How wonderfully condescending of you. But useful. "You wouldn't happen to be one of those other women wanting to shine a light on the senator's sins, would you?"

"Me? I'm just an informed source. Gotta go; my ride's here." Tyler hung up.

An informed source who may have slept with Van Drizzen and wanted to see him get his, Lacey thought. Esme's death was a good excuse for all sorts of sources, informed and otherwise, to kick up the dust, spread rumors and innuendo, and float trial balloons. No doubt Van Drizzen's political opponents were waiting to see where the dust settled. Lacey dialed Van Drizzen's office. Doug Cable refused to take her call. Instead she was passed off to a junior press flack who offered a very polite "No comment."

Within a half hour after Lacey's call, the senator's office issued a statement that he and Mrs. Van Drizzen were separating amicably, but he was hopeful of an eventual reconciliation and asked the press "to respect his family's privacy in this difficult time," *blah blah blah.* The statement categorically denied that there was any connection to Esme Fairchild's death.

Mac sent a photographer to take pictures of the moving vans outside the Van Drizzens' stately McLean home. *The Eye* planned to rerun photos of the senator's wife wearing the Bentley scarf and the Bentley scarf Esme planned to buy, side by side. They were intended to let the readers draw their own conclusions. A leak from the coroner's office informed Trujillo that Esme was strangled with a silk scarf.

"Tony, what kind of scarf was it?" Lacey demanded.

"Hey, man, don't torture me. Don't pull this fashion clue stuff on me."

"What did it look like?"

"Caked with grime and mud. You saw the body."

"It would help if we knew what brand it was. There might be a label."

He groaned. "I'll work on it."

Lacey's head was spinning by the time Jeffrey Bentley Holmes called from New York, his voice full of concern. "I just heard some awful news. Is it true your car was the target of that insane explosion?"

"Luckily it wasn't my car. I'm fine." She heard him relax. "But it gets worse." She noticed that her desk was a disaster and Honey Martin's flowers were dead. Balancing the phone receiver on her shoulder, she dumped them in the trash can.

"What?" The concern was back.

"Your mother paid me a visit yesterday."

He whistled. "What did she do now?"

"I know this sounds loony, but she tried to buy me off." Lacey tried to move the papers around into organized stacks, but it was a losing battle. "Apparently I'm not a suitable match, whatever that means. I told her we only had dinner. Once."

Jeffrey sighed. "I'll double whatever she offered you if you just ignore her."

"She's done this before?" *Of course she has.*

"I'm afraid so. And unfortunately, there is simply nothing I can do about her. I should have warned you, but I never even told her about you. I don't know how she found out."

"Maybe she's having you followed."

"Mother? She's not that organized. She's really quite harmless. Yet annoying." His exasperated tone changed. "Lacey, let me make it up to you."

"I don't know if anything in the world can salve my wounded pride. I usually pass muster with boys' mothers."

"Dinner tomorrow night. Any place you want."

"That's a start."

She felt herself smile and noticed Trujillo crossing her path. She swiveled her chair away from him and looked out the window at Farragut Square. "How about something relaxed, casual, where they serve great Mexican food?" *And it doesn't cost a month's rent.*

"You're on." They said good-bye, and she thought about how much she needed a relaxed night out. Of course, that wasn't what Stella would say she really needed.

"Smithsonian, you got a date?" She heard Trujillo's boots stop behind her chair.

"You are so nosy, Tony."

He spun her chair around. "But I'm right. You're grinning like a Cheshire cat. Who is it?"

"Jeffrey Bentley Holmes, if you must know."

He stood back, alarmed. "One of the infamous Bentley Boys? I mean, that family has not got a good record with women. You know that better than anyone."

"He's not like the rest of the family. I hope."

The horror of the Bentleys spurred Tony to action. "I'll take you out for a steak, Lacey. On me."

She laughed. "And deprive the rest of the female population of your divine company?"

He smirked and started rearranging the papers on her desk so he could sit there. "It would be a sacrifice I'm willing to make."

"You're cruising for a bruising, Trujillo."

"You are really going out with him? What about Vic?"

She froze for a moment. *Indeed, what about Vic?* "You are not my duenna."

"Perhaps you need one. Is it over with Vic?"

"Vic who?"

"Do you have your cell phone?"

"You know I do. I'm ignoring it."

"Let me see it." Lacey moaned and produced the little monster. Tony punched in some numbers. "Now I'm on your speed dial."

"You and the rest of the world, Trujillo, but what if you have a hot date?"

"*If?* Simple. I'll just tell her you're my ailing mother."

Lacey hurled a copy of the morning paper at him. He ducked and ran away, but not before he cast a forlorn look at Felicity's empty desk.

Something needed to be done, and Lacey needed help. There was no privacy in the newsroom, so Lacey ducked into the Mayflower Hotel to use the telephone. She had just enough change for the call. She thought briefly about using her new phone, but cell phones could be monitored. She would answer if it rang, she decided, but she wasn't touching it except in an emergency. She hesitated for a moment, then picked up the pay phone and dialed.

"Brooke, it's me. I need your help, and Damon's too."

"Lacey? What's that noise behind you? Wait—are you calling from a pay phone?"

"Yes." Lacey said. She felt like a jerk, but she didn't care. She did not want this phone call traced or monitored. "Indulge me."

"Okay, we're there for you. What's up?"

"I need the sort of convoluted, conspiracy-crazed thought processes that only you two have."

"I'm flattered," Brooke purred. "Go on."

"I have to hide something that I don't want found. It needs to be taken to a self-locking storage facility."

"Your car?"

"No, that's locked up at the garage. Just come over at nine, possibly with Damon and his most trusted confidants, if he has any."

"You're thinking about a diversion?"

"A diversion? Sure, whatever."

"Right, we'll need at least three cars to throw off anyone who might be watching."

"Three cars?" Someone was waiting for Lacey get off the phone. *Why doesn't he have a cell phone like everyone else on the planet?* She hoped he wasn't listening to her conversation. "I don't really think anyone is watching."

"Come on. The FBI's Undertaker is knocking at your door. He may not care if you personally get blown up, but he wants to be around to pick up the pieces and bag his quarry."

"And that quarry would be?" Lacey turned to look at the person behind her. He ostentatiously looked at his watch.

"Whoever killed Esme Fairchild is undoubtedly the same person who is at the heart of the mysterious computer adjustments in the appropriations budget. This killer is at the core of the congressional ring of sleazeballs preying on the tender young flesh of innocent interns."

"You say that with such relish," Lacey said. Since she and Lacey had conducted a bit of surveillance work in the spring, Brooke was more than ready to taste a little adventure. She spent her days looking for loopholes in federal regulations and writing briefs that were anything but brief. Life as an attorney was not colorful enough for Brooke Barton, Esquire.

"And it almost sounds plausible when you say it, Brooke. But please, don't jump to any conclusions," Lacey said, although she knew there was no way that was going to happen.

Back at the office, Lacey returned a call from the woman who administered pensions for retirees of the old ILGWU. Her name was Sal. "Oh, yeah, this is your lucky day, Ms. Smithsonian.

Miss Dorrie Rogers turns out to be a Dorothy Rogers who qual-
ified for a pension. She stayed with the Bentley company until
she retired fifteen years ago."

"Is she still alive?"

"Oh, yeah. I already called her about you wanting to contact
her. Sharp as a knife. Not like some, you know. She never married, no family. Kind of a shame. But a union member all her
life."

"Can I call her?"

"You're cleared for takeoff." Sal rattled off Miss Rogers's
phone number.

Lacey dialed, then listened to the phone ring. A raspy voice
answered. "I've been waiting for your call," the voice said,
after Lacey introduced herself.

Miss Rogers explained that after the initial contact by Sal at
the pension office, she had, with the help of an aide at her
assisted-living facility, surfed the Web in the home's library
seeking information on Lacey Smithsonian and found the stories
in *The Eye.* "I guess you're interested in what happened to
Gloria Adams."

"Yes, please, what can you tell me?" Lacey knew she was
being too eager.

"What makes you think I know anything?"

"You were her roommate. I'd like to know more about her.
And I'd love to meet you. Anyone who knew my aunt Mimi is
someone I want to meet."

Although her health was frail, Dorrie was sound of mind,
and she remembered her few contacts with Mimi vividly.
"Well, I suppose any niece of Mimi Smith's is all right with me.
But it's not the kind of story I'm going to tell on the telephone."

Dorrie Rogers resided in a facility in New Jersey, near
Princeton. "It's a tomb for the living. We just haven't been em-
balmed yet." Lacey made arrangements to visit over the weekend. At Dorrie's suggestion, they agreed that Lacey would
claim to be a remote relative, a Miss Lacey Smith, when she
came to visit on Saturday afternoon. Miss Rogers also mentioned that visiting relatives usually brought a little something

to show that they cared, flowers perhaps, or a box of chocolates. But of course, she sighed, she had no real relatives left in the world. Lacey got the message. She would take care of shopping for Dorrie Rogers tomorrow. Right now she had a diversion to attend to.

Lacey Smithsonian's

FASHION BITES

When Bad Clothes Happen to Good People

Sometimes it just happens. You think you're wearing a great outfit, or an okay outfit, or at least something you're not ashamed of. Then it happens. You realize that what looked like a good idea in the dim light of dawn has turned out in the cruel light of day to be a fashion disaster. You may or may not actually look that bad to others, who, after all, have their own fashion disasters to worry about, but your clothes have suddenly turned on you, the little traitors, and they're making you feel awful.

It's probably not true that all eyes are upon you, staring in horror and then looking away in embarrassment from your fashion faux pas, your disgraceful hanging hem that suddenly gave way, the disgusting coffee stain on your white slacks, or the unexpected gap between overstressed blouse buttons—but then again, maybe they are. Nip that nasty wardrobe malfunction in the bud—now.

Why did this happen? Perhaps it's because you have forgotten just how bad those treacherous clothes really are. You've enabled them. You've made excuses for them. You've lied to yourself and said, "I know this skirt made me look fat before, but I've lost five pounds. It's not the skirt's fault." Oh, yes, it is. That skirt hates you, and skirts gathered at the waist hate everybody. And here are some other turncoats to watch out for.

- *Incorrigible stain suckers.* You thought that stain came out in the wash, but you were wrong, because you ironed them in the dark early in the morning on a towel on your dining room table because you were too lazy to get out the ironing board. Those slacks were hiding that stain like a terrorist in a spider hole. And white slacks just love to guzzle black coffee, spaghetti sauce, and ink. They like the taste. They'll find more.

- *Knee-high hose under your skirt.* No one will notice? Trust me, people will notice—when you sit, when you walk, when you bend over to buckle that shoe that won't stay buckled (another little traitor). You may think it would be fun to feel like Marilyn Monroe—until you've had a Marilyn Moment with a sudden updraft up your skirt on K Street. And men will bear me out here: Marilyn wasn't wearing knee-high hose.
- *The closet calamity waiting to happen.* That polyester of unknown origin that drapes beautifully on the hanger? Go ahead, put it on—and just watch it stretch or shrink or bag or bulge or creep up in very unflattering ways, all while you're wearing it. How does it do that? *It's alive!* This stuff belongs in a dark closet in a horror movie, not yours.
- *The sentimental favorites.* That adorable miniskirt you loved in college, the frilly blouse that made you feel so dressy once upon a time, the little cropped top you had such a fling with one summer long ago. You still love them, but they have a secret: They hate you. They are *so* over you. They think you're a little, well, *old* for them now. And if you take them out on a date, they will break your heart. There is only one cure: You must be brutal. You must cut them out of your life.

Lacey's Law: When bad clothes happen to good people, fight back. Toss them, give them away, turn them into rags, or give them to Goodwill. If you don't they will haunt you with the tenacity of a polyester monster from the back of the black lagoon otherwise known as your closet.

chapter 21

Lacey took the precaution of shutting all her blinds before Brooke's team arrived at her apartment. She had taken down her hair and changed into jeans with her new butter-colored sweater, the better to be spotted. If anyone was following her that was okay, diversion-tactic-wise. And the match had been undisturbed—she felt safe for the moment.

Remembering her hostess duties, she was prepared with three dozen Mrs. Fields cookies and several six-packs of sodas. Alcohol would not be a good idea for a conspiracy meeting. And just in case they were all on the Atkins diet, she had picked up some fresh strawberries and a stack of protein bars. *Yeah, right, I'll be eating those myself for the rest of the week.*

She had just a few minutes to call Miguel to ask him to lock up the Gloria Adams pattern and the still unfinished dress.

"Are you kidding? Hello! I am guarding it with my life, and several of my friends' lives. You think I pay no attention?"

"I love you, Miguel."

"Love you too. You are going to be fabulous. Now, I have things to do. See you later, sweetie." She hung up and hoped she had thought of everything.

Brooke showed up right on time. As per her instructions, the others showed up spaced at irregular intervals. Damon arrived about fifteen minutes after Brooke, dressed in black. He was followed by a couple of friends, all in black, and then three more guys showed up, more casually dressed in blue jeans and shirts, like construction guys after calling it a day. Damon introduced them all by code names. Like the rest of the team, Brooke was dressed in stylish burglar black. Lacey thought they didn't have to be quite so obviously coconspirators. Men in Black, *the alternative version.*

"Okay, what's our scenario, Lacey?" Brooke flipped her blond braid over her shoulder and whipped out a Palm Pilot.

"This may be crazy—"

Damon interrupted her. "We wouldn't be here if we thought it was crazy. I really believe some people are just like lightning rods for the truth, and you may be one of them."

Lacey was beginning to feel very foolish.

"You're certainly dressed like a lightning rod," Brooke put in. "Don't you have anything in black?"

"I wasn't dressing for anything as dramatic as a covert operation," Lacey said. "I just need a few things moved to a safe location. A storage unit or something. It's important that they not be found." She picked up several manila folders that contained all the Gloria Adams documents, letters, and patterns. "First, I'd like copies of all the documents to be put in different locations. The originals are already taking up residence in a safety deposit box at Burke and Herbert Bank and Trust. I brought them there after work."

Damon took one set and leafed through them. "Smart move, Smithsonian. This way, if anything happens to you, we still have the evidence."

Brooke stepped in quickly to reassure Lacey. "But nothing is going to happen to you; we'll make sure of that."

Lacey wasn't terribly reassured. She showed them Aunt Mimi's black Bentley suit. She had already taken the jeweled button covers off and secured them in the safety-deposit box. They may be only costume jewelry, but Hugh Bentley seemed very fond of them.

"I interrupted a clumsy break-in attempt here Tuesday night," Lacey said, watching Brooke's mouth fall open. "It may have nothing to do with the explosion, but Hugh Bentley wants this suit and he wants it bad." Nobody cracked a smile. Nobody said, "Who's Hugh Bentley?" Nobody said, "That old dude?"

That was good, but somebody with a code name asked what made it so valuable. "Bentley asked me to donate it to his museum and offered me a trade: two couture dresses, my choice, worth many thousands of dollars. I said no. This suit was the original prototype for one of his most famous suits. It was designed in 1943 by a young designer named Gloria Adams. Bentley put his name on her designs, and then she disappeared. By the way, Damon, none of this is for publication yet, because it is not proven yet. And it's my story. If it is a story."

"Okay, but someday I'm going to write about it—and about tonight's adventure. But only after the truth comes out. Deal?"

"After my story is published." *He'll make me look like a lunatic.* "Anyway, we'll talk about it later. Are you still interested?"

"Of course, but—"

"Damon, darling, she's obviously in danger, someone tried to break in, and someone tried to blow up her minivan." Brooke looked soulfully into Damon's eyes. He softened instantly. "And she doesn't even have a minivan!"

Lacey took back the floor. "I believe this suit and other materials can prove that Hugh Bentley stole Gloria Adams's designs and made his fortune by dancing on her bones."

"She's the one who disappeared from the factory during the war?" Damon asked. "You think he killed her? But you didn't put that in your story in *The Eye*."

"You can't print it. There's no way to prove it yet. Maybe never. But his early reputation was based on her work, and now he wants to enshrine his reputation in his self-named museum. I have original patterns, letters, photographs, and supporting materials from Gloria Adams. If all these materials are destroyed, then Hugh Bentley will have won. And this trunk. I also need this trunk moved." The code-named crew stared at the trunk, waiting for the explanation.

"Oh, Lacey, Aunt Mimi's trunk?" Brooke asked. "But why?"

"There are irreplaceable things in there. They may not all be Adams designs, but they are priceless to me. They could be stolen or destroyed in Bentley's drive to obliterate the evidence. If Hugh finds out that this was Mimi's trunk, he would be just as happy to destroy it. He denies that he knew Mimi, but I know that after Gloria disappeared, Mimi made his life miserable during the war by having his factory investigated. I know that sounds crazy now, but it was deadly serious during World War Two. They never proved that Hugh Bentley was involved, but two of his drivers went to prison for two years for smuggling contraband nylons."

"Obviously," Damon said, "they rolled over and took the rap for Bentley, for a price. Now the Bentley Museum has an extra forty million because of a snafu in the appropriations bill."

"But what does this have to do with Esme Fairchild being found dead at Huntley Meadows?" A guy Damon had introduced by the code name Turtledove spoke for the first time. A huge man, he looked like he was a mixture of a dozen ethnicities. He was hard-muscled, dark-skinned, with wavy black hair. He had beautiful bones and a deep, seductive voice.

"It's a funny thing about connections, Turtledove. They are not always apparent," Damon suggested. "Things that happened back then may have created a vortex of evil that still swirls around us unseen. Swirls around Lacey. And Esme. And the trunk."

"Vortex of evil, dude." Turtledove grabbed a Coke. "Fair enough. I'm there."

Lacey kept her thoughts to herself and tried not to smile. They made her paranoia seem very pale—and positively justified.

The team got to work planning. Lacey carefully packed Aunt Mimi's suit inside the trunk. Copies of all the patterns and materials went with Brooke, duplicates with Damon, and another set inside the trunk. Two of the others also took copies, sealed in manila envelopes. The entire team whipped out their cell phones and exchanged numbers. They looked like a phone commercial. Lacey was embarrassed, but she pulled out her own for show. Brooke's eyes went wide and she almost smiled, but she said nothing. Turtledove and another guy, code-named

Hawkeye, carried the trunk down to the service dock, with Code Name Daisy and Code Name Gibraltar as lookouts, and loaded it into an anonymous white van for its trip to a self-locking, high-security storage unit in Fairfax County owned by the Bartons.

Daisy and Gibraltar followed the white van in a black SUV to make sure it wasn't tailed. In the meantime, Brooke, Lacey, and Damon strolled into Old Town for a late-night margarita and an order of nachos, just in case Lacey was being followed. Another member of the crew, a large man with a shaved head, Code Name Rosebud, stayed behind in Lacey's dark apartment to see if anybody would try to break in, and to monitor incoming calls on the answering machine.

After dinner Brooke and Damon escorted Lacey back to her apartment. Rosebud reported that nothing happened. A couple of hang-ups, and a guy named Vic left a message saying hello. Nothing else. Lacey sighed. *Vic calls and I'm out playing secret agent. Figures.*

"Vic? Lacey, I think you have something to tell me," Brooke said. "Not to mention your break-in attempt and your new little toy . . ."

"Please, Brooke, some other time." Brooke acquiesced but threw her a meaningful look before heading out, holding hands with Damon.

Lacey was glad that Mimi's trunk was secure, but the apartment felt lonely without it anchoring the living room. And the sofa bed was empty too. Stella's off-and-on boyfriend, Bobby Blue Eyes, was back in town—and Stella was making up for lost time. After the crowd was gone, she sat out on her balcony to look at the Potomac. She noticed the dim red glow of a cigarette in one car in the parking lot far below, but the driver never emerged or started the car to leave, and eventually the glow went out. Maybe it was Turtledove watching over her under orders from Brooke. *Or maybe not.* Lacey shivered, went inside, and locked the balcony door.

*   *   *

Lacey decided on Friday morning that she was sick of being a lily-livered coward. In an act of defiance, she chose an arrest-me-red vintage suit from the late Forties. The jacket had a nipped-in waist that draped long over her hips. The skirt was slightly flared with side slits. It was sexy and attention-getting and she didn't care. She teamed it with a sassy little bag that sported red roses swimming in a field of yellow and red.

She showed up at Stylettos for her final Forties hairdo with a present for Stella: a gift certificate at the stylist's favorite leather store in Georgetown. Although Lacey could not imagine what on earth Stella might possibly lack in the world of leather, her stylist was thrilled.

"Mmmm, leather. You really know the way to a girl's heart. I'll treat myself this weekend. Thanks, Lacey." She kissed the certificate and tucked it into her cleavage.

"It's the least I could do," Lacey said. "Thanks for looking out for me."

"No problem. Your sofa bed is pretty comfortable, considering."

"Considering what?"

"Considering I don't usually sleep alone."

"Right. How is Bobby?" Lacey was led to the shampoo bowl. She put a towel around her shoulders and sat down in the chair.

"Fabulous, and I'm not sharing." With that Stella got down to the serious business of creating a Forties look to complement Lacey's bold choice in suits. "There's only one thing we can do to your hair that will hold its own with that suit—Rita Hayworth!" She pronounced it as if it were law. Lacey had been prepared to be a little rebellious today in her saucy red suit, but the mere mention of the goddess of *Gilda* sent a shiver up the back of her neck.

"Okay, Stella, make it pure danger."

Stella took over, washed Lacey's hair, applied styling gel, and made her sit under the hairdryer for forty minutes.

Lacey enjoyed her coffee and the latest edition of *The Eye Street Observer,* especially its photos of Mrs. Van Drizzen and the matching Bentley scarves. Her "Crimes of Fashion" column was missing; Stella had already cut it out and passed it around the salon. She saw it tacked on a bulletin board near the front door.

CRIMES OF FASHION

No Such Thing as a Fashion Clue?

By Lacey Smithsonian

You are what you wear—aren't you? Your clothing is a clue to your personality, your lifestyle, your many moods. But believe it or not there are some people who believe that there is no such thing as a fashion clue. Most of them are men and some of them are cops, the very people you might think would appreciate a fashion clue. Make a sports analogy and they can analyze it and categorize it and beg for more, but throw them a fashion clue and they call it a foul.

But not you, stylish reader. You observe people every day and draw conclusions based on what they wear. Think you can decipher a fashion clue? Here are a few test questions for those who dare.

Your normally over-the-top casual coworkers start wearing suits and ties, heels and hose. What does it mean? Are they looking for a new job or a getting a promotion? Are they going to a funeral after work or a wedding? When a friend suddenly stops wearing makeup, puts on weight, and wears baggy clothes, is she depressed, pregnant and elated, getting in touch with her inner slob, merely following a fad, or joining a cult?

Even experienced fashion observers might not know for sure. But they would know these are clues. *Fashion clues.*

So when it was discovered that Esme Fairchild planned to go to a fancy boutique to purchase an expensive Bentley's silk scarf the same day she disappeared, and she was later found strangled with a silk scarf, that too is a fashion clue. A clue that even the most fashion challenged could not miss—unless you're a fashion-clueless detective. . . .

Approaching minute forty under the hair dryer, Lacey realized she should call Mac to tell him she'd be late, as if he couldn't tell. She gingerly pulled out her new cell phone and pressed one button, hoping it was the speed-dial code for Mac, not one of the other dozen numbers already in her phone. She slipped out from underneath the hood.

To her relief Mac answered on the first ring. Lacey explained that her hair styling session was running longer than usual. "Today's the last day, right?" Mac asked. "For your multiple-personality hairdo thing?"

"That's right."

"I hope it's a good one; I'm sending Hansen over there."

"Wait a minute; you want him to take photographs over here?"

"Yeah, your pal Stella suggested it the other night over fried chicken. She said it was your idea. It's all set."

The bobby pins came out, and the curls spilled down. Stella attacked with brushes and sprays and enough attitude to raise Rita Hayworth from the dead. Sure enough, the result was moody and curly and smoldering. Stella tilted Lacey's head back to just the right angle in the mirror, and there it was: a hint of Rita Hayworth as the free-spirited heroine of *Gilda*. Parted on one side, it was Rita, but not Rita's red; it was Lacey's own light brown with Stella's rich golden highlights. All she needed was attitude.

"Oh, my God, that's it!" Stella yelled. "Lacey, that's it!"

"What? What is it?"

"It's the hair to go with the Gloria Adams dress. This is it."

Lacey cocked her head. It was definitely the look for the dress. *Who knows? Maybe this time someone on the street in D.C. will even turn around to look at me.*

Hansen chose that moment to pop into the salon and stare at the lady in red. As soon as Stella saw the cameras, she started applying blush to her own cheeks and spiking her hair with extra gel. By the time she was finished, she looked rather like a proud mad scientist with her latest creation. Happily for Lacey, Stella was the focus of the photos this time, and Lacey was seen only in profile, the better to show off the hairstyle. The shoot went more smoothly without Mac and Trujillo second-guessing the photographer. But Stella more than made up for it.

At the office the reaction to Look Number Five was generally favorable, in that timid, asexual, Washingtonian way, although Tony Trujillo's eyes went perceptibly wider when he saw her. But he had his doubts, all of which he had no trouble sharing. "I don't know, Smithsonian. You really want to waltz into the tiger's cage looking like that?"

"Like what?"

"Like one of those babes they painted on bombers in World War Two."

"Oh, Tony, you think I look glamorous!"

He grinned. "Just call me if you get into trouble."

"What kind of trouble could she get into?" Mac wanted to know.

"Smithsonian kind of trouble," Trujillo said. "She's going to dinner with a Bentley. And tigers don't change their stripes."

"Don't worry; I'm a tiger tamer."

"You bringing a pair of scissors with you?" Tony prodded.

"That's not funny."

"No, it's not." Mac stepped into the fray. "From now on there will be no scissors, no fooling around, and no exploding vehicles. Isn't that right, Smithsonian?"

"Mac, you must be psychic."

He favored her with one of his wise parental looks. "Let's keep it that way." He marched off as Tony sat down in Felicity's chair and leaned back.

"By the way, Tony, is there any more news about the scarf? Is it a Bentley?" Lacey said.

Tony kicked his feet up on the desk. "I know nothing. Gary

Braddock is totally pissed that we printed the leak, so the gag is on."

"How about Van Drizzen, anything new?" Lacey opened drawers and put her bag away.

"Only that the press guy, Cable, isn't talking to *The Eye* anymore. You know him?"

"Gum-chewing, Metro-screaming psychopath? Yeah, I know him."

"Mutual admiration society, I see. What's up with that?"

Lacey didn't get a chance to answer. A riled Peter Johnson paid her a visit. "What the hell are you doing on my beat again?"

She and Tony exchanged looks. "Does this have anything to do with Van Drizzen?"

"Listen, Miss Smithsonian, you can play dress-up." He who knew nothing about how to dress sneered at her vintage red power suit. "But don't play reporter on my territory. The Hill isn't your beat."

Her face burned as curious faces from the newsroom were drawn to today's episode of *The Daily Planet, Eye Street Observer* style. Trujillo started to step in, but Lacey was having none of it: this was her fight.

"I take it you mean my story on the Van Drizzen affair. Here's a tip for you, you insufferable prig," Lacey said. "Why don't you ask Doug Cable why he's trying to pin the blame for the whole appropriations bill mess on a dead woman who can't defend herself? Maybe Cable had something to do with rearranging the numbers on his laptop, being the lapdog of Senator Van Drizzen, who just might have been in bed with the Bentleys, as well as with Esme Fairchild." She threw her copy of *The Eye* at him. Mac stormed up the aisle, a fresh cup of coffee in his hand. No one spoke for a moment; then Mac broke the silence.

"Those might be very good questions, Johnson. Get on it."

Being in a snit was one of Johnson's talents, and he was working on a big one. "But they won't talk to *The Eye!* Not even me! Because of *her.*"

Mac grimaced and rubbed his jaw. "If everybody liked us, we wouldn't be doing our job. Now go find someone who will talk to you."

That afternoon Hansen presented Mac with a proof sheet of all the Smithsonian shots, which was ordained as the big Sunday LifeStyle piece. Hansen could do very nice work, but he couldn't resist at least one eye-rolling or eyes-shut-mouth-open shot in every batch. Mac actually consulted Lacey's opinion on the photos of her five looks, which she chalked up to the power of the red suit. They wrangled over the exact choice for a half hour before they finally agreed on the five shots.

Lacey finished her last assignment of the day, dredging up glowing adjectives for the big makeover story and lauding her stylist, Stella, as a genius. *There'll be no living with her after this.*

chapter 22

Lacey waited for Jeffrey at the entrance of her building. She didn't know how she felt about letting him into her apartment. She loved her place, with its view of the Potomac River from every room, the building's slight shabbiness notwithstanding; it was as comfortable as an old chenille bedspread. But certainly it would never measure up to a Bentley's standards.

Despite Trujillo's earlier fear, she had no intention of wearing the red suit to dinner. After dark, it was a suit that would say, "Hey, sailor, how about a hot date," and she preferred to speak a little more softly tonight. She selected instead comfortable old blue jeans that were snug and flattering in an innocent girl-next-door kind of way. And a cherry-red sweater with a V neck and a fitted midriff; it was sexy and reliable and it had never betrayed her. It was warm enough for sandals. She grabbed a shoulder bag, and against all her better instincts tossed in the new cell phone.

Jeffrey pulled into the circular drive in the last vehicle Lacey ever expected to see a Bentley driving: a battered old pickup truck. She hopped in before he could get out and open the door. He smiled. "You look great. I'm really glad to see you in one piece," Jeffrey said.

"Me too. Where's your mother?" She looked into the back of the truck.

"Gee whiz, I don't know! Mom, are you back there?"

Lacey laughed. She was ridiculously relieved. "I didn't expect to see a Bentley in a good old American Ford truck."

"It's Mike O'Leary's old truck. A Ford truck man from way back. I finally convinced him to break down and buy a new one if I promised to give the old one a good home."

"O'Leary, the cop who busted the young delinquent Bentley Holmes?" Jeffrey nodded as he pulled into traffic. "Okay, tell me what happened next to the young demon seed. I believe we left him standing on the church steps having a spiritual crisis."

"At dinner," Jeffrey promised. "Where to?"

Lacey navigated them to Taquería Poblano, a cozy place that featured colorful surroundings, great margaritas, and a friendly staff. It was located in the Del Ray neighborhood of Alexandria and always seemed to be packed. Jeffrey ordered two margaritas. Lacey specified hers on the rocks, no salt, while a muffled ringing sounded nearby. She looked around. *Somebody answer that damn cell phone!* It took her another minute to realize that the annoying sound was coming from her own purse. She ripped open her bag and retrieved the irritating hunk of plastic and metal. "I'm so sorry. It's new, what with the explosion and all," she said to Jeffrey by way of apology. Into the phone she said, "Hello?"

"Are you okay?" This was not an entirely new side of Tony Trujillo, Boy Scout and protector of womenfolk, but it was a much more intrusive side.

"I'm fine. What do you think you're doing? And who gave you this number?"

"You did, remember? Chill out, Smithsonian; I'm just checking. I'm standing by. If you're in trouble, signal me."

"Honestly, I'm okay."

"You have a history of provoking homicidal maniacs."

She held the phone up. "He's worried about my safety."

"It's true, you know," Jeffrey said, licking salt from his glass. "I might be some kind of maniac."

"Don't worry, Tony; I have a steak knife."

"As long as you're armed, man. I'll leave you to your dinner." Tony hung up. Jeffrey waited for an explanation.

"The cavalry is waiting in the wings to rescue me from you. Just so you know."

He sighed and leaned back into the booth. "Ah, the curse of the Bentleys strikes again. Now you have a taste of what it's like to belong to the family. Women scatter like hunted prey. Men surround the castle with clubs and torches. So, is this guy your boyfriend?"

"No, that was Tony Trujillo, my buddy from work, police reporter. He's written just as much about Esme Fairchild as I have. But no one's gone after him." Lacey felt a little irritated when she realized this. "No one blows up Tony's Mustang. Why am I so special?"

"You should see how irritated you look. But Lacey, I honestly don't think my family had anything to do with the bomb in the minivan."

"Not even on aesthetic grounds?"

"Do you have a boyfriend?" It was the subject they had avoided the first time. She kept trying to think of Jeffrey as a source, but it was getting more difficult.

"That's the million-dollar question. Kind of, sort of, I don't really know. He's been out of town getting a house ready to sell to his ex-wife. Or maybe he's buying what the ex-wife is selling. What about you? Do you have a girlfriend?"

"Not at the moment. Although my mother keeps throwing girls named Muffy at me."

"I know the type." She immediately thought of Tyler Stone, beauty, breeding, and bucks, a closet full of chichi shoes, the type poor Jeffrey was probably destined for. "I met someone your mother would love. She works for Senator Dashwood."

"That sounds like Tyler Stone."

"Oops. You know her? Washington is such a small town." *Or maybe being rich is its own small town.* Lacey realized she should tread carefully here.

"Our families know each other, yes. Mother would like that. Tyler would definitely be 'suitable'—she's pretty and she knows all the right people. But Tyler"—Jeffrey shook his head—"is not my type. Besides, she doesn't make me laugh."

"Nothing like a good minivan explosion to lighten the atmosphere."

"That's not exactly what I meant, but you nevertheless always make me smile." He favored her with one of his dazzling smiles. Lacey noticed a young brunette at the next table sneaking looks at Jeffrey while her boyfriend was figuring out the bill. "But I didn't take you out to dinner to explain my family. Or talk about all my nongirlfriends."

"Then tell me about O'Leary. You're fifteen, at the church, St. Timothy's."

Jeffrey visibly relaxed and continued the story he began at their first dinner together. "A large hand clamped down on the back of my neck as I stood at the back of the church and a familiar, oddly musical voice whispered in my ear, 'So, Mr. Jeffrey Bentley Holmes has come to see how the other half lives? All right. I'm going to escort you to your seat. And you are going to stand when we stand, kneel when we kneel, and sit when we sit. And you're not leaving till I give you permission. Do you understand?' "

Lacey pictured the big Irish cop with the skinny young heir. It was hard to keep from giggling. Jeffrey had no idea that Officer O'Leary ushered at the eight-o'clock Mass, still in his police uniform. Nobody left early at St. Timothy's when O'Leary ushered. "He more or less put me on display in the middle of the church. It was excruciating. After the Mass—and I stayed to the very end—O'Leary collared me again. He told me that if I had any money, they served coffee and doughnuts and juice in the community hall after the service. I took it as an order. I was afraid he would tell my mother where I was. To destroy your mother's Mercedes is one thing, but sneaking into Mass with the townies was something else entirely."

"So exactly what religion is your family, Jeffrey?"

"Country club. First Church of Christ, Golf Pro. I barely remember being inside a church of any stripe before that day."

"Did you buy those doughnuts?"

"I was too shy that first time. I went to prep school, and I didn't know anybody from public school or the local Catholic school. O'Leary guided me to the community hall and sat me down with his kids. His daughter, Katie, was a blue-eyed, redhaired doll. I didn't dare stare at her under the gaze of her dad. His son, Kevin, was a year older than I was, and he looked like a pretty tough guy himself. I figured he was probably going to take a shot at me as soon as he heard I was part of that Bentley clan. But then O'Leary brought over a tray full of doughnuts and milk and set them down. The only thing he said was, 'This is Jeff. Jeff Holmes.' "

"He didn't tar you with the Bentley brush," Lacey said. "So O'Leary turned out to be a pretty cool guy. And the other one never kicked your ass?"

"Rappoli ushered the nine-thirty Mass. Still does. And he keeps threatening to straighten me out. Still could."

"How did you two wind up buddies? And don't leave out the juicy parts about you and O'Leary's red-haired daughter."

He shook his head sheepishly. "Katie. Kathleen Maureen Bernadette O'Leary. I had a terrible crush on her for years. But I was too afraid of O'Leary to even approach her, and you know how embarrassing my mother can be. Katie's engaged to a great guy now."

"So nothing?" Lacey was so disappointed for him. *Men are such fools.*

"We're great friends," he said, a faint hint of regret in his voice. "I had never been in much of a regular family situation before. Before long I knew all of the O'Learys, Peg, Mike's wife, the kids. Actually, I secretly thought of myself as an O'Leary. By eighteen I think I thought of myself as Catholic. It came as a shock a few years ago when Mike pointed out that I was not, in fact, a baptized Catholic."

"That O'Leary's big on facts, isn't he?"

"Very. I decided to study to become a convert. That, of course, nearly caused a nuclear meltdown in my family. You would have thought I was becoming a monk and tossing away my shares of Bentley Enterprises to the church, as well as depriving my mother of grandchildren."

"I think you ought to tell that to Tyler." They both laughed.

"Anyway, a retreat seemed the perfect way to get away from

all the noise of status, the cacophony of class that seems to be the prevailing mantra in my family."

"What happened?"

"Mother had palpitations, Hugh had a fit, Aunt Marilyn stopped speaking to me. Aaron was merely snide and condescending; he's thinks it's very funny. The upshot is, I dropped the subject, at least in public. And now I'm in the process of converting anyway."

"Oh, my God. How do they like that?"

"It's a secret conversion. Just me and God are in on it. And the O'Learys. And now you."

"Your secret is safe with me." She realized that sounded foolish, considering her job. "At least that particular secret." Jeffrey laughed. "I'm the only Catholic left in my family," she said. "They all lapsed somewhere along the way."

"Good. Now it's your turn to talk," Jeffrey said.

She hesitated for a moment. "If you must know, my family always acted like I was a changeling, the spawn of wayward gypsies. And that the real Lacey Smithsonian was out there somewhere, probably running a cheerleading camp, teaching the little gypsy girls how to shake their pom-poms."

"I'm sure they appreciate you."

"Of course. In the way anthropologists appreciate a specimen of an exotic culture. Lucky for me my sister, Cherise, was a cheerleader and has a fabulous boyfriend who is expected to pop the question at any minute, at least according to my mother. And she drives a minivan that no one will ever blow up. Or maybe it's an SUV; I forget."

Platters of steaming steak fajitas arrived, and they dug in. "Will you be taking time off until they catch the guy who wired your car? I think you should."

"No. I can take care of myself." *Oh, really? Keep telling yourself that.*

He looked doubtful. "It's about the Fairchild thing, isn't it? And now it's that Adams woman from the factory. Who do you think did it?"

"The incident of the minivan? I haven't figured it out." Was he just trying to weasel out information for his family? She didn't want to think that, but she couldn't rule it out.

"I see," Jeffrey said quietly. He reached for her hand. "You have such small hands."

"But they create such big problems. Or so I've been told," she said, drawing them back.

"Don't be afraid of me, Lacey. Maybe I could talk to them," he suggested.

"And say what? 'Please don't blow up Lacey's car or try to break into her apartment, even if you do think they are aesthetically unattractive'?"

"Someone tried to break into your apartment?" He was definitely alarmed now.

"Only sort of. It's okay; I sleep with a baseball bat beside me." *Oh, that sounded good.* She could just imagine what Stella might say: *Sure, shoot yourself in the foot again. Handsome quarterback, there's the pass, but Smithsonian fumbles, and she's out of the game.*

They agreed to an early night, as she had major plans for the next day, which she declined to share. As Jeffrey turned into the circular drive to drop her off, her heart lurched. She recognized a familiar green Jeep Wrangler in the parking lot, and someone was sitting in the driver's seat. *Oh, this is great timing,* she thought. Jeffrey escorted her to the door and kissed her on the cheek.

"I can protect you," he said. "I'm pretty good with a baseball bat."

Lacey imagined Jeffrey and O'Leary with their posse of choirboys coming to her rescue and laughed. "Not tonight, thanks."

Then he looked her in her eyes and kissed her for real. She didn't feel a need to stop him. She kissed him back and wondered if they were being observed. He let her go reluctantly. "Good night, then."

"Sweet dreams, Jeffrey." She wanted to tell him how genuinely nice, how truly decent he seemed. But she knew that would be the wrong thing to say.

Lacey waited for Jeffrey to drive off. And then she waited in the lobby for the driver of the Jeep to stroll up the front walk. Her heart pounded, heat pulsed through her veins, and chills ran up and down her spine. She'd felt something a little bit like it only a moment ago, when Jeffrey kissed her, but they were two different thrills in terms of velocity. That one warmed her; this one made her dizzy.

Vic had been out in the mile-high sun, obviously not bothering with sunscreen. Some dangerous high wattage lit those green eyes, contrasting with his tan skin. His blue jeans and blue work shirt revealed hard muscles that had been at work, presumably on behalf of the former Mrs. Donovan. He looked so good—and so annoyed. She opened the door for him and she wanted him to say something wonderful, like maybe he had missed her.

"So, Lacey, out having a hot date?" That wasn't what she had imagined he would say.

"Not exactly. He is sort of a source. Sort of." *Until that kiss . . .*

"Do you always kiss your sources? Not that it's any of my business."

"It's not like you and I have an agreement."

"We don't?"

"He kissed me, and you would have to pick that moment to arrive. And hello, Vic, long time, no see." Why was she so irritated? she wondered.

"I said I'd be back." Warm breath tickled her neck. His voice teased her.

"Right. I vaguely recall that. Pretty long ago. How was Steamboat?"

"The aspen are all gold now. Same old grandeur. But it was lots of work. The house is almost right for the new buyer."

"That would be Montana, the ex–Mrs. Donovan?" Lacey couldn't help the slight edge in her voice. She walked in slow motion toward the elevator and Vic followed her. She pushed buttons and they rode up to her apartment. "So you're all done with, um, whatever you're done with?"

"I might have to go back to take care of a few more details."

Details like Montana Donovan, or whatever she's calling herself these days? "Then she'll have time to come up with a few more excuses to keep you there."

"It's not like that. You would like her."

"Only men say stupid things like that, Vic. Besides, I've met Montana, remember?"

"You have? I don't remember. You're not jealous, are you?"

"I'm not if you're not. Did you kiss her good-bye?" She unlocked two locks and opened the door for him.

"She kissed me," he mocked her. "You have nothing to be jealous of. Do I?"

Lacey didn't think so. But she wasn't about to tell him that. She merely cocked one eyebrow at him. He swiftly took her in his arms and kissed her till her head swam. He smelled enticingly of spice and exhaustion. She wanted to cling to him, but he broke the moment, entered the apartment, and went directly to the refrigerator. He selected a Dos Equis for himself.

"I see you still have my favorite beer. Do you want one?"

"No, but ice water would be nice." Lacey shut the door, set her purse down, and collapsed on the sofa waiting for him, slipping off her sandals and curling her feet under her. "Have you talked with Stella?" *That would be Stella and the Girls, the amazing one-woman Dupont Circle news bureau.* Vic had gone to Stella in the past for breaking news on Lacey.

He strolled back, beer in one hand, ice water in the other. "But I did call you first. Your machine is probably flashing. You weren't around, so we grabbed a pizza, she and Bobby and I. I can't wait to see the Sunday newspaper and Stella's masterpiece." Lacey could just imagine that gabfest. Stella loved nothing so much as an attentive male audience. "Then I decided to come over and see you in person."

"Okay, what are you so amused about? Talk, Vic."

"Stella tells me she's been doing your hair all week, slaving over a hot curling iron for you."

"Slaving? That witch. It was her idea."

"Something about turning you into a 1940s screen goddess

for some fancy ball. I don't know what that's all about, but it came up in the conversation. And I've always liked 1940s screen goddesses."

"Is that all?"

It turned out also that he'd already checked out DeadFed dot com. "It's trash, but I always read it to make sure you're not in the headlines. But of course, my hopes were dashed. There she is, Lacey Smithsonian and the Amazing Exploding Minivan. I'm not sure I even understand what that was all about, either, but why the hell can't you stay out of trouble?"

"Those are the words I've been dreaming of hearing."

He moved next to her and smoothed her hair off her forehead. "I like your hair. It's nice, sexy. Stella does nice work."

"Stella is a piece of work."

He moved in close to her and gazed into her eyes. "So how is your car?"

How is my car? What a sweet talker! "The Z is at the garage. My mechanic is keeping it locked up for me, boarding it like an old dog at the kennel."

"You need a new car. And I don't want you driving that thing till I check it for explosives. Most mechanics don't know what to look for. But have him make sure your brake lines haven't been cut, things like that. And if you insist on keeping that old dog, excuse me, beloved vintage classic, you should install an alarm system. I'll look into it for you."

"Aye-aye, sir! Any more orders, *mon capitaine*? I haven't seen you in two months and all you want to do is lecture me."

"That's not all I want to do." He looked at her pointedly. She could feel the heat rise in her face, estrogen pumping, thumping, coursing through her body. He had the most distracting effect on her. He touched her face with his fingers delicately, as if she were made of china, then her hair, then ran his fingers down her neck and drew him to her. He kissed her, sending delightful shock waves running through her. She wanted the moment to linger, there in her living room. He let go. *What is it with this guy?*

"Of course, if you could only stay out of trouble we might

be able to, um, catch up with each other. Now that I'm back. Like I said I would be."

"Why do you always assume everything is my fault?"

"Good question. Maybe it's not your fault; maybe you're just like a gigantic magnet for trouble."

"Shut up." She kissed him hard, willing him to extend the moment. But he pulled away.

"Damn, I'm tired," he said. "I just drove fourteen hours today. Too tired to do what I would like to do. And too tired to argue."

"Yeah. We'd probably just wind up in a big fight." She was disappointed and relieved at the same time.

Vic reached out to set his empty beer bottle down on Mimi's trunk without looking, which normally doubled as her coffee table. And then he noticed it wasn't there.

"What happened to the thing, the trunk you had here? I thought that trunk was really important to you. And where do I put my beer in case I have to kiss you again?"

"It's in a safe place. I hope." He stood up and placed his beer on the end table.

"Okay. I sense there is a long story here. Back in a second." He opened the fridge and helped himself to another beer. "Have you not been to the grocery store since I left? It looks like the same provisions you had two months ago."

"The moving crew cleaned me out. There are some crackers and cheese and summer sausage if you're hungry. Or I could cook something," Lacey lied. "I suppose Montana cooks?"

"Montana cooks up a lot of trouble." He stood up. *Aha, I knew it.* "And you attract trouble." He returned with a box of crackers, a block of cheese, and a knife. "Why don't you tell me what's going on?"

And things were going so well, with all that kissing and stuff. They ate all the cheese and they drank all the beer, and they talked till after midnight.

"Let me get this straight." He looked at her through travel-weary eyes. He had been on the road for the last four days. "All you have to do to summon up a dead body is look in an old trunk? And bam, there she is, a sixty-year-old mystery. Most people, Lacey—and this is not a criticism—but most people would find this interesting stuff for dinner conversation. They would not proceed to the point of provoking people to blow up their cars."

"That sounds like a criticism to me."

"By the way, when you were thinking about securing the trunk and taking it to a safe location with such an ingeniously convoluted plan, did you think about your own safety, even once?"

"I really don't want to talk about this anymore, Vic. I have to get up at the crack of dawn." He opened his sleepy eyes wider. "It's a long story," she protested.

"It's a long night."

She explained about Dorrie Rogers and her plans to visit the one woman who might help her understand what happened to Gloria Adams. Vic didn't like it. He didn't like the part about the Bentleys, the missing woman, and the dead intern. And he especially didn't like the part about her impetuous trip to New Jersey to see someone she didn't know, who had been involved in this mess sixty years ago. "I'm sorry, Vic, but this isn't about what you like."

Lacey and Vic said good night in a state of detente. There was another kiss, another moment when they both knew they'd be in Lacey's bedroom in another ten seconds, but they both pulled back. It would be too easy, she thought, and it wouldn't solve any of the issues between them. *Stella will think I'm out of my freaking mind.*

She laid out clean sheets and towels for him and gave him a new toothbrush. She had laid in a supply of extras after Stella's surprise overnighter. Vic insisted that she needed protection and offered to go to New Jersey with her. But Lacey knew he was too tired for another road trip. Besides, she would be safer out of town than at home. Vic finally agreed.

Their relationship was so full of unknowns at this point, full of longings, missed signals, and misunderstandings. The bedroom was off-limits for the moment, they concluded, but spending the night on her sofa, he announced, was the only decent thing to do. After all, he had ratcheted up all her fears, as if there were a troll waiting under the Woodrow Wilson Bridge, just waiting to get his claws on her.

The next morning she awoke to the smell of coffee. Vic opened the door to her bedroom and delivered a cup, along with a plate of freshly toasted English muffins and a slice of cheese. Lacey smiled at the sight of him. She forgot she was wearing her favorite black satin nightgown with the oh-so-revealing décolletage.

"Coffee and breakfast in bed, this is great."

"Smile like that and I will delay that trip of yours."

She felt herself blush and she nearly upset her coffee. *How could Montana let you go?* she thought. But then, she reasoned, *Vic probably only behaves like this when your life is in danger.*

Vic sat on the side of her bed with his own cup of coffee and gave her a few more personal-safety lecture points that he had neglected the night before.

"Nothing is ever easy, is it?" she said.

"Not with you it isn't." They heard the toaster pop. Vic headed for the kitchen.

The moment was gone. *Enjoy the little things,* she told herself as she picked up the muffin. She briefly reflected that for the second time that week someone had sacked out on her popular sofa bed. *I'd better buy a trundle bed before tourist season.*

chapter 23

The weather was back to blisteringly beautiful and she could think of better things to do than head up Interstate 95 to the New Jersey Turnpike in a rental car. As much as she loved her burgundy-and-silver Nissan 280ZX, it was rather noticeable and rather old, and the mysterious minivan bombers must know by now they had gotten the wrong car. While the engine might run forever, its supporting cast of metal, plastic, and rubber parts was proving to be less durable and more delicate. Now she was in some sort of big navy blue box. It said Ford on the trunk and she was grateful not to be driving a big white box, like a refrigerator on wheels.

Vic offered again to go with her, but she refused. She let him drop her off at the rental place and check out the car, which made him feel better.

As she drove, Lacey kept scanning the traffic in her rearview mirror. She didn't think she was being followed. She was beginning to wonder if she had overrated the whole minivan episode. Maybe it really was Felicity's fault after all. It irritated Lacey that everyone, even including her, and most of all Vic, simply assumed she was behind things like that.

Lacey was negotiating the Jersey Turnpike traffic when the cell phone rang and nearly scared her to death. She'd forgotten to turn it off before she started. She ignored it and its persistent annoying ring, which she realized apparently replicated the opening five notes of some vaguely familiar classical piece of music. She managed to get it out of her purse and click it off.

It's bad enough lugging you around, she thought; *I'm certainly not going to answer you, especially while driving.* Every driver in Virginia and the District seemed to be on the phone all the time now, and it drove her crazy.

She pulled over at one of the turnpike rest stops for a quick break, a cup of coffee, and a fill-up for the big blue box. An apple-cheeked young man of about twenty-one pumped her gas. She did a double take: He was so neatly dressed with his blue slacks, white-and-blue-striped shirt, and blue tie, neatly knotted with the tail tucked between his shirt buttons, that Lacey couldn't help herself; she told him how nice he looked, even though smudged with oil. With golden-brown hair and ruddy cheeks he looked like a *GQ* model, but his voice was pure Jersey. His nod to self-expression was rolling the sleeves up over his muscular biceps.

"You think I'd dress like this if I didn't have to?" But he smiled at her as he filled the tank. "Company makes us."

God bless company dress codes. She glanced around to get her bearings. It didn't help. All the Jersey Turnpike stops looked the same to her; she wondered if this was the Molly Pitcher or the James Fenimore Cooper. The cell phone on the passenger seat accused her silently. She turned it back on just for the break and it rang immediately. It was her third cell phone call. Who had her number? For a start, Brooke, Damon, the trunk moving crew, Tony, and Mac. And Vic. She realized she should have asked Mac not to pass it around. At least it couldn't be Stella. Or could it? "Hello?"

"Ms. Smithsonian. Where are you?"

"Who wants to know?"

"Agent Braddock, FBI."

"Top of the morning to you too, Agent Braddock. I'm at a gas station."

"A gas station where?"

"On the road. Why, are you following me?"

"Evidently not, or I wouldn't be calling you."

"How did you get my number?"

"Douglas MacArthur Jones, your editor."

"His friends call him Mac. Is there something I should know, Agent Braddock?"

"Negative. Is there anything I should know, Ms. Smithsonian?"

"I cover fashion. I'm on a fashion-related story and you scoff at fashion clues. So why the big surveillance?" The spiffy attendant handed her the credit card slip to sign.

"If we were surveilling you, Ms. Smithsonian," he said reasonably, "we would know where you were. I'm just keeping in touch. And by the way, I'd never scoff at a fashion clue."

"You're not going to tell me not to leave town, are you?"

"No." He said it with a heavy sigh, as if he had heard this line a lot and he didn't find it particularly clever.

"It's a little late for that anyway."

"You will call me if you uncover any more trouble, won't you?"

"If I require the services of the Federal Bureau of Investigation I will certainly let you know. 'Bye." With that she turned the damn thing off and drove the rental car over to the parking lot in front of the rest stop.

Travelers weary from the endless Jersey Turnpike can count on the Woodrow Wilson or the Richard Stockton or any number of other interestingly named rest stops to refresh them for a few minutes. They supply their own unique entertainment. Lacey was struck by how many basically attractive people she could see in the most extreme fashions. Sky-high heels and tiger-lady nails for the women, and muscle shirts and gelled pompadours for the men, and impressive physiques on both, bursting out of skintight clothing. It was definitely not D.C. *Hunks and babes wearing funny clothes—there's a column in there somewhere.*

The rest of the drive to Dorrie Rogers's assisted-living facility east of Princeton was uneventful. But Lacey couldn't help feeling uneasy. Braddock's call had awakened her imagination once more. Fighting paranoia was hard. What if Agent Braddock thought she was actually onto something important? That thought made her feel better. *Bravado is good. If I'm in danger,*

I must be on the right track. Who knew fashion could be this fun?

She pulled into a small shopping center a few blocks away from Dorrie's home to pick up some fresh flowers and freshen up. She reluctantly turned the cell phone on again. Of course it rang. This time it was Vic.

"Are you playing games with Braddock?"

"What? You know him too?" Vic seem to know entirely too many people in law enforcement everywhere he went.

"We've crossed paths before. I figured he'd be in on your little escapade. We traded information."

"I don't like the way that sounds."

She could hear him chuckle. "He says you're a bit prickly."

"Ha! *I'm* prickly? He doesn't hang around with many reporters, does he?"

With a little extra time on her hands, Lacey sat down at a small coffee shop to relax, take in the crowd, and peruse *The Post*. The Style section featured a retro stylized sketch of the First Lady's outfit for the gala, designed by Aaron Bentley. It was described as a creamy ivory silk with "splendid embroidery." So Aaron had given *The Post* the exclusive. It wasn't surprising that he hadn't given it to her, considering the negative press she had thrown at the Bentleys, but still it grated on her nerves.

A familiar popping sound made her glance over at an intense man sitting near her wearing a white Izod shirt, khaki pants, and Topsiders without socks. He was chewing gum and blowing bubbles between sips of coffee, reading *The Post. Good grief, what's he doing here?* She decided to take the offense.

"Are you following me, Cable?"

He jerked his head up, stared at her in surprise, and snarled, "Me? What the hell are *you* doing in New Jersey?"

"Communing with nature. And you?"

She stood her ground silently while he compulsively blew another bubble. "Okay," he finally said. "This is off the record. Mrs. Van Drizzen is here visiting her son."

"I thought she had the furniture moved back to Arkansas or wherever they're from."

"She did." Cable glared at her and upset his coffee onto the paper. "I'm here to try to convince her to go back to the senator before next year's race. She has to stick with him through this scandal mess. A mess you made a lot worse."

"Just following leads. And why blame the appropriations mess on Esme Fairchild?"

"To take the heat off the affair. Duh. Besides, the little tramp may really have diddled those figures for all I know. She's my number one suspect."

"Is that a quote?"

"Like I said, off the record. For all I know, you're following me. I never want to see you again, Smithsonian. And if you spill one word about this, I will strangle you."

"Under the circumstances, Mr. Cable, that is a very poor choice of words." She pulled out her cell phone. "Want to repeat them to the FBI?"

"Go to hell. You and your crummy paper." He grabbed his coffee and paper and stormed out. He jumped into a white Toyota Camry and roared out of the parking lot.

She was shaking and had to sit down again to calm her nerves. She tried to concentrate on the paper, but she couldn't finish the story; she stuck it in her bag. Maybe she would look at it later. Lacey finished her coffee and a protein bar, then spent a long moment trying to remember where she parked her big bland blue box of a rental car.

chapter 24

Lacey bought a large box of Godiva chocolates and an armload of fresh fall flowers, making sure it was large and colorful with lots of cheerful yellow and orange trumpet lilies and scarlet chrysanthemums. She didn't think Cable or anyone else had followed her to Eastwood Greens, the facility where Dorrie Rogers lived. She locked the rental car while balancing a few other little items for Dorrie in her arms. It seemed like a nice enough place, Lacey supposed, but it was an impersonal low-slung brick building. Opening the large glass-front door, Lacey caught a whiff of pine-scented cleaner mixed with an institutional medicinal smell, as if vaccinations were the order of the day. The linoleum floors were polished but not homey. Lacey stood before a large cheerful receptionist with bright pink blush painted on her cheeks and too much eyeliner on her wrinkled eyes.

"Dorothy Rogers? Why, I can't remember the last time she had a guest. And who did you say you are?"

"Lacey Smith—I'm a distant relative, actually. We'd really lost track of Great-aunt Dorrie. But when I heard she was here and I was near the area, I simply had to visit."

"Why, that's just lovely, dear. And you've brought her such a beautiful bouquet." The woman got the attention of an aide nearby who was pulling dead flowers out of a vase. "Chandra, would you please take Miss Smith to the dayroom? I believe Dorothy is in there." The young woman showed Lacey to a large room, where she was met by a tiny woman with wire-framed glasses that enlarged her eyes. She was pushing her rollator, a walker with wheels, a small seat, and a basket, in which she carried magazines and box of Kleenex.

"Aunt Dorrie?" Lacey asked. She hoped she was right.

"Why, my, oh, my, it must be my little great-niece, Lacey Smith," she said, and she managed to give Lacey a wink behind the aide's back. "My dear, you are all grown up."

The aide looked surprised. " 'Dorrie'?"

"Oh, it's an old family name, Chandra; I haven't been called Dorrie in at least twenty years. Everybody here calls me Dorothy, Lacey, and I don't let anybody call me Dot."

Dorothy Rogers looked quite frail, but she had eyes that sparkled with energy and humor. Lacey thought she had probably started out at five feet tall, but she was considerably shorter than that now. Her iron-gray hair was cut in a short Dutch-boy bob with bangs framing fierce brown eyes. Her face was wrinkled, but she looked lively. She rarely had visitors, it seemed, and Lacey guessed she was going to make the most of this one.

"Let's sit awhile; let me show you off. Wait till they see I've got my family visiting me."

This sunlit room was more inviting than the reception area, and the furniture looked fresh and clean. Lacey sat on a moss-green velvet sofa, while Dorrie eased herself into a rose-striped satin wing chair. She steadied herself with her hands; then Lacey offered her the flowers and two small packages. "I brought you a little something, Aunt Dorrie."

The old woman laughed with delight. "Would you look at this booty! Chandra, please go get me a vase for these flowers."

The aide went in search of a vase, and several older women watched with interest. Dorrie picked up the gold box with green ribbons. "Godiva chocolates! You're pretty bright, Lacey. You're from the smart side of the family. It's so pretty, I'm going to save this for later. Now what else did you bring me? It's too much." Her hands reached eagerly. "I swear this is better than Christmas."

Dorrie carefully opened the other small package, setting aside the pink satin ribbon. Her hands were large for her small frame and heavily veined, but they were deliberate and dexterous, the hands of a seamstress. She lifted the top of the box and folded back a layer of pink tissue paper to reveal three pairs of soft slipper socks in pastel colors. Dorrie clapped her hands. "You must know that old people have cold feet. These are very pretty." She put one of the socks on her hand and admired it. Then she carefully put them back in the box and tucked them along with her chocolates into the basket of her rollator.

"Mimi always liked warm socks," Lacey said.

"Ah, yes, Mimi. You look like her," Dorrie said, studying Lacey. "Not her hair, of course—her hair was the most beautiful auburn, a real dark Irish red."

Chandra returned to the room with a large vase full of the colorful flowers, artlessly arranged, which caused quite a stir among the other occupants. "I think those are some of the prettiest blossoms I've ever seen," Dorrie said. "I'm going to write to your mother and tell her what a smart and pretty great-niece I have." The old woman was obviously performing for the crowd, or maybe herself. Lacey took it upon herself to re-arrange the flowers with a bit more care.

Dorrie suggested they should go where they could talk more privately. Before leaving the day room, however, she made sure to introduce her "great-niece" to several groups of women in the room. She waved to them and gestured Lacey into the hallway.

"They're all supposed to be deaf, but you'd never know it by the way they gossip. News travels at the speed of light around here. So come to my room." Dorrie gave one last look into the dayroom at the old people. "Besides, it will just make it more interesting for them to wonder what I'm telling you. After you are gone I can make up anything I want."

"Just make it a good story," Lacey said. "I'm a sucker for a good story." They walked down the hallway, took a right past the windows overlooking the garden, and found Dorrie's cozy room.

Painted a soft peach with white trim, it was large enough for her bed, a small sofa and matching easy chair, and a faux-wood dinette set. There was also a tiny kitchen and a handicapped-accessible bathroom. The bed had a handmade quilt with matching pillows, and a bright yellow handmade rag rug lay on the floor. Dorrie wheeled over to her easy chair. Lacey followed behind, carrying the vase full of flowers. "Just put those down on the dining table. It's Formica; you can't hurt it," Dorrie said.

Once they were settled, Lacey pulled out the pictures of Gloria and the two photographs from the picnic at Great Falls. Dorrie traced the images with her fingers. The photos seemed to have the same effect on her as on Honey Martin. "So young. Why, I wasn't half bad-looking, you know. Look how young we all were."

"Full of life," Lacey agreed. Then softly, "What do you remember about Mimi?"

"I met her only a few times before Gloria went missing, at that picnic for one. It was a beautiful day, around Easter, I think. Mimi had heard I didn't have plans, so she told Gloria I should join them for the weekend. You see, my mother was dead and my father worked two jobs and he was seeing a widow at the time. There wasn't any room for me. But after the city and the factory I was happy to spend a couple of days in Virginia. Gloria said it was a town, Falls Church it was called, but it sure seemed like the country to me."

"You were Gloria's roommate, but you two weren't really friends. Is that right?"

Dorrie nodded. "We were thrown together because of the war, like so many people. I was a fabric cutter and Gloria was a draper with higher ambitions. We both could sew better than the average factory girl. I was pretty glad just to have a job, but Gloria thought she wasn't rising fast enough." Dorrie moved around in her seat as if to get up. The clock with extra large numbers indicated it was three o'clock. "Now what kind of hostess am I? Can I get you a cup of tea? I usually put a kettle on the stove this time of day."

"That sounds great, but why don't you let me do it?" Lacey

said. She filled the bright red kettle with water and put it on the stove. She located Earl Grey tea bags and a couple of cups.

"I like it with some sugar, and there are some cookies in the cupboard," Dorrie instructed.

"When we talked the other day, you said you been waiting for this call for fifty years," Lacey said, as she stood by the stove waiting for the water to boil.

"Yes. Oh, my, yes. It seemed that somebody would care someday. Of course, Mimi cared about what happened. But at the time I wasn't really sure of what I knew, and I was afraid of losing my job, or worse. If I went missing, there would be no one like Mimi to come around and ask questions. My father would have missed me, I guess, but he sure wasn't one to go stirring up trouble."

"Mimi thought it had something to do with the black market and Hugh Bentley."

"You'd have to be deaf and dumb not to notice certain things," Dorrie said. "Gloria complained about the rationing and government restrictions on clothing, like L-85, but she managed to get little treasures from Hugh Bentley—fine red wool for a coat, and there was some silk, I remember. It was different for the rest of us."

Dorrie explained that their landlady demanded most of their coupons to buy food for the boardinghouse. Still, they managed to save a few to pool among friends for little parties.

The Bentley factory turned out inexpensive rayon dresses by the thousands. Many of them were cheaply made copies of the clothes that actors wore in popular movies. But for wealthy clients, Hugh Bentley always managed to provide premier materials, the kind you could get before the war. When he did this he said he was "exhausting the available stock," because new stocks of wool and silk were supposed to go to the war effort. Nearly all the 100 percent virgin wool was commissioned by the armed forces. Companies advertised that their remaining stock was all that was available "for the duration," until the war was over. But Hugh Bentley's stock, Dorrie said, never seemed to go down. He was a magician, pulling fine materials out of a hat, waving his magic wand and producing bolts and bolts of forbidden silk and increasingly rare wools.

"He was definitely involved in the black market?" Lacey asked as she brought in a tray with the cups of tea, sugar, and spoons. Dorrie put in several spoonfuls of sugar; she liked it extra sweet. And she had a taste for chocolate-covered graham crackers.

"Oh, he had to be, but no one could ever prove it. Although they sent those poor boys to prison for driving deliveries."

"Yes, but Bentley never went to jail."

"He skated scot-free his whole life."

"Tell me about Gloria; what was she like?"

"The way she ran after Hugh Bentley scandalized me." Dorrie clicked her tongue, still slightly scandalized. "We worked together in Hugh's design studio. It was really just a big room with mirrors, sewing machines, table, and dress dummies. It was much better than working on the factory floor. Hugh had big ideas to do more than make dresses. He wanted to design them, make a name for himself."

"And he did, didn't he?" Lacey said.

"Yes, he did. He could cut and tailor nicely—after all, it ran in the family. But he wasn't quick about it, not like Gloria. She was like lightning. Gloria would get an idea and she would be grabbing for a pencil to get it down. Napkins, envelopes, sometimes she would even use the underside of her smock." Dorrie shook her head at the memory, as if it were the nuttiest thing. "You could see her mind catch on fire. She would not be happy until she had a complete picture and pattern pieces drawn out. For Hugh it was harder. He didn't have the flair for it."

"Did Hugh put his name on her designs?"

"Oh, yes, that was their deal."

"They had a deal?"

"She called herself Hugh's 'secret weapon.' And he kept all of those sketches of hers. He probably had enough ideas for five years after she disappeared."

Eight hours a day with Gloria Adams would have been enough for Dorrie, but housing was scarce and the factory had a rooming house. "That's how she and I wound up as room-mates," Dorrie explained. "I was quiet back then, but she was a talker. Even when she was drawing a design, she always kept up a running conversation. 'Do you like the sleeves, Dorrie? Should I give them a contrasting cuff? Do you think I should use piping and big buttons or small?' Or she would ask what I would like in an evening gown. As if I would ever have the oc-casion to wear an evening gown. Gloria would wake me up just to ask me questions and I would have to put my pillow over my head to get her to stop bothering me. I needed my sleep," Dor-rie complained. "Gloria was enthusiastic, but it wore me to a frazzle."

"Do you remember the last time you saw Gloria Adams?"

"It was May eleventh, 1944. It was a Thursday." The way she said it, so sure, so simple, let Lacey know Dorrie had gone over the details of that day in her mind a thousand times.

Dorrie didn't know that she would never see Gloria again, but she had a bad feeling that day. Orders were rushed; there was always so much work to be done for the war effort. *Don't you know there's a war on?* was the catchphrase. And Dorrie had been pulled from her regular job to work on a special proj-ect for Hugh Bentley, helping to prepare his fiancée Marilyn Hutton's trousseau. Nothing as insignificant as World War II would be allowed to intrude on the beautiful debutante's wed-ding.

There was a large handsome wardrobe trunk in the design studio, navy leather banded in beige with bold brass fittings, which Dorrie was slowly filling with Marilyn's new clothes. There were traveling suits, dresses, and slacks for a stay in the country. There was beautiful lingerie made in forbidden silk in-stead of rayon, but Dorrie knew better than to say anything.

"I didn't really mind," Dorrie said. "Not to be bragging, but I was a whiz with a needle and I was fast and careful. The trousseau was a treat to work on. And my, wasn't Marilyn pretty? She looked like a movie star. But I have to say there were lots of headaches working with Miss Marilyn Hutton be-cause she was so thin and required so many fittings. She kept losing weight before the wedding, but I guess that was just bride's nerves. It seemed she was constantly on edge, and I wondered if she knew about Hugh's trifling with Gloria."

"You knew they were having a love affair?"

"It was certainly love on her side," Dorrie agreed. "You would have to be blind not to see it. And I was not blind. The things I overheard in that room! Gloria refused to see reality; she was convinced that Hugh would throw Marilyn over for her, even though the wedding was six weeks away, and she could see me working on the bride's trousseau." Dorrie decided to open the box of Godiva chocolates. She offered one to Lacey, who politely declined. "This is delicious."

"Did Marilyn do anything about the affair?"

"Not that I could see, although she certainly tried to keep Hugh busy with wedding plans, the engagement photo, the party, things like that. I was working on the wedding gown that day, and to make things more hectic, Belinda, Hugh's little sister, always seemed to be underfoot."

"But wasn't Belinda in school?"

Dorrie thought for a while. "Maybe after the wedding. But she visited the factory quite a lot. She was going to be a junior bridesmaid and she was driving me nuts about what she was going to wear. She was always wanting something. Belinda was a pretty little thing, but what a pest."

That day, May 11, Dorrie had cut the pattern for Marilyn's wedding gown out of a bolt of white silk. Belinda was in the studio, wheedling for a white silk bow for her hair. Hugh told Dorrie she could certainly part with some scraps of silk, meaning that she had to do whatever the brat wanted. Gloria came running in late, buttoning her smock as she entered the studio. Hugh had given her an especially cruel task: to fit Marilyn's wedding gown, a traditional white silk gown, on the dress form. But then Hugh stormed in with sketches in his hand and a sample of a very different material: a beautiful embroidered ivory silk.

"It wasn't the silk I'd been cutting for Marilyn. This silk was so much richer than hers. Lacey, I'd never seen anything like it, not during the war, anyway." This was a story that had clearly been replayed in Dorrie's mind for years. The story that Lacey had waited for. "I don't know where he got the sketches. Maybe from her purse. They were Gloria's sketches, all right, but of another wedding gown, a real dreamy creation using acres of ivory silk. It was shameful, really, considering the war, but there were exemptions for silk for wedding gowns. Hugh insisted that the dress in the sketch be made for Marilyn. Gloria said it was her own wedding gown, and if he wanted to see it march down the aisle of the Episcopalian church he would have to see Gloria in it. Nobody else. They had a terrible fight. They carried on like I wasn't there."

Dorrie did what she always did: kept her head down and acted deaf, blind, and dumb. She was used to feeling invisible. Marilyn was supposed to arrive for a fitting soon, and Belinda was in and out of the studio. Gloria and Hugh were shouting like maniacs. Dorrie never understood why Gloria was convinced that Hugh would marry her. The lunch bell rang and Dorrie happily grabbed her sack lunch and her thermos of coffee for a quick half-hour retreat. But before she left she heard Gloria say, "You have to marry me, Hugh. There'll be a huge scandal if you don't, and I don't care who knows about it." Dorrie ran out but she had heard enough to tickle her imagination.

Dorrie deliberately delayed coming back from lunch to avoid an ongoing scene. When she returned everything was quiet, but the workroom looked like a hurricane had hit it. The trunk was gone and Marilyn's clothes were stacked on wooden worktables. The pieces of white silk that had been pinned to the dressmaker's dummy were on the floor, but the sash that Dorrie had cut out that morning was missing.

"I just stood there with my hands on my hips, looking at the disaster, wondering where to start. Hugh came back, looking flustered. I didn't say a thing. He told me that Gloria had a tantrum and was sent home to cool off. He trusted me to be discreet. Gloria usually got to take the afternoon off after fighting with Hugh. But the workroom had never been such a mess before. He told me the missing trunk was damaged and a replacement would be coming. Marilyn came in and told me she had a frightful headache and we would have to fit the dress the next day.

"Sure enough, a new trunk arrived in a day or two, and we filled it up with Marilyn's trousseau. She even had nylon stockings and alligator pumps. I wore ankle socks and saddle shoes."

"What do you think happened to the trunk?" Lacey said before taking a sip of her now lukewarm tea. She had gotten so wrapped up in the story that she'd forgotten about it.

"At first I thought Gloria must have damaged it in their fight, like maybe she took a pair of shears to it and gouged the leather or something. Later I realized that wasn't like Gloria. She would just as soon go after Hugh with the scissors as that beautiful trunk."

Good for her, Lacey thought. *Scissors can be a girl's best friend.*

"What did you think when she didn't come back?"

"I didn't worry at first. She had spent several nights away before, and she never told me where she spent them—as if I didn't have a pretty good idea. But when she'd been missing for four or five days, that's when I really began to worry. Gloria never came back."

"Did you report her missing to the police?" Lacey asked.

"No. Hugh said he did, but I think he was lying."

The next week Hugh asked Dorrie if Gloria had made a version of her secret wedding dress design, the one with the embroidered silk. He knew her habits pretty well by then. Gloria liked to present him with the finished version so he could see the entire effect. She didn't trust his imagination to fill in the details. "I was scared to death. I knew she'd pinched two bolts of that beautiful ivory silk embroidered with a pale-green-and-gold-leaf border pattern. Of course, it was black-market silk. There were five bolts and Gloria took two, bold as brass. And now here's Hugh Bentley himself saying real nice things to me, like all of a sudden I was a person and not the invisible little monkey in the room. He was saying I was really valuable to his work because I knew my place and I was smart and a first-rate seamstress. And it would be a real help if I could find that wedding gown of Gloria's."

Hugh generally didn't mind when Gloria took the materials. It was understood that she was working on some new design. But what Hugh didn't know was that Gloria had designs she did not share with him.

Gloria used to keep her secret projects in a locker. Dorrie said she really didn't know anything about the wedding gown, but she told him about the locker. He broke the lock off the door and there it was, hanging up with the green-and-gold embroidered train looped over a separate hanger. The hem wasn't in and the sleeves were not quite finished, but anyone could tell it had star quality. Every stitch was perfect.

Dorrie stood up and indicated to Lacey that she should move to the dining table, where a large box rested. The box was covered in blue watered silk, emblazoned with the Bentley logo in gold script. Lacey recognized it as the type used decades ago by expensive department stores. The type of box that Mimi had liked to store things in.

Dorrie used her walker to slowly inch to the table. She lifted the lid to reveal news clippings and photographs, and beneath them, what looked to be a large piece of material protected by layers of tissue paper. Dorrie unwrapped the material and spread it out carefully on the table. Lacey gasped when she saw it.

No one could have guessed it was sixty years old. It was still lovely. Ivory silk, with the embroidered pattern of pale green and gold leaves. Lacey's fingers longed to touch it. Dorrie picked up a newspaper clipping about Hugh and Marilyn's wedding with a photo of the bride wearing the dress. The clipping had yellowed, but the wedding couple were Hollywood handsome.

"He told me to fit it to Marilyn, you see. We had to fill in the bust a little, and make the neckline higher, but it was a beauty. Marilyn was gracious about it, but I could tell she didn't want Gloria's dress. As you can see, the picture doesn't do justice to the material."

Lacey examined the old clipping. "Did Hugh put this dress in his collection?"

"No. It was intended to be one-of-a-kind, and he made sure that it stayed that way. And it was the war, after all. A lot of women didn't want something so extravagant. It didn't seem patriotic, and lots of girls got married in a pretty dress or a suit and a wide-brimmed picture hat. Everyone was trying to do their part for the war effort. Well, nearly everyone."

Lacey turned her attention from the material and looked up at Dorrie. "I took it," Dorrie said, answering Lacey's unasked question. "After the dress was finished, Hugh locked up the remaining bolts of the silk. He said he didn't want anyone else using it, and he never wanted to see it again. Can you imagine that? Why, it would be a sin for all of that beautiful fabric to be lost forever. So I took what was left from the wedding dress." Dorrie sat down at the table and sifted through the various items in the box. "It didn't really occur to me that something terrible had happened until Mimi Smith showed up. But when she did I knew Gloria must be dead. I knew that it must have happened on the eleventh, the day the trunk disappeared."

"What did Mimi say about your idea?"

Dorrie looked down at her hands, rubbing them as if they were cold. "That's a terrible thing. I didn't tell her."

chapter 25

"You didn't tell her?" Lacey had to sit down. Tears overflowed Dorrie's eyes, and Lacey forced herself to be quiet while the old woman continued. One day a couple of weeks after Gloria vanished, Mimi Smith popped her head through the door of the workroom. She had tried to find her friend Gloria, "Morning Glory," she called her, but no one seemed to know where she'd gone. Gloria Adams hadn't gone home to Virginia, as Hugh Bentley had suggested. And it didn't really hit the factory girls until the papers reported that Gloria had disappeared.

"I mean, who would care about a factory girl, even if she had pretensions to be a designer, even if she'd had a dalliance with the boss? Only your aunt Mimi, and she somehow came up with a reporter. But I didn't say anything about the big scene with Hugh and Gloria, or the mess afterward, or the trunk. I had a job, a pretty good job, and I needed to keep it. I knew it wouldn't take much for me to disappear too."

Mimi told Dorrie and the reporter that she was afraid Gloria Adams had uncovered some unsavory information about the black market. Bentley denied any knowledge of black-market activities. Nevertheless, investigators from the Office of Price Administration poked their noses into every part of his operation.

There were many theories around the factory about what happened to Gloria Adams. The black marketeers had gotten her, or some Nazi spy. The Bentley factory girls were scared to death: They all started walking home in twos and threes. Still, according to Dorrie, some of the girls thought that Gloria was sent away to have a baby. It seemed reasonable, especially after all the gossip about her and Hugh Bentley. Some people thought that maybe she had married a GI on leave. But Gloria never returned to the rooming house to pick up her clothes and effects. Finally Dorrie boxed them up and sent what she could to Gloria's family in Virginia.

"I always felt bad about not telling Mimi. I haven't done many good things in my life. Don't get me wrong; I haven't done that many terrible things either. But not speaking out about Gloria was the worst. It's too late, but I've been waiting to free myself of it." She sighed deeply and pulled a tissue from the box to wipe her eyes behind the huge lenses. "Mimi was smart. I thought she and that reporter would find out the truth without my getting involved. I wasn't smart. I wasn't brave."

"What do you really think happened to Gloria that day?" Lacey's head was spinning.

"Gloria left Hugh Bentley's factory in the trunk. That's what I think. And I kept thinking about that missing sash. Maybe they tied her up with it. I've kept those thoughts for more than fifty years. I kept hoping Hugh would die so I could tell someone. But he's like the devil."

"I guess if she left in the trunk, she wouldn't be there now," Lacey mused as she picked up her cup and rinsed it in the sink before returning to the table.

"No chance of it," Dorrie agreed. "They're too smart. They probably dumped her in the sea. Or the East River. Isn't that where mobsters are supposed to dump people?"

"What about Marilyn, Hugh's wife?"

"She was always decent to me. She had her own worries. She always suffered from those crippling headaches. She was a little rich girl, but I think she was sweet. Can you believe she still sends me a Christmas card every year?"

"And Belinda Bentley Holmes?"

"A selfish child. But just a child. After the wedding I never saw her again." Dorrie, lost in thought, mindlessly munched on a cookie. Lacey fingered the beautiful embroidered material that lay on the table. It was heavenly—too bad it had such a shady past. Then she remembered that Hugh had told her that the First Lady would be wearing vintage silk that had been in the vaults for decades. She retrieved her bag and the article, *The Post*'s exclusive.

"Dorrie, I have a terrible feeling about that silk," she said as she showed Dorrie the paper.

Dorrie took a magnifying glass out of the pocket of her over-size blue sweater and examined the newspaper's sketch. "Very ladylike."

"I think you'd better read it."

The old woman traced the words with her index finger until she was finished. "It must be the same material. Oh, my Lord. I don't think the First Lady would want to wear it if she knew where that silk came from." Lacey was silent.

Dorrie took a pair of scissors and snipped off a piece of silk about six inches wide, enough to show the entire embroidered pattern. Then she folded the rest of it carefully and gave the larger section to Lacey. "You take it. I'll keep this piece for my memories."

"Oh, Dorrie, I don't know. What do you think I should do with it?"

"You're young and smart like Mimi; you'll think of something. But somebody should tell the President's wife that there's blood on this silk."

Lacey wasn't sure how she could possibly make that happen. She was only sure that the afternoon had slipped away and that she needed to get going. She had a long drive back to Virginia. Dorrie said not to worry about leaving her alone, that she would have company: She always ate dinner with her boyfriend. She laughed at the expression on Lacey's face. Dorrie said it was a good thing she liked older men. "He's ninety and still a pretty good kisser. I may be old, dear, but I'm not dead."

Lacey kissed the old woman on the cheek when they said good-bye at the front door. "Now you come back and tell me how it all turns out," Dorrie said. "I've always wanted to have a great-niece."

chapter 26

Lacey was too exhausted to drive back to Virginia. And her stomach was complaining about not being fed, so she pulled the blue box into the lot of a small Italian restaurant called Gina's, somewhere on the outskirts of Princeton. She was greeted by a hostess who hastily stubbed out her cigarette in an ashtray.

"Alone?" The woman raised her eyebrows in surprise. She was on the shady side of sixty, her skin olive and her raven locks exuberant. She wore years of too many rich dinners, liquor, and cigarettes on her face, but her eyes were kind.

"I'm on a business trip." Lacey shrugged. "And I'm hungry."

"No problem; I have a nice table for you. This is my place, so if you need anything, you just holler for Gina." She led Lacey to a small table where the clean white-and-pink tablecloth was covered with small holes caused by cigarette burns. *Must be Gina's own table,* she thought. Lacey ordered the chicken Bolognese. "That's a good choice," Gina approved. The woman returned to her bar, where she lit a Camel.

The meal was a delicious antidote to the draining session with Dorrie. Now all Lacey wanted to do was stretch out on a firm bed and chill. A motel was her first thought. Unfortunately, the other night over nachos, Brooke and Damon had regaled her with stories about a Washington journalist named Danny Casolaro, investigating what he said was a massive government conspiracy. The last thing he told his friends was that if anything happened to him it was no accident. Shortly thereafter he was found dead in the bathtub of the blood-spattered bathroom of his motel room in Martinsburg, West Virginia, where he was supposed to meet a source. His wrists were slit and his notes were never found. The cursory investigation declared it was a suicide, although his friends and family, not to mention DeadFed, did not believe it. And there were other stories of investigative reporters killed in motel rooms. DeadFed featured a whole directory of them, but the main attraction was the late Danny Casolaro. Lacey's thoughts grew gloomier and bloodier at the idea of pulling over to a roadside Bates Motel.

I've got to stop reading that damned Web site. Curse you, Damon Newhouse. But then she had a happier thought. *Journalists never seem to die at a bed-and-breakfast. At least not on DeadFed.*

Just then Gina stopped by with the bill and to ask if Lacey needed anything else. And as a matter of fact she did. Sure enough, Gina had a friend who ran a bed-and-breakfast just a couple of blocks away. The kindly restaurant owner made a phone call and in twenty minutes Lacey was checked into an old Victorian mansion with her own cozy room and bath. She breathed a little easier, and she called Vic at her apartment on her new cell phone. She explained that she couldn't drive home because she was too fried. Donovan agreed with her, but she couldn't tell whether he sounded annoyed or concerned. "I should have gone with you," he said. He promised not to tell anyone where she was, including the FBI.

After wedging a chair under the doorknob of her locked door and tucking her phone under the pillow where she could grab it in a hurry, Lacey finally went to sleep. Despite her exhaustion, her sleep was restless, filled with dreams of Gloria Adams in a silky blue dress. She kept hearing the voice of Marie, the psychic, crooning in a soft, singsong Cajun voice, "We're planting morning glories in the trunk, in the trunk." Lacey tried to look into Gloria's face, but it turned into the black hole where Esme's face used to be and the wraith danced away into the mist.

Lacey pulled herself awake at seven the next morning. The

chair was still propped against the door and the cell phone was still under the pillow next to her. After a quick shower and the accompanying breakfast she was on her way. The silk package in her trunk was weighing heavily on her mind. The conjunction of the two words *silk* and *trunk* was giving her chills. Her life seemed to be far too full of too much silk in too many trunks—Marilyn's, Gloria's, Mimi's, Dorrie's, and now hers. She drove into Princeton, where she saw a small crowd entering a Catholic church, and she thought about Jeffrey. She stopped for the eight-o'clock Mass. And remembering the famous Officer O'Leary, she stayed until the last hymn was sung.

"You can't do anything with it, Lacey. It is the story of an old lady, the kind of story that you love, but it's just a story. People can say anything when they're old." Vic was cooking himself an omelet for lunch in her kitchen when she showed up at her apartment. He had stayed the night to make sure that no one tried to break in. He looked perfectly restored, while she felt like a limp rag, although she hoped she didn't look like it.

"Must you always be right? It's so annoying."

He laughed and tended to his concoction, which was dripping with cheese and redolent of bacon and onions. "I'll split this with you." Vic poured her a cup of coffee from her old stainless-steel percolator. "You ever consider a coffeemaker?"

"I like that pot. Coffee comes out fiercer."

"Like you. Okay, let's think about what Dorrie Rogers told you. Let's say that Hugh clocks this Adams character in the head. Stuffs her in the trunk. Then what? The trunk is gone. Not only is it gone, it is sixty years gone. It's not like he's going to keep it around in his trophy room. He dumped it in the ocean, in a landfill, or maybe he burned it in the woods. Believe me, Lacey, it's nowhere. And then there's always the possibility . . ."

"What?"

"That he didn't kill her. I know that ruins your story, but all the evidence is circumstantial. Worse, anecdotal. Maybe she left on her own. Maybe he paid her off and she changed her name, had his baby or not, started a new life. Married someone else. Or got hit by a truck on the Jersey Turnpike."

"Say she did start another life—a tiger doesn't change its stripes, Vic. So if Gloria Adams became Jane Doe she would still have been sketching designs somewhere on this planet. Somewhere there would be a great female designer who looks just like Gloria Adams only with a different name. She'd be as famous as Edith Head or Coco Chanel. But that didn't happen. And don't tell me I wouldn't recognize her work, because I would. Her style was that unique. Besides, none of this changes the fact that Hugh Bentley took her work and never gave her any credit. His most brilliant collection was based on her designs and he's been living on it all these years."

Vic split the omelet with a spatula and served it on her Franciscan Desert Rose plates. "All right, let's say Hugh Bentley is a murdering bastard. What do you think you can do?"

"Just one thing: Wear Gloria's design. In front of Hugh Bentley at the gala—just like the telltale heart. And no one else in the world may know what happened to Gloria Adams, but God knows, Hugh Bentley knows, and I know."

"You left out that Dorrie Rogers knows, and now I know." He grinned like a handsome pirate. Lacey left out that Miguel Flores will know and Stella Lake will know, which meant it would stay a secret for only so long. He dug into the omelet.

"By the way, this is delicious," she said.

"I have hidden depths."

She smiled at that. "There is possibly one other thing I can do. You know Gary Braddock? The Undertaker?"

"Yes." He looked at her doubtfully.

"It's time to call the FBI. Besides, he's on my speed dial."

After they cleared the plates away and cleaned up, Lacey spread the creamy vintage silk fabric that Dorrie had given her on her dining room table. She cut three good-sized pieces from it, each large enough to see the embroidered flower pattern. The largest piece she placed in a box and tied with string. Then she called Brooke.

"Lacey, what's up? I haven't heard from you in days!"

"I need something secured again. Can you assemble the League of Justice for me?"

Vic interrupted from the kitchen. "You're nuts, you know that?"

"Excuse me, Brooke. A little static on the line." She covered the receiver with her hand. To Vic she said, "Do you have a better idea?"

He put his hands up in the air in surrender. "I'm going to finish the dishes."

"Lacey, do you have a man in your apartment?" Brooke demanded, her voice quavering with excitement. "The pheromone jammers must be weakening; is it Code Green again?"

"Very funny. I'll tell you later."

Vic made the call to Braddock after Lacey hung up with Brooke. "He wants to meet us at the Krispy Kreme on Route One at four o'clock," he said as he handed back the phone.

"You're joking. Doughnuts?" She was not impressed by the Bureau's choice of clandestine meeting locations.

"Sorry, I guess all of the spooky underground parking garages were booked."

Lacey decided to change into khaki slacks with a black knit sweater, so she would look casual but not sloppy. She also decided to freshen her makeup. Vic stood by the bathroom door watching her. "Aren't you ready yet?"

"I'm taking ten minutes, okay? I'm always careful how I dress for the FBI. The Undertaker can amuse himself watching the doughnuts march through the amazing waterfall of glaze."

"Are you grumpy?"

Lacey looked at Vic. "I'm exhausted." She squinted in the mirror at her pale face. Blush was definitely in order.

"Well, I hope Krispy Kreme is ready for this vision of loveliness."

"Has that smart mouth ever gotten you into trouble?"

"Many a time," he said, "but I talk my way out of it." He nuzzled her ear on their way to the door.

And that'll get him into trouble too, she thought.

*   *   *

Vic drove, and Lacey fought sleepiness on the short drive to Northern Virginia's celebrated palace of doughnuts. Once it had been famed as the northernmost outpost of the Krispy Kreme doughnut empire. But first they had a small mission to accomplish.

Brooke had agreed to meet her for a handoff of the package in front of the Old Town library. Lacey gave her the box and told her to secure it. Lacey had kept the largest piece of the silk in her apartment, sealed in a plastic bag and hidden in the back of her bookshelf. The third small piece was in her handbag, folded in a white envelope.

Brooke looked pretty in a sky-blue sundress topped with a crocheted white sweater. The weather was too warm to give in to wearing nylons and heavy clothing. Her bag with its tropical motif betrayed a desire for the late summer to linger, with its newfound romance with Damon Newhouse. Brooke did not look the part of the serious young barrister today. Instead it looked like the warning code for amorous adventures was bright green. *Green for* go.

"I know you have to go now," Brooke said. "But I predict we are going to have a long girls' night out. Soon." She looked meaningfully at Vic Donovan, who sat in the driver's seat of his Jeep Wrangler. He looked casual and handsome waiting there with his sunglasses on. His curly dark brown hair spilled over his forehead, giving him a rakish look. "You've been holding out on me." It was an accusation.

Lacey just groaned. "Okay, Brooke, I promise. You know what to do with this package?" Brooke rolled her eyes dramatically. At that, Lacey dashed back to the Jeep.

The heavenly aroma of baking dough hit them as soon as they pulled into the parking lot at the Krispy Kreme doughnut factory. The neon sign in the window proclaimed HOT DOUGHNUTS NOW, the rallying cry of Krispy Kreme fans everywhere. Lacey could see FBI agent Gary Braddock, a.k.a. the Undertaker, sitting with his back against the booth wall and looking out onto Route One. He was sipping his coffee and hefting a glazed doughnut. He seemed oddly peaceful, and he was not wearing his characteristic black. Instead he wore khaki slacks and a light blue knit T-shirt that seemed to intensify the azure gaze of his eyes. That gaze, no doubt, struck terror into the hearts of those he interrogated. He looked as lean as a greyhound. *That doughnut diet must be working,* Lacey thought.

Vic waved to the agent, signaling that they would join him after succumbing to the siren song of sugar and dough. Lacey sauntered over to the table and took a seat opposite Braddock. "This is hardly my idea of a clandestine meeting place," Lacey said.

"I didn't realize it was supposed to be clandestine," Braddock said. "Besides, if you have nothing useful to tell me, I still get something out of this—hot glazed doughnuts, a little round piece of heaven." He lifted his coffee cup to her.

She pulled out the piece of silk from her purse. "I'll make this simple. This material is leftover black-market silk from World War Two. From Hugh Bentley's factory. It figures prominently in the disappearance of a young woman."

"I read your story on Gloria Adams."

"And her possible murder a long time ago."

Vic joined them, setting down a coffee in front of Lacey with a chocolate glazed doughnut and the same for himself.

"I'm working on the Esme Fairchild murder," Braddock said. "Why do you think I would be interested in a sixty-year-old disappearance?"

"Let's just say murder might run in the Bentley family. And this black-market silk is twisted up in the murder scene. And the motive. And next week's headlines."

"And how would you know all that?" Braddock fixed her with his cool blue gaze.

"A witness was there the day Gloria Adams disappeared, but that isn't the urgent part." Lacey reached into her bag and produced *The Post* article describing the fabric that would be used in the First Lady's outfit for the opening of the Bentley Museum of American Fashion. And a copy of the news clipping and photo of Hugh and Marilyn Bentley's wedding in June of 1944.

Braddock looked at her expectantly. Vic escaped to the counter for more doughnuts and fresh coffee.

"When the First Lady opens the museum doors on Tuesday afternoon, she is expected to wear a new dress and jacket by Aaron Bentley. It's supposed to be vintage silk. Based on what Hugh Bentley and a confidential source told me, I believe it will be this material. There were five bolts originally, and I can account for two."

"The same silk? That's pretty interesting, but why should anyone care now? This is so long ago that all the suspects must be dead too, and raising the dead is a little out of my line."

"Oh, the suspects are very much alive. And this material is covered in blood, figuratively speaking. If the First Lady knew that, she might not want to wear it. The witness to Gloria Adams's last day just wants the First Lady to know the story, and so do I. If the First Lady's already seen a sample of the Bentley silk for her dress, she'll know if it matches this piece. Then she can decide if she wants to wear the silk. We think it's the right thing to do."

"So this isn't about the Esme Fairchild case. If you're looking for a Boy Scout or someone to restore justice in a sixty-year-old crime, Smithsonian, I'm not sure the Bureau can help you."

Vic returned carrying a tray with more doughnuts and slid in next to Lacey. The agent wanted to know what would happen if no one told the First Lady the tragic story of Gloria Adams, and she wore the outfit.

"She could just read all about it in *The Eye Street Observer.*"

"Ah. She might not enjoy that. And this is all based on fashion clues?"

"Major fashion clues. And old people with long memories."

Braddock gazed at the ivory silk. "Memories. Mark Twain once said he had an excellent memory; he could remember things that never happened. And if this material disappeared, then where would your story be?"

"Oh, please, don't tell me you think I'm that stupid." She was so annoyed she took another doughnut off Vic's plate.

Braddock looked at Vic for guidance. Vic shrugged. "She likes to cover all her bases."

"Then there's more material." Braddock smiled. "And you think I'm the right person to relay this information?"

"*The Eye Street Observer* doesn't have a lot of pull at the White House," Lacey commented. Vic started to laugh, but she threw him a look and he swallowed it.

The Undertaker was known for his sense of style. He was the FBI equivalent of a flashy dresser. He eyed the material closely, clearly unwilling to touch it with sticky fingers. Lacey realized it was time for her to shut up and let the silk speak for itself, if it had anything to say. "It's a shame; it's really quite beautiful." Braddock paused to consider another doughnut and decided against it. "Do you know how cold cases are solved, Lacey? Times change, circumstances change, people want to get even, they get religion, they want to close the books. They don't want to go to their graves uncleansed."

Lacey folded the material up and placed it back in the small white envelope, then handed it to Braddock. He slipped it into his pocket.

"I'll pass the information along with my personal recommendation to view it seriously," he said. "Beyond that, no promises."

On the way back to her apartment, Lacey was contemplating a long afternoon nap when she was struck by panic. "Oh, my God."

"What is it?" Vic swerved the Jeep in alarm.

"The Bentleys' big gala is tomorrow and I don't know if my dress is ready."

"Is that all? Lacey, honey, you'd look good in anything. Or nothing at all." He kept his eyes on the road. "Do you want to go for a drive? If you like B-and-Bs, I know one—"

"Are you crazy? I didn't even bring the stupid cell phone. I have to go home."

Lacey was relieved when they got back to find a message from Stella on her answering machine.

"First of all, why don't you get a cell phone?" Stella scolded. "And second, oh, my God, Lacey—"

"There are a lot of 'oh, my Gods' going on around here," Vic cracked.

"—the dress is done, and it is totally . . . well, like words totally fail me, and when has that ever happened, you know?" She continued: "We're bringing it over for a final fitting tonight and, you know, a styling session. Be there at five." Stella clicked off.

Lacey looked at her watch. It was five minutes to five. She glanced at Vic and saw him fumble with something in his pocket.

"By the way, since you're playing dress-up tonight, this might be a good time to give you this. I picked these up at a little shop in Steamboat." Vic handed her a small box inside a plain brown bag. She opened it up. It was a pair of simple antique drop earrings with pearls and diamonds.

She felt tears sting her eyes. "Vic, they're beautiful." She immediately put them in her ears and walked over to the mirror in the hallway to admire them. They swung gently and picked up the light.

"Hey, don't cry! I don't think they're real," Vic said, following her. "But I think they're real pretty and they show off your face."

She threw her arms around him and gave him a kiss. He tightened his arms around her and, in one of those moments of perfectly bad timing, someone knocked at the door. Lacey groaned. The styling team had arrived.

chapter 27

"Lacey, darling! We're your SWAT Team," Miguel said as he swept through the door with armloads of bags and boxes. "Special Wearables And Trappings, right, Stella?"

"I thought we decided it meant So We're A Terrific Team," Stella said.

"Oh, that too," Miguel said, handing too many things to Lacey. "And you're not Tony," he said to Vic. "I thought Tony would be here, but you'll do. I'm Miguel, and you are?"

"I'm Vic, and I'm leaving," Vic said. Lacey looked stricken while the others watched with interest. "Don't worry; I'll be back," he said with a grin. "I'll go down to the store for more beer. You'll need it."

"So you're the babe from Colorado? I've heard so much about you," Miguel said. "Hurry back."

Vic left chuckling, and the SWAT team set up shop in Lacey's spare bedroom, the one she called her office, though she mostly used it as extra closet space. It was only a dress rehearsal to see if there were any last-minute alterations to the Gloria Adams gown, but Lacey was thrilled to finally have it in her hands. She sent Miguel and Stella out of the room after Miguel had shown her all the details. She wanted a long moment alone with the gown.

It was as magnificent as if Gloria had lovingly tended every stitch. The morning-glory blue seemed to have a life of its own. She wondered if she could possibly live up to it. Lacey stroked the impossibly soft material and admired the intricate shooting-star beadwork. The gown evoked a scene from the decade it belonged to. She could imagine a big band playing in a bandstand. She lifted it carefully and swayed to the music she heard playing in her head. "Sentimental Journey." It was time to see if the magic would last.

In a rustle of blue silk it was over her head and zipped up the side with an invisible zipper, not a period touch, but a welcome detail. It fit snugly over the midriff, but it didn't pull or bind. It hugged her like her own skin. In that moment, Lacey knew the utter indulgence of the exquisite couture dress built specifically for her. More than her tailored vintage clothing, it fit her perfectly, down to the last millimeter. Even the hem was perfect.

The gown seemed to make her eyes glow. She slipped on the wicked shoes, the impossibly expensive Scarpabella shoes that she had lacked the heart to return. Her cheval mirror held her glance and showed off the way the dress flowed like a blue stream, undulating with sparkling beads of shooting stars. It was one-of-a-kind and it was hers. She still wore the antique earrings Vic had picked out for her, all by himself she hoped, in Steamboat Springs. Simple pearl-and-diamond drops, the baubles caught the light and picked up the blue of the silk. That was all the jewelry she needed. A necklace and bracelet would be too much; they would take away from the intricate beading.

"Hey, Lacey, you stuck or something?" Stella's voice broke the spell.

Lacey took a breath, shook her curls, and swept into the living room like the star they expected her to be.

"Oh, my God." For once, Miguel was without a snappy retort.

Stella was momentarily speechless, but soon recovered. "If you ever get married, it's got to be that dress."

Lacey looked around, but Vic was gone. Miguel caught her expression. "He brought up Dos Equis and then he left. I think all this girly stuff was too much for him. His loss, Lacey. Just look at yourself."

It figures, she thought. *Every time we try to get together there's some detour.*

"So what do you think?" Stella demanded.

"It's unbelievable, you guys."

"Tomorrow's the big day. I want you at the salon at noon." Stella inspected Lacey's hands. "Manicure, pedicure, hair, and makeup." It was a command, not a suggestion.

"That's pretty early, Stella." Lacey wondered how to broach this to Mac, who wouldn't have a clue how long it would take to prepare for a gala like this. He would expect her to work a full day and rush over right after work. And there was the Tremains' makeover to cover. Luckily, that was scheduled to start at nine in the morning. Lacey figured she could bop over to the exclusive and pricey Georgetown salon early for the pre-makeover interview and then let Hansen take the photos later. Stella broke into her thoughts.

"Miguel and me, we've got to get to the Building Museum for an early training session."

"Huh? What training seesion?" The glorious redbrick building was the site for the gala, and "Sixty Years of American Fashion."

"We didn't tell you?" Stella looked supremely satisfied with herself.

Miguel jumped in. "We're going as catering staff. You know, hoisting silver trays with champagne flutes. I have a friend and I knew he must need extra help, so it's a perfect cover to keep an eye on those rotten Bentleys. And your dress."

Stella reached into her leopard-skin bag and pulled out a tiny camera. "It's digital."

"But you can't take a camera in while you're working," Lacey protested.

"Watch me. Oh, sure, we have to wear white shirts and black pants or skirts with a little cummerbund." Stella fondled the small camera. "But I figure I can just wear it on a string like a necklace. I'm going to the ball, and I'm going to see you in the dress that poor dead woman designed. And I'm getting pictures."

"Where does it say in the story that Cinderella's fairy god-parents go to the ball?" Lacey asked.

"In the footnotes, my dear," Miguel said. "Now take off that gorgeous creation and let's go over the details."

After the SWAT team had gone home, Lacey called Marie. "Hi, Marie, it's Lacey."

"Hello, *cher*. What's up?"

You are the psychic, Lacey thought, *why don't you tell me?* "I was just wondering if you've had any feelings about tomorrow? Or about me?"

"Let me think. You and tomorrow? No, it's clear as a bell. Why, something going on?"

"Oh, nothing special," Lacey said. *Clear as a bell. That can't be good.*

On Monday morning Lacey dutifully arrived at the very expensive Northwest D.C. salon known as Portfolio to chat with a couple of nervous-yet-excited makeover candidates. Willie Tremain was fretting over a cup of coffee while Annette excitedly looked at nail colors. Each had a personal stylist who eyed them hungrily, flipping their hair this way and that, making pronouncements. *Thank God Stella doesn't work here. Any more attitude and she'd be lethal.* Lacey wore a pair of black tailored slacks and a black blouse to fit into the very upscale scene and to avoid any sniping about her appearance from the stylists. Her blown-dry hair was smooth and curved slightly under. She looked like a completely normal Washington career woman.

"You, my dear, are *so* not about your gray hair," said one tall thin man to a nervous Willie.

"I'm not?" Her eyes widened as he proclaimed that she would have a warm brown hair color, perhaps with highlights. "But I'm used to the gray."

The other, more petite male stylist brushed Annette's hair back and declared, "You have cheeks and eyes. Who knew? Why are you hiding them? And why not go darker? An audacious auburn. Honey, this hair color is totally nowhere. But I will take you somewhere."

Annette merely giggled. With a blank check from the Bentleys to do whatever they wanted, the Portfolio stylists were giddy with the possibilities. Lacey took notes as Annette bubbled. But Willie was apprehensive. She reluctantly okayed the new Autumn Chestnut hair color. "I feel like a lamb to the slaughter."

Lacey ducked out of this rarefied atmosphere to make it to Stylettos by noon, but not before she saw concealer wipe away the storm clouds of years that had gathered under Willie Tremain's eyes.

A harrowing cab ride delivered Lacey to Stylettos for the works. Stella was on full boil as she pin-curled Lacey's hair and scolded her for the dark circles under her eyes. "I thought I told you to get a good night's sleep. What happened? Was it Vic? Or that gorgeous Bentley guy? In either case, I can forgive you."

"No, I just didn't sleep well. And Vic was at his place. Don't ask. We're not . . . We haven't sorted out our relationship yet."

"What relationship? No sex, no relationship. Duh! I'm beginning to think the two of you are retarded."

"I just don't want to get hurt." Lacey reached for a magazine to get Stella off the subject.

"So join the human race. Getting hurt is a fact of life. Besides, you need it. It's good for you."

"And what about the circles under your eyes?"

Stella dipped her comb in some gel before sectioning off a layer of Lacey's hair. "I got a good excuse. Bobby's keeping me happy. Now, that's a relationship." Stella snorted when Lacey laughed. That snort left nothing to the imagination.

Lacey swept through the newsroom at three, typed up part of her makeover story on the Tremains, and batted her false eyelashes at a stunned Trujillo before breezing home to add her own final touches.

The look must be working, she thought as she got ready. Trujillo was speechless, Mac's eyebrows froze in midflight, and Peter Johnson actually stepped in a wastebasket and fell down. *Could they be thinking, who's that mysterious woman and what has she done with Lacey Smithsonian?*

Lacey Smithsonian's

FASHION BITES

Valuable Vintage—or Just Old Clothes?

Many fashionable women are climbing onto the vintage clothing bandwagon. Even glamorous movie stars, who could afford the most exclusive designer duds, are scarfing up the really primo finds, then wearing them only once—at the Academy Awards. Suddenly your best friend outshines your brand-new, two-hundred-dollars-an-ounce little black dress with her fabulous fifty-dollar Ginger-Rogers-look-alike dancing dress from Value Village. Is this fair? In a word, no. But you too, style-savvy shopper that you are, can open up a whole new-old world of one-of-a-kind clothing, if you have an eye and appreciation for vintage.

The benefits of that rare find—aside from the thrill of the hunt—consist not only in wearing that unique, wonderfully tailored garment that you alone possess. A vintage suit or evening gown also carries with it something of the spirit of the original owner and the style icons of her era. Was she a beautiful WAC officer yearning to look like Katherine Hepburn? A sassy Fifties career girl with just a hint of Audrey Hepburn's gamine charm? And who was that handsome Cary Grant–type on her arm? (Okay, they were somebody's Aunt Betty and Uncle Bob from the Bronx, but a girl can dream, can't she?)

Why do vintage clothes seem so good, so much better made than today's? Well, they *were* better. A great 1940s suit used a lot of skilled American labor. But it's also because most of the bad, cheesy, everyday garb from the

Forties, Fifties, and Sixties has already been turned into rags or rugs, made into patches, or sewn into quilts. Previous generations were thriftier and made the most of their clothes. What we find in the better vintage stores now are the survivors: clothes that were treasured, tended, and loved. They were their owners' good clothes, the worn-once-a-year evening gown, the Sunday-go-to-church dresses, the funky little vacation togs complete with South American embroidery that the owner simply couldn't part with. After all, Aunt Betty had her dreams, too.

Here are a few things to keep in mind when you shop for vintage clothing:

- *We've grown.* Vintage clothing was generally sized for smaller people, so rejoice, you petite sophisticates. Older styles come in sizes that will fit you, but don't freak out if they carry a size that sounds huge. A "sixteen" from 1945 may well translate into today's eight. It doesn't mean you are fat. Of course some vintage clothing comes in larger sizes and there are stores that specialize in it, but they are harder to find. You must try these clothes on to be sure they fit, but be gentle. Which brings us to the next point.
- *The fabric is willing, but the thread is weak.* You will find fabulous fabrics, wools, crepes, silks, linens, and marvelous covered buttons, but beware, the fifty-year-old thread will break immediately after you buy that new-to-you garment. Check for weak seams, fallen hems, and broken metal zippers. Have them all fixed at once, not piecemeal, or it will drive you crazy. Bring along a small sewing kit and some safety pins, just in case. Letting it all hang out is not the look you're aiming for.
- *Remember, vintage clothing is a vanishing resource.* At the rate it is being bought up by people who don't deserve it (like you do), it is becoming harder and harder to find. Treat these delicate finds with respect and love. Someone else cared enough to save

them for you. Surely you can return the favor. Someday you can explain why this dress—or one just like it—was so breathtaking on Rita Hayworth way back in 1946.

chapter 28

Red lips, Rita Hayworth hair, heartless high heels—and the Gloria Adams dress. Lacey's eyebrows arched knowingly in the mirror, giving her a certain power. She had a moment of hesitation, but the memory of Mimi soothed her. *Don't be silly,* Lacey imagined her saying. *Wear it for Gloria and for me. And for that old bastard.*

Lacey felt like a five-star general in the Women's Army of Fearless Heartbreakers. "Take no prisoners," she told herself. "Your mission is to hunt down and corner the enemy: Hugh Bentley."

The entire world had changed since the morning in 1944 that Gloria Adams vanished. As Braddock said, cold cases break because circumstances—and people—change. Perhaps Hugh Bentley had grown too old or too tired to lie. She hoped so.

The earrings that Vic had given her added the final touch. She'd never looked so *femme fatale* in her life, thanks to the talents of Stella and Miguel. No doubt they would take all the credit. A tiny beaded purse with a strap long enough to wear on her shoulder carried keys, money, lipstick, as well as a small notebook and pen. After all, she was still a reporter covering an event. She tried to stuff the stupid cell phone in but the purse was bulging unattractively and there was no room it. She had a moment of regret, but decided firmly against it. The purse still had to hold one more thing: a scrap of silk.

A knock at the door signaled Vic's arrival. She opened the door languidly and was mesmerized. He was wearing a tuxedo.

The white shirt contrasted with his darkly tanned skin. Almost any man looked good in a tuxedo, but Vic, who looked fabulous in skintight jeans and T-shirts, made her heart take a swan dive. He looked extra dangerous. *The pirate king goes to the ball.* She wanted to run her fingers through his dark wavy hair. She found it hard to breathe. He had insisted on driving her, but she had no idea that he would be dressed up.

He whistled in awe at the sight of her. "You plan on kissing your sources in that getup?"

"I hadn't thought about kissing until just now."

"So this is the telltale-heart dress? You look beautiful, Lacey." He touched the earrings that she wore, then caressed her neck. The warmth of his hands sent liquid fire down her spine. "I thought they would look good on you." He leaned in and kissed her until she forgot all about the gala. Then he released her too soon.

"You look pretty good yourself, but why are you wearing a tux?"

"I was just about to tell you. I'll be there tonight. Extra security."

"What? Wait—don't tell me—Stella suggested it!"

He just smiled. "Okay, I won't tell you."

Lacey playfully swatted him on the butt in response. "As much fun as I'm having with all this foreplay, I guess we had better go. Are you ready?"

She nodded and grabbed a matching silk wrap provided by Miguel. *Ready or not, we're dressed to kill.*

The National Building Museum had been the site of numerous presidential inaugural balls, and it wore its stately elegance with ease. The enormous redbrick building had been built to house the Pension Bureau in the 1880s. A terra-cotta frieze of weary Civil War soldiers banded the entire building. For tonight, the Great Hall had been transformed to accommodate one hundred and fifty tables of ten at the "Sixty Years of American Fashion" gala. Each paying table would net $10,000 or more, bringing in more than a million dollars for the museum—

and much more than that in publicity. *Vanity Fair* magazine was in attendance, as well as *Vogue, Elle, W, Entertainment Tonight,* and *Access Hollywood,* along with a few of the more sobersided media venues. Even *The Eye Street Observer* had bought one of the pricier tables. Lacey was very curious to see what her publisher, Claudia Darnell, would be wearing. She hoped her fellow reporters would blend in and not look so much like . . . well, reporters.

Inside the main door, a string quartet played as dignitaries arrived. Lacey was on her own after Vic dropped her off and vanished to do his job. The massive Corinthian pillars soared and golden light suffused the room. As if the Great Hall were not grand enough, a team of Hollywood set designers had donated their skills for the event. Lighting designers had taken the theme "Night of a Thousand Stars," and the room glittered. Each of the round tables was covered with a gold cloth, featuring a low centerpiece of roses the color of rich cream.

The security was ample yet subtle. Guests passed through metal detectors and guards at the entrance. Numerous men and some women wore small earpieces and identifying security pins on their lapels in addition to their sober evening dress. Vic was just one of dozens. He was across the Great Hall and did not see Lacey, but she saw him flash his killer smile at a young woman who was blatantly flirting with him. Lacey's heart skipped a beat, but she told herself he was just doing his job and she had to do hers—observe the clothes and the crowd, and watch for an opening to confront Hugh.

She located *The Eye*'s table. Lacey found that she was seated between Trujillo—*how did he get an invitation?*—and Mac. It was apparent that Claudia Darnell wielded enough influence to land a table inside the eight Corinthian columns, which framed a small fountain at the center of the enormous Great Hall. Claudia knew where all the skeletons of scandal lay buried, including her own. She was always accorded special treatment, even if her newspaper wasn't.

Between most of the numerous smaller Doric columns that lined the perimeter of the Great Hall were mannequins dressed in evening gowns and placed on marble pedestals. There were designs from all the important American couture houses. The Three Bs, Bentley, Blass, and Beene, were there in strength, but Lacey also spotted stunning examples of Bonnie Cashin, Victor Costa, and more current designers like Ralph Lauren, Donna Karan, Tommy Hilfiger, Badgely Mishka, and Isaac Mizrahi. Classic Hollywood costume designers were well represented; she spotted Edith Head, Irene, Adrian, and Orry-Kelly, and there were others she would have to read her program to recognize.

It was as if the court of Louis XIV had been reincarnated in the mannequins in this room. It was the definition of conspicuous consumption, and Lacey found herself dazzled by all the eye candy. The Gloria Adams dress she wore could have taken its place among the treasured gowns. As the string quartet played, the room pulsed to life. Predictably, most of the crowd was wearing black, the men uniformly clad in tuxedos, the women glittering with diamonds. Lovely though they were, they blended into each other, though there were a few brave women offering bright spots of color.

Tony Trujillo materialized beside her. "Smithsonian's wearing glad rags tonight. I didn't think you could top the red suit. But you've done it."

Lacey's attention was momentarily caught by Penelope Mandrake, the Bentleys' museum director, who, though dressed in a stretchy black evening gown and wearing crystal chandelier earrings, still clung to a clipboard. She slid past Lacey without a glance, checking off names.

"No one knows how to relax in this town," Trujillo said. "Except me." He lifted a glass of champagne off a waiter's tray. The dapper reporter wore his tuxedo with a black shirt and a silver and black bolo with a large turquoise in the knot. He noticed her staring at it. "Turquoise goes with anything where I come from." He grinned and moved off in the direction of a pretty young blonde.

Lacey went in search of Annette Tremain and her mother, Willie, but she didn't have to look very hard. Drawn to the

small circle of photographers and television lights surrounding
the newly made-over mother and daughter, Lacey veered in for
a closer look. Willie, in a lilac crepe dress sporting a V neck,
simple lines, and cape sleeves that floated over her chubby
arms, looked every inch the prosperous Virginia matron. Her
makeup was subtle but glamorous and, as promised, the gray
had been washed away, taking a good fifteen years with it.
Willie looked pleasantly bemused.

But for Lacey, the big news was Annette Tremain, who simply blossomed under the guidance of a clever hairstylist, an expert makeup artist, and the genius of a Bentley evening gown.
When Lacey first met Annette, she had looked positively ane-
mic. Now her green eyes sparkled with the knowledge that she
was the center of attention, perhaps for the first time in her life.
Annette's newly auburn hair was tamed in a chic updo caught
with sparkling gems. Aaron Bentley himself had selected her
dress, a simple pink satin sheath with thin straps and a low
neckline. The dress would make a really thin woman look like
a plucked chicken, but it showed off Annette's shapely arms
and ample décolletage.

"Lacey!" Annette ran over to her and gave her a quick hug.
The dress seemed to have unleashed the effusive Southern belle
in her. "Thank you. I owe this all to you." News cameras leaned
in and whirred as she spoke.

"There is no need. Bentley's did all the heavy lifting. And
you look wonderful, really wonderful."

"But it never would have happened without your story on
Gloria, as sad as it was. I shouldn't say it, but at this moment I
am in heaven." Annette sighed happily.

And I'm not going to ruin it for you, Lacey promised
silently. She wondered what Annette would think if she knew
what Lacey had learned about Gloria's last day. *Would she be
so grateful to the Bentleys then?*

"And, oh, look at you," the new Annette continued. "That is
the most incredible dress. I've never seen anything like it. And
that color is heavenly." Annette's eyes and mouth suddenly
went as wide as two cups and a saucer. "That's morning-glory

blue, isn't it? Oh, my God, that dress—it's Great-aunt Gloria's! It was her color. She wrote about it in her letters. Lacey, how on earth did you do that?"

"Someday I'll tell you about it, but now I think your public is calling."

A photographer was trying to get another shot of Annette and her mother. They happily complied. Lacey moved back to *The Eye*'s table to jot down a few notes. She had the table to herself; everyone was milling around, admiring one another's finery.

"May I join you?" It was Gary Braddock, the Undertaker, exquisitely turned out in a shawl-collar tuxedo that looked as natural on him as blue jeans did on Vic. He could have stepped out of a glossy magazine ad. *This is a man who owns tuxedos, not a man who rents.*

"Agent Braddock. You peacock, you. I take it you're working tonight?" Lacey asked. "Or perhaps you're a supporter of the new museum?"

"Maybe I just like looking at beautiful women in beautiful gowns."

"Strange words from an FBI agent."

"I'm sure there's a story there," he said, nodding his head at her gown.

"The same story. This is a Gloria Adams design."

"I hope you are right about that silk you gave me. I try as often as possible to avoid looking like a fool."

"Don't be silly. I'm sure you had it checked out." He smiled and conceded a tiny nod. "Thank you, Agent Braddock. You are a doer of good deeds."

He laughed. "Now please stay out of trouble."

She rolled her eyes, exasperated. "You've been talking to Vic again, haven't you?"

"You have a history, Ms. Smithsonian." He leaned close. "Off the record, though, I helped interrogate Razor Boy last spring. You do nice work with scissors." He smiled and sauntered off.

Just once I stab a killer and they never forget, Lacey thought.

Claudia Darnell waved to Lacey and moved gracefully to *The Eye*'s table. The celebrated publisher of *The Eye Street Observer* wore a one-shouldered ivory gown that played up her golden skin and her still-drop-dead-gorgeous-at-fifty-something figure. Dangling blue topaz–and-diamond earrings brought out the aquamarine of her eyes and caught the light as she tossed her head. Her platinum pageboy was pulled up in a chic chignon.

"I gather from our coverage that you're caught up in another little drama. Exploding minivans in front of the office. Make sure you're careful—explosions are good for circulation but hazardous to reporters." Her smile revealed pretty white teeth. "By the way, that's a wonderful dress you're wearing. I don't recognize the designer."

"She's practically unknown." *Only one person needs to recognize it.*

"Perhaps *The Eye* can shine a light on her talents. We'll talk later." With that, Claudia joined a distinguished gray-haired gentleman that Lacey recognized as a recently divorced senator.

Mac, *The Eye*'s resident fashion disaster and connoisseur of old corduroy jackets, showed up wearing a tuxedo and looking very distinguished indeed, much to Lacey's surprise. His wife, Kim, wore a black gown that played up her shapely petite figure. Her thick black Asian hair fell in a high ponytail that shimmered with well-placed glittering beads.

"Evening, Lacey. No explosions tonight?"

"Don't tease her, Mac," Kim said, and flashed her an apologetic smile. They moved on to schmooze with the paper's executives.

Marilyn Bentley came into focus. She was wearing a long-sleeved white gown with silver beading to show off her snowy mane. She took one look at Lacey and stopped cold. "Where did you find that dress?" she asked, trembling.

"I had it made. Do you like it?"

"Oh, dear, my head." Marilyn touched her temple, then moved quickly away.

Someone tapped Lacey on the shoulder. She half expected to see one of the Bentleys, and was surprised to see Brooke Barton, Esquire, a vision in vintage, and Technicolor at that. The young attorney wore a strapless emerald-and-pale green ball gown from the Fifties with a nipped-in waist and a bustled bow catching up the back of the skirt. Her blond hair cascaded down her back in loose curls. Brooke looked like a mermaid who had shucked her fish tail and gone to Prince Charming's ball. Next to her, firmly in tow, was Damon Newhouse in a black suit with a black shirt and his serious glasses—and a goofy grin every time he looked at Brooke.

"I'm so proud of you, Brooke!" Lacey said. "Where on earth did you get that fabulous dress?"

"You told me I couldn't wear black, and I didn't have time to go shopping. This was Grandmummy's. Can you believe it? Mother had it boxed away in her disaster of a walk-in closet. It fits me perfectly—well, with a little help from a merry widow," Brooke said, referring to the restrictive undergarment she was poured into.

"It's gorgeous."

"You're not so bad yourself."

"What did your mother think of you wearing your grandma's dress?"

"Oh, she got all teary-eyed and she went on and on about her mother and Grace Kelly and how no one really looks like that anymore. But I do, of course. That's what she said, and then the tears started all over again."

Brooke did a movie-star spin to make the skirt fly, and several attractive men looked her way. *Never underestimate the power of the dynamite dress*, Lacey thought.

A photographer asked them to smile while he snapped away. Behind him was Aaron Bentley. Cordelia Westgate was nowhere in sight. "Lovely. Take another," Aaron instructed the man. "Good evening, ladies." He moved closer to Lacey, creating an intimacy she did not care for. "Lacey Smithsonian, intriguing as

always. Now, I would say that spectacular dress you are wearing is vintage, but to my eye the fabric looks quite new, and in
such a lovely color. But it looks like it could be one of Dad's
early designs. You look quite beautiful tonight."

She didn't know what to say and she didn't know what he
was up to. "Thank you."

"I mean it; you look fabulous and so different in this crowd
of baa-baa black sheep. Washington fashion is an utter snore,
my dear." Aaron smiled at her and took her elbow, steering her
away from Brooke and Damon. "But not you, Lacey. Look, you
and I have gotten off on entirely the wrong foot. I think we
should start over." He picked up a flute of champagne from a
waiter carrying a silver tray. The waiter turned out to be Stella,
who winked at her behind Aaron's back. He offered the glass to
Lacey, but she refused. "Nothing for me, thanks."

Stella whispered, "Sparkling apple cider on the left, miss."
Lacey took the one she indicated. Stella winked again, then momentarily disappeared behind one of the mannequins, set down
her tray of drinks on the platform, and took out her tiny camera. She crept close to Lacey and Aaron and snapped several
shots. Aaron seemed not to notice, and Lacey tried to keep a
pleasant look on her face. She willed herself not to react to
Stella's antics, but she noticed a look of disapproval from several ball-goers. A waiter taking pictures of the guests violated
some invisible class barrier.

"You mean you don't mind the articles that I've written?"
Lacey asked.

He surprised her by laughing. "Hell, yes, I mind your articles. But I would rather have you with us than against us. Come
on; Dad wants to talk to you."

"Oh, I'm sure I will see him sooner or later."

From out of a sea of black-clad revelers, Miguel popped up
in the background, a yellow rose pinned to his starched white
collar. As he hefted his silver tray of hors d'oeuvres with one
hand and proffered napkins with the other, he raised one eyebrow in acknowledgment of her. Lacey felt that she passed the

test for his approval. He was more proficient with his tray than Stella, and soon he melted from her sight.

"Please. I promise you it will be painless," Aaron said, with a gleam in his eye.

"Where is Hugh?"

"Upstairs at the private reception." Lacey felt her eyebrows arch in a question. Aaron shrugged. "We've taken the pension commissioner's suite for a private retreat out of the hustle and bustle. Dad has a lot of energy—hell, more than me—but he is in his eighties. I know he'll be eager to see you in that fabulous gown, though."

Her curiosity got the better of her; she agreed to go up and see Hugh. She steeled herself for the encounter. This wasn't the way she had visualized their meeting. She had hoped to engineer an accidental encounter in the heart of the Great Hall, with a thousand eager eyes to register Hugh's guilty reaction to Gloria's dress. Lacey turned her head quickly to see if perhaps Miguel or Brooke was watching her leave. She caught a glimpse of Stella being chewed out by another tray-bearing waiter. Miguel had swooped in to Stella's aid, but neither was looking toward Lacey. She had also lost sight of Vic, Braddock, Brooke, Damon, anyone who might be useful. Aaron was pulling her gently out of the eye of the crowd to the perimeter of the room. Lacey felt a twinge of unease.

"By the way, where is Jeffrey?"

Aaron did not disguise his look of annoyance. "At the head table. With Tyler Stone."

"Tyler? From Senator Dashwood's office?"

"Yes, she's a charming girl."

Lacey craned her head toward the table, which was staged on a platform above the crowd. It was set aside for the Bentleys and other gala sponsors. Jeffrey was as handsome as ever, and Tyler was making her own fashion statement in a bold black-and-white gown, rather reminiscent of the young Jacqueline Kennedy. Very simple, very elegant. Tyler had a protective hand on his arm and he seemed to be enjoying himself. *So Tyler's not his type? What did he really want from me?*

"They make a lovely couple, don't they?" Aaron said. "I expect they'll be making an announcement soon."

"But I didn't think he was seeing anyone." Although Lacey had no claim on Jeffrey, she felt a stab of dismay. Despite Tyler's obvious pedigree, there was something grasping about her. It couldn't really be true? Miss Trust-fund Baby and Jeffrey, the white sheep of the Bentleys? He had flat-out denied it. Her puzzlement must have shown on her face.

"I forgot, you two are friends, aren't you? Well, maybe they'll invite you to the wedding."

Fighting to regain her composure, Lacey changed the subject. "Where's Cordelia tonight?"

"I haven't the faintest. She was supposed to be here, but I haven't seen her, have you?" Aaron placed his hand a little too intimately in the small of Lacey's back and steered her to a stairwell off the hall. "It seems your scoop on me and Esme upset the beautiful Cordelia and she's broken off our relationship."

"I'm sorry."

"Don't be. I'm not."

Lacey had to lift her skirt so she could navigate the shallow redbrick steps, worn in uneven grooves. She didn't trust herself not to stumble in those beautiful but treacherous high heels. At the top of the stairs they turned to the right and passed the "Private Reception" sign. Aaron opened the door to the suite. She had seen the trio of elegant icy blue-green rooms with their lofty ceilings before, while visiting the museum. A long country table in antique pine was laden with food and drink and decorated with fine linen tablecloths and napkins in rich jeweled colors, emerald, sapphire, ruby, and gold. The crystal stemware was heavy and the china plates creamy, trimmed in gold. Elaborate silver candelabras twined with ivy and cream roses sat on either end.

Hugh Bentley sat like a king in a leather club chair near the fireplace, which was set with a flower arrangement rather than a fire. He held a wineglass in his hand. All that was missing was the court jester, Lacey thought. *Maybe that's my role.* Hugh rose and bowed slightly.

"Why don't you leave us, Aaron, and see if our dear Cordelia has deigned to arrive. I'll call you in a bit. We can't miss the speeches. We have to make a few of our own."

Lacey glanced around the room. She noticed Hugh's silver-tipped walking stick leaning against his chair. Yet another example of the Bentley taste in antiques, its handle sported an intricately carved silver lion's head. And Hugh with his silver mane was the very image of a regal old lion himself. Aaron shut the door and was gone.

chapter 29

"Have some Champagne, my dear." Hugh indicated the bottle in a silver bucket. She declined, and she could see his eyes linger hungrily on the dress. "That is a most remarkable gown, Ms. Smithsonian. Would you mind turning around so I can see the full effect?"

Lacey spun slowly around, light catching the beading on the dress and the diamonds in her earrings. She heard him sigh, a long, low utterance that could have been a moan. She turned again to face him.

"And just when I thought you couldn't pull another rabbit out of the hat. I always wondered what it would look like properly made. It quite takes my breath away."

"You know the designer then?"

"Unmistakably Gloria Adams. Now do tell me how you came by the pattern. Because the dress is new, isn't it? It's been made specifically for you, the way it caresses you, the way the skirt flows. It is beautifully made."

"I have questions of my own, Hugh."

"Then we will exchange information. First, may I offer you something? Some wine, perhaps?" His arm waved toward the buffet. But Lacey couldn't risk alcohol clouding her wits.

"No, thank you."

Hugh stood up and walked over to the reception table and laughed. "I wouldn't poison you, you know."

"I didn't think you would, Hugh." *Takes too long. Unless it's cyanide, and then where would you hide the body? No trunks here.*

Hugh poured himself a glass of port and sat down again. "Do sit down, my dear." Lacey sat down opposite him. "I tried to produce that dress myself—well, something similar, in lilac. It didn't work. I had misunderstood its lines. But Gloria . . ." He swirled his port, gazing into it as if it were a window into the past. "It isn't too late to enshrine that dress where it belongs, in the Bentley couture collection," he said finally.

Will he stop at nothing to get it? she wondered. After all, he took Gloria's wedding gown for Marilyn. "Gloria Adams designed your first collection," Lacey stated simply.

"Yes. And no. Her designs inspired the line, but we were a team. Of course, they had to be tamed somewhat for mass market."

"Yet only your name was on them."

"That was the deal. It was my factory. She was my . . . well, you might say protégé. And mind you, young woman, I am a designer. The best of my kind." His voice rose, then softened. "But Gloria was one of a kind."

"And what about my aunt Mimi?" She knew she should pursue Gloria, but family loyalty and sheer curiosity had to be satisfied.

"Your great-aunt was a beauty, but she proved to be quite a problem. It must run in the family."

"Because she started the OPA investigation?"

"You do your homework." He lifted his glass to her. "Mimi could be far too straitlaced about certain things."

"She knew right from wrong," Lacey said, feeling the blood rise in her face.

He chuckled. "Oh, there are so many shades of right and wrong."

"Black and white. Mimi never wore the black suit. The suit she always said was a Bentley's Original. She knew you'd stolen the design from Gloria."

"That woman could really carry a grudge." Hugh shook his

head at the memory of Mimi Smith. "Perhaps I can tell you something you don't know, Ms. Smithsonian."

"Please do, Mr. Bentley." She wanted to wring the story out of him, but she knew that she had to let him tell it at his own pace.

"I recognized that suit the instant I saw it on you. I also knew that Mimi's suit never came with the gold-embroidered Bentley's Original Premiere Collection label, that every stitch was labored over by Gloria herself to impress me, and it did. And it is the only one."

"But wasn't it your first collection?"

"That suit was never made in black for the Bentley line. And the jeweled button covers, Gloria had those specially made. She took the stones, the pearls and rubies, from a pin I had given her. She told me it was too big and ugly and she had 'improved' it. God, she was nervy." Hugh laughed at the memory.

Lacey remembered one of the letters from Gloria that described how she had improved the smock she had to wear. "But surely it was just costume jewelry."

"No, my dear. The stones are real. Perhaps they aren't the finest jewels, but they are real and, of course, those button covers are one-of-a-kind. They were made by a jeweler in Greenwich Village. So you can see that your suit is quite rare." *Finders keepers,* she thought. He had been playing with her from the beginning. "And it is rather valuable. With its historical implications, quite valuable. Shall I tell you what that suit might be worth?"

"No, please don't." What something was worth was always in the mind of the beholder. The suit had belonged to Mimi; therefore it was priceless to Lacey. She was grateful that it was locked away in storage and Hugh couldn't get his hands on it. *That bastard.*

"Did you have a romance with my great-aunt?" she asked.

"I certainly tried to, but she said no. And kept saying no. She didn't approve of the little fact that I was engaged." Lacey laughed inwardly. *You go, girl!* "I confess that my engagement was essentially a family arrangement. Rather like a merger.

Marilyn and I have been very happy, as it turned out, but in the beginning I'm afraid I failed to take it very seriously." He paused momentarily to shift his weight and sip his port. "In those days I had to travel to Washington on business quite a lot. We had government contracts, and there were all those clothing regulations and all those brand-new bureaucracies. I met Mimi at the Office of Price Administration. She introduced me to her friend Gloria, a 'budding designer,' she said, and I hired her. And Gloria turned out to be a brilliant addition to the factory."

Lacey took a deep breath. "And then you and Gloria had an affair."

"My, my. Who have you been talking to? I suppose you have proof? But then again, why wouldn't you—you have the suit and that incredible gown. You seem to have a gift for this sort of thing." He looked away and nodded. "Yes, we had an affair. It was quite . . . passionate. Gloria was wild, and hungry. And ambitious. And once she sank her teeth into an idea, she never let go."

Lacey had picked up a picture-perfect strawberry from the buffet table; it exactly matched her polished fingernails. She was poised to pop it in her mouth.

"You remind me a little of Gloria, as well as Mimi. And that brings me to my point." Hugh cleared his throat. "I'd like to offer you a job with Bentley's."

Work for Hugh the B? "You what?" She could feel her jaw drop. "A job with Bentley's? In what capacity?"

"Whatever you like, my dear. Communications director or something. Write your own job description. Research on our competitors, or fashion trends, or the next big thing. I think you would be good at that, very good. And the compensation would be outstanding, I promise you."

"I don't understand." She realized she had forgotten to breathe for a moment.

"Bentley's is a global company. Expand your horizons, Lacey. You could see the world in style. Think of it, traveling to Paris and Milan. Fashion Week in Paris—ah, that's something you should experience."

"Paris?"

"Why not? We have quite an operation in Paris. You could be based there if you like. I suppose you've seen Paris on a tourist's budget? Well, this would be something quite different."

Living in Paris? She had always longed to see Paris. But there was no chance of *The Eye* ever sending her abroad. New York once a year was a struggle. The glamorous life of the fashion world, seductive and multifaceted, beckoned to her with its promise of parties and travel and beautiful clothes. Part of her had always wanted glamour. *And Paris?*

chapter 30

Hugh Bentley steadied himself with his walking stick and stood before her. "You'd stay in the best hotels, wear fabulous clothes, experience life at its finest," he promised. "A little pied-à-terre in Montmarte? I can see you there now—"

Lacey thought for a long moment, the strawberry still in her fingers. She had no idea how long she stood there, frozen. Hugh seemed to have all the time in the world. But then she wondered what strings were attached. Even halfway around the world, she realized there would still be strings attached, strings held by Hugh Bentley. He offered her a glittering ruby apple—with a poisoned worm hidden inside. She put the strawberry down.

"So Paris would be—my purchase price? If you could buy me?"

"Quite the contrary—your talents would be priceless to me. You would be fairly compensated."

"You think you can shut me up?"

"Not at all. You'd be speaking for Bentley's. You can say whatever you please. So what do you say?"

"Did you order the car explosion at my office?"

"My dear, that's hardly my style. I have many other powers of persuasion."

"Money? Dreams? Glamour?"

"Money makes dreams come true. You must have dreams of your own."

Lacey took a deep breath. *It must run in the family,* she thought, remembering Belinda's offer. "I do have dreams, Hugh

Bentley. And I would never work for you. It would be a nightmare." Hugh took a step back. "Now please tell me what really
happened to Gloria Adams that day, May eleventh, 1944."

He sighed. "She went away, Lacey. It became apparent that
she wanted more than I was willing or able to give. Although
there is so much I can offer, if only you could see."

"She wanted to marry you."

"That was a problem." Hugh looked directly at Lacey. "She
thought she had the upper hand because she was a brilliant designer. But I had learned from her and needed her less and less.
In the end, I didn't need her at all. Just as perhaps my offer to
you was also unnecessary."

"What about the black market? She threatened to go public."

"Not much of a threat. I was a respected businessman with
connections in Washington, and who was she? Just a factory
girl. But if you must know, she chose differently than you. I
sent her away. It was costly, but we came to an agreement."

"Where did you send her?"

"To Mexico, and then after the war to Europe, Rome, London. Paris for a while. She became—a painter. You've seen her
sketches, I suppose."

Gloria never mentioned painting in her letters, Lacey
thought. "And she never came back?"

"No, that was part of the deal." Hugh flipped open his cell
phone and hit a number. "Bring Chevalier up, would you?" He
waited for an answer, then put the phone away.

"Is she still alive?"

"We've been in touch over the years. You'll see."

"What about the silk for the First Lady's outfit, the one she's
supposed to wear tomorrow at the museum opening? That fine
embroidered ivory silk—I imagine it came to Bentley's in 1944
via the black market. How many people died because of it?"

"You know nothing about it! That silk is mine and mine
alone."

Lacey withdrew the small piece of lovely fabric from her
bag and held it out for him to see. "This silk. Aaron gave an exclusive to *The Post* describing the ensemble."

"I've tried to be accommodating, but I've become quite tired of our negotiation, Ms. Smithsonian." He reached out for the fabric, but she snatched it away from him and tucked it into her décolletage.

Aaron opened the door, smiling, accompanied by Chevalier. "How are you two getting along?" He looked at them and his smile faded.

"Aaron, I want Chevalier to put Lacey in touch with Gloria Adams, the woman she's been writing about. She longs to learn about the end of the story. Please arrange it. I'll come downstairs with you."

Lacey saw Aaron's face harden and she realized that maybe she should have taken Hugh's job offer. Everything was moving too quickly now.

They marched her to the elevator for a silent ride down to the first floor. Aaron had a tight grip around her waist and shoulders. And Chevalier had her wrists. Hugh led the way.

"I've changed my mind about the job," she said, but she knew it was too late.

"The offer has been withdrawn," Aaron said. When the door opened the music was loud, but the crowd was louder. The string quartet had yielded to a blaring swing band. They were in an exclusive area cordoned off from the main party. Lacey hoped to catch someone's eye, but the three men surrounded her. "We are ejecting you from this party, Ms. Smithsonian. I trust we won't be seeing you again." Aaron looked hard at Chevalier. "He will take care of you—properly this time." Lacey stared at the beautiful Chevalier, his face shining cocoa-brown, his expressionless round dark eyes, and a sick feeling welled in the pit of her stomach. His navy tuxedo was set off by a pale blue ascot made of silk.

Hugh tapped his lion-headed cane on the floor. "Good night, my dear. It has been a trip down memory lane." He gazed again at Gloria Adams's creation. "A pity you didn't take my offer." He turned to his son again. "Nothing rough—I want that dress. Call me when it's done."

I'm in the lion's cage now, she realized, and her heart started beating a samba. *And the lions want my blood—and my dress!* Aaron let go of her waist to transfer her to Chevalier's care. "Don't make a scene," he snarled. "Or it will get ugly." He turned to go, leaving Chevalier with the instruction, "Save the dress for Hugh."

Chevalier yanked Lacey's left arm, pulling her off balance with her right arm suddenly free. She impulsively grabbed the soft silk ascot from his neck. It revealed the scar of a long-ago tracheotomy, the raised lumpy tissue pale against his chocolate skin. Something Miguel said clicked into place. Something about a beautiful black woman wearing a silk scarf to cover her scar, screaming and kicking him in the head. An angry light illuminated Chevalier's blank eyes as he realized what she had done. He let go of her, clutching his throat to cover his one physical imperfection. He growled.

"Oh, my God. You killed Esme Fairchild! With your scarf!" Lacey shouted. And she realized that the Bentley's robbery was indeed an inside job. "Miguel!" Lacey yelled at the top of her lungs. *Where the hell is he?*

Chevalier's lips curled into a smile. Moving slowly and deliberately, he reached for the blue ascot, but she was too quick. She backed away from him, kicking off the beautiful shoes so she could run. She scooped them up in one hand. A few people were beginning to stare. "Miguel," she yelled again. "Stella! Vic!" *Where the hell is everybody?* Aaron Bentley had disappeared into the crowd. But Hugh had been detained just a few feet in front of her by an aging admirer.

Lacey rushed toward him, and before he could react, with her free hand she grabbed the lion-headed walking stick. Chevalier was right behind her.

"Wait a minute; what's going on?" Hugh demanded. "Chevalier, I told you to—" Lacey put Hugh between them, and Chevalier froze in Hugh's glare. Lacey dodged around one of the giant Corinthian columns. He started after her again. She tossed one shoe at him. It missed and she heard a crash from a nearby table, so she hurled the other one, the heel striking him in the forehead. He grunted. She tried to weave through the crowd but the throng was too dense and she was stuck. Lacey stopped, turned, and flipped Hugh's walking stick in her hands to swing it like a baseball bat. She felt a small button under the lion's chin and tested it. Out snapped a small deadly-looking blade about six inches long from the top of the cane. "Whoa! How did you get past security?" she said aloud. *Trust Hugh Bentley to have another little secret.*

Chevalier was right in front of her. She swished the cane like a sword with both hands, holding him back for a moment. The crowd, aware that something was happening, circled around them, but the music was deafening. Somewhere close by there was the flash of a camera.

"Hot damn, Lacey, what's happening?" The dulcet tones of Stella's native New Jersey sounded like heaven to Lacey. "This is great. Smile!"

"Where were you?" she yelled, adrenaline still coursing through her.

"You disappeared, and we all went looking outside. Vic's still out there looking for you. Boy is he mad."

"Stella, this is not the time for a long story. You have to call security *now!*"

Chevalier grabbed for the cane above the blade. Lacey jerked it back. "Get Miguel too, Stella—to identify this creep."

Chevalier moved in again, but no one jumped in to help Lacey. *What's wrong with these people?* "This isn't the floor show," she yelled as Chevalier again lunged for the cane. Lacey jerked it back sharply, but he had grabbed it and was holding on tight. Stella latched on to Lacey's end of the cane and they managed to yank it away from the angry Chevalier. He grimaced, then shrieked in pain as the blade sliced through his palms. He clutched his bleeding hands, grabbing the handkerchief from his tuxedo pocket. Lacey looked around wildly for help and spied Miguel through a gap in the crowd, offering champagne to an elderly politician. She yelled for him again and this time he heard her, plowing through the mob to her side.

"His scar, Miguel. Look at his throat." Lacey pointed the cane.

Tray in hand, Miguel stared at Chevalier, who stood at bay, panting, wiping his bleeding hands on his tuxedo jacket, and Miguel's usually impassive face flashed into that of Miguel the Avenger.

"It's her! The filthy bitch who stomped on my head."

Miguel threw his tray of champagne flutes in Chevalier's face, dove and body-slammed Chevalier. Lacey held the cane protectively over her friend, ready to stab like a bullfighter if it came to that.

Suddenly Miguel was down and Chevalier scrambled to his feet, poised to kick Miguel in the head the way he had at Bentley's Boutique. Lacey lifted the sword cane and stabbed it down as hard as she could. She thought she'd missed—but Chevalier seemed to have trouble swinging his leg. They both looked down at his foot, puzzled. She had stabbed the blade clean through his black patent-leather Bentley's tassel loafer—and his foot. He was nailed to the floor and he howled like a trapped coyote.

Chaos reigned for all of thirty seconds in that small corner of the Building Museum while the band blared on. Miguel jumped up and put his fist in Chevalier's gut and doubled him over, still pinned to the floor. People in black gowns and tuxedos started screaming and retreating. Lacey looked around for her shoes but couldn't find them in the hubbub. She became aware of videocamera lights glaring in her face, and then realized the composition of the observers had changed. She heard clicking and saw a ring of weapons drawn at the four of them, at her and Miguel and Chevalier and Stella. Orders were issued to freeze. Lacey looked past the lights and saw Gary Braddock, part of the ring of pistols. Trujillo stood behind him, no doubt taking notes. Hugh and Aaron Bentley were nowhere to be seen.

"No more sharp objects, Ms. Smithsonian. It's always fun until someone gets their eye poked out," Braddock said.

"They offered me a job! In Paris!"

"How dare they. Care to explain?" he asked her. "Upstairs, I think."

"Wait! Aaron and Hugh will get away—"

"I don't think so. The speeches are starting—and they're making them."

Someone in uniform assisted Chevalier in hobbling away to a waiting police car, the walking stick still impaling his shoe. His tuxedo was smeared with blood from his hands, and he was spitting obscenities at Miguel and Lacey. She was hustled off for questioning, up to the now-vacant pension commissioner's suite. Miguel and Stella were also taken away for questioning somewhere else.

The small commotion at the end of the hall did nothing to stop the gala. It went on without another hitch, without Lacey. The Bentleys shared the spotlight and drank in all the glory.

Upstairs, after taking Lacey's statement, Braddock finally allowed Vic in the room, then left to question Chevalier. Vic took one look at her, his face a thundercloud of concern. "My God, Lacey. I thought you'd been kidnapped. What the hell happened?"

It was much too complicated to explain. She looked down at her bare feet. "I lost my shoes," she said in a small voice.

He gathered her up in his arms and didn't let go for a long, long time.

chapter 31

The following day, the First Lady was unexpectedly unable to attend the opening of the Bentley Museum of American Fashion. She sent her regrets and the Vice President's wife in a plain blue suit, who cut the designer ribbon. The entire Bentley family, minus Jeffrey, was at the Second Lady's side, smiling for the cameras. If they were disappointed that the First Lady did not appear and wear the highly touted outfit of vintage silk, they did not betray it. All the major entertainment media were in attendance, but the story took second place to the news that Esme Fairchild's suspected killer—and Lacey's attempted abductor—was also one of the Bentley Bandits: the mysterious "woman" in Chanel.

Although suspicions of Bentley involvement with Esme's disappearance were mentioned in the press, the Bentleys made no statement and referred all inquiries to their lawyers.

After Braddock finally turned them loose, Vic had taken Lacey, still barefoot and in Gloria's gown, to a twenty-four-hour diner in Arlington, listened to her story over and over, then drove her home just before dawn. He also offered to buy her a new pair of shoes, but she refused to tell him how much they cost. Vic spent another night on her sofa bed. Lacey roused herself to go to the office at about three in the afternoon on Tuesday. She had missed the museum opening, but she didn't care.

Mac, who stayed on the story till an extra edition was on the street, was bleary-eyed, but crusty as usual. "Thanks to you,

Smithsonian, no one but Claudia and my wife got to eat dinner at the fancy gala. Do you know how much that cost per plate?"

"I'll buy you a doughnut."

"No need. Hell of a story, but generally journalists are supposed to stay outside the action. News to you, I know."

She had already checked out DeadFed, which in its own inimitable way led with "Smithsonian Blades Again." The cutline accompanying its photo read, "Don't Cross Her." Mac handed her the special edition of *The Eye*. The front page showed her wielding the sword cane in a dramatic standoff with Chevalier. The headline: "*Eye Street* Reporter Nails Suspect in Fairchild Killing." *The Washington Post* buried it in Metro: "Suspect Questioned in Intern's Death."

She raised her eyebrows. "Where did you get the photo?"

"Stella Lake. She's pretty good. She made me pay the going rate, too."

"Of course." It made perfect sense. A hundred professional photographers there, all willing to watch her get killed for a photo, and Stella gets the only front-page picture?

"By the way, we're wanted upstairs. Let's go."

The last time she was summoned to the sixth floor for a meeting, her stomach had been twisting in a ballet of flip-flops. But today she was too tired to care. She and Mac exited the elevator and turned into the plush executive suite and conference room, so different from the rest of the paper's offices. A fresh pot of coffee and a tray of Krispy Kreme doughnuts were placed temptingly on a side table. Mac helped himself to a chocolate glazed and Lacey poured herself a cup of the aromatic brew. Full strength, not decaf.

Claudia Darnell walked in, looking well rested and relaxed in an aqua silk pantsuit. Her platinum locks brushed her shoulders. "I have mixed feelings about this, Lacey," she said. "Great story, but I don't like you putting yourself in danger. It's a bad habit."

"I completely agree," Mac said.

"It won't happen again." They looked doubtful. Lacey shrugged her shoulders. "How could it?" she said. There was a knock at the door, and Agent Gary Braddock was ushered in. He handed Lacey a paper sack. She peeked inside and gasped. "My shoes!" She looked them over: not even a scratch. "I thought I'd lost them forever." She fell to her seat with relief. After all, they weren't even paid for yet. And they were still beautiful. She felt herself tearing up and had to bite her lip. She'd imagined them adorning Hugh's trophy room.

"Too beautiful to be swiped from an evidence locker. Scarpabellas, very nice. And well built, apparently. By the way, there will be no official statement, but it is my understanding that the White House is very grateful not to be involved in any ancient black-market scandal that might touch the Bentleys. The First Lady says thank-you."

"She's very welcome. But what did Chevalier say? He killed Esme, he must have, but why?"

Agent Braddock glanced at Claudia. She nodded, and he pulled up a chair and selected a doughnut. "There are going to be leaks in this story; that's a given. So here's leak number one: In light of your gallant yet extremely foolhardy role in all this, I'm going to tell you what I know off the record, and then I will deny it." Aaron and the rest of the Bentleys, he said, were spinning the events at the gala as expertly as any Washington politician, painting Chevalier as a criminal mastermind. "They have released a statement of their gratitude to you for uncovering a killer in their midst, as well as a thief and a kidnapper. They deny any intent to harm you."

"Bastards," Lacey muttered, refilling her coffee. "I'd be floating in Esme's swamp right now if they had their way."

"Aaron Bentley explained to us that you were being escorted out, but it was just a misunderstanding. He was shocked to find you upstairs, which was off-limits to the press." Braddock's delivery was deadpan. "Once they realized that you were on the trail of the evil Chevalier, all was forgiven."

"And the Bentleys get off scot-free. Again."

"They're rich and powerful. On the other hand, you're pretty good with edged weapons. The sword cane, by the way, is called a 'flick stick.' Victorian. Collector's item. Hugh wants it back, of course, but we're keeping it for a while."

"What's Chevalier saying?"

"He's implicating Aaron and several other designers in a string of robberies designed to get rid of old slow-moving stock, clean up on the insurance, and then rake in a little more money from fencing the stolen goods." It sounded to Lacey like a lovely scam: Get paid twice for the same merchandise.

There had been no robbery scheduled for the D.C. store, and Chevalier hadn't participated in any of the previous holdups. He'd been in charge of "subcontracting" them, Braddock said. But he thought this time he would enjoy leading one, dressing up as his favorite drag character, "Lady Chanel." Chevalier, it seemed, had a checkered past. But things spun out of control, starting with Miguel Flores calling the police, and while his crew was scooping up jewelry and leather goods, Esme Fairchild walked into the store. She was there to collect her scarf.

She recognized Chevalier, even in drag. Esme was amused, not frightened, and Chevalier recruited her to help him get out of the store as the police were approaching. He told her it was all a publicity stunt. He quickly took off the Chanel suit and scarf and stashed them in an expensive leather bag, stolen from the store. He also slipped into a pair of men's slacks and a turtleneck shirt to cover the old tracheotomy scar on his throat, and topped it off with a leather cap. They slipped through a side door into a hallway leading into the office building, and a security guard helped them leave because, after all, they looked like such normal people. Chevalier thought she was crazy, he told Braddock, but she seemed to be enjoying the whole thing, as if it were a big adventure.

Esme clearly thought there was something in this robbery that would benefit her, but she started getting too clever, asking questions, drawing conclusions, and Chevalier soon understood that Esme was learning too much about the boutique robbery scam. She was already getting on his nerves while they were driving away in her navy blue VW Cabriolet.

Chevalier felt he had to do something about her. She told him she was going to use her role in the getaway to get what she wanted from Aaron Bentley. She seemed to think she had recruited Chevalier to her cause by helping him slip out the back. She drove out onto some tree-lined road; opened her cell phone, and called Aaron. "Honey, I just saved your ass big-time," she told him. But then she started demanding things. She said she knew all about the botched inside-job robbery. She wanted a big job in New York; she wanted Cordelia out. She wanted this; she wanted that. They talked for a while, then she handed the phone to Chevalier, saying that Aaron wanted to talk to him.

Chevalier said his boss was furious that he would dare stage a robbery at the same time the Bentleys were in town trying to win favors from Washington. Aaron started screaming at him and told him to take care of Esme. Chevalier, the jack-of-all-trades, didn't know how, but Aaron insisted that he "do something to keep her quiet." He ordered Chevalier to "take care of it permanently and not to bother him with the details." After all, the whole situation was all Chevalier's fault.

"Why didn't the Bentleys just get rid of him?" Lacey asked.

"He says he's got too much on them to be cut loose," Braddock said.

Esme didn't have the sense to be scared, according to Chevalier. They took her car to a country road in Maryland where he told her Aaron would meet them. He assured her that everything would be fine. He got out of the car and walked around to the driver's side to get his bag, which sat on the floor behind Esme. She kept chattering on about conquering New York City with the Bentleys and replacing Cordelia Westgate as their spokesmodel. In the meantime, Chevalier quietly opened the leather case and pulled out the scarf he had worn earlier. With one smooth, fast motion he slipped it around her neck and pulled tightly. He kept pulling until she stopped struggling. He called an old friend in D.C., a former associate in the armed robbery division of the Bentleys' far-flung empire, and asked him to dump the body and get rid of the VW Cabriolet. He said he didn't want to know what happened to them or where they went, so long as they were never found. Then he called a cab.

This was the same friend he later told to do something to make Lacey Smithsonian stop writing exposés about the Bentleys, but he neglected to make sure that his contact knew exactly who she was or what kind of car she drove. Nor had Chevalier stipulated what the friend should do to make Lacey stop writing. Apparently he was following Aaron Bentley's "take care of it and don't bother me with the details" model of criminal conspiracy. Braddock laughed, and took another doughnut. Braddock was having a good time leaking this story, Lacey thought. *No wonder criminals open up to him—he appreciates a good story.*

After the minivan explosion, Chevalier realized too late that his friend was an idiot. An idiot who had dumped Esme Fairchild's body in a little-known wildlife preserve in Virginia, less than ten miles from D.C. but in another world, far across the Potomac. Being a professional criminal and a lifelong D.C. resident, the idiot friend assumed no one ever went "way over there." No one, of course, except every birdwatcher, deer and beaver enthusiast, and nature lover in Northern Virginia, many of whom had been in a position to observe Esme's body the morning it floated to the surface of the shallow waters of Huntley Meadows. And Agent Braddock himself had presided over the idiot friend's arrest less than two hours ago.

Tony Trujillo is right, Lacey thought. *Most criminals are too stupid not to get caught. But that doesn't explain the Bentleys.*

chapter 32

On Wednesday afternoon, a large bouquet of roses and orchids arrived at *The Eye* for Lacey. She immediately assumed they were from Vic, who had returned to Steamboat for the closing on his house. Lacey had driven him to Reagan National Airport. He left his Jeep in her care. "Don't kiss any sources while I'm away. I want to be your main source," he had whispered before he kissed her and headed toward his concourse.

She opened the note attached to the flowers. *With desperate apologies, Jeffrey.* Of course; Vic wasn't a flowers guy. She called Jeffrey to thank him and he said—after casually mentioning that his mother had arranged his date to the gala with Tyler Stone—if there was anything in the world he could do, he would.

"Anything?" she asked. There was something, but, Lacey warned him, it could be very hard on him and his family. She described Gloria's last day, about how there was a trunk, and if it still existed there might be DNA evidence: a hair, a bloodstain. He said he would get back to her.

Jeffrey called her back the next week and invited Lacey to come up to the farmhouse he had inherited from his maternal grandmother, the repository of most of the Bentley family's castoffs. It was located in a green and wealthy pocket of Connecticut. There were trunks in the attic, Jeffrey said, that had been there forever. If she wanted to, they could open them together.

"It's a deal, but I can't believe we will find anything dramatic," she told him. "A hair is probably the most we could hope for."

"You're right, but we need to exhaust the last possibility."

She was suddenly reluctant to drag Jeffrey into the Bentley mess. *He's the only decent one in the whole family. Why try to ruin his life too?* "You don't have to do this."

"Yes, I do, so I can sleep at night," he said. "And so you can too."

"You have been talking to O'Leary again, haven't you?"

"He thinks it's a good idea, to put all our minds at rest."

"Jeff, it's going to be like busting into Al Capone's vaults. Nothing will be there."

If they found nothing, they agreed to have a good laugh over dinner. "Bring your friend from the paper, if you like. And a camera. If Al Capone's vaults are really empty, we'll have a witness."

Tony's Mustang took a right at a small sign that said STONE-HAVEN FARM and rumbled down a perfectly manicured tree-lined lane. The "farm," as Jeffrey had so quaintly called it, had a grandiose cobblestone circle drive in front of the imposing three-story stone-and-stucco home. The house was large and lovely and very old-money Connecticut. Lacey realized it had been used as the backdrop of some of the Bentley ad campaigns. She remembered one in which gentlemen rode up the circle drive on polo ponies while women in evening wear emerged from Jaguars.

Trujillo pulled the Mustang up into the covered entryway and parked. "Who knew that jockey shorts and T-shirts could buy all this?" he said, referring to the only Bentley items that he ever bought.

The door opened and Jeffrey greeted them. A large man with an Irish face full of freckles stood behind him, his sandy-red hair turning white. He smiled warmly.

"Mike O'Leary, Lacey Smithsonian," Jeffrey said. "And Tony Trujillo, am I right?"

"Pleased to meet you." She shook O'Leary's giant mitt.

"So here is your beautiful swordswoman, Jeff," the big man said. "I love a woman who can stand her ground and come right to the point."

"I see your reputation precedes you," Trujillo chipped in.

"And I love a man who ushers Mass in uniform," Lacey said. "Good for the collection plate."

"Well, not so often in uniform since I retired from the force," O'Leary said with a grin. "But I still make 'em give. She's all right with me, Jeff. You sure you want to show her the chamber of horrors?"

Jeffrey just smiled. They followed him and O'Leary into a large center hallway that opened to an impressive stairway with a landing midway up to the second floor. The polished floor had wide planks partially covered with Oriental carpets and a runner up the stairway. To their right were the formal dining room with a stone fireplace, the breakfast room, the butler's pantry, and the kitchen. A small bathroom was tucked underneath the staircase. To their left were a living room with a fireplace and a grand library leading out to a stone patio accessed through French doors. A vista of rolling green hills spread away beyond them.

"Just like my place," Trujillo said, and Lacey elbowed him in the ribs.

Upstairs were five spacious bedrooms and three bathrooms. Jeffrey explained that the servants' quarters were situated over the three-car garage. They were occupied by a housekeeper and her husband, the groundskeeper and maintenance man. Jeffrey had given them the weekend off. The other employees lived off the grounds.

The door to the attic was at the far right end of the third-story hallway. They ascended the narrow attic stairs quietly, moving into a large open room. It had never been finished, but it was insulated. There were many stacks of boxes and rollaway dress racks. One corner was reserved for holiday decorations: Halloween, Thanksgiving, Christmas. There was also red, white, and blue bunting for the Fourth of July, or perhaps it was all merely set dressing for Bentley advertisements. Jeffrey said the house was seldom occupied. He visited on the occasional weekend when he wasn't working.

They stopped en masse when they reached the trunks piled at the far end of the attic. They lifted rolls of old carpeting that had been stacked on top of them. As Jeffrey said, there were five, some larger than the others. All had been top-of-the-line steamer trunks in their day, leather wrapped and brass fitted, but now they were dark and dusty from neglect. Lacey thought of her own vintage trunk, which had been restored to its place of honor in her living room. It could have been a smaller sibling of these five trunks.

They started opening them one by one. All the trunks were locked, and Jeffrey had been unable to locate the keys. But not surprisingly Jeffrey, the builder, and O'Leary, the former policeman, had a knack—and the proper tools—for lock picking. The first two trunks were soon efficiently broken into. One was full of family photos, keepsakes, and letters to Jeffrey's grandmother. The second contained a cache of exquisite handmade baby clothes, perhaps Belinda's when she was a little girl, and some later things that must have belonged to Jeffrey. He lingered over a small red cowboy hat and a pair of boots that looked like they might fit a child of three or four. He handed the hat to O'Leary.

"Ah, you made a darling little cowboy, Jeff," O'Leary said.

The younger man grinned. To O'Leary he said, "Let's start on the large dusty one over there." He pointed out an old trunk with rusted hinges that looked as if no one had opened it for a long time.

The sound of an engine in the driveway drew Lacey to a small dormer window. She saw an impeccable blonde emerge from the driver's seat of a champagne-colored Mercedes.

"Jeffrey, I believe your mother is here."

"That's very odd. She didn't tell me she was coming." He looked puzzled.

Lacey heard the front door open, heels clicking on the hardwood floor. "Jeffrey! Jeffrey, where are you?"

"I'd better see what she wants." He rolled his eyes and then headed down the attic stairs.

In Jeffrey's absence, Tony helped O'Leary pull the trunk away from the wall. The locks and hinges on this trunk were not so easily picked. There were three locks and they seemed to be rusted solid.

The soft murmur of voices became louder. An agitated Belinda was clattering up the stairs. She was awfully agile for someone in her seventies, Lacey thought.

"No, Jeffrey, get them out of here! They don't belong here. What on earth were you thinking?" Belinda's angry voice carried up to the attic.

Trujillo, O'Leary, and Lacey all exchanged a look. O'Leary shrugged. He put a large flathead screwdriver to the lock as Belinda opened the attic door and started up the attic stairs. After three flights she was breathing heavily now, and she came to a stop and stared at the whole group.

"Mother, calm down. I invited them," Jeffrey said as he followed her up.

"You had no business doing that! All you people, please leave my home!"

"It is my house now," Jeffrey said. "You have no right to speak to my guests that way."

"Make them go!" Belinda cried. She saw Lacey. "You, you're nothing but a troublemaker. Do you know what happens to troublemakers? They must be dealt with. And my family knows how to—"

O'Leary stepped between them, his face ruddy with anger. But Tony's gleeful look merely said, *This is what we came for.* He looked ready to whip out his camera. Lacey knew Belinda, in her mid-seventies, was all bark. But she had plenty of bark left.

"What are you doing with the trunks?" Belinda demanded.

"We are opening all of them, Mother. It would help if you know where the keys are." Belinda merely stared at the rusted trunk O'Leary had been trying to open. "We want to know about Gloria Adams."

She turned on her son. "What do you need to know about her? Nothing! Nothing at all! She was going to ruin everything. There's nothing else you need to know. Make them go, Jeffrey—now!"

The others were waiting for his sign. Belinda seemed to have run out of steam for the moment, and Jeffrey helped her sit down on the trunk full of her mother's letters. Jeffrey nodded to O'Leary, who leaned hard on the screwdriver under the rusty hasp, and the trunk gave a groan of wood and metal.

"Not that one," Belinda screamed, "you can't open that one! I'll tell you about Gloria Adams. She was a tramp!" She looked at her son, her eyes wild. "Gloria Adams was going to stop the wedding, Marilyn and your uncle Hugh's wedding. Something had to be done."

"Mother, let me take you downstairs."

O'Leary leaned harder and pried off the first hasp with a loud pop. He started on the second. Lacey held her breath.

"She was going to ruin Hugh. I heard all of it; I was there. She said she was going to have his baby and he would have to marry her." The words tumbled out of Belinda as if they'd been bottled up for a long, long time. "Marry her, she said. Marry her. When he told her that was ridiculous, she said at least she could destroy him."

Lacey glanced over at Mike O'Leary. He was listening intently and nodding.

"Your aunt Marilyn walked into the room. She had come in on the train from Connecticut and she was there for their engagement picture to be taken."

Lacey tensed at the mention of Marilyn's name. Somehow part of her believed Hugh when he said he had really cared about Gloria, and Lacey always thought that perhaps Miss Hutton, the beautiful debutante, had played a part in this drama.

Belinda took a breath. "The photographer was supposed to arrive shortly. It was a big mess. I was her junior bridesmaid, did you know that? I had a beautiful dress of pink organdy and a matching picture hat. I carried a small bouquet of pink roses and lilies of the valley. I even had pink organdy gloves. But there was Gloria Adams, such cheap goods. That little tramp said she knew about the fabrics and the payoffs and the names to go with the black-market business that Hugh ran. He tried to calm her down; he said he would take care of her baby. She would have money, but he would have to send her away. He said it would be adopted and she could come back to work. But then she said if he took her baby away she would tell everybody who it was that really designed his new line of clothing. It was awful. They were all just running around the studio, shouting at each other. Gloria started tearing up Marilyn's beautiful wedding gown. Marilyn was in tears; Hugh was frantic." Belinda stood up again. "Someone had to take care of it, Jeffrey."

Jeffrey pulled up an old leather club chair and helped Belinda sit down again. He knelt and took her hands. "Mother, if Hugh took care of it, we have to find out. It's time we found out all of Uncle Hugh's secrets."

"Hugh? He didn't take care of Gloria. I did." Belinda looked over at O'Leary, who had just popped the middle lock open. "Please don't let him do that."

"How did you 'take care' of her?" Lacey asked.

But Belinda's eyes were glued on the trunk. O'Leary popped off the third hasp. The hinges were stiff, but he pried it up carefully. A layer of yellowed material was visible in the trunk. He snapped on a pair of latex gloves. Lacey and Trujillo stared, mesmerized, and Jeffrey hugged his mother tightly. There was silence. Only the whir of the attic fan could be heard, and a slight breeze disturbed the dust floating in the air. The stiffened material looked like pattern pieces stuck together. It rustled as O'Leary lifted the layers and then carefully pulled them back from what lay beneath.

There were several gasps, but not from the ex-cop, and not from Belinda, who knew what was there. Lacey felt her breath turn ragged as she watched. Her throat was so tight it ached, but she couldn't pull her eyes away. Lying quietly in the trunk were the remains of a woman's body.

The corpse was mostly bone and skin—its fluids had long ago soaked into its fabric wrappings, her clothes, scraps of silk, but it still had the wild curly black hair that had been Gloria's trademark in life. She was tucked up on her side in the fetal position, and a stained silk sash was still tied around her neck. Her hands were reaching up for the sash. She wore a discolored smock, once blue, that identified her as a Bentley's factory girl. Gloria Adams had not run off with a soldier, she had not gone to Europe to paint, nor had she met her end in some dark alley. She had never really left the Bentleys at all. And it was true that Hugh had known exactly where to get ahold of Gloria.

"Holy Jesus and Mary, Mother of God, this is an unholy mess," O'Leary finally muttered in a low voice.

"She was going to ruin everything," Belinda said. "I had to do something. Hugh tried to stop me, but I don't think anything could have stopped me that day. I took the silk, and I twisted it and twisted it. Until it all stopped." Finally exhausted, she sat back down in the club chair and said she needed something to drink.

O'Leary gently took Jeffrey by the arm and said he had to make some phone calls. He suggested that Jeffrey call the family attorneys. Belinda said he should call Hugh, because Hugh always knew what to do. Lacey knew that this was much worse than Jeffrey had imagined, but like a festering sore, the secret of his family was finally lanced. They had uncovered the dark heart of the Bentleys.

"Jeffrey, I'm so sorry," Lacey said. She felt shaky and weak, and she was grateful when he came and put his arms around her.

"It's not your fault." Jeffrey looked at her clearly. "I'm sure your aunt Mimi would be proud of you. And Gloria too. And so am I. We wouldn't be here if not for you."

Lacey couldn't help herself; she burst into tears and sobbed into his shoulder.

chapter 33

Lacey said later to Trujillo on the long drive back to Washington that she couldn't understand why the Bentleys didn't just dump the body in a landfill somewhere years ago. He pointed out that most killers screw up in disposing of the body—like Chevalier's subcontractor. And if you're a killer who happens by dumb luck to have gotten that part right, he said, you're safer leaving it where it is rather than moving it. *But nobody knows why people do what they do,* Lacey thought. Maybe the Bentleys just thought that no one would ever think to look for Gloria there, in the picture-perfect farmhouse in the picture-perfect countryside. After all, everyone had assumed that if Gloria hadn't simply run off, she was taken away in the night by some monster. *And we're not monsters, are we? No, no, we're the beautiful Bentleys.*

In the weeks following the discovery of Gloria Adams's body in the trunk in the attic, teams of lawyers swarmed around the Bentley family like worker bees supporting their queen. So far nothing official had been done, no charges had been filed, and they were all still free, as Lacey had predicted they would be. It would be months, perhaps years before anything like justice was served to Belinda Bentley Holmes. Perhaps never.

Senator Van Drizzen and his wife patched things up very publicly, and the charming, gum-popping psycho Doug Cable joined an unwary presidential campaign.

Chevalier, who turned out to have a lot of names, not just one, was happily telling the police in two states and the District every interesting story he knew about criminal conspiracies on the part of Hugh and Aaron Bentley. Trujillo and Lacey milked the story for several front pages and photo spreads, although Tony predicted privately that Hugh and Belinda would never be indicted, considering their age and their money. Aaron was another story, but he had put together a legal team that could stop a tank. Jeffrey resigned from the company and was on a retreat in a Franciscan monastery in Northern Virginia. It was really only a few miles from Lacey's apartment, but she hadn't seen him since the day in the attic. He seemed sad and distant on the phone, and she decided to let him call her, if he ever wanted to again.

Gloria Adams's remains were finally released to the care of her family. Jeffrey quietly arranged to pay their funeral costs, much against the advice of the family's attorneys.

With all the media attention on Gloria, the funeral in Falls Church was larger than expected. The reporters outnumbered the friends and family, and Lacey attended with Vic, who finally, he said, was free and clear of Steamboat Springs and his ex-wife. A small group from *The Eye Street Observer* was also on hand, including Mac and Trujillo. Wilhelmina and Annette Tremain were front and center, next to the polished wooden coffin, which was draped in a blanket of blue silk morning glories.

Even Duffy, Mimi's old beau and a former reporter himself, attended to see how the story ended. But Dorrie Rogers, whom Lacey had never identified in her stories, didn't come, saying she was too old to travel. She told Lacey she was satisfied that the story had an ending, but she was still afraid of the Bentleys.

Lacey had half expected to see Jeffrey there, but of course he wasn't. She was sure he would have considered it in bad taste to appear, and in any case he was still on his retreat. But she was surprised to see Mike O'Leary there, with his wife, Peg. The big Irishman hugged her. "This whole thing is tearing Jeff up, but he'll come out of it stronger; you'll see. I always thought I knew all the Bentley dirt, but I was wrong, wasn't I?

He always believed there was some terrible secret that had to come out. But he'll heal. He's not like the rest of them."

And there was one other mourner Lacey was surprised to see: Honey Martin with her housekeeper and companion, Ruby. Honey wore a proper navy overcoat, an ancient pillbox hat, and gloves. Ruby wore a stylish gold raincoat.

"Mrs. Martin, I didn't expect to see you here," Lacey said.

"Well, I didn't either, and yet here I am. Perhaps I judged Gloria too harshly, and it was such a long time ago. Do you like the silk flowers? Of course, I would have preferred to send a blanket of fresh fall flowers, but that young Miss Tremain thought that this would be more fitting, and in a weak moment I agreed."

"You provided the silk morning glories? That's very nice, Honey."

"I wanted to do something, although it's not really very much. I fear that Annette has a romantic streak, just like her great-aunt Gloria."

"I think Gloria would love the blue morning glories."

"Come on, old lady," Ruby said. "I've got to get you home." Her housekeeper jingled her car keys.

Wilhelmina Tremain couldn't help telling everyone that she had known all along that those wicked Bentleys had done away with her poor aunt Gloria. The reporters, including Tony Trujillo, were more than willing to listen.

Annette had retained much of the unexpected sparkle she had displayed at the big gala. She was looking very grown-up and feminine, and she was wearing a sharp burgundy suit and shoes that actually had something like heels.

"Of course, it is all so tragic, Lacey. But I think I might try to write a book inspired by the short, sad life of Gloria Adams, my great-aunt. Only I'll have a more upbeat ending, you know? Maybe she will go off to Paris and become a great designer and have lots of men and live happily ever after and that'll be her big revenge on those dastardly Bentleys."

"So it's a romance?"

"Absolutely. A major romance. Only I'm not telling Mother

yet. She would be shocked." Annette smiled shyly at Lacey. "I
know that most of the Bentleys, the old ones anyway, are a horrible bunch of murderers. But in a weird way they gave me
back my own life. I was just rotting away, but they opened my
eyes. The Bentleys really changed my life. . . . Oh my, you
aren't going to quote me, are you?" She suddenly looked horrified at the thought of seeing this conversation in the paper.
Lacey imagined the headline: "Murder Victim's Niece Thanks
Killers!"

"No, no. You're completely off the record. You save it for
your own book. And I'll want an autographed copy."

Lacey trudged back over the uneven ground to where Vic
stood among the trees, tall and resolute, sunglasses hiding the
amused expression she knew was in his eyes. "Annette is going
to write a novel. Based on Gloria Adams, but with a romantic
ending. A big, juicy, old-fashioned, bodice-ripping romance.
What do you think of that?"

Vic put his arm around her shoulders and kissed her forehead. "I think it's time we worked on our own big romance. A
little bodice ripping sounds perfect. For a start."

SIGNET

COMING IN SEPTEMBER 2004
FROM SIGNET MYSTERY

MURDER SHE WROTE: DESTINATION MURDER
by Jessica Fletcher & Donald Bain   0-451-21284-3

Mystery writer Jessica Fletcher takes a ride—and solves a murder—on the Starlight Express in this special 20th novel in the *USA Today* bestselling series.

WILD CRIMES
edited by Dana Stabenow   0-451-21286-X

An all-new anthology featuring wild men, wilder women, and the wildest crimes imaginable. Stories from Margaret Coel, S. J. Rozan, Loren D. Estleman, Laurie R. King, Dana Stabenow, and more.

EARLY EIGHT
A Working Man's Mystery
by L.T. Fawkes   0-451-21285-1

Terry Saltz is trying to get his life in order with an awesome double-wide trailor and a sweet carpentry business. But trouble follows him everywhere, and when a woman in the bar pool league turns up dead, it must be time for Terry to solve another murder.

**Available wherever books are sold, or
to order call: 1-800-788-6262**